"Shana Galen is an amazing writer, and weaves together a story filled with mystery and romance."

—Mrs. Q Book Addict

"Probably one of my favorite historical romances. The plot was amazing and Shana Galen's writing technique kept me intrigued from beginning to end."

—Readaholic

"Well-written with detail and depth. A fast-paced page turner, it has humor, romance, belonging, sweet sensuality, betrayal, family duty, true love and adventure and will you not want to put it down."

—My Book Addiction and More

"A very interesting time period and Shana Galen has done a wonderful job of portraying… both the English Regency and the French Revolution as backdrop."

—Debbie's Book Bag

"LOVED it! Passion is much more fun when there's some play involved."

—The Book Faery

"Wonderful!! Witty, romantic and adventurous. Beautifully paced, full of action, charming dialogue and pure fun. Well done, Shana Galen!"

—Bookfoolery and Babble

"Marvelous! I was enraptured from the first page."

—Readin' and Dreamin'

The Making of a Gentleman

SHANA GALEN

sourcebooks
casablanca

Published by Sourcebooks Casablanca, an imprint of Sourcebooks, Inc.
P.O. Box 4410, Naperville, Illinois 60567-4410
(630) 961-3900
FAX: (630) 961-2168
www.sourcebooks.com

Printed and bound in Canada
WC 10 9 8 7 6 5 4 3 2 1

For my daughter, who kept me company throughout the
writing of this book with her kicks, hiccups,
rolls, hiccups, flutters, and (have I mentioned?)
hiccups. For you, Bellaboo.

One

ELEVEN-YEAR-OLD ARMAND HARCOURT, THE COMTE de Valère, should have been asleep. He was well aware nothing incited his nanny's wrath more than when she looked in on him late at night and found him still awake. Armand did not consider reading a vice, but Madame St. Cyr, his nanny, had other ideas.

And so, with one eye on his book and the other on the door, Armand hunched over a candle and read with the sort of desperation one might expect from the starving wolves described in his novel. He knew he should go to sleep before he was caught, but the beasts were just about to attack a little girl. How could he be expected to put the book aside now?

Armand's voracious eyes gobbled up the words. Halfway down the page, he began to hum. The song was something patriotic and vaguely familiar. He turned the page, still humming, and realized the song was growing louder.

He raised his chin and allowed the book to dangle from his fingers. Was that singing he heard?

He cocked his head, vaguely aware of the hollow thud the book made as it dropped onto the plush rug beside the bed.

Heart knocking dully, Armand snuffed out his candle and rose to his knees. His fingers shook slightly as he parted the drapes beside the bed.

At first he saw nothing. The lawn below was dark and peaceful. The stars in the sky flashed and twinkled. Then he looked at the fields. Dots of orange light burned and danced, coming closer. Closer.

The singing grew louder and shapes emerged from the low-hanging mist. Several dozen men and women, most carrying torches, marched in a jagged line for the château.

In surprise, Armand dropped the draperies back in place.

For a full five heartbeats he sat rooted in place. He did not know what the peasants marching toward him meant, but he feared it. Hadn't his father, the duc de Valère, moved the family from Paris because of peasant uprisings?

Surely the same could not be happening here. The château was always quiet—a refuge for Armand.

But the singing grew louder, rising and falling into chants. Armand held his breath.

"*Mort à l'aristocratie!*"

Death to the aristocrats!

Terror sliced through him, leaving him cold and shaking, and he scrambled out of bed, tripping over books and toys littering the floor of his room.

Bastien—Bastien would know what to do.

A door on the opposite side of the room joined

the brothers' chambers, and Armand raced toward it. Flinging himself against it, he grasped the cold metal handle in one hand and wrenched the heavy wooden door open.

He stumbled into his brother's room. "Bastien!" Armand gasped. "Bastien, wake up."

The room was as black as a starless sky, and Armand groped wildly until he reached the bed.

"Bastien!" He clawed at the sheets, but the bed was empty.

His twin was not there.

Armand swore and immediately covered his mouth with both hands. Madame St. Cyr would have his head if she heard him.

Madame St. Cyr! Of course! She would know what to do.

He raced for the door to the corridor, opened it, and stepped into its gray-shrouded length.

Immediately, he began coughing as the smoke tickled his nostrils and curled into his lungs.

Armand looked about in confusion. Smoke? Where had it come from?

The image of the peasants carrying their torches sent him reeling. He did not want to accept what he knew must be true: the peasants had set the château ablaze.

Terror threatened to weaken and buckle his knees, but Armand forced himself to stand. He looked over his shoulder at the safety of his room, but how long until the smoke—until the peasants—infiltrated that last sanctuary?

He must get out, must escape the château.

The windows in his room were too high, and the peasants would be at every door. That left the secret tunnel.

Bastien used it all the time. He was always sneaking out of the château to embark on some adventure or other. Often he took Julien, their older brother, with him.

Armand didn't mind being left behind. He preferred his adventures between the pages of a novel.

But there was no safety in books now. He must escape before...

He squeezed his eyes shut.

No, he would not think of that.

"You go that way. I'll go this."

Armand opened his eyes and whipped his head in the direction of the unfamiliar voices.

"If you find any of the aristos, kill them."

Armand pushed a hand against his mouth to stifle a scream.

❧

London, 1801

Armand shot upright, the sound of his scream still echoing through the room.

He clenched his teeth until his jaw ached to stop the sound, but it was too late. He had roused the house.

Again.

Reluctantly, he rose from the floor where he had been sleeping and stood in his breeches—feet bare, chest bare. He could hear frantic footsteps approaching already, and he had to force himself not to fist his hands. No one was coming to beat him. They were coming to soothe him.

In his mind, he saw a hand reaching out, touching his shoulder, patting it weakly. He shuddered in disgust at himself, at his weakness.

He wanted to call out—to stop them—but he could not.

Somewhere deep in the recesses of his mind, he knew how to speak. He even had a vague recollection of the sound of his voice. He knew what it was to scream, even the joyful release he felt when he did it. But the word to describe this? Even though he could sometimes think it, his mouth refused to curve around the word. For years, his survival had depended on muteness. Now, he could not seem to make his mouth remember how to form syllables, words, coherent sounds.

It was one of many things he could not remember how to do. Or maybe he just didn't *want* to speak. Maybe he feared what he'd reveal—those terrors that hid in the forgotten caverns of his mind.

The door to his room banged open, and his brother Julien strode in. Julien spoke, but Armand tried to focus too late. The words sounded like a low hum, and Armand stared at his brother blankly.

Julien frowned and tugged a robe closed over his bare chest. His hair was tousled and unruly, and his face was peppered with stubble.

This man—tall, imposing, and commanding—did not resemble the boy Armand was beginning to remember. No, that was not quite true. The Julien in those faded, misty memories was also commanding.

But the harder Armand grasped at the memories,

the more quickly they blew away. He clenched his hands in frustration, wanting the childhood memories to stay. But he could not choose...

Julien looked about and blinked at the bright light in the room. Armand kept several lamps, the fire, and a half-dozen candles burning at night. He disliked dark, closed spaces and would not tolerate them. Thus, even though the air outside was chilly, his window was wide open—the parted draperies flapping in the breeze.

"Armand?"

This time Armand forced himself to listen, to focus. "Are you well?"

Armand stared at his brother and strained to make sense of the words. Long ago, he had ceased even trying to comprehend what others said to him; it was safer, better. Now he had to battle daily to master the skill once again. As a youth, he easily plucked words from his vast vocabulary. Now those same words hung just out of reach.

His brother did not seem to expect a response and was looking about the room as if inspecting it. Armand saw his gaze pause on the open drapes, the candles. But Julien would find nothing amiss. Nightmares did not leave evidence.

Finally, Julien seemed satisfied with what he saw, and he stared at Armand again. "Is everything all right?"

This time Armand nodded. He knew this phrase. He had heard it too many times. He might have spoken, but he knew the words would come out as little more than unintelligible grunts.

Armand's nod answered his brother's question, but

it did not eliminate the worry in Julien's eyes. Armand hated that he was the cause of that worry—that he was the cause of these all-too-frequent late-night gatherings. He hated his lack of communication and the way he was often treated as a fool or a child. He was no idiot, and he was no weakling either. Not anymore.

"Julien?"

The image of her came faster than the words. Images were easier for him. *Woman. Soft. Julien's.*

Finally the name: Sarah. Armand sighed. It was going to be another gathering.

Julien's woman appeared in the doorway, her white robe held closed at the throat and her brown hair falling over her shoulders. She was Julien's wife. And the slight rounding of her belly indicated she would also be the mother of his child.

Julien turned to the woman. "He's fine, Sarah." He turned back to Armand. "Another nightmare?"

Armand did not respond, knew no response was expected of him. He was ashamed. Ashamed to bring them here. Ashamed that he could not make it through the night without the nightmares.

He gritted his teeth and felt his hands ball into fists. His instinct was to send them all flying back to their beds. He could rant and roar, punch a hole in the wall. He looked at the other holes he had made.

No, that was the coward's way—the same as hiding.

The woman stood in the doorway and studied Armand, her dark eyes thoughtful and kind. She had always been kind. When he had first arrived in London, she had taken him to see his mother, in this very house. He had thought his mother was nothing but a fantasy he dreamed up in that dank cell where he rotted year after year after year.

The years ran together, and so did the memories and fantasies. Armand did not know what was real, what was conjured. His mind played tricks on him; tricks that kept it occupied and drove him half mad.

But his mother had not been a fancy or a whim. She was real, though not exactly as he remembered.

Nothing was as he remembered.

Sarah came into the room now, her small white hand still clutching the robe at her throat. Crossing to Armand, she stood beside him. Armand's eyes flicked to his brother. Julien watched his woman protectively. Armand wanted to tell him he would never hurt Sarah, but his attempts at speech would more than likely scare her.

She reached out and took his hand, and Armand braced himself.

The image of fire leapt into his mind—*Hot. Hurt. No!*

But because Julien was watching, Armand endured the pain and allowed her to hold his hand. He knew this was intended to be comforting, but it made him grind his teeth. Her closeness—anyone's closeness— was awkward and almost unbearable.

"Armand," she said quietly. He darted his gaze to her, then back to his brother.

"Armand, Julien and I have been talking," Sarah said quietly, "and we think it might help your recovery if you had a tutor."

Armand glanced back at her.

Tutor?

The word was familiar to him. He could not remember

the last time he heard it, but it was a word he liked. *Tutor*, he said in his mind, rehearsing it as though he would speak it. *Tutor*.

She squeezed his hand warmly, causing another searing bout of agony. "Would you like a tutor? Someone to help you remember how to speak?"

She was looking at him, and he stared back at her. Julien was behind her now, his hand on her white-clad shoulder. Her hair fell over that hand in soft waves, and Armand wondered if it was as soft as it looked. He once had a rat in his cell, and he had made it into a pet. Its fur had been soft and brown like Sarah's.

"Armand, do you remember Monsieur Grenoble?" Julien asked. "He was your tutor in Paris."

Something about the name caused Armand's heart to speed up. He did not know who or what Monsieur Grenoble was, but the memory was pleasant.

Before.

This Grenoble was from before the years of hell. Before the dark prison, the frequent beatings. Before he had been left for dead.

Sarah was smiling. "I think he does remember him," she said to Julien, turning her head to look over her shoulder. "Did you see the way his eyes lit up?"

Armand was aware they were speaking of him. They did this often, and he hated it.

He jerked his hand away from Sarah's, and she turned back to him. "I'll begin making inquiries tomorrow," she said, reaching out to pat Armand's arm. "We'll find someone extraordinary." She lifted on tiptoe to kiss his temple, and Armand dug his fingers into his thighs. This time it was not just her touch that pained him, it was her scent. She smelled sweet, like apples or peaches, and the feminine smell of her was almost more than his senses could handle.

When she stepped back, he could breathe again.

"Good night, Armand."

Julien watched him for another moment then followed her out the door.

The door closed behind them, and Armand looked about the white-walled room. He had paced it and knew it was three times the size of his prison cell—bright and sunny during the day, shadowed but not menacing at night. There were pictures hanging on the walls—between the holes he had punched.

Flowers. Field. Color.

He could not remember the names of all the colors.

Armand considered lying down and going back to sleep, but tonight the sound of the peasants singing was too loud. It echoed in his head, and Armand closed his eyes to block out memories of that night so long ago.

But the song would not be silenced, and even opening his eyes and staring at the flickering candle would not burn the images from his mind. The flame rose and fell, hissed and smoked, danced before his eyes—just as the fire had danced in the night sky so long ago.

The fire had danced as Armand's life burned to ashes.

Two

FELICITY BENNETT STOOD IN THE PARK IN THE CENTER
of Berkeley Square and stared at the mammoth town
house before her. She had never seen a house with so
many windows, and in this gray, dreary city, she had
never seen one so white. London's morning fog had
yet to burn off and hovered oppressively around the
other town houses, shrouding them in gloom. But
the fog did not deign to touch this house. The white
façade glittered in the shaft of sunlight just emerging
from the fortress of low-hanging clouds.

Felicity took a deep breath. It was not like her
to be intimidated, and if she did not muster her
courage soon, walk across the park, and knock on
that door—that mammoth door with the golden
lion's head door knocker—she was going to be late
for her appointment.

Late for what was to be her first day of employment.
That would not do, especially after all the pains she
had taken to arrive punctually. There was the hour-
long walk from the rectory to the posting house, the
eight hours on the mail coach—crushed between a

portly woman and a man who sounded as though he might cough up his lungs—and the harrowing hansom cab ride to her present location.

She had traveled all night without sleep and with little more than a small wedge of cheese and some three-day-old bread for sustenance. Every muscle in her body ached and her belly felt like a hollow pit, but she would not allow her fatigue and hunger to surface. She pushed them down and focused on the time ticking away.

Her father always said there was no time like the present, and Felicity always agreed. But that was because she did not mind cooking dinner or studying her mathematics or sweeping the floor. She did very much mind going to work for some snooty aristocrats who, if they were like all the others she had known, would be condescending and hypocritical. In short, Felicity did not look forward to a life of servitude.

But really, what choice did she have? The alternatives…

She almost jumped when she saw a movement to her right. She turned sharply when a man dressed in tight breeches, a fitted coat of navy superfine, and a stark white shirt with a perfectly tied cravat stepped out from behind one of the trees in the park and beckoned to her. Felicity blinked at him, certain he was an illusion—fervently *hoped* he was an illusion. Could she ignore him? Could she pretend she hadn't seen him?

He beckoned again, this time adding an impatient glare, so with a furtive glance at the town house, she hurried to meet him. "What are you doing here?" she whispered, stepping behind a tree and hoping she was out of sight of the house. "You shouldn't be here."

"My fiancée finally arrives in Town, and I'm not allowed to see her? Rubbish." His words were only slightly slurred, which was a good sign. And his fine clothes another good sign. Perhaps he was winning at the tables. Perhaps he would leave her in peace.

"How did you know where I would be? I haven't even met the family or secured the position."

He winked at her. "I have connections." He tapped the jaunty hat tucked under his arm. "Don't you forget that." He reached out, probably to poke her arm, but she quickly moved out of his reach.

He chuckled and gave her a long perusal that made her want to pull her cloak tighter over her bosom. "They'll like you." He nodded. "And they're rich. Very rich. Just what we're looking for."

That was not at all part of her criteria, but she didn't contradict him. "I only hope the pay will be adequate. How much did you say you owe the creditors?"

He grinned. "Anxious to get rid of me, are you?" He leaned closer, and she could smell the spirits on his breath. "I told you. For twenty-five pounds I will make our little agreement go away." He snapped his fingers, and she jumped in spite of herself. "If you can't pay up by the first of the year, well, then, prepare to have the banns called, *darling*."

She shuddered. Once the idea of marrying Charles St. John had been her favorite fantasy. Now, she would avoid it at all costs. Why hadn't her father seen through him? Why hadn't she? Twenty-five pounds might as well have been a million, but she had to find a way to earn it.

"I understand the conditions. And you stay away

from the house." She gestured to the town house behind them. "If they see you with me—"

"Yes, yes." He waved a hand. "A"—he squinted at her—"what's your position again?"

"Governess," she said through clenched teeth. Would he not just go away!

"A new governess should not be engaged. The quality don't like it." He leaned in again, and she held her breath. "The quality won't like me. Pay up, or I might just knock on the door and introduce myself. See how long your fancy position lasts then."

"I'm certain that won't be necessary," she said, but he was already moving away.

"I'll find a way to speak to you in a day or so. I'll send a note or prowl around the garden."

"Charles, no—" She was wasting her breath. He was already too far away to hear her. She sighed and swallowed back the frustrated tears that stung her eyes. How she wished her father was still alive. How she wished she could have been there at the end, snatched her father's pen away, done something, *anything* to prevent her betrothal to that—oh! She couldn't think of a word bad enough.

She watched Charles St. John stroll away, his hat now on his head at a rakish angle, and tried to pretend this would not end in disaster. Of course, that was no way to think before she went into that elegant town house. She had to be confident. With that in mind, she lifted her small valise, squared her shoulders, and began marching toward the huge structure. It grew larger the closer she came, towering over her like an alabaster oak. Her heart began to pound, and her legs wobbled like jelly, but she clenched her jaw and kept walking. She was no coward, and she bore her gaze into that ornate door knocker. Finally she stopped before it, her eyes level with those of the gold lion's. He looked friendly—in a violent, hungry sort of way. She reached toward the open mouth, complete with sharp golden teeth, grasped the heavy ring dangling there, and rapped three times. Hard.

Her hand dropped to her side, and belatedly she wished she had a basin of water with which to wash the grime from her face. Surely she could not look as bad as she felt...

No matter. The wealthy and titled rarely stooped to acknowledge the likes of her—daughter of a poor vicar. She heard the sound of a lock being turned, and the door yawned open to reveal a tall, distinguished man in black.

"Good day," he intoned. His voice sounded as friendly as the lion's teeth looked.

"Good day." Felicity's voice came out in a squeak, and she automatically cleared her throat. "I mean, good day. I'm Felicity Bennett. I'm here to see—"

Oh, Lord. What was the name of the lady of the house? The meeting with Charles had flustered her, and now she could not remember the details of the letter of employment. One would have thought she had committed it to memory, given the number of times she read that letter, but the small, vital detail of the lady's title had apparently danced away.

The butler raised his eyebrows, and Felicity smiled tightly. "I have an appointment with Lady—" She drew the word out, hoping the title would come to her. But, no, her mind remained a fresh slate.

Curses!

"Duchesse," the butler corrected, and immediately Felicity remembered. "The duchesse de Valère," he intoned.

"Felicity Bennett." Her tight smile did not waver. She was probably not as obsequious and fawning as the usual visitors to the house, but neither was she an imbecile. She knew the correct forms of address. "I'm here to see Her Grace."

The butler nodded, his expression giving nothing away. "Her Grace is expecting you." He stepped aside and opened the door wider to reveal a cavernous black-and-white marble vestibule as large as the rectory that had been her home. Wide stairs curved gracefully before her, leading to the upper floors. The interior was as impressive and as beautiful as the exterior promised, and the vestibule glittered with light. The sun was streaming in through a small window above the door, the light flashing off the crystals in the chandelier, sending a rainbow of sparkles across the sea of gleaming marble.

The scene was so pretty it drew Felicity inside.

"Leave the valise there." The butler pointed to one side of the door. "Is that the extent of your luggage?"

Felicity blinked, his voice tearing her away from the small, glittering rainbows. She realized she had expected the house to look gaudy and pretentious, but that was not the effect of the décor at all. Everything—from the chiseled marble statuette of a Greek woman on a pedestal to the cream upholstered Sheraton chair in the corner—was tasteful and inviting.

Everything but the butler, who was still looking at her.

"Pardon? Oh, no. My trunks should arrive later today or tomorrow." She set the valise on the smooth marble. In it, she had packed a change of clothing and all she held precious—a portrait of her father, her mother's Bible, and her sheet music. Removing her bonnet, she placed it on top of the valise.

She should probably have packed another change of clothes, but she could not bear to be away from her favorite pieces of music, even though she had no means with which to play them. Besides, she did not trust the men she had engaged to transport her trunks not to lose or damage the contents.

No, in the end she had decided it was better to sacrifice fashion than her precious music. Not that what she wore was going to matter, she thought as the butler motioned for her to follow him up the staircase. His black livery was of better quality than her Sunday dress.

At home in Hampshire, the pretty white muslin with a puff of a sleeve always garnered her compliments, especially when she paired it with the dark blue cloak she wore now. The blue of the cloak matched her eyes and contrasted nicely with her blond hair. But from all she had seen today, her clothing was sadly out of date.

Not that it mattered. No one cared what a governess wore. She was not going to be attending balls and soirees. She would be teaching a young boy. Boys liked to play in the dirt and run in the gardens. Perhaps it was best then that her clothes were more serviceable than fashionable.

As they reached the top of the stairs, Felicity searched the portraits hung in the corridor for one of a small boy. His name she remembered: Armand. It was a sweet name, conjuring the image of soft brown hair, a gentle smile, and rosy lips. The duchesse de Valère had been vague about his age in her letter of employment, but Felicity imagined him to be six or seven.

The butler rapped sharply on the towering white drawing-room doors then pushed them open. "Miss Felicity Bennett," the butler announced.

A woman was standing in the center of the room beside a bright yellow chintz sofa and across from a beautiful pianoforte. She turned when the butler spoke, and to Felicity's surprise, her smile was warm and inviting. It even appeared genuine. "Thank you, Grimsby. Will you have Mrs. Eggers send tea?"

The butler nodded and closed the doors with a flourish.

"You must be Miss Bennett," the woman said, stepping forward and holding out her hands. It was an unexpected gesture and a surprising one. The woman greeted her like an old friend.

"Yes." Felicity hesitated only a moment before moving forward and placing her hands in the other woman's. The woman's hands were slim and soft but firm. She led Felicity to the sofa, gestured for her to sit, then took the chair upholstered in cream opposite.

Felicity sat, belatedly realizing she should have curtseyed. Their greeting had been far too informal. But perhaps this was not the duchesse. Felicity narrowed her eyes. The woman's celery-colored gown was of the best material and the newest style, but it was plain and unpretentious. Not at all the sort of thing one would expect a duchesse to wear.

In fact, the woman did not look very much like a duchesse at all. Certainly, she was pretty. She had wide brown eyes and glossy brown hair, elegantly but simply styled. Her face was honest and open with high cheekbones and full lips.

She looked like a normal person, Felicity decided. Surely this was not the exotic duchesse de Valère, wife of one of the richest and most mysterious ducs in England. Made even more mysterious because his title and his ancestry were French.

"I don't look much like a duchesse, do I?" the woman said, and Felicity's heart stuttered. Had the woman read her thoughts?

"I haven't been the duchesse for long, only seven months. Before I married the duc, I actually held a position similar to the one you will occupy. I was a governess."

"Oh." Felicity tried not to seem surprised, but it was not every day a duc married a governess. Felicity attempted to imagine being married to a duc. Being the wife of a man who owned all of this. She glanced about the room with its polished wood floors, its thick Aubusson carpets, its heavy drapes, and its expensive art. She was not certain she would *want* responsibility for all of this.

Except for that pianoforte. It drew her gaze. How long had it been since she'd had the opportunity to play an instrument of that quality? Possibly never of *that* quality, but far too long since she had indulged in playing.

"It's a bit much, isn't it?"

Felicity glanced back at the duchesse, unsure how to respond. It was the most beautiful room she had ever entered, but the little porcelain plate on the table could have probably fed some of her poorer neighbors back in Selborne for a month or more. If she had even a tiny fraction of the wealth on display in this one room alone, she would not be here now—penniless, homeless, with almost all she owned in the world in a valise at the bottom of the staircase.

"It's lovely." And how her fingers itched to touch those pianoforte keys. She could already hear the music in her mind.

"But intimidating." The duchesse smiled. "The first time I was ever in this room, I cast up my accounts because I was so nervous."

Felicity's eyes widened. "Oh."

"In front of the duc."

"Oh!" She clapped a hand over her mouth to keep from laughing.

"It's all right. I want you to laugh." A tap sounded on the door, and a servant entered with the tea service. As the duchesse spoke, she set the lovely china on the table, poured the tea, and offered Felicity a large slice of what looked to be sinfully delicious cake. Felicity took the cake and forked up a large bite. It was vanilla and cinnamon, and as soon as she tasted it, her stomach growled with pleasure. She wondered if it would be rude to request a second piece. Felicity eyed the cake and decided to sip her tea delicately. Perhaps she could make this slice last longer.

"I want you to know," the duchesse continued,

"that I understand how daunting all of this can be."
She gestured to the room. "Please feel free to come to
me if you need support or encouragement. I'm afraid
your task will not be an easy one, but I'll help in any
way I can."

The servant slipped away, and Felicity decided now
was as good a time as any to ask a question. "Can you
tell me more about the comte de Valère? What will
my duties be as governess?"

The duchesse frowned slightly, and Felicity
wondered if she had said something wrong. "I
wouldn't say your title is *governess*. You're more of a
tutor. The comte no longer needs supervision."

"I see." Felicity supposed she had been wrong to
picture little Armand as so young. Only, she thought
the titled usually sent their sons to Eton when they
were older. But obviously the current duchesse must
be the duc's second wife. In which case, the boy could
be any age.

"I understand you have quite a background in
education," the duchesse said. "Your aunt, who
recommended you, said you taught at the parish
school near your home. The village of Selborne. Is
that correct?"

"Yes. My father was a Methodist minister who
believed in education for the poor. He raised money
for a free parish school, and then spent much of
his own salary to keep it furnished with books and
other supplies."

"That's quite admirable. Your aunt said your father
had passed away recently."

Felicity looked down, hoping the sudden sting

behind her eyes would not turn into full-fledged tears. "He'd been ill for a long time."

"So it was not unexpected, then." The duchesse's voice was kind, and the tender tone pulled at Felicity's heart.

"No." At least her father's death had not been unexpected to him. He had apparently known how ill he was and that he did not have much time left. She, however, had thought his cough would pass. It had lasted too long, but that was only because her father overexerted himself and did not get enough rest. If only he would have rested...

If only he would have confided in her the severity of his illness and his plans for her, she would not have agreed to visit her aunt. She would have been with him at the end, and perhaps this whole business with Charles St. John might have been avoided.

The state of their finances was dismal, but her father's solution to provide for her even worse. Unfortunately, he must not have known that Charles had debts of his own, that he was an inveterate drunk and gambler. How could her father have known? Charles had fooled everyone. Ignorance she could forgive, but it was harder to forgive her father for signing a betrothal agreement without even consulting her. How could he give his daughter away as though she were one more piece of property?

And now here she was, in this ornate drawing room, seated across from a duchesse, sipping tea.

She supposed life could be worse.

Much worse.

"Well, we are happy to have you. Your aunt is the

particular friend of a woman who is like a mother to me. When she recommended you, I knew we must hire you. And it was fortunate for us that you could arrive on such short notice. We want you to get started imme—What is it Grimsby?"

Felicity turned to see the taciturn butler standing in the doorway. "A question for you, Your Grace."

"What is it?"

"I am afraid it is from the workmen in the nursery."

"Ah. Can you tell them to wait?"

"Yes, Your Grace." The butler took a step backward and then paused. "Though they did say it was a matter of some urgency."

The duchesse sighed loudly and rose to her feet. Felicity quickly followed, noting as she did, the slight rounding revealed when the duchesse's gown had tightened over her belly. The duchesse was expecting. "I'm sorry." The duchesse spread her arms sympathetically. "I'm sure this will take only a moment or two."

"Of course." Felicity took her seat on the sofa again and tried to sip her tea. It was very good, much better than what she had been used to at home. Of course, she and her father were lucky to have tea, she reminded herself. Her aunt Robbins had six children, and with eight mouths to feed, tea was the last thing her cousins worried about.

Felicity smiled, thinking about her aunt and uncle and their big happy family. When Felicity's father passed away, her aunt had offered her a place in their home, but Felicity did not want to be a burden. And then when Charles appeared, waving that marriage agreement, her options became even more limited. Nothing but money would make him and that loathsome document quietly disappear. Oh, she could refuse to marry him, but then she would be in a worse predicament than she was now. How would she survive? No respectable man would marry a woman so scandalized. And who would hire one with such a reputation? Her aunt, seeing Felicity's dire situation, had helped her secure this position.

Felicity looked about the drawing room again, marveling. Who would have thought she would end up here?

She allowed her eyes to rest on some of the impressive paintings and ran her hand over the expensive fabric on the sofa. But what she really wanted to do was to play that beautiful pianoforte. And, coincidentally, here she was, all alone. And there it was, waiting to be played.

She angled her body so she could better admire the instrument. It was very fine—definitely much better than any she had ever played before. Far better than the one she had learned on—an ancient instrument that had been her mother's.

Her mother had been her teacher, as well. But that was years ago. Now both her mother and the pianoforte were no more. Her mother had died of consumption, while the pianoforte was sold two years ago to cover some debt or other.

The clock on the mantel ticked away, and still the duchesse did not return. The longer Felicity sat staring at that pianoforte, the more her fingers itched.

Surely it would not hurt anything to study the pianoforte more closely.

Felicity rose, one eye on the drawing-room doors and one eye on the pianoforte. When she was beside it, she reached out gingerly and brushed her fingers along the spine and the raised fallboard. The wood was smooth and cool to her touch. When she pulled her fingers away, not a speck of dust lingered.

Cautiously, Felicity circled the instrument, admiring it but watching the drawing-room doors. She did not think the duchesse would mind if she simply *looked* at the instrument.

But playing—well, that was something else entirely, Felicity thought, even as she sat on the plush bench before the black-and-white keys. It was considered quite ill-mannered to play someone else's instrument without first asking permission.

Felicity stroked the keys, caressing them individually. In her mind, she heard the sound each would make, and still, without pushing down the keys, she began to play her favorite sonata. She was not even certain of the title of the piece. It was something her mother had loved to play and something Felicity had not heard in a long time.

Gently, Felicity increased her pressure on the keys until the music was more than just a figment of her imagination. She pressed lightly, dampening the tones she heard, but it did not matter. The music was beautiful.

She closed her eyes and pictured her mother's hands on the worn keys of their instrument at home. She pictured her mother's face as she played each measure of the piece.

Here was a difficult section. Her mother's brow furrowed in concentration.

Here was a lively section. Her mother smiled, and her fingers seemed to fly over the keys.

Felicity's own fingers flew over the keys, as well. She was vaguely aware she was playing the instrument at full volume now. She was aware, but she no longer cared. Whatever scolding she might receive was secondary to the music. She could think of little else. The very notes themselves snared her and held her captive. She must finish the sonata. She could not breathe if she did not hear the next note and then the one after that.

She played with her eyes closed, knowing the sonata so well she did not need to look at her racing fingers. Even after all this time, she made no mistakes. Once she heard a piece, she rarely did.

And then when the piece was almost complete, her back prickled. She opened her eyes and stared straight ahead.

A man stared back at her. He stood just inside the door of the drawing room, his hands fisted at his sides. His shirt and breeches were of the latest fashion, but he wore no tailcoat or waistcoat, and his shirt was open at the throat. Even more surprising, he wore no stockings or shoes. His clothing was clean and neat, but his hair was in disarray. It was long and free of any binding. The brown locks were clean, though, and they fell over his shoulders.

It was his eyes that stilled her fingers. They were the deepest and darkest blue she had ever seen and framed by long, thick lashes and a dark slash of brows. There was something in those eyes that sent a shock straight through her.

Not a shock of fear, though the man was big enough and powerful enough to be a threat, if he chose that course.

The shock was that of recognition. This man loved music as much as she. Felicity could see it in his face, in his eyes. And the shock of seeing her own passion reflected back at her froze her hands.

Suddenly, the music ceased, and silence washed over the room.

Felicity stared at the man, and he stared back.

And then he began to howl.

Three

ARMAND KNEW THE SOUND FRIGHTENED THE GIRL, BUT it roared out of him before he could seize control. He was angry at the sudden silence.

He had been sitting in his brother's library, staring out the French doors into the garden, when the music began. He liked the garden—the fresh air and open space. He often worked there, planting shrubs or flowers, but today he simply stared, pretending he was out of the city. Free of the confines of these walls. Free of the confines of his mind. He had to concentrate to keep images from spilling into that mind.

At first the music had been quiet, and he thought it came from a neighboring home. But gradually the sound grew in volume, and as it did, Armand was on his feet, moving out of the library and into the vestibule.

He had to find that sound—either to make it stop or to make sure it continued. He stood in the center of the black-and-white marble and tried to picture all of the rooms in the home. He was picturing the instrument that made the sound and trying to remember if he had seen that instrument in the house. He could have remembered the name of the instrument if he'd tried, but words could be dangerous. Still, the sound it made was something he knew.

Finally an image of the drawing room and the instrument flashed into his mind. Instantly, he was on the stairs, taking the steps two at a time. When he reached the drawing-room door, he paused.

What if he opened the door and the music stopped? What if this was not really music at all but something from his imagination?

It had happened before. In prison the solitude caused vivid illusions. He heard voices, music, even saw images he would have sworn on his life were real. But when he went to touch them, to test their authenticity, they vanished into the dark cell.

What if this music vanished, as well?

Armand stood with his hand on the door and thought it over. A maid dusting nearby watched him. He could tell by the way her gaze darted away when he looked at her he made her nervous. He wanted to ask if she could hear the music, but he could not.

Behind the doors, the music grew louder, and Armand couldn't stand it another moment. He turned the knob and stepped inside. And to his surprise, the music continued. He could see where it came from now—a woman was seated at the instrument he had imagined. She had...

Yellow. Yellow hair.

That was not the right word for the color, but the less he thought about the words, the better. He could

not risk speaking. He could not survive another term
in prison—the blackness, the stink, the maddening
loneliness. He would die first.

The woman before him now played violently,
leaning into the keys and swaying from side to side.
Her eyes were closed, and she did not see him enter.

Watching her, Armand's breathing slowed and his
thoughts focused. It was almost like staring into a fire.
What was the word? Bewitch? But the music was not
all that drew his attention.

The woman. He could not look away from her.

Did all women have cheeks that smooth or necks
that long? He had never noticed before. And what
about her yellow hair? He liked the way the sunlight
seemed to melt into it.

And then she opened her eyes. They were blue—
the exact blue of the sky he had imagined all those
years when he was caged in prison. He had always
known that the sky could never be that perfectly blue,
but imagining it so kept him sane. He must be imagining this woman's eyes now. But then she blinked at
him, and he knew this was real.

And then the music stopped. The woman stilled,
and Armand felt the absence of the music like the pain
he experienced when his hand crashed through a wall.
The woman was looking at him, and he wanted to tell
her to keep playing.

He opened his mouth to tell her, to beg her. *Don't
stop. More music. More fingers moving.*

Her eyes widened—those perfectly blue eyes—and
she leaned back, and it was then that Armand realized
he was howling.

He tried clenching his jaw, but the sound wouldn't stop. Mortification ripped through him.

Silencesilencesilencesilence.

In desperation, he turned and smashed his knuckles against the drawing-room door. The splintering pain stopped the sound, but the damage had been done. The girl stood and stumbled back in an effort to get away from him.

Armand wished he could start all over again. He did not mean to startle her. At times he behaved little better than a monster, and he hated it. Hated his momentary loss of control. He turned about, looking for his brother or a servant who might reassure the woman, but no one was near. Even the maid he had seen earlier had fled.

The woman stumbled back again, tripping over the piano stool. She fell on the floor, and Armand moved without thinking. She held up a hand and scooted back—farther away from him. "Stay back," she ordered. "I'm warning you…"

Scared. Her eyes looking at him. Fear.

Anger swept through him, and he lunged forward and took her hand. She shrieked when he touched her, and though the sound hurt his ears, he did not release her. He would show her he was not always a monster. He held her gently, as gently as he had held his pet rat. He was so careful with her hand it took him a moment to realize she had removed her gloves.

He was touching bare skin.

His own skin began to heat where it met hers, and he glanced into her sky blue eyes.

She had stopped shrieking now and was staring

at him. Her gaze darted between his hand and his face, and she was absolutely still. Armand would have thought her a statue if he did not feel the warmth of her skin.

She looked down at her small white hand encased in his larger one, and Armand followed her gaze. Gently, he squeezed her hand, hoping the gesture was reassuring. Sarah and his mother did this to him all the time, and he figured it was supposed to soothe.

She did not begin shrieking again, and he judged the action a success.

But the girl was still on the floor, so Armand stepped back and tugged slightly, showing her that he wanted to help her to her feet. She nodded, seeming to understand, and he pulled harder. She rose to her feet and stood before him. "You may release me now."

He had forgotten to focus, and her words washed over him without meaning. And then when he tried to focus, his body would not allow it. She was too close; that much Armand realized immediately. She was so close he could see the dark rim of her sky-colored eyes. He could smell her scent, and normally that overwhelmed him. But not this time. He wanted to move closer, to inhale more deeply.

He looked into her eyes again, just as she tried to pull back her hand, and that was when he realized he was still touching her, still holding onto her.

And he realized something else, as well: he felt no pain.

Her touch caused him no pain!

In surprise, he pulled her hand to his chest. She

resisted, but he was stronger, and her hand touched the material of his shirt just under his throat.

And still no pain.

It didn't make sense. Touch always pained him. *Whywhywhywhy…?*

He pictured her hand on his bare flesh and lifted it to his cheek. A few weeks ago, he had shaved the beard he had worn for years, and now he had Julien's valet shave it again every few days. The valet had shaved him this morning, and his face felt raw and vulnerable. He braced himself in anticipation of the fresh pain her fingers would cause on that sensitive skin, but when he pressed her flesh to his, he felt only the warmth of her skin and the softness of her fingers. He had never felt anything as soft as this woman.

He looked into her blue eyes again. They were huge and round, but she did not look afraid. There was color in her cheeks—the word eluded him.

Red. Red on white.

Armand wondered how that colored skin would feel under his fingertips. Surely if her hands were soft, her face would be even softer.

And as soon as the question occurred to him, he knew he must have the answer. In one swift movement, he wrapped an arm about her middle and pulled her close. She resisted at first; he felt the tension in her body and the instant stiffening. Armand would not force her—could not imagine forcing any creature to do something against its will—and so he allowed his hold on her to relax. She must come to him, or else he would let her go.

The image of her moving away flashed before his

eyes, and he gritted his teeth. But as much as the idea displeased him, he could release her.

But when he relaxed his hold, she did not move away. She looked up at him, her face only inches from his. He could feel her warmth all over now, and her scent wrapped around him like the silk robe Julien had given him.

Her breathing was rapid, causing her chest to graze his with each intake of air. She was soft everywhere, round everywhere, and Armand felt a hard stab of something he had rarely felt before—need, want, desire. She blinked, tilted her head to the side. "What do you want?" Her voice was quiet and light now. It tinkled like bells.

It also trembled, and her body shook with it. Without taking his eyes from hers, Armand pulled her close again and slowly, ever so slowly, laid his cheek against hers. It was as soft as he had anticipated—softer than the fur of his pet rat, softer than any material he could think of. For four heartbeats, he relished the feel of her skin against his.

And then he was aware of another feeling—the feel of her body pressed to his. The feel of her breath in quick gasps on his neck. The yielding of her flesh against his. He knew her mouth was mere inches from his, knew if he turned his face slightly, he could press his lips to hers. He had never had the impulse to kiss anything or anyone before, but now he felt as though this was something he must do.

And at the same time, he knew he could not—knew that by holding her like this, he had gone too far. There were Rules in this new society—Rules he did not always obey, but Rules, nonetheless. He broke them frequently and mostly without intent, and he knew with certainty he was breaking one now.

He should release her. He should step away, allow her to go—

"Armand!"

Feeling like a naughty child, Armand sprang away from the woman and rounded on the doorway. His defenses were up, and he was ready for whoever the enemy might be. Attackers always came from behind. But instead of an assailant, his brother's woman stood there, her mouth open slightly. The maid Armand had seen dusting outside the drawing room was standing just behind her. Without turning, Sarah ordered, "Go fetch His Grace, please. Be quick about it."

The maid bobbed her head and ran away while Sarah stepped into the room and closed the door behind her. Armand clenched his fists. He hated closed doors. Sarah looked immediately at the yellow-haired woman, who was now leaning against the instrument, her slim, pale hand against her cheek where he had touched her with his own. The sunlight came in through the window and moved in her hair. It looked almost as though it were on fire. Armand had to resist the urge to go to her again.

"Are you hurt, Miss Bennett?" Sarah asked the woman.

Miss Bennett. That must be her name. He memorized it, thought he might try to say it alone in his room tonight.

"No, I'm fine," she answered in that same light voice. "I-I don't think he meant me any harm. I—" She waved a hand as though to fan her face. "I don't know quite what happened."

"Why don't we sit down?" Sarah said. But before the women could reach the chairs, the door swung open and Julien rushed inside. He wore his riding boots and coat, and his hair was windblown.

"What's going on?" His eyes took in the scene quickly, and when they met Armand's, Armand scowled at him. Now, more than ever before, he wished he were free to speak. Language was becoming clearer to him every day. He *could* speak. At one time he had spoken several languages, read them, as well. But then everything had changed. Words were forbidden, dangerous. He'd pushed the skill of speech far away, and when he occasionally wanted it, language was murky, something grasped at in a muddy pond. Plunge as he might into that pond, the object eluded him. Or did he allow it to elude him?

"I walked in," Sarah was saying, "and Armand had Miss Bennett in his arms."

Julien whirled toward the yellow-haired woman. "Did he attack you? Are you all right?"

"Yes, I mean, no. That is to say, no, he did not attack me, and yes, I'm quite well."

"What happened?"

She did not speak for a moment, and then her eyes met his. Armand knew an important question had been asked, and he saw now she was considering her answer. He looked away, certain no matter what she said, in a matter of moments she would be whisked away, and he would not see her again.

And perhaps that was for the best. He did not trust himself if she played that music again.

"I think the gentleman"—Armand turned to see that she gestured to him—"was overwhelmed by the music I played."

His head hurt from focusing so hard. A tool— hammer—pounded behind his eyes, but he willed himself to listen, to understand.

"Music?" Sarah said, her brow furrowed. She had moved closer to Julien, which did not surprise Armand. He had yet to see them together in a room when they were not near one another, usually touching. "What music?"

The girl's cheeks colored further, turning from a lighter shade of red to a darker one. "I'm sorry. I was playing the pianoforte. I haven't played in some months, and I'm afraid I got quite carried away. When I opened my eyes, he was standing in the doorway. The look on his face was…" She paused, glanced at him again. "I don't know how to describe it, but I think he enjoyed the music. Unfortunately, when I saw him, I was startled, and I stopped playing. It was then he began to… ah…"

"Howl?" Julien said.

She nodded. "It took me by surprise, and I stumbled backward, tripping on my skirts. At which point, he helped me to my feet and then…" She bit her lip, and Armand saw the color of her cheeks turn even darker. He wondered how dark they would go. "He sort of held my hand and then…" She reached up and tucked a piece of yellow hair behind one ear. "He put my hand to his cheek."

"He touched you?" Julien asked. "Voluntarily?"

Wordswordswordswords.

Some he knew, some he did not. Armand knew they were discussing him again. He hated this, hated they were doing it in front of her. He considered marching out of the room indignantly, but that would mean leaving Miss Bennett. He wanted to hear her voice again, see if her cheeks turned any darker. He could not seem to look away from her.

"Yes, he…" She looked at Sarah. "When you entered, he had pulled me close. I think to press his cheek to mine."

Sarah shook her head. "He *wanted* to touch you?"

"I think so." She looked down, obviously uncomfortable. Armand again felt the urge to go to her, this time to protect her.

But Julien and Sarah were staring at him now. *Damn it.* Obviously he had been right about breaking The Rules. This was the look they often had on their faces when he broke a Rule.

"I'll take him downstairs," Julien said and gestured. "Armand, let's go."

Armand fisted his hands. He would go when he wanted, *if* he wanted. He did not take orders. A gasp sounded across the room. "That man is Armand?" he heard her ask, but this time her voice was neither light nor high. It was heavy and disbelieving.

"Yes," Sarah answered. "If you'll just give me a moment, I'll explain everything."

But Armand did not wait to hear anything further, little as he understood it all. He understood that tone in her voice, and it made him remember who he was. What he was in their eyes—disgusting, revolting, monster.

Giving his brother a shove as he passed him, Armand strode out of the drawing room.

Four

"I CAN EXPLAIN," THE DUCHESSE SAID, HOLDING UP A hand. "There's no need to be afraid."

Felicity stared past her, at the drawing-room door where that man had just exited. That *man* was Armand? That *man* was her charge? She had imagined a little boy, sweet and shy—not a full-grown man with chestnut hair and cobalt eyes. Not a man who was taller than she, stronger than she, and—dare she think it?—a man who made her heart race.

With a curse, the duc strode after his brother. Felicity glanced at the duchesse. "I wasn't afraid." Oh, no, far from it. Though perhaps it would have been better had she been afraid.

The duchesse blinked. "Weren't you?"

"I own that I was startled at first, but I could see he meant me no harm. He was simply…" She gestured, finding it difficult to put the emotions she had seen on his face into words. "He was moved by the music. Enraptured by it."

The duchesse nodded absently. "Music. Yes. I don't know why we didn't think of it before." She tapped a finger to her chin and then gave Felicity an assessing look. "And you can play the pianoforte?"

"Yes. I apologize for not asking first. I saw it and was tempted. It's been so long since I was able to play."

"That's quite all right and, now that we've seen Armand's reaction, a talent in your favor. I don't suppose you would still be interested in the position?"

Felicity blanched. "Your Grace, I had assumed you were looking for a governess. That—man—is far from need of a governess."

The duchesse sighed. "But he does need a tutor. Please, won't you sit down and finish your tea?" The duchesse gestured to the sofa Felicity had occupied before, and then, without waiting for Felicity to agree, resumed her seat on the chair.

Felicity had little choice but to comply with the duchesse's suggestion. One did not refuse a duchesse her request even if one did not care overmuch for titles and peerages. She had only to glance about her at the opulent room or the view from the windows overlooking Berkeley Square to know that title or not, this family was wealthy and powerful—and not to be ignored.

Felicity peeked out those large windows at the peaceful view of the square as she crossed to the sofa. She sat and straightened her skirts. But she did not lift the tea cup or take another bite of the cake, though her throat was parched and her stomach protested. At that moment, she wanted nothing more than time to think about this governess position that was not a governess position, about this man who was not at all the boy she had envisioned.

Felicity bit her lip. She rather thought she wanted more time to think about the man than the position.

"I was hoping to tell you about Armand before you met him," the duchesse said, lifting her tea cup and sipping delicately. "He's my husband's brother. Until they were recently reunited, they had not seen each other for twelve years. They were separated during the revolution in France. Their family château was attacked, but the boys were able to escape. My husband and his mother, the dowager duchesse de Valère, who also lives here, escaped together. Neither brother had any idea if the other lived. In fact, there was a third brother, Armand's twin, and we still don't know whether or not he survived the attack. Unfortunately, the boys' father, the duc de Valère, was guillotined in Paris shortly after the attack, so we know his fate."

Despite her own desire to escape, Felicity could not help but find herself drawn in by the story. An attack on the family home. Brothers separated as children and reunited as adults. Their poor mother. "It's fortunate the two brothers were reunited."

"It is, but the circumstances are quite tragic. My husband found Armand—I suppose I should refer to him as the comte de Valère—rotting in a cell in Paris only a few months ago. He had been left there, forgotten for... well, I don't know how long. Possibly twelve years. You see, when we rescued the comte, he was unable to speak."

"But he can make sounds. He's not a mute." Felicity finally relented and lifted her cup. It seemed as though hours had passed since the tea had been poured, but it was still warm.

"No. He is capable of speech. My husband assures me before the attack, the comte spoke and read several languages, including French and English. But we have not heard him speak since he was rescued. I think that, when he chooses, he can understand our conversations. And I think he can speak, but for some reason he does not want to. We need a tutor to gently coax language out of him again."

Slowly, carefully, Felicity set her tea cup on the saucer. "Coax language out of him?"

"That's not all," the duchesse said hurriedly. "He needs lessons in manners and social etiquette, as well. Your aunt said that in Hampshire you oversaw something of a finishing school for the girls. We hoped the skills you taught there might also be useful for Armand—the comte. As you saw, he has forgotten many of the social graces."

Felicity swallowed, feeling as though the beautiful drawing room was closing in on her. This was no little boy. This was a man. How could she coax a full-grown man to speak if he did not want to? And how could she teach him social graces? It was true she had tutored some of the village girls in etiquette, but to say that she ran a finishing school was nothing more than extreme exaggeration. God bless her aunt. She had obviously wanted to help her niece, but now Felicity would have to reveal the truth. "Actually," she began. "I wouldn't call it a finishing school."

"Well, that was a disaster," the duc said as he strode through the doors. The duchesse turned to look at him, leaving Felicity in midsentence. "I can't imagine what got into him. I—" His eyes met Felicity's. "Oh, you're still here."

She smiled wanly, watching as he turned to his wife for explanation. Not surprisingly, the duc looked a good deal like his brother. Both had dark hair and blue eyes. Both were tall and long-legged, but the duc was trimmer, more refined. He wore a tailcoat, a cravat and... shoes. The comte, despite his years in prison—or perhaps because of them— was larger and more imposing. And his eyes—those passionate, wild eyes—were darker blue, cobalt in color and filled with mysteries. Unlike the duc's carefully styled hair, the comte's was long and unruly. She wondered if he had cut it since escaping prison.

"Of course she's still here," the duchesse said, rising. She went to him and linked her arm with his. "I've hired her to tutor Armand."

"What?" The duc looked from his wife to Felicity and back again. "Do you really think that's wise?"

The duchesse turned to him, and for a moment Felicity thought they had forgotten she was present. "Julien, we have been working with Armand for months. We have tried everything, and nothing gets through to him. Nothing. But this young lady appears, and within moments of her playing the pianoforte, Armand reacts. She did more in the space of ten minutes than we have in hundreds of hours."

"Then we'll bring someone in to play for him. Hell, I'll get him a whole string quartet if that will help."

The duchesse lowered her voice. "We have someone to play for him. Miss Bennett is obviously an accomplished musician and a tutor. She's precisely what we've been looking for."

Now the duc looked past his wife to study Felicity again. She smiled tightly, feeling now might be the time to mention that she was not as accomplished as they might think. "Actually," she began again.

"I don't like it," the duc said, looking at his wife again. Apparently, they *had* forgotten she was there. "I don't trust Armand with her. I don't think it's safe."

"Very well, then we shall have a chaperone with them at all times. I can sit with them or your mother or one of the servants. But I have to tell you truthfully, Julien, I'm not concerned. I have been alone with Armand dozens of times, and he has never behaved inappropriately. None of the servants has ever complained of inappropriate behavior."

"And yet today you walked in here, and he had Miss Bennett in his arms."

Felicity felt her cheeks heat again. She could not deny the truth of the duc's statements. The comte's behavior toward her was far from appropriate.

The duchesse waved a hand. "He was overcome by the music he heard. Perhaps he was surprised by the sight of a pretty girl. I don't know, but what I do know is Armand was touching her voluntarily. It may not be appropriate, but it is progress."

"Progress toward what?" the duc asked darkly.

"Recovery. And don't crease your brow like that." She touched the line between his brows lightly. "Miss Bennett will be perfectly safe. As I said, we'll have a chaperone with them at all times."

"I don't know."

"Well, Miss Bennett does. You're not afraid, are you, Miss Bennett?" The duchesse turned to her, and Felicity could see she was waiting for her to repeat her earlier declaration. It would be easy enough to repeat. She was not afraid of the comte. She supposed she should have been, but she had seen in his eyes he meant her no harm. She had been unnerved by him, made breathless by him, but she had not been frightened.

She opened her mouth to say as much, but then realized that if she confirmed the duchesse's statement, she would be doing nothing less than accepting employment as the comte's tutor. While she might not be afraid of the man, she could not imagine spending hours in his presence, coaxing him to speak. She had no idea how to even begin a lesson like that!

No, she should tell the duchesse she was afraid, or she could not accept employment. And then—

Felicity paused.

Precisely. And then—what?

Where would she go? What would she do? Marry Charles? Oh, she would rather try to teach the occupants of Bedlam than marry Charles St. John. And the only way to be rid of him was money. This position—strange as it might be—would provide her that.

Felicity glanced at the duc and duchesse again. The position might not be what she had anticipated, but her father had often said God made a way. Perhaps this was His way. And what other employment could she find on short notice? Charles wanted money before the end of the year, only two short months.

But could she really help the comte? How did one

teach a man who had been imprisoned for twelve years to speak again, to live again? What did social graces mean to a man who had endured all of that?

"It's all right, Miss Bennett," the duc said, breaking her long silence. "You're under no obligation to accept a position. We'll pay for your return passage—"

"I want to stay," Felicity said quickly, feeling as though she had no other choice. She *needed* this position.

"Oh, wonderful!" the duchesse exclaimed, clasping her hands together.

"Are you certain?" the duc asked, looking dubious.

"Perfectly," Felicity answered with a brisk nod. Mentally, she wished she would stop sounding so confident. She was terrified she was going to be a complete failure. But she had to try. She had to succeed.

"Very good, then," the duchesse said. "Do you think you can begin tomorrow?"

"Absolutely. Right after breakfast." Her heart pounded a little faster at the prospect of seeing the wild, handsome comte again, but she tried to tamp down her excitement. She was here in a professional capacity. There was no room for schoolgirl crushes. She was the schoolteacher this time.

Or at least until the Valères realized how inadequate she was for the position.

⤫

Several hours later, Felicity sat at a small dressing table in her room and gazed at her reflection in the looking glass. Her heart was pounding with nervousness. The duchesse and her housekeeper had showed her the house and grounds and then escorted her to this room. Felicity expected to be led to a small cupboard suitable for a servant, but this room was of a decent size and amply furnished.

It had a small bed with a brass head- and footboard, a clothes press, and this pretty dressing table. The wood was light brown and gold in color and complemented the walls, which were papered in a simple yellow design. The curtains on the windows were white with yellow stripes, and the coverlet was white satin. With a cheery fire in the fireplace and a vase full of daisies—where had those come from?—on the bedside table, the room was comfortable and warm. It was probably the nicest room Felicity had ever occupied and certainly the cheeriest. She rose, went to the window and looked out on a small garden in the back. It was winter, the middle of November, and there was not much green to be found, but the ground was clear of snow. The winter had been mild thus far, but Felicity could feel the chill coming off the glass. The sky was growing dark, the shadows in the garden lengthening. She squinted when she saw something move in the shadows.

Charles? Her heart slammed in her chest. *Please, no…*

Felicity leaned closer to the window and peered hard at a small gate in the back of the garden. As she watched, it swung open, and two silhouettes crept forward. One was a large man, stout and solid, with arms the size of ham hocks. The other was a child; at least, she thought so at first. Then he stepped into the light streaming from the town house, and she could see in his hard expression that he was no child. He was diminutive in size but gnarled and wrinkled in appearance.

The two men moved stealthily forward, and Felicity realized she was holding her breath. What were they going to do? Burglarize the house? Should she alert someone?

The men crept forward and finally knelt down beside a flower bed flanking the house. All greenery was almost completely absent from the bed, and the men took out trowels and began to weed.

Felicity shook her head and went back to the dresser. How silly everyone would have thought her if she had told the duc and duchesse she was afraid the gardeners were burglars. She needed to stop thinking foolish thoughts and ready herself to go down to dinner.

The duchesse had asked Felicity to eat with the family, which surprised her greatly. She had assumed she would eat with the upper servants. Now she went to the clothes press where she had placed all of her belongings, opened the heavy drawer, and studied the bare shelves. Her blue cloak was folded and lay on one shelf, as well as another day dress, which she would wear tomorrow. On another shelf there was an assortment of under things—a shift, a night rail, a pair of stockings. On the third shelf was her music.

She frowned at the music then down at the white muslin gown she wore. She *knew* she should have brought a change of clothing. Her dress was a day dress, not at all suitable for dinner with a duc and duchesse. Without any jewelry, it looked utterly plain and terribly simple. It would have been providential if the remainder of her luggage had arrived before dinner, but she suspected it might be another day or so.

With a sigh, Felicity went to the door, pausing at the bedside table to gaze at the portrait of her father beside the vase of flowers. She wondered vaguely how much the duchesse paid for fresh flowers in the midst of winter, and those thoughts reminded her of the garden.

Curious as to what the two gardeners had done with the flower bed, Felicity pulled the curtains back and stared down. The garden was empty, and it was too dark to observe any changes in the landscape. The shadows were long now as twilight crept in, and Felicity assumed the gardeners had ended their work for the day. She was about to drop the curtains back into place when her skin prickled, and she stared at the gate the men had opened earlier.

The small, gnarled man stared back at her. His expression was surprised, and she realized he had been watching the house and happened to notice her at the window. His eyes were hard, expression fierce, and Felicity gasped then dropped the curtains.

But she lifted them again immediately. Why should she be the one to turn away? She was doing nothing wrong. That man, on the other hand, did not appear to be gardening at all. Perhaps her fears about burglary had not been entirely unfounded.

Felicity stared out into the violet evening, but the man was gone. Had she simply imagined him at the gate, or had he run away that quickly?

With a sigh, she dropped the curtains again and rubbed her eyes. She was probably overly tired. The journey from Hampshire to London had been long, and her meeting with the comte quite a shock. Doubtless a good night's sleep would chase away shadows and phantom gardeners.

Straightening her gown once more, Felicity opened her bedroom door and started toward the dining room. She hoped she remembered the way. Her room was in the back of the house on the second floor. This was the same floor the family slept on, and as Felicity walked past the other rooms, she wondered who was behind the closed doors. She wondered how close the comte's room was to her own.

The heavy runner that lay over the polished wood floor muted her steps and made a shushing sound under her slippers. The candles in the sconces on the wall flickered as she walked past them, giving the illusion that the paintings on the walls swayed and danced. Felicity studied each as she passed. There were no family portraits, only paintings of landscapes and still life. Felicity tried to imagine what it must have been like to lose everything so violently. Had the duc managed to save any portraits of his family? What about the duchesse? She had said she was a governess. Did she also have a family? And had they suffered similarly in the revolution? Or perhaps she was English? Unlike the duc, the duchesse had no French accent.

Felicity reached the stairs and descended, pausing on the first floor. Here she had to walk down a little corridor that ended before the drawing room. The grand staircase was before her, rising majestically from the vestibule. She could already see the glow from the crystal chandelier. But from behind the closed door of the drawing room, she heard the tinkling of laughter.

Should she go into the drawing room and wait to be summoned to dinner or go directly down to the dining room?

"Oh, curses," she muttered.

"Exactly," said a voice behind her.

Felicity swung around and stared at a tall, elegant woman with black hair and green eyes.

The woman gripped Felicity's arm to steady her. "What are we bemoaning?"

"I—ah—" Now this woman looked every bit the duchesse. From the regal way she held her head to the refined clip of her words, this woman was an aristocrat through and through.

The older woman smiled. "No matter. Come inside."

Felicity blinked and then allowed herself to be led into the drawing room, where the duc and duchesse were settling on the couch. Felicity nodded to each, her cheeks heating a bit when she saw the tender look the couple exchanged. There was something romantic about the warmth and obvious love the duc and duchesse shared. In an age when marriages were often arranged, it was charming to see a marriage based on love.

"Rowena, this is Miss Felicity Bennett," the duchesse said as soon as Felicity entered. "She's the tutor I engaged for Armand."

"Ah," the elegant woman said, crossing to a table where glasses filled with a burgundy liquid stood waiting. Felicity noticed the duc also held a glass.

"And, Miss Bennett," the duchesse continued, "this is the dowager duchesse of Valère."

Felicity curtseyed. "It's a pleasure, Your Grace."

She had not intended to curtsey, considered the gesture ridiculous and demeaning, but somehow it felt appropriate with this woman. One look at her, and it was obvious she was the duc's mother, and yet her accent was aristocratic English. Felicity recalled reading the duc and his brother were only half French. Their mother was from a prestigious British family, which was why the *ton*, decidedly unenthusiastic toward the French, had welcomed the Valères so warmly.

Felicity saw now everyone had dressed for dinner. The duchesse wore a gown of midnight blue with matching sapphires about her neck and dangling from her ears. The dowager wore a simple black gown, elegant in its clean lines. The duc wore a navy tailcoat and breeches, and his shirt and cravat were of the starkest white.

"Oh, dear me, no." The dowager handed Felicity one of the glasses. "The pleasure is all mine. My daughter-in-law speaks very highly of you. We are all expecting great things."

Felicity's heart felt as though it were sinking into her belly. "I'll do my best, Your Grace."

"Of course you will." The dowager sipped from her glass. "But do not expect me to be patient. I have waited twelve long years to have a conversation with my son, and now that you are here, I find myself growing impatient."

"*Ma mère*." The duc's deep voice captured everyone's attention. "Miss Bennett is not a miracle worker. You'll have to give her time."

Felicity was thankful someone understood. Everyone

was looking at her, so she smiled and sipped a bit of the liquid in her glass. It was Madeira and quite good.

"Now that you have met my brother," the duc said, "do you have any plans for commencing instruction?"

It was a good question, one she would have asked herself if she had been in the duc's place. Felicity wished she had had more time to formulate a plan. As it was, she had an idea, but was not at all certain how successful it would prove. "I had thought I might use pictures and link them with words," Felicity said quietly. "If you would be so kind as to furnish me with some paper, I will draw images and the words. For example, I might draw a cat, show the comte the picture of the cat, and then teach him the word."

It had been a vague idea in the back of her mind, but now that she said it aloud, it seemed very promising. She could draw a dozen pictures tonight in preparation for the lessons in the morning. Felicity smiled, but no one around her spoke.

She cleared her throat and took another sip of Madeira. Finally, the duc rose and went to a side table where a decanter of burgundy liquid sat. He refilled his glass, and then turned to her. "We've tried that. It didn't work."

Felicity blinked. "Oh." Suddenly, her legs felt unsteady and too light to support her body. She wished she could sit, but no one had invited her to do so, and the dowager was still standing. Then another idea hit her like a ray of sunlight. "Perhaps I might show the comte actual objects, for example, a flower, and teach him the word that way."

The duchesse smiled weakly. "We've tried that, as

well. However, just because a method did not work for us, does not mean it will not prove beneficial to you. After all, you have already forged a special connection with the comte."

Felicity glanced at the pianoforte on the other side of the room. She had been studiously avoiding looking at it until now because she was afraid seeing it again would cause memories of being held in the comte's arms to return. But her fears were for naught. The incident this morning seemed to have happened in another lifetime, to another person.

In fact, Felicity was certain it had only been the passions aroused by the music that had caused her to feel anything more than surprise when the comte had taken her into his arms. It had just been the residual passion of the music that made her heart race.

And then the drawing-room doors opened again. The comte stood framed in the doorway, dressed much as he had been this afternoon. He wore no tailcoat and no cravat, but his shirt was clean and starched. The sleeves were rolled at the wrist, and Felicity could see the bronze-corded skin of his arms. His buff breeches were tight, showing off legs that were muscled and well-shaped. But he wore no stockings or shoes. Many men would have looked ridiculous with bare calves and feet, but it only made the comte look more masculine. His one concession appeared to be his hair. The unruly mass she had observed this morning had been caught back in a neat queue, hinting at a thin layer of civilization beneath the overwhelming air of feral sensuality. He glanced at her, eyes smoldering with primitive heat, and the room reeled. Her ears rang with a whooshing sound, and she fumbled with her glass. Not knowing what to do with her hands, she lifted the glass to her lips and drank deeply. But the Madeira was finished far too quickly.

She looked down, surprised to see her glass was empty. Then she looked up again, into the cobalt eyes of the man in the doorway, and she found she was still very, very thirsty.

Five

SEATED ACROSS FROM THE YELLOW-HAIRED WOMAN, Armand was having difficulty focusing on dinner. There were many Rules to eating with others, which was why he generally preferred to eat alone in his room. Some of the Rules, however, were vaguely familiar. Armand thought that if he reached far enough back into his murky memories, he might remember having learned these Rules.

But there were so many memories. And many were bad, very bad, and Armand did not care enough about the Rules for eating to go to those places.

Only now he wished he wasn't such a damn coward, because the woman was following all the Rules effortlessly, and he had to think and remember. He could not use his fork and spoon and watch her at the same time. Frustrated, he finally threw them aside and picked up the meat with his hands.

He looked up between bites and saw the eyes of the others at the table dart away from him. That was another thing. The Rules said you could not stare outright, but his family would watch him with sidelong looks. He had known this would happen, as well. He rarely ate with his family, and tonight he had not just come down to eat, but he had changed clothes and pulled his hair out of his eyes. He even put on one of those neck cloths—for five minutes. But it cut off his breathing, and he had torn and shredded it.

How did his brother stand being confined all the time?

Armand glanced at Julien and saw his brother watching him, a scowl on his face. Armand wanted to tell his brother he had nothing to worry about. Armand was not going to hurt the woman. He just wanted to be in her presence, and he wanted her to make that music again. He would find a way to demand it.

"Miss Bennett, you said you come from Hampshire?" His mother spoke now, breaking the silence Armand had been enjoying. It seemed he was the only one who preferred silence over noise.

"Yes. My father was a vicar in Selborne. He passed away recently." As she spoke, the woman's gaze touched on all of those seated at the table except him. Armand saw she was careful to avoid meeting his gaze, and when she did so, her face turned a light shade of red. He liked listening to her voice, liked watching her talk. And for some reason, he liked seeing her cheeks color when she looked at him.

"And your mother?" his mother asked. "Is she still alive?"

"Unfortunately, no. She passed away when I was only ten." She lifted her wine glass, then glanced in his direction, and set it down again. Armand wondered at the gesture. Why would she lift her glass and then set it down again? Did she want a drink and then suddenly change her mind? Why would a glance at him change her mind? Did he repulse her as he did so many others?

"Armand obviously appreciated your playing," Sarah said, signaling the footmen to remove the course and bring in the next. It was cheese and nuts, and Armand was grateful. One Rule he knew—cheese and nuts meant the ordeal of dinner was almost over.

"Did your mother teach you?" Sarah asked.

"Yes, she was an accomplished musician and had an enormous talent. She could hear something once and then play it perfectly."

"How extraordinary!" his mother said.

Armand sat perfectly still, his heart pounding. They were speaking of music. Now was his chance to ask the woman—Miss Bennett—to play again. But how? Frustration infused him like heat from a warm coal. Logically, he knew he was safe here. There was no danger in speaking. But he could not make himself do it. The words clogged in his throat, and panic rushed through him. Angry at his own weakness, he gripped his fork and bent it.

"I'm fortunate enough to have the same gift as my mother," the woman was saying, "though I do not always play the selection perfectly the first time."

Armand took the bent fork and clanked it against his plate loudly. Everyone looked at him. Normally, he tried to avoid attention, and now he remembered why. The feel of everyone's eyes on him made his skin crawl. He had the urge to reach out violently and rip away the eyes. Instead, he clenched his hands around the fork and glared at the woman who had caused him to endure this discomfort. The fork snapped in two, but the woman stared back, seeming unperturbed by his glare. He would have to think of a way to see her cheeks color again, but now he wanted to communicate a different message. He dropped the fork pieces and pointed at her.

Ah, there was that red color he so enjoyed.

"Armand is trying to communicate with Miss Bennett!" Sarah said in a hushed whisper.

Armand ignored her.

Armand showed the woman his hands again then turned them down and pretended to play the instrument she had played earlier. He glanced into her eyes, saw she had seen his movements, and waited. What would she do now? Would she make the music again?

The room was silent; even the footmen had frozen with their plates of cheese and nuts held aloft. Finally, Miss Bennett looked away, toward Julien. "He wants me to play again."

Armand felt like smiling. She had understood! Good. Now she would play again.

Immediately.

But she remained seated, her gaze on his brother. "Do you think I should?"

Recognizing her interrogative tone, Armand turned to Julien. Not surprisingly, he found Julien watching him thoughtfully. Armand raised his eyebrows at Julien in a gesture of impatience, and Julien actually smiled. "If you don't mind playing, Miss Bennett, I don't see why we shouldn't enjoy some music after dinner." He turned to the frozen footmen. "But first, the last course."

Armand sighed and thrust back in his chair. Why must he be forced to wait? He refused the cheese and nuts and glared at his brother in an effort to make him eat more quickly. His efforts were not rewarded. Julien's movements actually seemed to slow down.

Finally, after an eternity, the family adjourned to the drawing room, Armand leading the way with his mother beside him. He was vaguely aware he should take her arm, as Julien took Sarah's, but the discomfort of her touch was not worth obeying The Rule.

They reached the drawing room, and Armand would have arrowed for the instrument, but his mother caught his elbow and tugged him over to the couch. "Sit here. You should be able to hear very well beside me. And"—she gave him a pointed look—"I have missed your company." She took her place beside him and patted his arm. To his annoyance, Armand had to crane his head to see the yellow-haired woman and the instrument—pi… something.

Think! Idiot! Word!

In a flash, it came to him—pianoforte!

The woman went directly to it.

"Is there anything you'd like to hear?" the woman asked, looking at each of them in turn. Armand did not understand the question, but he nodded at the pianoforte to encourage her to begin.

"Why don't you play the piece you began this afternoon? Obviously, Armand enjoyed it," Sarah said.

Miss Bennett nodded and raised her hands. Seconds later, Armand was once again captured. Almost

involuntarily, he closed his eyes and allowed the music
to take him away. The music made him believe there
was a time when he had been an innocent child, a
time when he had been happy, a time when *prison* was
a word and not his life. When he heard the music, he
could almost forget the years he had spent crammed in
a cell and all but left for dead. He could pretend they
had never happened.

The music slowed and paused, and Armand opened
his eyes again. Around him, everyone smacked their
hands together. He frowned at the sound they made
and was about to rise to make her play again, but her
hands lowered, and a new song began. From the first
notes, the song was familiar to Armand. He could not
say how he knew it or when he had learned it, but he
found himself anticipating the notes before the woman
played them.

His eyes met Julien's, and it was obvious his brother
knew the song. Was it something they had learned as
children? Armand stood, needing to move nearer to
the pianoforte, to the source of the music. Seeming to
sense his need, his mother released him. Armand edged
forward, and the yellow-haired woman watched him
as he came closer. Her sky blue eyes locked on him,
and she offered a small smile. She did not seem afraid,
but Armand could sense his brother moving nearer.
He was always aware of anyone behind him. And
though he trusted the people in this room, he would
never relax with his back unprotected.

The song continued, and now words tickled the
recesses of Armand's mind. Not so much words as
ghosts of words he had once known.

Au clair de la lune…

Were those the actual words? He rehearsed them in his mind. He had no idea what they meant, but they seemed right. As the woman began to play the third verse, he began to sing in his mind.

Au clair de la lune
Mon ami Pierrot
Prête-moi ta lume

The last few words escaped his lips, and he flinched at the sound of his voice. A gasp sounded somewhere in the room, and the woman stopped playing. Armand was frozen in shock and disbelief. He had spoken. True, his voice had sounded hoarse and brittle as ancient parchment paper. And he had not been singing or speaking so much as rasping out words through vocal chords that choked on every syllable.

But he had spoken. He had used words. His gaze went directly to his mother's, and he saw the sheen of tears on her cheeks. It had not been simply his imagination, then. She had heard.

He opened his mouth to speak again, then quickly shut it.

No!

Silencesilencesilence…

Must control. Control words.

He knew secrets, things he must keep to himself.

He looked at his mother, saw the eagerness in her eyes, and looked away.

Angry, he slammed a hand down on the pianoforte. The instrument was not harmed, but he saw the woman jump at the action. He had frightened her. Again. Was that all he could do? Frighten and terrorize? He had fewer manners than a dog, and he sounded like a creature one might find in the Tower Menagerie. Sometimes he wished Julien had just left him to rot in that prison.

Without a backward glance, Armand strode out of the room.

❧

Felicity blinked as the drawing-room door slammed in the comte's wake. For such a silent man, he could certainly make a great deal of noise when he chose. Slowly, she turned to observe the others in the room—and then found herself wishing she had kept her eyes on the piano keys. Everyone was staring at her!

"Well, I imagine that isn't an everyday occurrence," she said brightly, her voice sounding tinny and false in her ears.

The dowager sniffed and dabbed her eyes with a white lace handkerchief. The duc went on scowling, but the duchesse smiled. "No, no it isn't." She rose. "Miss Bennett, this is further proof we did the right thing in employing you. I can't believe the progress—"

"Progress!" the duc all but shouted. "How is this progress? You saw what happened. He doesn't *want* to speak."

"But he did," the duchesse said, her voice still even. "And he will again. Somehow Miss Bennett is able to break through whatever is holding Armand back."

"Everything is moving too quickly," the duc stated, pacing in front of the pianoforte. Felicity watched him stalk, his movements reminding her of a caged lion she had seen once in a traveling circus. "He's already been pushed to the limits of what any man could endure. *Should* endure. If we aren't careful, he's likely to have a setback."

"And if we're too careful, he'll never take any steps forward."

"Better that than for him to revert to what he was!"

The duchesse shook her head. "He won't revert. Julien—"

He took three long strides and was at her elbow. "Sit down. You don't need to overtax yourself. You need to think of the baby."

"The baby is fine, and I'm fine. And *Armand* is fine. Stop being so overprotective."

"Stop being—I am *not* overprotective."

"Yes, you are," the dowager said, standing now. She waved a hand. "And in case you are wondering, I am fine. I do not need to sit down."

The duc scowled. "*Ma mère…*"

But the dowager ignored him. "Miss Bennett," she said, turning her gaze on Felicity. Felicity sat straighter. For the past three minutes she had contemplated slinking out of the room. She doubted anyone would have noticed her absence. After all, this seemed a family discussion. The duchesse could inform her in the morning that her services were not required.

"Miss Bennett," the dowager repeated, and Felicity jumped to her feet. "I am impressed with the changes I have seen in my son. Before tonight, I had not heard his voice in twelve long years. If this is what you can accomplish in one evening, I look forward to seeing your progress"—she eyed the duc—"in a week. I shall see you at breakfast, Miss Bennett."

"Yes, Your Grace." Felicity curtseyed as the
dowager swept past her. A moment later she realized she was now alone with the fuming duc and
the victorious duchesse. Neither was looking at her,
but Felicity began to make her own way out of the
drawing room. "I think I shall retire, as well. It's been
a long day." Of course, she need not have bothered
with niceties. Neither the duc nor duchesse was
paying her the slightest attention.

Felicity took the steps slowly on the way back to
her room. She was indeed tired. It had been a long
exhausting day and one full of surprises. And yet she
found her mind was a jumble of thoughts and ideas.
She doubted she would be able to sleep for many
hours to come. The prospect of lying awake, thoughts
of the comte flashing unbidden into her mind, was not
a pleasant one, but she had little choice but to retire
to her room. Perhaps tomorrow she might ask about
borrowing a book, but tonight she would have no
company other than those unbidden thoughts.

Perhaps if she focused on the tasks ahead of her,
she would put other thoughts behind her. Speaking
was only one of many things with which the comte
needed assistance. His manners were atrocious. Even
if she could not coax him to speak, perhaps if she
made improvements in his manners, then the duchesse
would be pleased. She had to find a way to make the
comte cooperate in order to keep this position. If she
lost it, how would she pay Charles his twenty-five
pounds? That would be almost her entire salary for
the year, so as it was, she would have to ask for an
advance. But she could not ask for an advance on

her salary until she had shown she had made some improvement in the comte.

She reached the top of the stairs and turned into the corridor leading to her room. It was dark, and she did not see the shadow move before her until the hand reached out and caught her wrist.

She gave a brief shriek before she was pulled hard and fast against a man's chest. She did not need to look to know he was the comte. She did not need to look, but she did. Her gaze traveled up his stark white shirt, over his smooth, bare throat, around his strong jaw, lingering on his soft mouth. Her heart sped up, pounding inside her ribcage like a trapped bird. Heat, white and razor-sharp, sliced through her.

She forced her gaze to jump to his. His eyes, deep and dark, met her gaze, and Felicity felt all the air in her lungs rush out in a sudden gust. They stood in the corridor gazing at one another for hours, or so it seemed to Felicity. But finally she pried her locked jaw open, parted her lips, and whispered, "What do you want?"

Images assailed her. His lips meeting hers softly, roughly… The comte bending her back, kissing her throat, caressing her hair, caressing…

Oh, dear. The heat burned, setting her on fire, making her breath come quickly. Did she actually want those things? If not, why was she imagining them—and why was she still standing in his arms?

And then, quite abruptly, she wasn't. He released her—all but her hand—and pulled her after him.

Six

FELICITY COULD NOT HAVE SAID WHY SHE FOLLOWED. She didn't usually follow men she did not know, especially those who pulled her into their arms, leaving her breathless. Not that that happened to her very often. Actually, it had never happened to her before today.

It would definitely be best if she continued along her way, retired to her bedroom, and locked the door. That would be the sensible thing to do.

Of course, that was not what she did. Instead, she followed the mysterious comte deeper into the darkened corridor and then down a back stairs, probably the one reserved for servants. The stairs were steep and narrow, and the faint light from the comte's candle did little to dissipate the shadows around her.

The stairs finally ended, and the comte pushed through a door. He did not hold it open for her, and it slammed closed in her face. "Cursed man," she muttered, opening the door and emerging to find him waiting on the other side with an impatient look on his face.

He turned his back to her and continued walking

through a second door, which Felicity could now see led outside. What was this? It had to be past ten. Where could he be taking her? And *why* was she still following? If he ended up strangling her and leaving her for dead in the garden, she would have only herself to blame for behaving as such a brainless ninny.

Then again, perhaps strangling her was not his plan, at all. Twice he had taken her into his arms. Perhaps his motives were more romantic in nature. And now that the possibility had occurred to her, hadn't she better turn back immediately? But of course she didn't because, to be honest, had the idea really just occurred to her? Hadn't she been hoping all along his plan was to kiss her? And what would her father, the poor vicar, think of her now? And Charles, her betrothed—well, she did not care what he thought of her. One day in London and already she had become a wanton.

She stepped outside, feeling the crisp night air quickly envelop her. It was cold, but not uncomfortably so. She had forgotten her cloak, and it occurred to her that fetching it might serve as an excuse for escape. But when her eyes adjusted to the darkness and she found the comte standing a few feet in front of her, he did not appear overly anxious to either strangle or kiss her.

He was staring up at the sky.

Felicity stood behind him and stared up, as well. The view of the night sky was certainly nothing compared to what she was used to in the country. The stars in London were muted and sparse, only the brightest managing to shine through the haze of lamplight and coal smoke that hung over the city.

Remarkably, it was the same night sky she had seen a hundred times. Strange that she should be so far away from home and yet be standing under the same sky.

The hair on the back of her neck prickled, and she turned to the comte. He was watching her, his eyes dark and intense. She did not think he wore any expression that was not intense. She cleared her throat. "It's pretty outside," she said, realizing it sounded trite but knowing not to expect a response in any case.

He continued to stare at her, giving no indication he had heard her. And she was supposed to coax him to speak? The dowager had wanted progress in a week. Felicity was not feeling optimistic.

"Do you like the stars?" she asked because he was still looking at her, and that look made her tremble inside. But she didn't want to think too much about whether the sensation resulted from discomfort or attraction. Perhaps a little of both.

"The stars," she repeated and gestured at the night sky. "Do you like them?"

He followed her gesture and looked up, and now she had a chance to study his profile. His face was classic in structure—straight nose, strong cheekbones, full lips. She had to stop staring at those lips. Or, if she could not, she should focus on how set they were. How hard. He might have the face of an aristocrat, but the way he stood, the way he moved, was primeval. No, there was nothing refined or elegant beneath the surface of this man.

And why did that make her heart race?

He was still staring at the night sky, and she turned her gaze back to the speckled inky black vastness above them. Safer that way. They stood in silence for some five minutes or more—long enough for her to feel the chill—before she wondered, once again, why he had brought her out here.

Thankfully, he did not appear intent upon strangling her. Nor did he seem to want to kiss her—which was a good thing, she told herself, ignoring the stab of disappointment cutting through her. So why direct her outside?

The breeze stirred the leaves in the trees, rustling them quietly, and she sensed the comte relax beside her. He seemed less tense, less fierce out here. She supposed that should make sense. After all, a man who had been locked up for twelve years would come to appreciate the freedom of the infinite night sky and the unpredictable evening breeze.

She turned and found him watching her again. It was dark now, the town house's lights behind them creating just enough glow for her to distinguish the look on his face.

She could only describe the expression as one of longing. And because her heart constricted when she saw it and her belly pooled with warmth, she started to speak before she did something ridiculous like throw herself into his arms. "I can see why you enjoy the garden. After all those years in prison, it must be refreshing to step outside any time you please."

He continued to stare at her, moving closer and studying her face. Felicity tried to ignore the heat she felt blossom in her cheeks and stared up at the stars again. The North Star was the most apparent, and she focused on its bright, steady glow. "I don't know what you must think of London. I only just arrived this morning and find it quite overwhelming." She knew she was babbling now, but he continued moving closer. She could feel his breath on her cheek.

"But I suppose if you were in Paris, the noise and…" She squeaked as he lifted her hand and cradled it in his. She still wore her gloves, but she could feel the warmth of his bare skin through the thin material.

"—and the lights and the general…"

He stripped off her glove, and now there was no barrier between his warm, calloused flesh and her own, which was cooler and surprisingly sensitive to his touch. As he had that afternoon, he lifted her hand and put it to his cheek. She could feel the stubble there, under her fingertips.

"The general, ah, general hubbub…" She tried to continue speaking as though what he was doing was not entirely inappropriate. As a woman betrothed to another man—however unwillingly—she should not allow this. In addition, as his tutor, she had more reason to stop him. This would be the perfect opportunity to teach him manners, but when she turned to rebuke him, those cobalt eyes were on her again, and her throat went dry.

There was curiosity in his expression, almost as though touching her hand to his face was an experiment. But there was passion there too. She had seen it this morning when he had interrupted her playing, and she saw it now. Saw he did not quite know what to do with it.

Oh, she could show him. She could lean forward and place her lips on his, and then—

And then her father would turn over in his grave! What was she thinking!

Summoning her father's face before her eyes, she finally found the strength to tug her hand out of the comte's grasp. Now she would go inside. She would go inside and go directly to her room and go to bed. Tomorrow they would start fresh and pretend none of this had happened.

"I'm going to go inside now, my lord," she said quietly, stepping back. "I shall see you in the morning." She said it forcefully, and she followed the words with a determined turn back toward the doors where they had exited. She had meant every word—until she felt his hand on her elbow.

Don't stop. Keep walking, she told herself, but she couldn't resist turning, just to glimpse the look on his face. Curses, but he had to be the most handsome man she had ever seen. How was she supposed to walk away from this wounded angel who aroused and unsettled her all at once?

How was she going to serve as his tutor if she did not start enforcing some discipline now—on herself, if not her pupil?

Be strong, she thought, and began to turn away again. She would have made it inside the town house at that point, too, if his hand had not reached out to stroke her cheek. The feel of his rough, warm finger on her cool cheek arrested her body and mind. It was one thing to have him scrape her fingers along his face and quite another to be touched by him.

Her knees went weak, her stomach fluttered, and she could not seem to find enough air to fill her lungs.

Without her permission, her eyes closed, and absent her sight, the feel of his hand against her face was that much more exquisite, that much more seductive.

Did he even mean to seduce her? Did he have any idea the effect he was having on her?

"You must stop," she breathed, trying to put some force behind her words. "This is not appropriate."

But of course he ignored her, and the finger trailed across her lips, sending a zing of pleasure coursing through her body. Oh, curses... She gulped in a breath and wheezed it out again. It seemed London was deficient in air, and she had inhaled the last of it. Her head was pounding, or was that her heart in her ears?

"You must..." But he was not going to stop. He had begun to trail that tantalizing finger down the slope of her opposite cheek. And here she had stood for a good three minutes and allowed him to touch her so intimately. *She* had to be the one to stop this.

Drawing upon reserves she did not know she possessed, Felicity wrenched herself away, stumbling back unsteadily. She would have caught herself, would have regained her balance and arrowed for the door but for the lump of dirt that caught her heel and sent her sprawling.

The comte made a sound of distress and rushed to her aid, but Felicity was no longer paying attention to him. She was studying the ground where she'd tripped. She had plopped in a neat, tidy garden. Granted, it was November, and much of the garden's blooms were dead or hibernating, but she could see where pin-straight rows had been planted and waited for spring to come again.

Except that amidst the rows, in what seemed to her a haphazard fashion, holes had been dug. They were quite deep but not evenly spaced. They appeared more destructive than anything else. The comte leaned over her, grasped her arm, but Felicity shook him off.

"Look at this." She pointed to the mound of dirt she had tripped over, leaning forward to peer inside the hole. The moon had not yet risen, or was shrouded from view by London's pervasive fog, and she could make out very little. But from what she could see, nothing had been planted inside the hole. Besides, who dug a hole, planted something within, and then left it exposed?

She glanced up at the comte and saw he had finished studying the hole she pointed to and now seemed to be cataloguing the others. She saw his gaze dart from one to the next and the scowl that accompanied what he saw reminded her of the duc, his brother.

"It's strange," she murmured. "Why would anyone dig holes like these? Certainly your gardeners…" She bolted up, her mind rushing back to earlier in the evening. "Those two men!" She glanced at the comte and saw he was watching her with interest. She did not know if he understood, but she continued anyway, working it out in her mind.

"I saw two men earlier from the window in my chambers. I assumed they were gardeners, but then they acted so suspiciously. I wonder if they were out here digging these holes. But why would they do this?"

It was a question apparently the comte had no answer for either. He merely glanced about the garden one last time, then took her hand and pulled her forward.

"Now where are we going?" she asked, slightly breathless as he pulled her along. But once they reached inside the house, he released her and gestured toward the stairway, indicating she should go up—back the way they had come. "But perhaps I should speak with your brother about what I saw earlier. It might be something of importance…"

But the comte knew what he wanted from her. He pointed to the stairs again and made a shooing motion with his hands.

Felicity clenched her teeth. Was she some child to be hurried off to bed? After all, if that was what he had wanted, then why had he dragged her outside? She opened her mouth to protest, to begin what she was certain would be the first of many, many lessons in manners, but he simply turned on his heel and walked away.

"Wait!"

But her command was ignored. Without looking back, the comte raised a hand and shooed her, once again, away.

And then he was gone, and she stood alone. She supposed she could search out the duc and duchesse, tell them what she had seen, but where to begin? And what if they were already abed? She was not going to wake them or risk rousing the house.

She would just mention it tomorrow at breakfast. And then, after breakfast, her lessons with the comte would commence. And she knew just where she would begin.

❧

Armand hated going inside again. He felt free outside. He could breathe outside. Months ago his brother had taken him to a house in a place called Southampton. The house had a name: The Gardens. Armand understood the words and the reason for it—the house had at least a dozen gardens, some wild, some straight and tame.

When Julien made him leave, Armand fought. He would have done anything to stay in that place, to work outside in those gardens. He had seen dogs on the property. He had always wanted a dog. But Julien had forced him to come back to London, and though this house had a small garden Armand enjoyed, he could not stop thinking of the house in Southampton. He needed to find a way to get back. And he would... after he had spent more time with Miss Bennett.

But tonight, escaping to The Gardens was not his problem. The garden here—what he thought of as his garden—had been violated. His brother must see it.

Armand found Julien in the library. Sarah had taken to retiring early, and after dinner, Julien could usually be found at his desk, pen scratching in his ledger.

Armand entered, but Julien did not look up from his work. "Give me five more minutes, *chérie*. This deposit doesn't add up..."

Armand stood, waited, aware he was not the one being addressed. Finally, Julien looked up and scowled. "Oh. What is it now? Run out of young ladies to accost?"

Armand didn't understand every word, but he comprehended the gist of them. And the tone—that he understood quite well. Armand wished he could remember his childhood, wished he could recall whether Julien had always teased him, always been so overprotective. Had he bantered back and forth with Julien?

He could not imagine doing so now. He could not imagine using words so carelessly, so freely. He knew what others thought of him—the maids, the footmen, the members of the *ton* who came to call on Sarah and his mother. He could see their discomfort in the looks they gave him and each other.

They feared him.

But the yellow-haired woman, Miss Bennett, had not feared him. He had not seen even a flicker of fright in her eyes. And yet, she was not comfortable with him. She avoided looking at him, fumbled with her hands, drank her wine too quickly. Did she pity him?

He had never cared what others thought, but for some reason he cared what Miss Bennett thought. He could not get enough of her sky blue eyes or the music she made with those talented fingers. He could not get enough of her touching him. For the first time in memory, the touch of another human being did not burn him.

He had taken her outside, showed the stars and his garden in what was probably a failed attempt to prove he was not some savage. He wanted her to see he had an appreciation for beauty and nature. Instead, he had made her uncomfortable enough that she tried to run from him. And then she had discovered the holes.

And that was why he stood in Julien's library now. Those strange holes in the garden had not been there last night. What could have caused them? Miss

Bennett had tried to tell him what she knew about it, but he did not understand everything.

No matter. He had his own ideas.

They had come. He could not say exactly who *they* were, but he knew it was someone from his past. They were here, and they were searching for...

Silencesilencesilence!

No, he would not even think the name. Even thinking it would be dangerous. Julien needed to see the danger. He needed to know they were no longer safe.

With that objective in mind, Armand crossed the room and unlatched the French doors behind Julien's desk. They led out to the garden, to an area where the family sat on warm summer evenings. Armand had tried to lure Julien outside on such a night and found his brother did not appreciate the quiet of the gardens as he did.

"I'm not in the mood to look at stars," Julien said, waving for Armand to close the doors again. "I want to finish these ledgers."

Armand pushed the doors wider and waited, arms crossed over his chest. He stared at the back of Julien's head, wondering if a swift smack against the hard skull would have any real effect.

Finally his patience was rewarded, and Julien turned and scowled at him. "You're allowing the heat in this room to escape."

Armand pushed the doors wider, stepped outside, and waited. With a long-suffering sigh, Julien heaved himself out of his chair and followed. "This had better not be about looking at some plant or other," he growled, stomping after Armand.

Armand led the way, smiling in amusement at his brother's mumbled curses. If he were Julien, he would not have traded the outside for sitting in a dark office, staring at lists of numbers for hours and hours. But he understood his brother considered any pursuit that was not monetary in nature a waste of time.

Finally, they reached the section of the garden where he stood earlier with Miss Bennett. It was darker than before, but Julien had carried a lamp with him and now he raised it to illuminate the ground where Armand pointed.

"What the hell?" He studied the holes then knelt down for a closer look at the biggest one. He glanced up at Armand, who stood with his arms crossed, feeling rather smug. "I don't suppose you did this?"

Now it was Armand's turn to scowl.

"Hmm. Doesn't look like the work of an animal."

Armand simply waited patiently, knowing his brother would eventually see the problem, the danger.

Julien rose, peered at another hole. "It can't be the gardeners. This is destructive." He ran a hand through his hair. "Or exploratory." He shot a look at Armand. "Digging for something? What would someone be digging for in our garden?"

Armand frowned, still having difficulty tracking his brother's rapid speech. Julien mimed digging with a shovel, and Armand nodded. Yes, now he understood.

Kicking at one of the mounds, Julien growled, "Why?"

Armand inhaled sharply, hoping his brother would not press the issue.

"I'll have the gardeners repair the damage in the · morning," Julien said, turning back toward the town house, but Armand made a sound that caused his brother to spin back around. He put a hand to his forehead and pretended to be looking into the distance for something. Julien watched him for a long moment then said, "You want me to have someone watch the house. You think this might be more serious."

Armand nodded.

Julien put his hands behind his back and walked slowly toward the town house. Armand followed behind, impatient for his brother's decision. Finally Julien paused at the French doors. "I'll have someone keep watch tonight."

Armand relaxed and started inside. As he passed through, Julien patted him on the shoulder.

Hot! No!

The pain was instant and intense. Armand jerked away, his skin burning where his brother had touched it. He rounded on his brother, fists high and ready to attack. But Julien already had his hands high in surrender.

"I'm sorry. I forgot." He spoke slowly and gestured for Armand to relax. "I won't do it again. My mistake."

Armand's shoulders fell, but he kept his wary eyes narrowed. The pain began to fade, and he nodded at Julien, let him know he was fine.

"Really, I'm sorry, brother. I forgot. For a moment, you seemed so—" He cut himself off, and Armand wheeled away. He climbed the stairs, feeling like an outcast. Worse, he felt as though he had brought danger here. The holes were danger. Everyone near him, including Miss Bennett, was in jeopardy. But damned if he knew how to save them.

Would he see Miss Bennett again on the morrow, or would she have disappeared by morning? It was probably best if she disappeared, probably best if he never saw those sky-colored eyes again or heard the magical music she made. If he saw her again, she would try to force him to speak. She had already done so. He could not risk it happening again. Now that the danger was closer, speech was even more hazardous.

If she were still in the house tomorrow, he would refuse to see her. She would go away if he refused long enough. It might be the only way to save her.

Seven

HER POSITION WOULD BE TERMINATED BEFORE SHE HAD even begun. Felicity fretted and paced the drawing room as, one by one, each member of the Valère household returned with the same news.

The comte would not see her.

He refused to leave his room, refused to acknowledge anyone's presence, refused to interact.

"He's done this before," the duchesse told her, while the duc stormed upstairs to harangue his brother into compliance. Felicity could hear the duc's rapid French echo all the way down in the drawing room, and it did not sound like he was having any better luck than either the duchesse or dowager duchesse had. "He withdraws into himself, sometimes for an hour, sometimes for days. I don't know what triggers it"—above them, a door slammed, and booted footsteps stomped along a corridor. The duchesse and her mother-in-law exchanged weary looks—"but I suppose it's understandable after all he's been through."

The drawing-room door burst open, and the duc,

looking as though he were ready to throttle someone, stormed inside. "He's not coming out. Don't ask me why. The man is as stubborn as an ox. I'm going back to my library." And he stormed out again.

Felicity blinked. It seemed to her that perhaps stubbornness was a family trait.

"I don't know what to tell you," the duchesse said, spreading her hands. "Perhaps he will be more sociable tomorrow."

Felicity nodded. But what if the comte did not come out tomorrow? The duchesse had said sometimes he stayed hidden away for days. Would they pay her for those idle days? What if the comte did not deign to leave his room for a month? Would she still have the position, or would she be forced to tell Charles she had been dismissed? Then what would happen?

She knew exactly what would happen. And if she refused to marry Charles, what then? If she returned to her aunt's house, she would only be a burden. She could not endure that. Nor could she endure having to explain to her aunt and her aunt's friends and her aunt's neighbors and *everyone she ever met from that day on* the man her father had promised her to, the man who had nursed her father in his last days, the man everyone thought was upright and respectable, was a gambler and a drunk and blackmailing her, besides.

How humiliating—for her father, God rest his soul, and herself.

She could not allow that to happen.

Panic began to creep in. She had to do something. But what?

The comte was a grown man—and not a small or

weak one at that. He could not be dragged or physi-
cally persuaded to do what he did not wish. For the
tenth time since she had arrived, she wished she had
not been wrong about the comte's age. It would be
so much easier to teach a boy of seven or eight. If
nothing else, he could be forced to leave his room.

So if she could not force the comte to come out, she
would have to persuade him using other means. She
could not go to his room. That would be improper,
and he would probably ignore her anyway. He had
ignored his own mother and brother.

She glanced across the room at the sunlight filtering
through the drawn curtains. A splash of gold hit
the pianoforte, and she smiled. If words could not
persuade him, then perhaps music could.

"Your Grace, would you mind if I played a piece?"

The duchesse shrugged. "Of course not. You
must play as much as you like—oh!" Her face lit like
a candle. "Oh! Why did I not think of that?" She
turned to the dowager. "Of course. If Armand hears
the music, it will certainly lure him from his room."

The dowager looked thoughtful. "Perhaps, perhaps
not. It depends how deeply he has withdrawn into his
shell. But I agree you should attempt it." She nodded
to Felicity. "Sarah, you go downstairs, and I shall stay
here to chaperone. I think the fewer people in the
room, the better."

"Very well."

The dowager took a chair in the back of the
room, where she would not be easily observed, while
Felicity settled herself on the bench at the pianoforte.
She lifted her fingers and noted they were trembling

slightly. What if the music failed to lure him out? What would she do then?

No, do not think of that. Think only of success. And what piece would bring her success? A sonata? An étude? A march? A fugue?

Felicity closed her eyes and pursed her lips. She was thinking too hard. She should just play. Play anything.

She set her trembling fingers on the keys and began, tentatively at first. The notes were quiet and slow, and her fingers felt stiff and awkward. She stumbled, played the wrong notes, played the wrong rhythm. The comte would never be drawn in if she continued to play this poorly. She had to let go, as she had the day before.

Her instincts told her to concentrate harder, focus more, but instead, she closed her eyes and forced herself to relax. She played several wrong notes, the sound clashing and making her cringe.

Feel the music. See the keys in your mind.

But the image that came to her mind was that of her mother. She looked impossibly tall, and Felicity knew this memory originated from when she was a young child. Her mother wore a yellow gown, and her long hair tumbled over the faded material like a shower of gold. She sat at a stool, her hands poised on the pianoforte, but she was looking over her shoulder and smiling. Felicity smiled at the memory. And then in her mind, she saw her mother turn back to the piano, saw her lift her long, slim fingers, and heard the music flow from those fingers.

Now, Felicity allowed her own fingers to move in time with her mother's. She didn't hear the music she played, only the music in her memory. She did not hear the drawing-room door open or the sound of footsteps stomping angrily into the room. But she felt a prickle rush up and down her back, and gradually, as the memory faded, she opened her eyes.

The comte was angry. It did not take much to discern that. His eyes blazed icy blue fire, his hands fisted at his side, and his barefooted stance was at once defiant and eager. Felicity forced herself to continue to play, though she would rather have run from the comte's glare. And then part of her wanted to smile. All was not lost. Her position was secure… for the moment anyway.

"My lord," she said, her hands racing over the keys almost of their own volition, "how good of you to join us."

He growled, his lip curling in anger, but he stomped to the piano and stood watching her fingers fly over the keys. "It's by Mozart, Piano Concerto Five in D Major," she told him.

He didn't respond, merely continued to watch her play.

"You didn't come down for your lesson this morning. Were you trying to avoid me or the lesson or both?"

He scowled at her, his glare fierce. She knew what he wanted. He wanted her to stop speaking and just play. But she was through allowing him to take the lead. As the tutor, she must lead, and he must follow. She slowed her hands, drawing out each note, making each one last. She could see the comte lean forward, anticipating each chord she played. And so she continued to slow her hands until the music finally stopped altogether.

In the sudden silence, she heard the comte's breathing and the scrape of the wood under his hands as he gripped the sides of the pianoforte. She looked up at him, met his gaze. How could his eyes be so dark blue? How could they be so intense, so passionate? Her back prickled again as awareness of him flooded through her. The room felt suddenly too warm, as though the sunlight seeping through the windows was burning her.

"You would rather I didn't stop playing." She raised a hand to her forehead to wipe a bead of perspiration away. When she saw his gaze followed the movement, she pretended to smooth her hair back into place. "If you want me to continue playing, why don't you just ask me?"

He looked at her for a long moment then waved at the piano. When she did not immediately begin playing again, he pointed more forcefully at the piano, jabbing at the keys. Felicity raised a brow. "I'm not at all certain I understand what you want, my lord. If you could just say it; that would help immensely."

He understood her. She could see in his eyes he knew exactly what she wanted from him, but he was not going to do it. He was not going to give her what she wanted. He pointed at the piano again, this time striking the keys and filling the room with the dissonant sound.

"No," she said, meeting his gaze and not looking away, not looking away even when he grabbed her arm to forcibly place her hands on the keys. "You must say it. Say, 'Play the pianoforte.'"

He pushed her hands down on the keys again, but

she pulled them out of his grip and placed them in her lap. "Perhaps that's too much to begin. I'll make your task simpler. One word. *Play.* That's all you must say. Just say, '*Play.*'"

He stared at her, and she could tell he was turning the idea about in his mind. He tasted the word, digested it, familiarized himself with it. But would he say it? Should she offer the French form of the word— no, that would make it too difficult. Keep it simple.

She watched him, her hands clutched in her lap. She willed him to say the word, said it a thousand times in her mind for him, but she kept her lips firmly compressed.

He continued to stare at her, his jaw clenched, his mouth closed in recalcitrance.

Her hopes sank. He would not say it. She could see in his eyes he would rather remain silent than attempt to say the word, even if it meant she would cease the music. She sighed. "Very well." As much as she wanted to continue to play, as much as she wanted to see the light back in those eyes, she could not give in now or she would never make any progress.

She sat back, saw the anger flash across his face. She might as well just continue playing. Her scheme would never work anyway. But she continued moving backward and began to rise. Before she knew what had happened, his hands were on her shoulders, pushing her back down. Behind him, she saw his mother rise, worry in her eyes. Felicity shook her head, though perhaps the dowager's interference was exactly what she needed. She allowed herself to be pushed back into place, but she wanted him to know she could be stubborn, as well. Determined, she folded her hands into her lap.

The comte pointed at the piano, and there was no mistaking what he wanted. "Play," she said. "That's all you have to say, and I'll play until noon." She leaned close, whispered the word. "*Play*."

He held her hands, and she felt his fingers flex, knew this was difficult for him. He was uncomfortably near to her. Too near—she could see the ring of violet around those cobalt blue eyes of his. Too near—she could feel his warm, sweet breath on her lips. Too near—she could smell him, the intoxicating mix of musk and man.

Curses! She was glad the dowager was just on the other side of the room, because who knew to what temptations she might succumb if she was left alone with the comte. She couldn't remember ever being so drawn to a man, had certainly never been drawn to Charles like this. But this man—this aristocrat, whom she had expected to abhor—drew her like no other. The comte said more with his eyes than most men did with a lifetime of words.

But she wanted one word from this man, and she did not think she was going to get her wish. She searched his eyes with her own, pled silently with him. And just as she was about to give up, to look away, she saw his lips move.

It was a slight movement, his lips forming the shape of the word *play*. She wanted to nod in encouragement, but she could not tear her gaze from his lips. She could almost feel them on her skin. They were full and generous, and she could imagine they would be soft and teasing on her lips—or her neck, or her shoulder—

She inhaled sharply. Where were these thoughts coming from? She had to put a stop to them!

He moved his lips again, and this time her skin prickled because she heard him whisper. She did nod now. "Yes, that's right. Just a little louder."

He cleared his throat and then he took a deep breath. "Play." The sound was as scratched as a child's desk but also husky and unimaginably enticing. She stared at him, watching those lips, hoping for more. But he released her hands suddenly and stepped back, rubbing the back of his neck. He seemed surprised he had spoken, shocked at the sound of his voice.

And then he turned and glanced behind him, almost as though he thought someone was waiting to pounce on him, to punish him. She feared he would leave, retreat to his room, but with a worried look in his eyes, he turned back to her. Inside she felt her heart leap with joy. He had spoken! He had actually done it! And he was still standing before her. She beamed at him. "You did it!" She jumped up and clapped her hands together. "You did it!" She had actually helped him to speak. Perhaps she would succeed at this position after all. Throwing back her head, she laughed with joy.

He gave her a wary nod, and then he pointed at the pianoforte. She laughed again. "You want me to play again. Of course you do." She whirled and settled herself back on the bench. Raising her hands, she grinned at him and played a happy little jig.

And then, because the piece was short and over far

too quickly, she played a longer piece she knew he would enjoy. It had always been one of her favorites. She wished she had thought to bring some of her sheet music down from her room, as those were pieces she would like to learn. But the comte did not seem to care what she played. He stood beside the pianoforte and stared at her fingers or alternately at her face.

She tried not to notice when he stared at her face, tried not to feel the heat course through her at the feel of his gaze upon her. She concentrated on the keys and then, behind the comte, she saw a movement.

His mother! Of course. She had almost forgotten the dowager was chaperoning them. The comte was probably not even aware of her presence, and perhaps that was a good thing. Tears were streaming down the woman's cheeks as she all but sobbed. Her eyes met Felicity's, and the dowager mouthed the words, "Thank you."

Felicity felt her own eyes sting—partly from the happiness she had given to the dowager. Partly from the thrill of seeing the comte's accomplishment. But mostly she was thinking of her father, missing him and the family she had once known. She had not expected this family to make her long for her own, had not thought aristocrats capable of the kind of warmth and love she had known as a child.

But now she knew she had misjudged most unfairly.

She also knew, without a doubt, she was more alone than she had ever been.

❧

Several hours later, Armand paced his room. He was exhausted, but he could not seem to relax enough to sit down. Before the afternoon was finished, he had spoken four words. Speaking each word had been a struggle. It was as though a massive rock rested on his tongue. All of his concentration and patience were required to move the rock, to force out even a single word. But he had forced them out.

And he was still standing. Nothing bad had happened. Yet.

But he knew something could happen. The holes were a sign. If he said the wrong thing, if the wrong person heard... No! These were the thoughts of a child. He was not afraid anymore.

But one thing had changed.

Speaking even those few words had been like a key on the padlock of his mind. Now, unwanted words and phrases from his past rushed at him, faster than he could comprehend them. Some were in English, others French. He thought some might even be Italian or another language. It was exhausting, and now that the door in his mind had been unbarred, he did not know how to close it again—if even for a short time.

And while he did not mind the racing words and phrases, what he did mind was the assault of images and memories that flooded him. Voices and faces that were wholly unfamiliar to him suddenly appeared. He saw taverns and houses and streets he could not place, men he did not know, and yet all of them seemed in some way to relate to his life before—before prison.

Images of his time in a cell attacked him as well; those he had more experience controlling. But what were these new images? Were they real? Imagined? Why did they not make sense?

He put his hands to his head and squeezed, trying to stem the flood. "Damn it." His raw, rocky voice broke the silence in his chamber, almost startling him. It did not sound like the voice he remembered. But then, the voice he remembered was that of a child's. This was a man's voice, and a raspy one at that. He knew with use it would grow stronger. Was that what he wanted? It was what Miss Bennett wanted. He had to give her credit. She was clever and inventive.

The music she had played this afternoon was an incentive, but that was not all that encouraged him to speak. Seeing her face, the way she smiled and her eyes crinkled at the corners, was more than enough to make him want to continue pleasing her.

No wonder he had said "Please," "Thank you," and "Yes" in addition to "Play." At this rate, he would be the most polite man in all of England.

For the moment, he didn't care. One thing he had no memories of was women. Oh, he could remember his mother well enough, and he thought a few of the fleeting images were also those of his nanny from years ago, Madame St. Cyr. But there were no other memories of women. Was that why Miss Bennett affected him so much? Was that why he could think of little else but kissing her?

Armand began pacing again. He did not think he had ever kissed a woman. He had seen Julien kiss his wife once, but even their very public affection had limits. It had been a short kiss on Sarah's mouth. But Armand wanted something longer and deeper. He did not know how he knew he wanted this, only knew the idea absorbed him. When he was near her, there were times he could think of little else. Were all men this way, or was this once again the monster in him rearing its head? Either way, his lips ached to feel hers underneath.

And that was not all that ached. Other parts of his body, parts he had never paid much attention to in the past, had begun to ache. He clenched his fists, noting how often they tingled, wanting to touch Miss Bennett's hair, her skin, her lips. He knew enough of Society's Rules to know touching her in those ways was not appropriate, and so he knew even more fully his other fantasies were far beyond the pale.

He imagined stripping her of her clothes. He had never even seen a woman naked—no, that was not true. He had seen a painting of a partially clothed woman and a statue, as well. But those were artist's renderings, not real women. Miss Bennett was real, with her curves and her softness. He wanted to see it all, to touch it all, to touch her.

But that would never be possible. Not with The Rules. He allowed the thought to sink in and to cool his heating blood. She was his tutor, nothing more. She thought of him as a pupil and probably as little more than a wild animal to tame. She would never allow him to touch her in the ways he wanted. Would any woman?

For now, he needed to clear his mind, to rid his head of the voices and images. He stepped out into the corridor and saw it was much later than he had thought. The wall sconces were already lit. Stepping back into his room, he realized he had forgotten to part the draperies and open the window. Amazing. The enclosure had not even bothered him. He parted them now. Dusk had long since faded into the dark night.

He had missed dinner and had not even known it. His stomach protested now, but he had long ago learned to control hunger and thirst. He ignored the sensations and made his way toward the servants' stairs. He wanted to be outside, in the blanket of darkness. He wanted to feel free—and be free of these thoughts and feelings. He would have to deal with them all again in the morning, of that he was certain. But tonight, he would put them aside.

He stepped into the garden and inhaled the night air. It smelled like London, like the city. He compared it to the country air at his brother's house in Southampton. He preferred the fresh smell of grass and hay to that of coal and too much horse manure, but the London garden was better than the house. He stepped out farther, looking up at the stars, and then remembering the night before, he glanced down at the ground.

The holes had been refilled and covered over. There was no trace of them now, and the earth appeared undisturbed. Maybe that would be the end of it. Maybe the holes were not what he feared. He wondered if Miss Bennett knew the holes were covered, wondered what would have happened last night if she had not tripped over one of those holes. Would he have kissed her?

He knew he would have. And he knew without a shadow of a doubt that if given the opportunity to kiss her again, he would take it. Society and its Rules be damned.

Something moved in the path ahead of him, and he froze, his senses alerted to danger. He felt the instinctive need to crouch, but he held himself stiff and upright, a growl rising in his throat. This was his home. The garden was his territory, his to protect. He would stop any intruder.

And then the shape became more defined—a long white gown like a beam of moonlight floated on the path. He squinted, and a yellow-haired woman walked slowly toward him.

Armand was almost convinced his mind was once again throwing images at him, but he knew this woman, knew she was no figment of his imagination.

Miss Bennett was still moving toward him, and he saw the moment she realized she was not alone. She stiffened and paused, her head tilting to get a better look. And then he heard her breath whoosh out, and she murmured, "Oh, it's you."

Since none of the words he had practiced seemed appropriate for the moment, he remained silent, watching her move slowly closer to him. His eyes were on her lips, and he almost willed her to walk away, because he knew if she continued on her current course, he would not be able to resist kissing her. But, of course, she did not walk away. She continued toward him, smiling because she did not know the danger she was in.

"I heard a noise and thought—" She waved a hand, dismissing the idea. "Well, I didn't realize it was you, my lord." She stopped before him now, and his hands began to itch. He had to clench them at his sides to keep from reaching out to touch her hair. It was so much like sunlight. Even in the moonlight it managed to shine. "We missed you at dinner."

"Yes," he rasped out. He was not certain what she was speaking of—he wasn't paying close enough attention—but in his observations, people often nodded and murmured, even when they were not really paying attention.

His efforts did not go unrewarded. She smiled at him, obviously pleased by what he knew were poor attempts at speech. "Very good. Soon we'll have you speaking in sentences." She was wearing some type of blue outer garment, and she pulled it closer around herself now. He was supposed to say something. He could tell by the way she watched him. He did not know what to say, so he stood mute. Feeling like a fool.

"It's cooled off quite a bit, so I suppose I had better go inside," she said, looking past him. He realized she must be looking at the house. "I'll see you in the morning for another lesson."

She started to move away, and he knew he should let her go. He should stand still and allow her to walk inside.

But he was not going to be able to do that. Before he could stop himself, he reached out and caught her arm. She looked back at him, her face showing surprise but not worry. He thought she should be worried.

"What is it?" She raised her eyebrows—a sign of interest.

"Yes?" he rasped out.

Now she frowned. He had confused her. "Yes…?"

He grasped her free arm and turned her toward

him, pulled her close enough so he could smell her scent and feel the warmth of her body. She was so warm. He wanted to pull her closer.

"No?" he said, his voice husky and low but less scratchy. She had to know what he wanted now. She was almost in his arms. Armand was painfully aware of how easily he could have her fully in his arms.

"I'm not sure what you're asking." Her voice was low and trembling, but he did not think it was from fear. He narrowed his eyes and studied her face. No, she was definitely not afraid. Should he take that as a yes?

He wrapped an arm about her body, pulling her hard against him. The sensation was so strong, he almost gasped. Her heat and her softness burned into him. Yet, he did not feel pain. He felt only longing for more. His eyes were on her lips now, and his hand had made its way into her hair. It was thick and soft. He had imagined it might feel warm, like sunlight, but it was cool to his touch.

He felt its fastenings and wanted to tug them out. He wanted that hair free, but he feared he had gone too far already.

"I think I know what you're asking me now," she said, and her voice sounded different. It was as dark and low as the night closing in around them.

"Yes. No," he repeated.

"Oh, dear. You don't make this easy. I should not say yes, but—"

He heard the word he wanted, and that was all it took. He lowered his mouth and touched his lips to hers.

The feel of her mouth against his was a shock at first. Her lips were so soft and so pliant—not at all what he had expected. He felt he could explore that mouth forever and, acting on instinct, he coaxed her lips open so he could explore further.

The sound she made in the back of her throat—a low moan—made his heart race and his blood thrum through his veins. He wanted… something. He didn't even know what he wanted, but his body hungered for it more than it had ever hungered for food or water or companionship in all twelve years of prison.

And then, quite suddenly, he realized he was hard, hard and straining almost out of his breeches. He wanted to push himself closer to Miss Bennett, to push against her. He struggled for control, grasped it.

And it was that moment she began to kiss him back. Up until that instant, she had allowed his kisses, but now she returned them—her tongue twining with his, her mouth locked with his, her arms around his neck.

His blood ran so hot and so heavy he feared he might lose his hard-won control. He was already thinking of pushing her onto the ground and then—what? He knew what he wanted to do next—was uncertain exactly how it would all work, but he had no fear instinct would show him.

And then another instinct kicked in—one he was familiar with from long years in prison. The hackles on his neck rose, and his body tightened, wanted to crouch. Something or someone was watching him.

He yanked himself away from Miss Bennett, tearing his mouth from hers and whipping around to scan the garden.

"What's wrong?" she breathed. "What—"

He saw it then. Saw the eyes watching him. Human eyes. No animal.

And he knew those eyes. Remembered them from another time, another life. With a howl, he charged.

Eight

FELICITY JUMPED BACK IN SURPRISE AS THE COMTE released her and charged toward the garden's gate. "My lord, where are you going? What's—"

And then she saw him—the small, gnarled man she had seen out of her window only last night. He was at the gate, at least until the comte charged him. She had to give the comte credit. He was quick and agile, and he almost caught the small, wrinkled man, but the intruder was quick and crafty himself. He ducked under the comte's arm, circled behind him, then darted back out the gate at a full run. The comte went after him, and Felicity, hand to her heart, hesitated between running to the gate and running inside to fetch the duc and duchesse.

Finally she pivoted and raced for the town house, entering through the first door she found open—a small, feminine parlor. Once inside, it was only a moment before she encountered a startled servant and made her request known. She bent to catch her breath and still her pounding heart, and then the duc threw the door open.

"Where is Armand?"

"He's—" Felicity tried to breathe, couldn't, and pointed at the garden. Without waiting for further direction, the duc slammed through the French doors and disappeared into the night. A moment later, the duchesse floated into the parlor. She was wearing a white silk robe, and her hair was a thick chocolate wave across her back. "Is something wrong? Where is the duc?"

By now Felicity had her breath back and was actually anxious to return to the garden. "His Grace went after the comte. There was an intruder in the garden."

"An intruder?"

"Yes. I must take my leave, Your Grace."

As she stepped back outside, she heard the duchesse call, "If there's an intruder, stay inside!"

But Felicity could not bear to stand idly by if something exciting was happening elsewhere. She raced to the garden gate, reaching it just in time to encounter the two brothers. Both looked winded, but neither seemed harmed. She looked at the duc. "Did you catch him—the intruder?"

The duc opened his mouth to answer, but the comte was the one who spoke. "Bad man," he said, his voice considerably less hoarse than earlier that day. Felicity blinked in surprise, and she and the duc exchanged a glance.

"I didn't teach him that," she said.

The duc was looking at his brother. "Who was it? A thief?"

The comte seemed to think for a moment, and then he repeated, "Bad man."

The duc sighed, looked at Felicity. "Did you see this man?"

"Yes. In fact, this was the second time I saw him. The first was last night. I saw him from my bedroom window. He and another man were digging in the garden. I thought they were the gardeners. I suppose that was a rather foolish presumption, now that I think of it. It was far too late in the day to be gardening."

But the duc was nodding. "The holes we found." He glanced at his brother, and Felicity felt her cheeks grow warm. Obviously, the duc did not know she had been present at the comte's discovery of those holes. But the comte had not seen the man that night, only his handiwork. Did he somehow recognize him from an earlier meeting?

She almost opened her mouth to speculate, then realized doing so would indicate that tonight was not the first time she and the comte had shared a stroll in the garden after dark. And tonight—there had been more than just stargazing.

Had she really allowed the comte to kiss her? Had she really just stood there while he pulled her against him, wrapped his arms about her, and ravished her mouth? There was no other way to describe the kiss. She had been kissed before—innocent pecks and even one or two more passionate embraces. But none of those kisses had moved her like this one. None of those kisses had claimed her mind and body so completely. She could still feel the last remnants of the fire that had pooled in her belly. Even the appearance of the intruder had not been enough to dispel it completely. The feel of the comte's arms around her and his mouth on hers lingered, as well. She had known his lips would be enticing, and they had been. Her mouth still tingled, and she ran the back of her hand along it to try and quell the sensation.

Fortunately, the duc did not notice her action. He was looking at his brother. "Did you see that man last night when you discovered the holes?"

The comte shook his head. "Bad man," he repeated, and Felicity was certain he must have seen the man before.

"I suppose I'd better station some footmen about the perimeter of the house tonight," the duc said, motioning for Felicity to precede him back to the house. "I don't want to take any chances. In the morning, I'll speak with some of the neighbors and see if they've had similar problems."

They entered the parlor, and the duchesse pounced on them. "Did you catch the intruder?"

The duc scowled. "You should be in bed."

She rolled her eyes. "I'm not tired. And how am I supposed to sleep with an intruder about?"

"He's gone now, and I'll station some footmen outside tonight to keep watch. I may hire some professional watchmen tomorrow."

"Bad man," the comte said again, and the duchesse's eyebrows rose considerably.

"Does Armand know this man? I'm still not entirely sure what happened." She looked from the comte to Felicity. "Our servant said Armand had gone after an intruder, but how did you know about the intruder, Miss Bennett?"

Felicity could feel the duc and duchesse's eyes bore into her and knew they were beginning to put the pieces together. She glanced quickly at the comte, realizing belatedly the gesture would only incriminate her.

"Oh, hell," the duc said under his breath.

Felicity was not certain if the comte understood the full conversation, but he understood enough to look chagrined. Still, he would not have to be the one to explain.

"I was walking in the garden after dinner," Felicity began, trying to decide how much to tell. In reality, she had been afraid Charles might make good on his threat of an appearance in the garden, and she'd hoped to shoo him away before anyone in the family saw him. She could hide her reason for being in the garden, but she could not deny she had met with the comte. The kiss they had shared, on the other hand, would remain their secret. "I was on my way inside, in fact, as it had grown dark. On the path to the house, I passed his lordship. I suppose the comte was planning to take a stroll himself. We stopped for a moment to... exchange pleasantries..."

Beside her, the duc blew out a breath, and she continued quickly, not wanting to look at him. She had a feeling he had guessed more occurred than just a stroll in the garden.

"And as we were... communicating, the comte seemed to notice the intruder. He stiffened and yelled, then ran after him when the man fled the grounds."

"Were you able to see the man, as well?" the duchesse asked.

"Yes. In fact, as I told His Grace, I saw him last night from my chamber window. He was digging in the garden with another man, and I assumed he was one of your gardeners."

"Are you certain it was the same man?" the duc asked.

Felicity nodded. "Perfectly. His appearance is quite unique. He's small—the size of a child, but his face is wrinkled and gnarled. An old man's face, though I don't think he could be over fifty. And his eyes— well, as I looked down into the garden last night, he looked up at my window. The look in his eyes was nothing short of malevolent."

"Really?" The duchesse shuddered.

"You should retire now," the duc all but ordered his wife.

"And the man who was with him? What did he look like?" she asked, ignoring her husband.

"He was tall and muscular. His arms were huge, like ham hocks. I didn't see his face as clearly, but I believe him to be younger."

"Very bad man," the comte said now.

Felicity glanced at him, then the duc and duchesse. "I really do believe his lordship recognized the man he chased tonight. He may also be familiar with that man's accomplice, the larger man."

"I agree," the duc said brusquely, "but unless Armand can give us more information, he'll be of little help to the magistrate."

"Perhaps I might work with him on that point tomorrow."

"That might be a better use of time than a stroll in the garden."

Felicity felt her cheeks flush but forced herself to meet the duc's eyes. She needed this position and could ill afford to give the appearance of any wrong-doing. She could ill afford to *engage* in wrongdoing! What had she been thinking in the garden? It was wrong to kiss the comte, for so many reasons. It would *not* happen again.

The duchesse laid a hand on her husband's arm. "It's been a long day, and I fear we are all over-tired. Why don't you and Armand retire, and I will see Miss Bennett to her chambers?"

"Fine," the duc growled, and Felicity could tell by the look in his eyes he wanted to say more but held back for his wife's sake. "Don't be long."

The duc pushed his brother toward the door, but the comte shrugged him off and went through the French doors, into the garden again. The duc shook his head in frustration and followed his brother. Obviously the comte was truly concerned about the men he called *bad*. She wondered what precisely made these men so bad. It couldn't be merely that they had dug holes in the garden. Those were easily refilled and restored. He must have recognized the men from somewhere else. But where? And what had they done that made them so detestable?

Could she manage to coax that information out of him?

"You and the comte have become quite close rather quickly," the duchesse said, interrupting her thoughts.

Felicity bit her lip and tried not to sigh. She had thought when the duc retired she would be free from scrutiny and questioning. Now it appeared he had been dismissed so his wife might question and scruti-nize in his place.

Felicity tried to smile. "I would not say we are close. We both happened to be in the garden at the same time."

The duchesse raised eyebrows above eyes that seemed to know far too much. "Just this once?"

Felicity swallowed. "Perhaps twice."

"Oh, dear."

Felicity clenched her fists at the duchesse's disapproving tone. "I assure you our meeting tonight was purely by chance. It will not happen again."

The duchesse did not look like she quite believed her, and Felicity stood there, feeling like a small, disobedient child. "You are attracted to the comte."

Felicity opened her mouth to protest, but the duchesse shook her head. "There's no sense in denying it. I can see it quite clearly. He's an attractive man."

Felicity straightened to her full height, which was still a bit short of the duchesse's. "Yes, but I am his tutor, and that is clearly a professional relationship." Not to mention—and she would not mention it—she was technically betrothed to another man.

"Precisely. I am happy you understand the comte needs you to act as his tutor at all times. I fear if your relationship were to become... entangled, it might be to the comte's detriment. He's vulnerable."

Felicity bit her lip to stop the retort on her lips from spewing forth. She did not think the comte was quite as vulnerable as the duchesse would have him appear. After all, it was he who, mere moments ago, had swept her into his arms and plundered her mouth with reckless abandon. Those steel arms holding her close had not felt particularly vulnerable.

Felicity cleared her throat. "I assure Your Grace the relationship will not become entangled. I know my position." Perhaps a hint of the bitterness she felt was betrayed in her voice, because the duchesse reached over to touch her arm.

"You know I was once a governess, as well, so obviously I don't mean to patronize you. I'm only thinking of what's best for Armand. If your feelings will not allow you to act in a professional capacity—"

"My feelings are purely professional," Felicity said, pulling her arm away. She could not afford for them to be anything more and keep this position. Not only that, but she would need another position in the future. For that, she would need the duchesse's recommendation. "I assure you, once again, that I know what is expected of me. There will be no more strolls in the garden."

"Miss Bennett—" the duchesse began, her voice beseeching.

"May I be dismissed?" Felicity asked, keeping her back ramrod straight, so straight she feared were she to bend, it might crack.

"Of course," the duchesse said with a sigh. "I shall see you in the morning."

Felicity nodded and strolled, head high, out of the parlor, into the magnificent vestibule, and up to her room. She managed to hold back her tears until she had shut the door, and then she could not stop them.

She had overreacted; she knew that even as she extracted a lace handkerchief from a pocket in her gown to dab at her tears. She sat on the bed and pressed the lace to her eyes. She had been in the wrong, and the duchesse had been kind enough to remind her of that gently. But the worst of it was she had put her position in jeopardy. She could not lose this position, and if she continued down her current path, that would be the inevitable outcome.

Foolish girl! she chided herself. Do you want to end up married to a drunkard who gambles away money and leaves you with a passel of hungry mouths to feed? Do you want to bring scandal upon your poor aunt?

No, and she should be ashamed of herself.

Then why wasn't she? Try as she might, Felicity could not regret what had passed between the comte and herself. How could she regret a kiss that had all but melted her insides with a liquid fire? On the other hand, would it not have been better never to have experienced that kiss? Surely, no other could match it. She would be forever disappointed.

Surely Charles St. John would never make her feel that way. He had kissed her once. It had been about two years ago—a quick kiss but not altogether dispassionate. Still, it had set her young heart racing. She knew he was experienced, had kissed other girls. He was a popular man in Selborne, and he had many of the village girls in giggles when he walked by. She had always thought him the most handsome, most charming man of her acquaintance. She pined for his attention, but she had too much pride ever to chase after him. Not all the girls held back, and he had always seemed more interested in the girls who flirted and wore their bodices low than in her.

Had her father made Charles promise to marry her?

If so, why had he agreed? Duty? Did Charles possess a sense of duty? He obviously had no honor. What kind of man demanded money in return for ending an engagement?

The kind who was always looking for a profit. Was that why he had cared for her father at the end? Had Charles, laden with gambling debt, returned home to Selborne, saw the ailing old vicar, and seen an opportunity to make a profit? If so, he had grossly overestimated the Bennetts' financial situation.

And that was why she was here, tutoring the comte de Valère. She must remember she was his tutor, nothing more.

And tomorrow, when she was forced into his presence for hours on end, she had best forget the way his body had felt against hers, the way his tongue had teased her lips apart, the way he had smelled…

Felicity fanned her face with the handkerchief and groaned. Was it too soon to ask for a day off?

He could not allow the bad men to come back. Armand was not certain what would happen if they did. Try as he might, he could not recall how he knew them or from where. But he knew they were evil. He wanted them as far away from his family as possible. Had his speech brought them here? No, they would have come anyway. He knew that. They were a part of his past, a part he had always known would never let him go.

Every night for a week, Armand spent the hours after the sun had set prowling the garden, keeping watch on the house. He knew his brother had hired watchmen, who paroled the town house's perimeter, but he did not trust anyone else with his family's safety. He had, somehow, brought these men here, and he was responsible to see they did no harm.

Julien tried to make him stop his nightly patrols, but Armand ignored him and went right back to patrolling. With his increased speech fluency, communication was easier, but mere words alone did not open the locks barring his memories.

Armand's nightly watches did not benefit him by day. Miss Bennett expected to begin her lessons with him directly after breakfast, and some days she continued teaching right until dinner. Actually, she did not teach so much as cajole, harass, and demand he say these words, use this fork, bow in this way.

Armand was tired of the lessons but increasingly drawn to Miss Bennett. His constant state of sleep deprivation meant his mind often wandered far from the object of the lesson for the day, straying into what he now knew was dangerous territory.

When she attempted to show him the correct way to hold a knife and fork, he forgot to pay attention and stared at her long white fingers instead. When she attempted to illustrate how he should bow after being introduced, he found himself staring down the front of her gown—at her… oh, he could not think of the word, and she had turned red when he had asked. And even now, as she encouraged him to say some word or other—he really should pay more attention—he was more intent on the shape of her pink mouth than what she wanted from him.

"Carriage," she said again, her lips curving ever so slightly as she spoke. "Now you try."

Why was it he had never noticed a woman's lips before? There was a maid pretending to dust in the corner of the drawing room even now. She was here as a chaperone, but Sarah had probably told her to pretend to be busy with her work. Armand flicked his glance to the young woman. He had seen her a hundred times, perhaps a thousand in the time he had been here, and yet he had never looked at her lips. He looked at them now as best he could, considering she was moving about, waving a long-handled thing with bird parts attached to it at everything she saw.

The maid's lips were nice, but nothing that interested him. He did not want to kiss them. He looked back at Miss Bennett. Now, her lips he wanted to kiss. He knew he was not supposed to kiss them. His brother had given him a long, rambling talk on that subject after that night in the garden. But Armand still wanted to kiss Miss Bennett's lips. And why shouldn't he? Julien undoubtedly kissed Sarah's lips.

Something to do with marriage. It was a word Armand knew, vaguely. A word from his childhood that had never interested him much. But that word had everything to do with why he could not and should not kiss Miss Bennett.

"My lord."

Her lips had thinned, and he glanced up into her eyes, which were not quite so bright blue at the moment. They had turned a darker, ominous shade.

"Miss Bennett," Armand rasped.

"Are you paying attention, my lord?"

It took him a moment to think how to respond, and then he nodded. "Yes."

"Oh, really?" She tilted her hair so a yellow curl that had come loose from the ball on top of her head fell over her shoulder. His hand itched to touch it, to take it between two fingers and feel its softness, but he clenched his knee instead. She was unhappy for some reason. He could tell by the way she had put her hands on the soft, rounded part of her body below her middle. He thought about asking for the name of that body part, looked at her face again, and decided otherwise. "If you were paying attention, then what is it we were discussing?"

This was a more complicated question than he was used to answering, and it took him a moment to take the words in his mind and translate them into speech. She was, as ever, patient. "You want me to talk."

"Yes. Could you be more specific?"

He frowned, uncomprehending.

"I mean, what word did I want you to say?"

That he did not know, and it came to him suddenly this was the source of her displeasure. He had not said the word she wanted. Damn. What was it? Finally, he shrugged. "The hell if I know."

She blinked, and her mouth—God, he loved that mouth—dropped open. "Pardon?"

Her eyebrows were pulled down over her eyes, and those pretty blue eyes were now so dark they were almost black. "I said, hell if—"

"Shh!" She cut him off with an angry swipe of her hand. "Where did you hear that phrase? I certainly didn't teach it to you, and it is not appropriate to use in the company of ladies." She motioned to herself and the maid, who was dusting a lamp with much more energy than Armand thought the lamp deserved. She was standing over him now and moved closer. "Did your brother teach you that?"

"Julien?"

"Yes. Did he teach you that word?"

She had said quite a few words, and Armand was not certain which she meant. "What word?"

In obvious frustration, she threw up her hands. "Oh, never mind! The word I wanted you to say was *carriage*."

Armand nodded. Why hadn't she just said so? "Carriage," he said. Now perhaps she would stop thinning her lips at him.

But his obedience did not seem to please her. She merely shook her head and sat on the furniture piece opposite him. Now was probably not a good time to ask what the name of it was. He would remember if he thought about it long enough. He supposed he should know what a carriage was, as well, but he could not picture the thing. Or perhaps it was an action—what Miss Bennett called a verb.

"What is carriage?"

Across from him, she lifted a brow, and he could see this had been the correct question. She appeared happier.

"It's a moving vehicle, pulled by horses. It transports you from one place to another."

He nodded as the picture formed in his mind. Of course. He'd known that. But sometimes he had so many words and images in his mind, it took a moment to sort through them. "Thank you."

She bit her lip, sighed, and he wondered what he had done now. "My lord—"

But the door to the drawing room opened, and Mrs. Eggers poked her head in. "Excuse me, Miss Bennett, my lord. I need Jane here for a moment." She pointed to the maid.

"Oh, by all means, Mrs. Eggers," Miss Bennett replied, sitting straight in her chair. "We shall be fine without her for a moment or two."

But Armand noticed the girl looked uncomfortable. She whispered to the housekeeper, "But Mrs. Eggers, the duchesse said I was not to leave them alone."

Armand saw Miss Bennett turn red again, but she ducked her head and traced the pattern on the... chair! That was the word! She traced her finger over the pattern decorating the chair. She was obviously pretending not to listen to the whispered discussion on the other side of the room, so Armand pretended he could not hear, as well.

"It's only for a moment. Do you want me to interrupt the duchesse to ask permission?"

The girl shook her head. "No."

"Good, then let's go."

The girl followed the housekeeper out of the room, and the door shut behind them. As soon as they were gone, Miss Bennett looked at him. "My lord, I hope you do not think I am choosing words randomly just to hear you say them. I am trying to aid your conversation so you might, for example, ask a servant to fetch your carriage at a ball."

Armand nodded, though he was hardly listening. It had occurred to him, as the drawing-room door closed, that for the first time since that night in the garden, he was alone with Miss Bennett.

It also occurred to him now might be a good time to have her answer some of his questions—questions, he imagined, that would make her cheeks turn that light shade of red.

Nine

THE COMTE SMILED AT HER, AND IMMEDIATELY, FELICITY felt the heat pour into her belly. Why did the man have to be so handsome? And why could she not stop noticing? She had worked for days—*days*—to forget the kiss they had shared the other night, and now all of those images and feelings were raining down on her as if it had been mere moments ago.

She cleared her throat. "As I was saying, it would be quite beneficial for you to be able to ask for your carriage."

"There are other words I would like to know," the comte said in his matter-of-fact voice. It was still raspy from years of disuse, but Felicity found the huskiness, combined with the infrequency of his speech, only made it that much more sensual when he did speak. But that was not what she should be thinking of now. She was his tutor, and she decided on the lessons, not the other way around. She found if she gave him too much freedom, he inevitably found a way to avoid the lesson.

"I'm certain there are hundreds of words we have yet to discuss," she said, standing. "But we can't go about our work in a haphazard fashion. Today we are discussing transportation and ballroom etiquette." She almost wanted to laugh at that last bit. What did she know about ballroom etiquette? The few assembly-room balls she had been to would pale in comparison with what she imagined the balls of the *ton* were like.

The comte frowned at her. "Carriage. Horse. I know these words. I want to know the word for that."

He pointed at her hands. She lifted them. "You know that word, my lord. It's *hand*."

He stood, and she felt the room tilt slightly. He did not appear quite so tall and magnificent when he was seated. "I know that word. I mean that place. The place for your hands."

She frowned at him. "The place for your hands? You mean the end of the arms?"

"No. Here, I'll show." He held out his hands in a universal gesture for her to place her own hands in his. She felt the room tilt again and knew the lesson was sliding away from her.

Wary, she placed her hands in his, and he then directed them back at her body, toward her hips. Oh! She understood now. She had inadvertently placed her hands on her hips, and he wanted the word now. Oh, dear. She could give him the word, but then she risked the very real possibility this lesson would turn into one on parts of the body. That she was not prepared to teach.

She lifted her hands away from her hips and shook them free of his light hold. "My lord, I think it best we adhere to our lesson on transportation. Perhaps another day we can discuss physical features." Yes, a day when she was no longer so attracted to him. In other words, never. "So, since you seem quite familiar with the word *carriage*, why not try using it in a sentence? Pretend I am a footman and you want to leave a ball. What would you say?"

But she could tell all her efforts at redirection were for naught. He was still staring at her hips, and the more his gaze bored into them, the warmer she felt. "I know the word," he said, gesturing to her hips, "but I cannot remember." He touched his own hips, slim and clad in buff breeches, and then, to her horror, he reached out and cupped hers.

"My lord, this is most inappropriate!" She tried to move back, but he held her firmly. She glanced toward the door, her heart pounding. The maid would return any moment, and then word of this would reach the duc and duchesse. The last thing Felicity wanted was another lecture from the duchesse. Especially when she had been trying so hard to keep her relationship with the comte purely academic. "Very well!" she said, hearing how breathless her own voice had become and hoping the comte did not notice. His hands on her body were burning into her, and her every impulse was to move into his touch, not away.

He glanced up at her now—thank God—his attention on her face rather than her nether regions.

"They are called hips," she said, hoping if he received the information he sought, he would release her, and they could return to their safe, banal discussion of modes of transportation. "This is a hip." She pointed to her right side. "And this is a hip." She pointed to her left. "The plural is hips. All right?" She tried to withdraw again, but to her dismay, he did not release her.

"Hips," he said slowly, his voice like worn velvet. The way he tasted words, rolled them over in his mouth, and then allowed them to drop from his lips like honey was far too sensual for her comfort. And did he realize despite all his years of silence, he still retained a French accent? She had never realized she was so attracted to French accents.

"My lord, truly, you should release me." She tried to sound firm and commanding, but she knew words without actions would probably mean very little. She must push away from him!

"Your hips are different than mine," he remarked, caressing her in a circular motion.

Felicity felt her breath come in a short gasp as liquid fire radiated from his touch.

"Yours are soft," he said, still caressing her. "And… what is the word? Round."

Now Felicity knew her cheeks were flaming—and not simply because his touch had that effect on her. "My lord, I am well aware that my hips might be a bit fuller than is considered ideal. However, it is most rude of you to point that out. In fact, it is usually best to avoid commenting on a lady's appearance except in very general terms."

But if he heard what she said, he made no show of acknowledging it. Instead, he ran his hands up her body to cup her waist. Oh, curses! This was really too much. Felicity tried to take a deep breath, to gather her strength to resist this sensual assault, but all the air in the room seemed to have evaporated. Perhaps she could open a window, anything to clear her hazy mind.

"And what is this part called?" the comte asked. "This part that is so little?"

Felicity narrowed her eyes at him. Was he doing this on purpose? Did he have some ulterior motive for complimenting her so, or was this his true opinion? The man was impossible to read. At times he seemed genuinely naïve and childlike, and at others he seemed to know far more than he appeared.

"That, my lord, is called a waist. Now, really, you should release me."

"Waste?" He looked into her face, and she could not help but notice his eyes were dark, dark blue. He was definitely not as naïve as he would have her believe. "As in 'do not waste the light'?"

She shook her head, tried to speak, and found her mouth was parched. "No," she croaked. "The spelling is different. This waist"—she looked down at his hands, noticed how bronze they appeared against her pale pink and white gown—"the one you are holding is spelled W-A-I-S-T. The other is spelled—"

"I like to watch your lips move," he said, lifting one hand to trace them and leaving a fiery path where his finger trailed. "They are soft and… more."

"Are they?" she breathed. "I mean"—she shook her head—"my lord, you are not supposed to do this."

He grinned. "I know, but I do it anyway. I can't stop myself." He leaned close, brushed his lips over hers, and Felicity felt all the air in her lungs trickle away. He pulled away, nuzzled her neck. "Do you want me to stop?"

Now was the time to assert her authority, to put him in his place and reestablish their relationship as purely professional. "Yes, you should definitely stop."

"Those are *the rules*."

"Yes."

"But that is not what you want."

"It is. I want to follow the rules." And she did. Truly, she did. It was only that he made her forget that from time to time.

"Then why does your breath come so quick? Why does your..." Now his hands traveled upward, and Felicity felt her heart ram against her ribs. The beating was so loud in her ears, she could hardly hear her own thoughts. And even as she knew she should wrench herself away from his explorations, her whole body yearned for his touch and actually leaned into it as he grazed her breasts and then cupped them with his hands. "What is the name for these?" he whispered.

She couldn't answer him. His fingers were moving over her, teasing and exploring. She wanted to lean her head back and give in to the sinful sensations, but she had to be the one with some restraint.

"They are soft here." He cupped the underside and traced the curve. "And hard here." His finger brushed over her nipple, and she moaned slightly. She dared not look into his face, but she knew he was watching her intently. "You like that," he whispered, his breath on her cheek.

"Too much," she admitted. "You should st—"

"Kiss you again," he interrupted, and then his mouth was on hers, his tongue exploring her as thoroughly as his hands. Her whole body was on fire, aching to feel his hands everywhere, his mouth everywhere. She wanted him more than she had wanted anything else.

But in the back of her mind, she knew they would be interrupted in mere moments. They were not alone—and thank God for small mercies—because she did not know what she would do, what she would allow him to do if they were.

With a force of will, she broke the kiss, and he was distracted enough that she moved out of his reach. He came for her, but she held up a hand. "My lord, we cannot do this. It is against the rules."

"Because we are not married?" He looked as disheveled as she. His eyes were dark, and his hair, previously neatly tied in a queue, was slightly awry where she had run a hand through it.

"Yes. Kissing and touching is only for married people. Like your brother and the duchesse."

"Then we should marry." He moved close again. "I want to touch you more."

Felicity blinked, shocked, but still managed to evade his hand as he reached for her waist again. "Y-you don't know what you're asking. We cannot marry."

"Why not?"

She shook her head. For a thousand reasons she could not begin to explain. Oh, why could they not stick to her lesson plans? Types of carriages and horses were so much easier to clarify. "This is a question you should ask your brother," she said finally, knowing it was the easy way out and not caring. "I can't explain it." .

"I see." He looked thoughtful for a moment then turned on his heel. "Julien!" he called.

Felicity blew out an exasperated breath and rolled her eyes. "Not this minute, my lord! We haven't finished with our discussion!"

But just as he reached the door, it opened, and the dowager duchesse stepped inside. "Am I interrupting?" she asked.

Felicity was never more thankful the comte was halfway across the room from her.

"Ma mère," the comte said, bowing to his mother then glancing at Felicity over his shoulder. They had worked on bowing earlier this week, and he obviously wanted her approval. She smiled and nodded. How did she tell him that was a rather formal greeting for one's mother? And yet she had noticed he was far more reserved with his family than he was with her. He never voluntarily touched any of them. Now that she thought of it, the few times she had seen his mother pat his hand or the duchesse touch his arm, he had stiffened as though in pain.

"How is your lesson progressing?' the dowager asked, still looking at her son.

He rose. "Very well. We are speaking transportation."

"Ah." The dowager met Felicity's gaze over his shoulder. "A very useful subject. And yet you look as though you are done for the moment." She eyed the space between them and the comte's obvious path for the door. "Are you finished for the morning?"

"No," Felicity said.

"Yes," the comte answered. Ignoring her, he went on, "I want to see Julien."

"Oh." The dowager nodded. "I'm sorry, but I think he is out."

"In the garden?"

"No, at his club or his solicitor's or some such errand. But if you were planning to take a respite, I could use your company, Miss Bennett."

Felicity raised her eyebrows. "Me, Your Grace?"

"Yes. I need to do a bit of shopping on Bond Street. I see your trunks have arrived, but no doubt there are a few necessities you need. Would you care to accompany me for a few hours of shopping?"

Felicity glanced at the comte then back at the dowager. It would indeed be a good idea to put some space between the comte and herself, especially after her latest lapse. And shopping would be a wonderful diversion. She had been to London once before but never to the shops on Bond Street. She imagined they were infinitely more varied than the one store in the center of Selborne. On the other hand, she did not have the funds to purchase anything. She had less than a pound to her name, and she could not justify parting with that on something so frivolous as a hat or a ribbon.

"That's very kind of you, Your Grace, but I think we should continue with our lesson."

The comte, however, had other ideas. He bowed again and arrowed for the doorway. Belatedly, he remembered to take his leave and called over his shoulder, "Excuse me." And then he was gone.

Felicity grimaced. "I'm sorry. We're still working on some of the finer points of interaction."

The dowager waved a hand. "Oh, do not apologize to me. I'm amazed at the progress you've made. Armand is interacting with me. He is speaking. You cannot comprehend how long I wondered if he would be locked away in silence forever."

Felicity smiled. "He is making progress, but I do not think it is all attributable to me."

The dowager nodded thoughtfully. "He is somewhat preoccupied by the incident earlier this week. Those men jarred something in him. They made him remember something."

"The duchesse said he sleeps very little. The comte spends much of the night guarding the house and garden."

"Yes. He is afraid of something. God knows what. Perhaps we will never know. I cannot stand to think what he must have suffered all of those years, alone and isolated. He still cannot bear to touch me or to be touched. It pains me I cannot even touch my own son."

Felicity nodded, sympathetic but also confused. How was it the comte could not tolerate the feeling of his mother's arm linked with his, and yet he seemed to have no qualms about touching her? And she had touched him, as well. She could vividly remember the feel of the muscles along his back as she ran her hands over it. Or the stubble along as his cheek as he pressed her hand to his face on that first encounter.

And yet, she could not very well bring this discrepancy to the attention of the dowager.

"However, it appears that, whether you like it or not, your lesson for the day has ended. I would so enjoy your company on my shopping expedition."

Felicity smiled tightly. How was she going to refuse a duchesse her company?

"No, no!" The dowager held up a hand. "I know that look. My daughter-in-law has already given it to me. She pled fatigue, but she has an excuse you do not. I will not take *no* for an answer. Fetch your wrap, and I shall see if the coachman has the carriage ready."

Well, there was nothing for it now. Felicity could hardly argue with a direct order from a duchesse. "I shall be down in a moment."

Ten minutes later, she had donned her cloak, fetched her reticule with its scant coins, and tucked her hair into a bonnet. And as she climbed into the Valères' well-appointed vehicle, she had never felt so poor or so simple in all her life. The carriage was huge and infinitely luxurious. The squabs had to be upholstered in velvet, and the carriage drapes were silk or satin, while the pillows were soft, jewel-toned, and equally expensive. Pillows in a carriage! She had never seen such indulgence.

She settled across from the dowager, glad the woman had decided to keep the curtains drawn. She did not relish the eyes of hundreds of commoners peering in on her in curiosity and awe. She, who was no better than they. The dowager tapped her walking stick on the roof of the carriage, and they were in motion. "I need material for several new dresses," the dowager began the conversation, "but I am not at all opposed to stopping at the millinery or glove-makers."

"Thank you," Felicity said, averting her eyes. Perhaps it would be better if the drapes were open. She could pretend to study the view of London. "I really have no need of anything at this point. I shall simply enjoy accompanying you."

The dowager was silent, and Felicity glanced up to see her reaction. She was tapping a thoughtful finger on the knob of her walking stick. "How bad is your financial situation, Miss Bennett? I would add the caveat, 'if you don't mind my asking,' but clearly you are going to mind, and clearly I am going to ask anyway."

Felicity felt her stomach tighten. This was precisely the reason she disliked the aristocracy. She had watched her father deal with them over the years, and they were always butting in where they were not wanted. "My financial situation is adequate, though it does not afford me the luxury of a new hat, dress, or gloves at the moment. Thank you for asking."

"I see. Exactly how much money do you have?"

Felicity gaped at her. Really! The gall of these aristocrats! "Excuse my rudeness, Your Grace, but that is none of your affair."

She nodded. "You are right, of course. I do not ask because I am curious, but because I feel some sort of motherly responsibility toward you. I know your father is gone, and you have only your aunt left to care for you. Did your father make no provisions for you before he passed away?"

Felicity cleared her throat and wished again the drapes were open. Perhaps she should open them? "He did provide for me, Your Grace. Unfortunately, those plans are not without some small defects." She loathed her betrothed, and he threatened to ruin her if she did not either marry him or pay him off. That was certainly a small defect.

"Would you mind sharing those plans with me? I would like to help you if I could."

Felicity smiled. The dowager really did seem concerned with her well-being. "You have already assisted me immensely, Your Grace, by hiring me as the comte's tutor."

"I am glad to hear it. Did your father leave you any money?"

The carriage bounced over a rough patch in the road, and Felicity gripped the cord at the window to steady herself. "No. My father was a poor vicar and had no money to leave. Instead, he made other arrangements."

The dowager merely raised a brow, but Felicity would say no more. She wished she could ask the dowager for help, but governesses were not supposed to be betrothed. Further, aristocrats hated scandal. Felicity had a feeling the dowager might not be so eager to help if she realized her son's tutor could bring scandal on her family. "I'm grateful to have the opportunity to tutor your son." Was now the time to ask for an advance on her salary? The dowager did seem to be in a generous mood...

"Yes." The dowager drew the word out. "But that is not all there is between you, is it?"

Felicity's breath caught. Had the dowager seen more than Felicity realized this afternoon? Curses! How mortifying to have the comte's mother see her in such a compromising position. Why had she not been more forceful and refused the comte's advances right away?

"I see by your silence I am not wrong on this point."

"Your Grace—"

"Let me speak for a moment, Miss Bennett. If age has afforded me anything, it is the right to speak my mind."

SHANA GALEN

Felicity nodded. The dowager was right. If she wanted to scold Felicity for the rest of the day, Felicity supposed she deserved it. And now there was no question of the salary advance. It would be grossly impertinent to ask.

"I have seen from the beginning, Miss Bennett, that my son is drawn to you. The way he looks at you, the way he reacted to you immediately. As soon as you stepped foot in our home, you changed things for him."

"And I'm very sorry to have done so. I certainly didn't mean to alter anything, Your Grace."

The dowager held up a hand. "Will you allow me to speak? I am not admonishing you. I am complimenting you."

Felicity blinked. She was not going to be scolded by the dowager? Perhaps the woman had *not* seen what had transpired in the drawing room this morning.

"That does not mean I approve of everything. My son does not know the boundaries of Society and, as a man, he is less likely to pay attention even if he did. You, Miss Bennett, do not have that luxury. You are alone in the world, and, as such, you must protect yourself."

"I am well aware of that fact, Your Grace."

"Normally, I would ask my son's intentions toward you, but I do not think he has advanced enough to comprehend that question. What does he understand about marriage? At this point, he likely understands only that he wants to take you to bed."

Felicity felt heat rush into her face and her throat close up. She felt she would surely combust from embarrassment. She had never heard such matters spoken of so frankly.

"Therefore, Miss Bennett, I must ask you—what are your intentions toward my son?"

Felicity opened her mouth and found no words came out. How could she possibly answer a question she had been so ill-prepared for? Was this how men felt? No wonder they tended to shy away from marriage.

"I-ah-I—"

"Do you find my son handsome?"

Felicity shook her head, speechless.

"Miss Bennett, we are both adults, are we not? Simply answer the question. You cannot be that naïve."

Felicity took a deep breath. The dowager was right. She must stop acting like a ninny. "Yes, I find the comte handsome. I do not know what woman would not."

"Many, I assure you. Most women of our acquaintance cannot see past the wounds Armand has suffered. They would rather die old maids than be saddled with an imbecile who cannot make bon mots to entertain everyone at the evening's soiree."

"Oh." Felicity had not thought of the comte's prospects in quite those terms. "But I am certain that given more time and encouragement, the comte will be—if not entertaining—certainly not an embarrassment to any lady of the *ton*."

"So then you have no designs on him?"

"Your Grace!" Felicity shook her head again. "I do not see how that would be at all appropriate. I am his tutor, nothing more. I am not of his station, nor do I aspire to be. I am no social climber."

"No one said you were, Miss Bennett. I hope you did not think I meant to imply such a thing."

The carriage slowed and halted, and Felicity heard the coachman jump down. A moment later, a footman pulled the door open and moved to lower the stairs. The bright afternoon light blinded Felicity for a moment. It had seemed as though days had passed in the carriage. And yet outside, the sun was shining, and but a few minutes had passed. "Close the door again," the dowager ordered. "I will let you know when we are ready to disembark."

"Yes, Your Grace." And the footmen shut them up in the dark again.

"I do not care about your title—or rather your lack thereof, Miss Bennett. When Julien and I fled from France, we had nothing but our title—little good that did us. Now the French government has abolished all titles, and we do not even have that. Oh, we retain it as a courtesy, but we are no better than you. Not that we ever were. What I care about is my son's happiness. That is all I have ever cared about. He seems happy with you."

"I don't know what to say, Your Grace," Felicity stammered, and it was true. She did not know what to say. The comte's title *did* matter, if not to her, then to all of Society, as well. She was nothing, no one. Any romantic link between her and the comte would be noted by Society, and she could only imagine what demands Charles would make then.

"Do you intend to pursue my son, Miss Bennett?" the dowager asked in her usual forthright style. Felicity did not think she would ever get used to it.

"No, Your Grace. I propose only to be your son's tutor. I have no higher ambitions."

"And if my son decides to pursue you? Ah... I see by that flush creeping back into your cheeks that perhaps my son *has* decided to pursue you."

Felicity pressed her lips together. There were some things even this brash dowager duchesse would not get out of her. She wished circumstances were different. She wished she were free to consider marrying the comte. But she was not. There was no point in pretending Charles St. John was not a very real presence in her life. One who, given the slightest opportunity, would exploit her connection to the comte and the Valères. She liked the Valères too much to expose them to Charles's loathsome schemes. She liked the comte too much to allow him to see what a sad, pathetic situation she was in. She'd rather lose the position and deal with Charles than be so humiliated.

"If my son decides to pursue you, Miss Bennett?" the dowager asked.

"Then he will be disappointed."

The dowager tapped her fingers on her walking stick for what felt like several minutes. Finally, she said, "Well, Bond Street will not wait all day. I have very definite ideas about the material I want for my gowns, and I have half a mind to have a new gown made up for you, as well, Miss Bennett."

Felicity's head whirled at the quick change in subject. Had the dowager accepted what she said? Had she not accepted? What did her silence on the subject portend?

"That is not at all necessary, Your Grace," Felicity

forced out even as the dowager tapped on the door
and the footman opened it once again.

"Do you have a ball gown, Miss Bennett?'

"I…" Felicity blinked into the sunlight as the
footman handed her down. "I do, Your Grace."

The woman raised a brow at her over her shoulder.
"Perhaps I should have said a ball gown made within
the last Season or so?"

"Ah…" When had her ball gown been made?
Three years ago? No, probably closer to four.

"I see."

Felicity did not care for the look on the dowager's
face. They stepped out of the carriage and into the
bright sunlight, and the dowager immediately entered
a dressmaker's shop. Felicity could only follow, and for
an hour or so, she trailed after the dowager duchesse
as she looked at hats and lace and silks and gloves and
spent more money than Felicity had ever seen.

Finally, the hour grew late, and the dowager told
her to wait in the carriage during the last stop. She
would only be a moment. Felicity sat in the cool, dark
interior and stared through a crack in the curtains at
the other shoppers on the street. Men and women
hurried about, their arms or the arms of their servants
filled with packages. She tried to guess what they might
have bought. That woman had probably purchased
new shoes. Hers were quite worn. That woman was
obviously admiring the hats in that window. And that
man with the woman in the garish red dress had a new
walking stick he was quite proud of—

Charles?

Felicity slunk down and slashed the drapes closed.

It was Charles. There he was, casually strolling down Bond Street, looking every bit the dandy. If he was so in need of funds, where did the money for that new walking stick come from? Better yet, what about that tailcoat or those boots? They were not the same ones she had seen him wearing the first day they had met in London.

She parted the curtains only enough to allow one eyeball a view of the street. With a frown, she noted the woman beside Charles. The lady—if she could be considered such—wore a low-cut dress, had an unnatural shade of copper hair, and wore quite a bit of rouge. Felicity had heard of the demimonde, women little better than prostitutes. Was Charles associating with one of these?

As she watched, he lifted his fancy walking stick and pointed to the Valère carriage. The woman turned to look at the conveyance and said something that looked dismissive. Charles frowned and started for the carriage, obviously intending to prove the woman incorrect.

Oh, no! Felicity dashed the curtains closed and threw herself back against the squabs. No doubt, Charles was coming toward the carriage. What should she do now? She could stay inside and hide, but what if the dowager returned while Charles loitered outside? What if he mentioned to her he knew Felicity?

Curses! Even if the dowager didn't return, he would surely speak with the footmen. They might feel obliged to mention her connection to a man who associated with demireps to the duc. She bit her lip hard then jumped out of the carriage. She had no choice but to intercept Charles and his companion.

The footmen called after her, but she ignored them and, dodging the cabs and carriages, made her way to Charles and the woman. He had seen her coming and now stood with a smirk on his face.

"Miss Bennett." He tipped his hat in a sardonic greeting. "I was about to leave my regards with your employer."

She swallowed the venom on the tip of her tongue. "How kind of you, but I think it better we spoke here."

He grinned. "I'm sure you do. And how rude of me." He gestured to the woman beside him. Now that she was closer, Felicity could see the woman wore not only rouge but lip and eye paint. She had a black dot stuck on one cheek. Felicity was more certain than ever the woman was a prostitute.

"This is Celeste," Charles said. "Celeste, this is my fiancée, Felicity Bennett."

Celeste waggled her brows. "Fiancée? Well, well, well…"

Felicity felt heat rush to her face. Not only had she been introduced to a prostitute—her fiancé's prostitute—but she had the additional embarrassment of being introduced as Charles's betrothed. Felicity tried to ignore the curious stares of passersby and hoped the conveyances in the street were numerous enough to hide her activities from the dowager, should she return before this odious business were concluded.

Charles's catlike grin widened. "Fortunate for you that you found me today. I was thinking it had been too long since we'd spoken."

"I have hardly had time to settle in."

"And yet the time grows short. Perhaps I should

charge you interest on that twenty-five pounds. That might make you work a little harder at acquiring it."

She clenched her jaw, holding back the words she wanted to say. "I assure you that I am working quite hard. Furthermore, I intend to ask for an advance on my salary."

He nodded. "That's the first intelligent thing I've heard you say. When will you have it?"

She looked away, accidentally meeting the gaze of Charles's companion. The woman sneered at her.

Felicity wished she could wipe the grin off the woman's face. She murmured, "I haven't asked yet..."

"Well!" Charles threw his hands up. "You're wasting my time."

"What does it matter when I give you the money? Why not tear up the agreement now? As soon as I have the funds—"

"Tear up the agreement?" He gave her a look of mock surprise. "What would your poor father, who is surely looking down on us even now, think? He begged me to marry you, to protect you, to—"

"Stop!" she hissed, her stomach roiling at the way he derided her father. "You took advantage of an old, sick man."

"He knew what he was doing."

"Oh, yes, you kept your true nature hidden from us all, didn't you? Lying about joining a regiment and fighting for your country, when all along you were in London, gambling and drinking and..."

He glanced at his companion. "Whoring?"

Felicity pressed her lips together, and the woman, Celeste, cackled.

"I'm afraid I won't make you much of a husband, Felicity, but in my defense, I have given you a way out."

"You're a scoundrel!"

He smiled. "Quite." He reached into his pocket. "Here is my card." He handed her a small white card with an address on it she did not recognize. "Send for me when you have some blunt. I'd like a partial payment soon. Very soon. Now, I think I see one of your Valères across the way. You had better go." He waggled his fingers at her.

She turned to look, terrified the dowager would be there, and when she turned back, he and the woman were gone.

Ten

"WHAT THE HELL ARE YOU TALKING ABOUT?" JULIEN said later that day as he handed his greatcoat and hat to the butler. "I just walked in the door, and you start in on marriage?"

Armand ignored his brother's foul mood. "What is this marriage? I want it explained."

His brother gave a half laugh. "Don't we all? Look, Armand, it's late, and I'm hungry. I've been wanting you to speak for months, but if this is your chosen topic of conversation, then we can talk about this tomorrow."

But Armand wanted Miss Bennett now, and there was no telling how long this marriage thing would take. He was not willing to put the discussion off another day. So instead of retreating to his room, he followed his brother up the winding marble stairs. As Julien walked, he conducted a brisk business with the servants—where was his wife, what progress had been made on the nursery, had the watchmen arrived for the night yet, he wanted food and drink brought to his room immediately…

He opened the door to his chambers, and all but

Armand scattered. Julien strode inside, and Armand followed, receiving a curious look from Julien's valet before he spoke. "Monsieur le Duc, you have ruined this cravat! *Mon Dieu!* Why do I put up with this?"

"Because I pay you well," Julien growled, surrendering to the valet's quick fingers. The valet tugged his tailcoat off, and Julien scowled. "Where *is* my wife?"

"Wife," Armand said, and Julien spun around then sighed. "That is what I want to discuss. My wife."

"Bloody hell, Armand. Do we really have to do this right now?"

Armand crossed his arms and waited.

"Fine," Julien brushed his valet aside. "Leave us, Luc. You can see to these clothes later."

"Of course, Monsieur le Duc. But do not throw them on the floor. Remove them carefully—"

"Thank you, Luc," Julien said, ushering the valet out the door. As soon as he was gone, Julien dropped his necktie on the floor and his tailcoat with it. "You want a wife?" Julien said, crossing to a table with a crystal decanter on it. "A valet is a lot less trouble." He poured a glass for himself and then another for Armand. "But not as much fun. I assume you are thinking of the fun part."

"I want to know about this marriage. What is it?"

Julien handed him the glass of amber liquid then slumped into a chair and eyed Armand warily. "Damned strange to be having a conversation like this with you," he said, sipping his drink. "For months you say nothing, now we're talking as if…" He gestured with a hand, seeming unable to find the words he wanted. Armand was glad it was not only he who struggled. Julien took another sip. "Why this sudden interest in marriage? Does Miss Bennett have anything to do with it?"

"Miss Bennett. How do I marry her?"

Julien sighed heavily. "That's what I thought. Did she give you this idea? No"—he held up a hand—"I can see where it came from. Not only your voice has awoken, I suppose."

"I don't understand."

"But I do." Julien leaned back in the chair. "Let me see if I have this about right. You like Miss Bennett."

Armand frowned.

"What I mean is you think she's attractive, pretty."

"I like her mouth and her eyes," Armand said. Finally it seemed his brother was beginning to understand. "And her hair. And"—what was the word he had learned today—"her hips. They are soft and round. And I like…" He put his hand to his chest and gestured. "I do not know the name for these."

Julien ran a hand through his hair. "I get the general idea. You like her, and perhaps you kissed her?"

"Yes."

"What did she say about that?"

"She confuses me. She seems to like it, and yet she tells me to stop. I can't recall all of her words."

"Let me guess. She said you couldn't kiss her because you're not married."

"Yes. I would like to kiss her and touch her and—"

"Are you going to drink that brandy?" Julien interrupted. "If not, I could use another glass."

Armand looked down at the untouched liquid in

his hand then gave it to Julien. He had never liked the taste of the amber drink anyway.

"Listen, Armand. I understand exactly what you want from Miss Bennett. I probably understand better what you want from her than you do. But she's right. You can't do the things you are thinking of without being married."

"It's against The Rules."

He nodded, drank. "Right. You have to follow the rules."

The Rules again. Armand wondered if he would ever understand all of them. Had he ever known them? Some did seem familiar. This marriage one did not, but it seemed simple enough. If he wanted to kiss Miss Bennett, if he wanted to see what lay under her dress, touch those parts of her, he would have to marry her.

"How do I marry her?" he asked.

"How did I know that was coming?" His brother groaned. "It's not that simple, Armand."

Now Armand groaned and clenched his fist at his side. It sometimes seemed his brother and mother made these Rules more complicated than they needed to be. It aggravated him, made him want to retreat back into his shell, and stay there. But that would not help him with Miss Bennett. He flexed his fingers and eyed one of Julien's walls.

Julien rose. "Don't do it. Sarah will have my head if you punch a hole in here."

Armand glared at him, and Julien held up a hand.

"I know it's frustrating, but think of it like this. What if we didn't have these rules?" He stood in front of Armand, looked him in the eye. "What if any man who wanted could kiss a woman and touch her? Then what would happen to Miss Bennett?"

Armand had not considered this. He had not considered that other men might want to touch Miss Bennett. But it made sense. Julien was the only man allowed to touch Sarah. No one had needed to tell him that. It was clear in Julien's every action.

"There's more."

Armand gritted his teeth again.

"If you... touch Miss Bennett the way you are thinking. If you—hell, we'll have to go into this more later—then she might become with child. Like Sarah."

Armand thought of Sarah's growing belly. He had forgotten that part about marriage.

"So there's more to marriage than just the fun part. There could be children, and that's why marriage isn't something to take lightly. If you were to marry Miss Bennett—or another woman—she becomes your responsibility. You have to take care of her, not just for a night or a week, but forever. And you have to take care of all the children. There could be many, and you would be responsible for all of them."

Armand nodded. He was beginning to understand why marriage was so complicated. He allowed his hand to unclench, but he did not feel any less irritated. "I still want her," he finally said.

Julien laughed. "Of course you do, but it's not that simple. Do you know if she wants you?"

Armand raised both eyebrows. "I had not thought of that."

Julien swallowed the last of his brandy. "You

can't just throw her over your shoulder and haul her off to church. She has to agree, as well. And there are other considerations."

Armand narrowed his eyes. "Other considerations? What does this mean?"

"It means you're not some peddler off the street. You are Armand Harcourt, the comte de Valère, son of the duc de Valère. You can't just marry anyone you please. There are rules about that, as well."

"Explain."

"It's too much to explain tonight, Armand, but suffice it to say that Miss Bennett is not of your station. She's pretty, she's talented, but she is not a peer. Who was her father? Not a duke, I can promise you that."

"So that is why you married Sarah?"

The look that crossed Julien's face was almost unreadable. "No," he finally said. "It's true that her family was nobility, but I didn't know that when I married her. So you're right. Rules can be broken. But let me suggest this to you, Armand."

Armand nodded, still trying to piece together his brother's last comments. Perhaps he should pay more attention to Miss Bennett's lessons. He did not understand words like *nobility*.

"Before you decide you're going to marry Miss Bennett and have no other, why don't you at least see what the other choices are?"

Armand shook his head. "I don't understand."

"Why don't you look around and see if there are any other ladies you might prefer more than Miss Bennett."

Armand could not imagine there was another

woman he would want more than Miss Bennett. He had, on occasion, met other women, and they had stared at him as though he were a monster. Miss Bennett had never looked at him that way, not even when he knew he had done something that should have frightened her.

"Where are these women?"

Now Julien smiled. "All over London, Brother. And you don't know how happy ma mère and Sarah would be to take you out and show you all of them. Are you up for that?"

Armand frowned.

"What I mean is, do you want to try it?"

"Will Miss Bennett be there?"

"No. She'll stay here." Julien clapped a hand on Armand's shoulder, and Armand gritted his teeth. "But I'll have Sarah accept one or two invitations. Simple things that don't have too many rules. No balls. We'll see how it goes."

"Very well."

"Good." His brother smiled, but before he could clap him on the shoulder again, Armand caught his arm and held it.

"But I'm going to marry Miss Bennett."

Felicity knew she should not be in the garden at this time of night. She was inviting trouble in the form of the comte de Valère. But, of course, that was precisely the reason she had chosen to come outside this late. She pretended, even to herself, she needed fresh air after a long afternoon of shopping, but now that she was alone amongst the flowers and bushes, she could be honest, couldn't she?

She *wanted* trouble in the form of the comte de Valère. She couldn't stop thinking about his caresses, his kisses... what might have happened if she had not stopped him this afternoon. And she was upset about her meeting with Charles. He was growing impatient, and she feared he would do something drastic if she did not give him money soon. At times she wondered if he really cared about the money or if he just enjoyed having power over her. Perhaps he wanted her to fail so he could humiliate her.

She was not going to allow that to happen. She had made steady progress with the comte. Now might be a good time to ask the duc and duchesse for an advance on her salary. The duc was often in his library at night. She would seek him out there.

She turned and made her way inside. The town house was quiet now and dim. It seemed almost everyone had retired early that evening. She had not seen the comte since the end of their lesson this afternoon. But she doubted the duc was abed, and so she did not hesitate to make her way directly to his library. The door was half-open, and she had her hand on the handle before she heard the voices.

"He specifically said the word *marriage*?" a woman's voice asked.

"Yes, but only because he's been made to understand marriage is the only way he can bed a woman. Don't look so shocked. He's a man with a man's needs, even if they've been dormant up to this point." That was a man's voice, and the unmistakable voice of the duc. He must be speaking with his wife. And, judging from what Felicity had heard so far, the comte had taken her advice and gone to speak with his brother about the prospect of marrying her.

She blew out a breath and shook her head. She didn't know if she should be flattered or frustrated.

The duchesse's voice rose again, and Felicity made to move away from the door. She was no eavesdropper and could see now was not the time to discuss an advance, but the duchesse's words stopped her. "She wouldn't be a bad choice for him. She has an easy temperament, and they do seem to get on well."

The duc made a harrumphing sound. "But who is she? She has no title, no place in Society. Not to mention, she's penniless. I don't want Armand used for his money."

There was a long silence, during which Felicity battled the urge to storm into the library and defend herself. How dare he assume she would use his brother that way! Is that the kind of person he thought she was? Was that how all aristocrats saw their "lessers"— as fortune-hunting schemers?

"If you recall, you did not know I had a title or a place in Society when we married, and that did not stop you."

"Clearly, I was swept off my feet."

"Armand is swept off of his feet, as well. That's been apparent since the first day Miss Bennett entered this house."

There was another long pause, and Felicity assumed it stemmed from the duc's inability to think of an argument against the duchesse's logic. After all, it was the comte, not she, who had made the first advance.

The duc's voice was low when he next spoke. "And how do we know whether Armand is truly swept off his feet or whether this is just his reaction to a pretty girl. He hasn't been around very many women."

"We have had dinner parties and other events where he has participated."

"Not like he participates now. We can't be certain he even noticed the women at those evenings."

"Well, he's noticed Miss Bennett, and so all the rest are really inconsequential, don't you think?"

Felicity nodded. Yes, she was beginning to like this duchesse a great deal. And she had stood and listened far too long. She would leave the duchesse to plead her case.

Not that she wanted her case pled. Did anyone ever think to ask if she wanted to marry the comte? Perhaps she would never marry. After being duped by Charles, she was not even certain she could trust another man.

Except that the comte was guileless, incapable of deceit....

"No, I don't think it renders the other ladies inconsequential at all," the duc answered.

Felicity stopped midstride. What? How could the man disregard the comte's reaction to her?

"At least we can't make that decision as of yet. It bears further testing."

"Testing? Whatever do you mean?"

"I mean, *chérie*—don't get your back up like that." There was a moment of silence and Felicity tried not to imagine what was occurring during that long moment. When the duc spoke again, his voice was soft and milder. "I mean, that we should take Armand out in Society, introduce him to women, see if any others spark his interest. I want to be sure there's something special about this Miss Bennett before we seriously entertain ideas of his marrying her."

Felicity stomped her slippered foot. As though the choice of whom she married was in any way *their* decision!

"I suppose that is not a bad idea, though I do worry how Armand will react in large crowds."

"That's the beauty of hatching the scheme now. Christmas is in a month or so, and much of the *ton* will be at their country homes. The city is practically empty."

"Hmm. Additionally, we can choose carefully which invitations to accept. I can select those which promise to be more intimate."

Felicity could only shake her head. Apparently all these people wanted was to throw Armand at every woman possessing a title within two miles! She wanted to allow indignation to flare up and rage through her, but that reaction was ridiculous. She did *not* want to marry the comte. Why should she care if he met other women? Why should she feel jealous? Not that she was jealous.

"I like that idea," the duc was saying, "but make certain these events are not so intimate that they don't attract the cream of the *ton*. We need to be sure those ladies we introduce to Armand have both position and fortune."

"And we're back to money again. Need I remind you, darling, both of our families were left quite penniless at the end of the revolution? You have managed to rebuild your fortune, or else Armand would have nothing."

"Hypotheticals don't concern me."

"No, why would they?" she said drolly.

"What does concern me is that Miss Bennett is in rather dire straits. Her father has passed away, and her only living relative cannot take her in. She needs money, and she knows Armand is worth a fortune."

"I don't think she knows any such thing. Even Armand doesn't know how much money you have put away for him."

"She can deduce he is not destitute. Not to mention, he is a comte."

"A title that means nothing, as the nobility was abolished in France."

"The title has weight here in England. It opens doors."

Again silence. Felicity clenched her fists angrily. Did they really think she cared one whit about the comte's money or his title? She *really* should walk away now before she threw open the door and said or did something she would regret.

"I do not think Miss Bennett has any designs on the comte's money"—Felicity could hear the duc begin to protest—"though I can understand why that would be a concern of yours. But you do realize the *ton* is full of ladies who are greedy. Every third conversation revolves Lord Such-and-Such and what he is worth per year. Nevertheless," she interjected quickly, probably to keep the duc from interrupting, "on the whole I approve of your plan. I will speak with Miss Bennett tomorrow about preparing Armand to go out into

Society. If she thinks he is making progress, perhaps we might attend a function next week."

"Good."

"But, Julien, when I say *we* might attend a function, you do realize I am including you."

Now there was an even longer silence.

"I don't see why I should have to go along. You and my mother are perfectly capable of—"

"Oh, no! I am not going to undertake this… this matchmaking endeavor alone. *You* are coming along. And you'll enjoy it, too."

"Doubtful. But perhaps I can be persuaded." His tone had turned low and teasing, and Felicity did move away from the door finally. She had eavesdropped long enough, and she did not want to overhear any of the duc and duchesse's private moments.

But what was she to think of what she had overheard? The duc was not in favor of a match between herself and his brother. The duchesse was not opposed to it.

And why did she care for either of their opinions? She was the comte's tutor, and that was all she would ever be. When this position was finished and she was a governess to some small boy or girl, the comte would not even cross her mind. She would not even remember his kisses and caresses and those intense cobalt eyes. Her body would stop aching for his touch. Wouldn't it?

She made her way up the wide stairs in the vestibule, taking her time. She had no book to occupy her mind, and she dreaded the long night ahead of her. She wondered if any of the servants were about in the kitchens. A warm glass of milk might relax her and keep her from tossing and turning all night, her head full of images of the comte.

She had just turned back and was making her way down the stairs, when something crashed. It was the sound of breaking glass, the sound of destruction.

Eleven

ARMAND WAS IN HIS ROOM, UNDRESSING FOR BED, when he heard the noise. For a moment, he felt like a child again, alone and confused on the night the peasants attacked his château. But he was no child now. His every instinct screamed to protect his family and this house. To protect Miss Bennett.

He went swiftly to the door, threw it open, and stepped into the dark corridor outside his bedroom. He could hear the calls of servants and his brother, and he headed in that direction. He walked resolutely, though images of the night of the attack flooded his mind. He had been in the corridor outside his room that night, as well. The corridor already filled with smoke, he had not been able to breathe or see, but he could hear—as he could now.

"Mort à l'aristocratie!" he had heard them call, and in that smoke-blackened corridor, two men—servants? Peasants? He would never know—had agreed to kill any aristos they found. Even at his young age, Armand had known that included him.

He wanted to believe God had helped him to escape,

but he didn't think he deserved God's mercy any more than the thousands of other aristocratic children killed in the revolution. So perhaps it was luck that helped him evade the attackers. He had slunk along the corridor, hiding in alcoves and crawling along the floor when necessary, until he reached the secret tunnel his brothers and he used to escape the château without their parents' knowledge. He would have preferred to hide in it—as part of him wanted to hide now—but he had forced himself to run through it, keeping his eyes open for any sign of Bastien or Julien.

There had been none, and he emerged alone and confused.

And scared.

That was the feeling Armand remembered better than any other. He had been so scared. He had not wanted to die.

If only he had known what lay ahead, perhaps he would not have been in such a hurry to save himself. There had been many nights after his escape that he wished himself dead.

But he was alive now, and he was not frightened. If anyone challenged him, he would challenge them right back. The sounds were coming from the vestibule, and Armand made his way to the stairs leading there. He was halfway down when he spotted Miss Bennett.

She had her hand over her heart, and he could see her chest rising and falling. Her hair was not as neat as he was used to seeing it. Usually her yellow curls were pulled smooth, caught up with pins in some sort of round knot at the back of her head. But tonight, many of those curls had escaped their prison and were down about her back. Her hair was longer than he had expected; pieces fell to the middle of her back.

Just then she turned and looked up at him, and he could see the fear in her eyes. They were still as blue as the first time he'd seen her, but they were wider and darker. He took the remainder of the stairs in twos and was quickly by her side. For a moment, he fumbled with his words. His mind would not cooperate, and he could not form a syllable. But he clenched his fists and forced his mind to bend to his will. Finally he managed, "Are you well?"

"Perfectly. I was on my way to my room when I heard a loud crash. Your brother is investigating." She pointed to Julien, who stood in the center of a growing group of footmen and other male servants. Sarah stood on the side, her face white and one hand protectively over her belly.

"What in God's name is going on?"

Armand turned to see his mother coming down the stairs. She wore a blood red robe, and her long dark hair was down about her face. For a moment his world tilted. With her hair down that way she reminded him of... something... someone.

He blinked, and the image focused. She reminded him of herself years ago. She did not look so old now, but her eyes were different—sadder. He could remember, more clearly than ever before, what she had looked like in those days leading up to the attack on their country château.

"Armand," she said, seeing him. "What is wrong?"

He held up a finger, and with a last look at Miss Bennett, continued down the stairs. He pushed past the servants and elbowed his way into the dining room, which opened into the vestibule. In the light of one of the lamps, he could see the glass from the window was shattered, and the window itself was broken near the top. The hole was square or rectangular in shape, and when he followed the path the object must have taken, he saw the scrapes and dent on the normally shining wood of the dining-room table.

Julien was bending near the table, and now he rose, holding a red heavy thing.

"It's a brick," he said, turning it over in his hands. Armand nodded. That was the word he had sought. Had it fallen off the house?

No, he immediately dismissed that idea. Something or someone had put the brick through the dining-room window.

"And there's a message scrawled on it," Julien said. "Bring me a light. Closer." One of the servants moved to stand beside Armand, who peered over Julien's shoulder. He could see the scrawl of words, but they made little sense to him. He might have pieced out their meaning, but it would have taken him far longer than it took Julien.

"Give us the Treasure of the Sixteen or"—Julien turned the brick over—"we will crush you." His eyes met Armand's. "What the hell does that mean?"

All the servants were talking at once, each more confused than the last at the meaning, but Armand found he could not breathe, could not move. Something about the words held him still.

"Again," he said quietly, and then when he realized Julien could not hear him, "Again!"

The room went instantly silent, and Julien gave him a long look. Armand pointed to the brick. "Again, *s'il vous plait.*"

Julien looked down. "Give us the Treasure of the Sixteen or we will crush you. Does that mean something to you, Armand?"

All eyes were on him. He could feel them prickling his back, but he ignored the sensation and held his hand out for the brick. It was heavy and solid when Julien placed it there. Small pieces of glass still clung to its edges, falling off as Armand shifted it in his hand. He stared at the writing, little more than black scrawl made by a piece of coal or ashes. He stared at the words until they began to make sense. The writer had misspelled *treasure*, forgetting the *a*. He did not know how he knew this, only that he did.

The Treasure of the Sixteen. Why did he know that? Why did it sound so familiar? The murky water in his brain cleared slightly, as though he had dropped the brick into it and could see the bottom for an instant. He stared into the clear water, and thoughts rushed into his mind as if placed there by a familiar stranger.

A room at night. A low fire crackling in the hearth. The stench of unwashed bodies and stale wine. Someone was talking, and he was not supposed to hear what they were saying. Strong arms clamped onto his shoulder, screeching pain as he was hauled upright and belted across the face.

Armand dropped the brick, and Julien cursed. "You almost hit my foot!"

Armand blinked and looked around. He did not

recognize the room for a moment. Where was the fire? Where was the wine?

"Armand, are you well?" Someone touched his arm, and he turned, ready to strike out, to defend himself, but caught himself just before he struck at Sarah.

His mother was beside him now, and just behind her, Miss Bennett, who looked more frightened than before. He wanted to tell her she shouldn't be afraid, but he knew nothing but howls would come out now.

He could not get the damn smell of that room out of his nose! And until the smell was gone, he could not forget that scene. He must forget it. To remember... He put his hands to his head and tried to squeeze the memory away.

The Treasure of the Sixteen.

No!

Images of prison rose up before him: his small cell, the dark hearth.

No!

He could not go back there. He would not go back there!

"Armand, no one is going to make you go back there." It was his mother's voice, and it snatched him from the memories. He looked down and into her concerned face. "Armand, did you hear me?" She held up a hand but did not touch him. He could see she wanted to, but he was glad she did not. He did not want to be touched.

He nodded at her question, though he could not have said at the moment what it was.

"You are safe here. Come, let us sit down." She motioned to one of the chairs, and a servant immediately pulled it out from under the table. Armand sat, put his head in his hands. The memory was fading, but it still pulled at him, still tore at him like tiny rat teeth.

"Bring us a glass of wine," someone said, probably his mother. The low murmur of voices rose up around him, but he ignored them and concentrated on ridding his mind of the terror, ridding his nose of that smell.

He heard the wine glass clink on the table before him and reached for it without looking. He downed the wine immediately, feeling its warmth spread through him.

Where was Miss Bennett? He looked up and around, his gaze catching on her yellow hair. She was watching him. Everyone else, his mother included, was focused on Julien, who had lifted the brick again and was studying the writing.

But Miss Bennett was watching him. He stared at her, willed her to come closer. And finally, she did.

She took the chair on the side opposite his mother. "Are you well?"

He couldn't answer, could only reach out and take her hand. He knew he was not supposed to touch her this way. Julien would say something else about marriage, but at that moment, Armand did not care. Only Miss Bennett could make that memory fade completely.

As soon as her warm skin touched his, the last ripples of the murky water in his mind stilled. He allowed it to still, not wanting to disturb the memories hidden there ever again. "Bad thoughts," he finally managed to choke out. His voice was raw and hoarse again, as though he had not used it in many years.

"Do the words on the brick mean something to you?"

"No," he said quickly and then could see in her eyes she did not believe him. His brother was looking at him, too, and Julien cleared a path through the servants to stand on the other side of the table.

"Did you have something to do with this?" Julien lifted the brick.

Armand shook his head. "I was in my room. I heard the noise and came down."

"But you know something." All eyes were on Armand again, and he could feel his skin heat with discomfort. He lifted a hand to loosen his necktie and realized he was not wearing one. His throat felt tight and constricted.

"No," he lied. "I do not know something."

"What is the Treasure of the Sixteen?" Julien demanded.

Armand did not dare look away, but he remembered a song Miss Bennett played on the pianoforte that morning. He played it over in his mind. Julien finally looked at the others. "Does this mean anything to anyone?'

"No, Your Grace," all voices echoed as one.

Frustrated, he tossed the brick on the table, and Armand clenched his fists to keep from grabbing it. He wanted to snatch that brick and throw it as hard as he could back through the window. He wanted it far, far away from him.

"Grimsby," Julien said, "go outside and fetch the watchmen. I want to know if they saw anything. And I want to know how this got past them. I'll have their heads." The butler nodded and rushed to follow Julien's instructions. "You"—he pointed to a pair of footmen—"check the rest of the house. Make sure all of the doors and windows are secure. You"—he pointed to a maid—"clean up this glass."

The orders continued until all of the servants were occupied. Through it all, Armand held Miss Bennett's hand. He should have been outside tonight. He would have been if he had not been so tired. His mind had been occupied with thoughts of marriage. What he should have been thinking of was protecting the house.

Julien slumped into one of the dining-room chairs beside Sarah. "Any idea who could have done this?"

"I think it is safe to assume that it might be the same men you have been paying the watch to protect us from," his mother said. "The men who dug up the garden."

Armand nodded. How he wished he had run a little faster that night when he had seen the man in the garden. If he could have caught that one, then none of this would have happened. He felt the water of his mind ripple again and forced it to still. But the momentary wave had confirmed something. The men in the garden and the Treasure of the Sixteen were related.

Miss Bennett was no longer holding his hand. She had released it at some point, but she was still seated beside him, and now she spoke. "I think the comte remembers something."

"Really?" His brother's tone was harsh, and Armand gave him a threatening glare.

"No need for sarcasm, Julien," Sarah said. She

looked at Armand and smiled, though the smile was tight. She was tired. "If you know something about the words on the brick, you should tell us, Armand. Explain why someone would throw that through our window."

Armand stared at her then looked at his brother. He could not remember. He would not. And, even if he could, the knowledge would not save them. The less they knew, the better.

"I don't know anything," he said, rising. Julien rose, too.

"You're lying. I saw your reaction. All of this means something to you. Tell me what."

"I don't know anything," Armand repeated, but he could see Julien was not ready to give up. Armand would make his brother give up. He slammed his fist onto the already damaged table, making it rock and groan. "Stop talking!"

But his brother was already around the table, and before Armand could react, Julien grabbed his collar and hauled him against the dining-room wall. "Tell me what you know, damn it! What the hell is going on?"

Rage had been building in Armand for days, rage and a feeling of impotency, and now he pushed Julien back. His brother was taken by surprise and stumbled, but Armand caught him, reversing their positions. He slammed Julien against the wall, rattling a painting but feeling the satisfying thunk of Julien's bones crash into the solid material behind him. "I could kill you," he hissed, reverting to French. For some reason, the language came easily to him now, the words falling off his tongue. "I could put my hands around your neck"—he put his hands on Julien's neck, felt the strong muscles beneath his fingers—"and squeeze every bit of life from you."

"Do it, then," Julien answered in French. "Kill me, but it won't stop the nightmares, *Frère*. It won't avenge the men who did this to you."

Armand flexed his hands. He wanted to hurt, to kill, to make someone pay for the pain even those brief memories had churned up in him.

"I didn't imprison you." Julien's eyes were bright and hard and never wavered. "I rescued you. I never, not for one instant, forgot about you. I never stopped searching for you."

Armand stared at him, the cold fire in his belly beginning to burn out.

"But now you've brought something back with you."

Armand's hands flexed, but his brother did not wince.

"And I need to know what it is. I can't protect ma mère or Sarah or Miss Bennett if you don't help me. What is the Treasure of the Sixteen?"

Armand stared at his brother for a long moment. The waters in his mind churned and bubbled then, resolutely, he stilled them. "No. I don't know." He released Julien and stepped back. His hands were moist, and he could feel the sweat on his back, his upper lip. The room had become too warm. He backed away from his brother, backed toward the stairs, toward the safety of his room.

Julien stepped forward. "Don't walk away from this. Don't walk away from me." But before he could move any closer, Sarah was in front of him.

"Julien, let him go."

"He knows something."

Armand turned to the stairs and began to ascend them, taking one at a time.

"Whatever it is, he either can't or won't remember. Leave him be."

"I'll make him remember." Julien lunged for him, and Armand paused. He wouldn't fight anymore tonight, nor would he talk. There was nothing left to say.

"No, you will not." That was his mother. Now she, too, stood in the gap between the two brothers. "You are doing more harm than good. Let him go. He will talk when and if he is ready."

He should have felt grateful to his mother, but he was beyond caring what happened to himself. This was his fault, and everyone knew it. He had not protected them; maybe he could not. He couldn't stop his gaze from seeking Miss Bennett. Would there be disgust on her face, fear, revulsion?

She had not risen from the table. She sat there, hands folded, worry in her eyes. And she looked—what was the word? He had heard Julien use it with Sarah—beautiful. She looked so beautiful it made him hurt.

But she did not look disgusted. She did not look at him as though he were to blame. That was, at least, something. And he continued upstairs to his bedroom, silently closing the door and blowing out the light.

For once, he wanted darkness.

⤜⤛

Felicity did not see the comte for two days. In that

THE MAKING OF A GENTLEMAN

time, she felt increasingly useless. The duc and duchesse were paying her to tutor the comte, but how could she do so when he would not leave his room?

And yet no one said anything to her. No one questioned her position. But without a pupil, she could hardly ask for an advance on her salary. At one point she received a note from Charles. It was riddled with threats and demands for money. She burned it in the hearth before anyone could see it and prayed he would stay away. But she was distracted and worried.

"Are you well, Miss Bennett?" the duchesse asked on the afternoon of the second day without the comte. She was serving tea, and Felicity realized she had not taken the cup the duchesse had held out to her.

She took the cup now. "Quite well. My head was somewhere else."

"We are all distracted of late. It will ease my worries when the comte rejoins us. When he does, I would like you to focus your studies on the social graces. I have accepted an invitation to Lady Spencer's musicale next week. Armand will be attending."

So the hunt for the comte's wife was to begin. Felicity set her tea cup on the saucer. It rattled slightly, and she quickly put it on the table. "Certainly, Your Grace."

"I thought a musicale would be the best place to begin, as we all know the comte's love of music. Also, he need not worry about dinner conversation or dancing, though that will come eventually. Do you know how to dance, Miss Bennett?"

Felicity swallowed. An image of the comte holding her in his arms while she showed him a dance step flashed through her mind. And after that, another image from two nights ago materialized—the comte, his shirt open to midchest, his blue eyes burning like those of an avenging angel. Never had she seen a man who was so powerful, so intense. When he had grabbed his brother, she had been terrified and also strangely aroused. What would it feel like to have that intensity focused on her—not in violence but in passion? After all, were they not two sides of the same coin?

The same hands that circled the duc's neck in rage could stroke her skin until it heated and burned. He had done it before, but he mustn't ever do so again. And she would speed that along when she helped him find another woman to marry, to bed, to put his hands on…

The duchesse was looking at her expectantly, and Felicity cleared her throat. "Pardon, Your Grace, what was the question?"

The duchesse gave her a quizzical look then repeated, "Do you dance?"

"Ah, yes, but not very well. I have never taught anyone."

The duchesse nodded, and Felicity could almost see her mental list of tasks growing. "Then I shall hire an instructor."

"Do you think the comte will agree to dancing lessons?"

The duchesse shrugged. "I have no idea. He can be stubborn, as you have seen."

Felicity thought of him closed in his room, refusing to come down, even after she had played for hours in an attempt to lure him. And then she thought of him the night the brick came through the window. "But I do not think it is all stubbornness, Your Grace. I think there are some things he *cannot* tell us. Some things he cannot allow himself to remember."

The duchesse set her cup and saucer aside now. "I agree, Miss Bennett. And I know the duc agrees, as well, but he feels so helpless to protect his family, and that frustrates him."

"I believe it frustrates the comte, as well."

The duchesse smiled. "You protect him. I like that, but I wonder if he needs our protection any longer. Perhaps we have protected him too long? Perhaps it is time some of the doors he has closed were reopened. They may open whether he wants them to or not."

"I saw him last night," Felicity said, not knowing why she revealed this now. "From my window," she hastily added when the duchesse's eyes widened. "He was in the garden, pacing, watching the gate and the house." She had been worrying Charles would make an appearance and had seen the comte instead.

The duchesse frowned. "It was pouring rain last night. I wish he would not do that. The duc hired extra men to watch the house. The window has been repaired, and we have ordered another table."

"Yes, but that does not erase the threat, not truly. Those men will not go away so easily. If we close one door, they will find another somewhere else. The comte knows this, and even so, whatever secrets he harbors, whatever secrets are hidden in his mind are too painful to bring to the forefront. He is willing to guard the house all night, to stand in the rain and the fog and the cold to protect us. That must tell us something about the severity of what he hides."

The duchesse looked past her, her eyes seemingly focused on something in the past. "I wonder if he will ever be healed, Miss Bennett. I wonder if anything— or anyone—can heal him."

Their eyes met, and then the duchesse rose. "I must speak to Cook. Please finish your tea. I shall see you at dinner."

The next morning, the sun was bright and warm, and when Felicity opened her drapes, the day seemed a reflection of springtime. She knew it was late November, but it did not look or feel so, and she donned a white day dress with yellow flowers then tied a yellow ribbon in her coil of hair. The dress was not nearly warm enough for winter, but Felicity did not care. It matched her mood.

She had taken her time dressing and knew she missed breakfast. It was no bother, because she was not hungry anyway, and so instead of making her way to the dining room, she went straight out to the garden. The air was crisp but not uncomfortable, and the sky was an endless sea of blue. She looked up, turning as she did so. No, she could not see a speck of white in the sky—not a cloud to mar the beauty of the day. She craned her neck farther to see if the moon had yet faded from sight and turned right into a very solid, very familiar form.

She almost stumbled back, but the comte caught

her before she lost her balance. To her disappointment and relief, his hands did not linger.

Felicity stood and straightened her dress. "My lord, it is good to see you out and about."

"Miss Bennett," he said with a nod. She smiled at his politeness, glad her lessons had taken root. But she also mourned the reserve in his eyes. Had she taught him that reserve?

"It's a beautiful morning," she said, looking at the sky again.

"Yes, beautiful."

She glanced sideways and saw his eyes were not on the sky but on her. Perhaps she had been too quick to think him reserved.

"What I mean to say," he added, "is indeed. It is indeed."

Still without looking at him, she said, "I have not seen you for some days, and yet our lessons are far from complete. Do you think you feel up to continuing them today?"

He sighed, and she could hardly blame him. A day of study indoors did not suit her mood either. "Perhaps we could have class outside this morning."

When she glanced at him, he was smiling. "I would like that."

"Good. Then shall we begin? The duchesse says you will be attending a musicale next week."

"A what?"

She smiled at him. "It's not as bad as it sounds. It's a party where music is played. Often there is a singer or singers who perform. Light refreshments are served."

"Light—"

"Tea, punch, small sandwiches, and such. I think you will enjoy the music. I thought we might discuss how the evening will go in order to prepare you."

"You will be there."

She shook her head. "No. I'm afraid I have not been invited."

"I don't understand."

She bit her lip, gave that vast blue sky one last glance. "I am not of your station, my lord. I have no money, no title, no connections. You are the comte de Valère, and as such, you have all three. I cannot go where you go, but I can make sure you are prepared for each event."

He frowned, the look on his face fierce. "But I want you there. I will go and speak to Ju—"

She reached out, touched his arm to stop him. "Please don't." She could think of nothing worse than having to tag along where she was not invited, being forced to watch the comte interact with other women who were more beautiful, more accomplished, and more wealthy than she would ever be. "I don't want to go. In fact, I think this is a good opportunity for you to meet other ladies. Do you remember our last conversation about marriage?"

The way his eyes darkened said he remembered perfectly. And the way his gaze flicked to her mouth told her the passions that had led to that discussion had not really waned either. "This might be your chance to meet a woman you would marry, a wife."

His eyes turned cold. "My brother has spoken to me of this, but I told him I would marry you."

Felicity's heart stopped long enough for her breath to catch in his throat. "My lord, that's not possible."

"Not possible?" He moved nearer, closed his warm hand about her wrist. "Or not desirable? Tell me which."

Twelve

"THAT IS NOT AN EASY QUESTION, MY LORD," FELICITY said. Her wrist tingled where his hand had closed around it. His fingers were rough and callused, not at all the smooth, effeminate fingers she would imagine an aristocrat to possess.

But then this man was not some refined aristocrat. He was feral, untamed, passionate. She glanced up into his eyes and saw all of that and more. She saw longing there—longing for her. He wanted her, and the thought made her shiver. She wanted him, too, but she was no wild creature. She knew the rules and knew she had to obey them, despite what her emotions of the moment told her.

"It is easy," he contradicted her. "Do you want me? Yes or no?" He was close to her now, and she could feel the heat from his body through her thin dress. Why had she not worn a cloak? Her head was spinning, and she felt faint from his closeness. She was no ninny who would really faint, but she had a feeling the sensation might be due to the blood rushing from her head to lower regions of her body.

"The question," she managed to whisper, "concerned marriage, not desire."

"What is the difference?"

For a moment, she almost wished they could return to the time when he could not speak. It seemed dealing with him was simpler then. Now he had so many questions, and she felt ill-prepared to answer them.

"Marriage is a contract, a legal joining," she said, even though she doubted he would understand all of the nuances of what she told him. "Desire is something fleeting. It comes and goes."

His hand moved lower, his fingers caressing the inside of her palm. Curses! She had forgotten her gloves, as well!

"Not for me. Desire is…" He paused, and she could see him searching for the word. "Continuing?"

"Constant," she breathed.

"Yes." He was watching her now and judging her. She did not know what he would see, but she knew what he should see—a tutor who insisted he learn the lesson for today. Even if that lesson was how to catch a bride who was not she.

"My lord…"

"Why do you not call me my name?" he asked. "Is that another rule?"

She wet her lips. How she would love to call him by his name. It was such a rich, sensual name. So French and exotic. How she would love to form her mouth around it. "Yes," she said then had to clear her throat to make the word come out clearly. "It is a rule. I must call you *my lord*, and you must call me *Miss Bennett*."

"Call me Armand."

Oh, dear. She loved the sound of the word on his lips. It was so dark and sweet. The light French accent with which he spoke was more pronounced on his name, and it sent a shiver up her spine. "I cannot," she whispered, trying not to allow him to feel her tremble.

"Once," he said, but he did not sound like he was pleading. He sounded almost as though he were commanding her.

"My lord." She glanced down, unable to hold out against the passion she saw in his eyes. "That would not be appropriate."

"What is your name?"

"Miss Bennett."

His fingers trailed over the sensitive skin of her bare palm again. "Your given name. Please."

She glanced up at him quickly, saw the light in his eyes and knew he was teasing her. He hated all the polite terms she made him learn, and if he was using one now, it meant he was trying mightily to persuade her. And perhaps she could use that to her advantage—to turn this into her lesson and away from the dangerous path they were both skirting.

"I will tell you, my lord," she said, stepping back and disengaging her hand from his, "if we can pretend we are at Lady Spencer's musicale."

His brows furrowed, making him look even more serious than usual. How she loved all of his looks—serious, passionate, intense, and now today, she had seen teasing.

"Here, you stand over by that bench, and I will pretend I am a young lady the duchesse wants to introduce to you."

"I don't want to pretend."

She gave him the same look she had given the girls who argued with her back at the small parish school in Selborne. "Go stand over there." She pointed, and with a long-suffering sigh, he did so.

But he was slouching, one hand in his pocket, and that would not do at all. "My lord," she said, shaking her head, "that will not do. You must stand straight."

He raised a brow and continued slouching. Felicity sighed. She supposed this was the best she could do for now. Posture was probably not at the top of the duchesse's concerns for the musicale.

"All right. Pretend I am being led over to you by the duchesse or your brother. You don't know me, but perhaps you have been admiring me all evening. And now is your opportunity to meet me."

"I do not understand the point of this pretend."

She gave him an exasperated look. "It is practice for the night of the musicale! Will you just try, my lord?"

He threw up his hands in surrender and then, to her dismay, shoved them both back in his pockets. Undeterred, she made her way slowly toward him. "You might smile at me, my lord. If you look so formidable, you will scare all the ladies."

"What is this *formidable*?"

"It means frightening and serious together."

"Hmm." He actually looked rather pleased with that description, so she was not surprised when he did not begin smiling at her. Finally, she stood before him.

"I am playing the duchesse now. Miss Felicity Bennett, might I introduce you to my brother-in-law,

Armand Harcourt, the comte de Valère. My lord, this is—"

But he had reached out and taken her wrist again. "I like how you say my name, Felicity. Say it again, Felicity."

She gave him the stern look again. "You should be calling me Miss Bennett. Only men and women who are related or who are engaged to be married may call each other by their Christian names."

"Marriage, again," he said, raising a brow.

She extracted her hand and went on. "As I was saying, my lord, this is Miss Bennett. You see, a lady is always introduced to a gentleman, even if he ranks above her. If you were being introduced to another gentleman, the order would depend upon—"

"Felicity?"

She paused and had to stop her heart from pounding in her chest. She loved the way her name sounded on his lips, like a whisper of cool sea air on a warm day. "Yes?"

"What do I do now?"

"I suppose a bow would be appropriate. And I might curtsey." She made a small one because she detested them.

"A bow?"

"Well…" She should probably not tell him this, but what if he saw others doing it and made some kind of wrong connection?

"Yes?" He had that brow raised again. How did he manage to do that? And why did it make it so hard for her to breathe?

"You could also kiss the lady's hand."

"Show me."

She cleared her throat and took a step back, recognizing that look in his eyes. "It is one option, my lord, and generally used more by men who are trying to be charming."

"What is this *charming*?"

"The opposite of formidable."

He nodded, and she was not certain what he made of her explanation. "Show me the hand kiss."

Now she had to pause. "I don't really know how to show you. I've never done it." Or had it done to her. She was simply not that irresistible. Either that, or she didn't know enough charming men. "But what I have seen men do is to take a lady's hand lightly, lean over—like a bow—and gently kiss her knuckles." At least she thought it was the knuckles. Perhaps it was the back of the hand?

"Knuckles?"

She held up her bare hand. Curses on her for forgetting her gloves in her hurry this morning! "These ridges."

"Ah." He held out his hand, and she placed hers into his. For a moment, he stood and held her hand, his gaze on her face. She was about to repeat the instructions, when he said, "What do I say?"

"Um…" She could think of any number of things she would like him to say, but those suggestions would not help matters. "Well, I have just been introduced to you. So you take my hand. Yes, you have that part, and I suppose you say something like, 'Delighted to meet you, Miss Bennett.' Then you bow and ah—kiss the knuckles."

He nodded, looking very serious. "Delighted to meet you, Miss Bennett." His voice was so low and husky the words sounded completely foreign coming from his lips. And then he bowed, and she felt the barest hint of his lips on her flesh. It tickled slightly, and she almost giggled like a schoolgirl. But she retained her composure and said, "And you, as well, my lord."

He had still not released her hand or risen, so she tugged slightly to let him know he should do so. When he did not cooperate, she pulled harder. "You should release me now, my lord."

"But you smell so good." And she felt that tantalizing brush of his lips on her flesh again. Her body trembled, and she wondered why his lips on such an innocuous spot as her hand should cause her this much reaction.

"My lord, you should stand and release my hand."

"Is that a rule?"

Was it? "Yes, I suppose it is."

He glanced up at her, his cobalt eyes so dark they were almost indigo. "I do not like rules."

Yes, well, neither did she at times. "Rules are made so that Society runs smoothly. If everyone did exactly as they pleased all the time, we would have chaos."

"Chaos," he repeated the word. "That is a bad thing?"

"My lord, you should release my hand."

Instead, he turned it palm up and leaned closer to… sniff it? "You smell so good. What is that?"

As she had used no lotions or powders that morning, she could not say. And even if she had wanted to speak, she would have most likely been silenced when he bent to kiss the tender palm of her hand. "My lord!" she hissed. "You should not."

But he was looking up at her with that teasing smile. "Why? You like it, do you not?"

"I do not like that you are breaking the rules."

"Hmm. Chaos." And he lowered his mouth to her palm again. The sensation was chaos—her senses were in tumultuous upheaval, and her body was straining to follow. The urge to give in to the chaos only intensified when she felt his lips brush her skin, and then his mouth parted, and his tongue dipped out to taste her.

Felicity struggled not to topple backward at the sharp stab of arousal that shot through her. What was this man doing to her? She tried to snatch away her hand, but he stubbornly held on. "My lord!" His tongue darted out again. "Armand!"

Now he looked up at her, and his blue eyes were so innocent. Oh, but she knew better. He knew *exactly* what he was doing to her. "I like it when you say my name."

"What you are doing is not appropriate. If you do this at the musicale, you, they—oh, I don't know what would happen!" The lady in question would probably faint. Or, considering what she had read about some of the ladies of the *ton*, she would drag the comte straight to bed. Felicity would have done that herself, except that she was not that kind of lady.

"I will not do this at the music. I will do it only with you." His lips skimmed up from her palm to the inside of her wrist, where he nuzzled the tender skin. Felicity felt her pulse racing, beating against his lips.

"You should not do it with me. You should probably do this only with your wife."

Now he looked up at her with interest. The interest made her wary, because she knew there would be questions behind it, but at this point, questions were better than the magic he had been working with his mouth on her skin. "What else should I do with this wife? I can think of many ideas—"

Felicity held up her free hand. "No, my lord. You must not divulge those to me. That is private." He frowned at her, and she added, "That is between a man and his wife only."

"But I want you to be my wife."

Felicity sighed in frustration and finally managed to pull away her hand. "We have been over that, my lord. We have discussed it," she said to clarify. "That is not possible. I am certain you will meet another woman who is more suitable for that position. In fact, it is my job to make sure that when you do, you impress her with your politeness and manners."

"Please. Thank you." He thought for a moment. "Delighted to meet you. Lesson over?"

She couldn't help but smile. "No, the lesson is not over. We haven't even discussed what you should do *after* you say 'delighted to meet you.'"

He grinned at her. "That is when I kiss the hand." He reached for her hand again, but she quickly tucked it behind her back and moved out of reach.

"Exactly, but then what?"

He moved closer, and she took another step back. "I will show you."

"No!" She held up a hand. "No, my lord.

Why don't we talk about it and leave showing for another time?"

"Words," he grumbled. "Too many."

And while she could sympathize with that statement, she knew it was the best course of action. Physical contact between them had to be kept to a minimum. And so she spent the better part of three hours explaining the protocol of introductions, rehearsing idle talk and chitchat, and giving him options for ending a conversation with a lady or gentleman. The comte seemed bored, but he tolerated the instruction, perhaps because they were outside and the weather was so lovely. He seemed happier outside, less tense and on edge.

Finally the dowager found them and asked Felicity to join her for a light tea. By then her belly was protesting the long hours without food, and she was more than happy to comply. But she promised the comte they would discuss the basics of fetching punch for a lady later. That suggestion made him look as though he had been shot with an arrow.

"I'm afraid you will have to postpone that lesson until the morrow," the dowager said. "The duc has agreed to escort his brother to Westin's. It is our hope the tailor can find something suitable for the comte to wear to the events we have planned."

Now the comte looked as though he had been stabbed with a knife, and Felicity gave him a sympathetic smile. She knew how he hated to be confined in the tight clothing in fashion for gentlemen, but there was nothing to be done for it. He could not attend the Society functions in shirtsleeves and bare feet. "Then

I shall see you this evening, my lord," she said and followed the dowager into the house. She was glad for the respite from their lengthy lesson, but that was not the only reason she was eager to allow the comte to go. She couldn't help but wonder what this untamed man would look like in a tailcoat and breeches.

The idea made her heart beat far too fast.

❧

Armand prowled the garden until the wee hours of the morning. He had not kept count, but he thought he had circled the town house at least one hundred times. On one of those circles, he had encountered his brother. Armand had expected Julien to ask why he was not in bed, but he did not. Instead, they circled the house together, and then Julien went inside.

But Armand knew even though it was very late, he would not be able to sleep. He could not get the image of the brick out of his mind. It had been a week since the incident. Why had the men not returned to carry out their threat? At his side, his hands clenched. If they did return, he would be ready for them.

When the pale colors of dawn lightened the shrubs of the garden, Armand finally abandoned his post to the hired watchmen and trudged to his chambers. His bed was made with fresh sheets and fluffed pillows, but he could not imagine crawling into it. For years he had slept on the hard floor, and with exhaustion setting into his bones, the familiar called to him.

Removing his shirt, he lay on the rug and stared up at the ceiling, watching the colors of the morning dance on the flat surface. In his cell, there had never been any light on the ceiling. He would go days, sometimes weeks, without light. He had become accustomed to it, and the light streaming through his window pained his eyes. And that was precisely why he refused to cover the windows. The pain of the light reminded him he was no longer in his cell. Not that he didn't know that already. He had never had a soft, thick rug in his cell. And his prison had never smelled as clean as this room. Everything here smelled of soap or wax or polish. The smells were strong but so much more appealing than those of unwashed bodies and excrement.

He closed his eyes and allowed himself to drift. As was becoming usual, the first thing he saw in his mind was Miss Bennett—Felicity. He liked that name. Someone had told him—or perhaps he knew it already—the name meant happiness. That was a good description for her. She was always happy, even when she was scolding him.

And how he liked for her to scold him, especially when it was because he was doing something to break one of her precious Rules. But then, he did not see the point in many of her Rules anyway. If he wanted to kiss her wrist—her small, sweet wrist—why should he not? He liked her reaction. He liked the way her sky blue eyes turned gray and smoky. He liked the way her cheeks turned not red—what was the color? Ah, pink. He liked that her blood beat faster. He could feel it against his fingers and lips when he put them to her wrist or her throat. She *wanted* him to break The Rules.

He began to imagine other ways in which they might break The Rules together and quickly had to turn his thoughts away. That path would only lead to frustration. Instead, he rehearsed the new words he had learned today, and gradually he began to drift off.

In the dream—Armand knew it was a dream, though he was powerless to end it or control it—he was a child again. He was walking through a crowded street in... Paris. Yes, he recognized this as Paris, though it was not the Paris he knew. This was a Paris filled with the hungry eyes of children and their mothers, standing on street corners selling their bony bodies for enough coin to buy a slice of bread. Not that there was any bread to be bought.

Armand picked his way through the crowds and the stench, keenly aware that though his clothes were soiled with soot and grime from his escape, they were still of better quality than any here wore.

He had paused once after escaping the château to turn around, and what he had seen had only made him run in the other direction. His home was on fire, flames shooting out windows and smoke billowing from the roof. He prayed Bastien and Julien had been away that night, out on one of their grand adventures, but he had no such hope for his mother and father.

Until the morning. He had hidden in the forest all night, and when sun rose, he had heard the unmistakable sound of his father's voice. Following that sound, Armand had seen his father, hands tied, led onto a cart with several of their neighbors. His mother, Julien, and Bastien were not with his father. When the peasants, who were insulting and spitting at his father the entire time, began to follow the cart, Armand did so, as well. From a distance. He knew enough to keep himself hidden. He did not want to be recognized.

The cart led him to Paris, where his father was unloaded and taken inside a building. He could not follow his father inside, and so he had stood in the courtyard, watching.

"Little brat, move on from there," a man in coarse clothing and with equally coarse speech yelled at him.

"Yes, sir," he said quickly, then, "What is this place?"

The man gave him a long look. "It's a prison. Don't you know that?" He leaned closer, his breath smelling of old wine as he smiled, showing yellow and broken teeth. "Who are you? You sound like an aristo."

Armand swallowed and stepped back. Something about the look in the man's eyes frightened him. The man turned to another guard loitering nearby. "Hey, Jacques, come here. I think we have another aristo!" He turned and swiped at Armand, but Armand was fast. He ran until he could no longer breathe, finding himself among the hungry children and the bony women. There were men, too. Men with knives and bayonets. Men who would kill him if he so much as opened his mouth. He could not speak again. Speaking was a death sentence.

And yet he needed food. His stomach grumbled, and his throat was as dry as sand. He needed food, and then he would have to think of some way to free his father from that prison. He passed a tavern where men were drinking, and wandered inside. He was immediately pushed aside, cuffed on the side of the head, and kicked. But he was too hungry and thirsty to care. The tavern was dirty, and he could see the lone barmaid was over-worked. She was thin but not as bony as the women he saw on the streets—and that gave him an idea.

She lackadaisically mopped at a spill on one of the tables with a dirty cloth then was distracted when a fight broke out among two of the patrons. She left her towel to watch the brawl, and Armand moved in and snatched up the towel. He began cleaning the table vigorously, and when the fight was over, he righted the chairs and the tables and wiped them down. Soon several of the men were telling him to bring them wine. At first, the barmaid tried to shoo him away, but he pretended he could not understand, could not hear. Eventually, she gave up, and he was soon sweeping floors, cleaning tables, and mopping up wine, among other liquids.

The tavern owner did not pay him, did not even acknowledge him, except to cuff him, but Armand was able to scrounge scraps of bread and sips of wine from time to time. It was better than nothing.

And every day he went to the prison, careful to stay away from the man who had tried to catch him that first day. He knew now that executions were happening in the square. Aristocrats were brought daily to lie down under a shiny silver blade. The men in the tavern called it Madame Guillotine, and Armand knew if he could not stop it, one day his father would lie down under Madame, as well.

It was in front of the prison that Armand first saw the little man. Despite his small size, he did not walk like a child, and he did not look like a child. He was old, even then, old and cruel. And his son walked behind him. His son was huge, three times the size of the father, and his eyes were glazed and stupid.

Those eyes met Armand's, and he heard a crash.

"No!" He sat straight up, his hands reaching out for something... anything. They caught the covers of the bed, and he blinked in confusion at the softness in his hands. Where? What?

The fog burned away with the sun pouring in through his windows, and Armand was brought back to the present. He was in London. He was at his brother's home. The tavern, the prison, the hungry children were far away and long ago. Those men were...

But they were not gone.

They were here in London, and they were looking for him. They wanted what was theirs, what they thought was theirs, and they would never stop until they had it.

Thirteen

FELICITY FELT AS THOUGH SHE WERE THE ONE WHO would be on display for all the *ton* to see. As she stood in the Valères' ornate vestibule, waiting for the comte to join the rest of his family, her heart thudded, and her hands felt clammy.

She was nervous, and she was not even going anywhere! It seemed she had so little time to prepare the comte for the musicale. She had done all she could, but how could she be certain she had not forgotten something? Had she remembered to tell him to address dukes as Your Grace? She thought she had. What about daughters of dukes? Had she gone over their honorary titles?

Curses! She had forgotten daughters of dukes, and surely Lady Spencer would have one or two at her musicale.

"Stop looking so worried," the duchesse of Valère said with a smile. "Armand will do fine."

Felicity swallowed the lump in her throat. "Of course he will. I'm not worried at all."

"You are pacing like an expectant father," the

dowager remarked as a maid draped a cape over her bejeweled black gown.

"Am I?" Felicity put a hand to her throat. "I suppose I am a tad nervous. Would one of you be so kind as to review courtesy titles for daughters of dukes with the comte? I don't know how it slipped my mind."

The duc raised a brow. "I don't even know courtesy titles for daughters of dukes." But Felicity knew that was not true. The duc of Valère was so refined, so elegant. She could not imagine he ever worried or stumbled through any type of social occasion. She, on the other hand, could sympathize with his younger brother. She turned and peered up the steps once again. Where was the comte? She was always nervous before any type of social gathering. Once she arrived, she inevitably relaxed and enjoyed herself, but there was always the worry her dress or her hair or her shoes would not be right.

Was the comte fretting over that now? What was taking him so long? Perhaps she should ask the duc to send a servant to assess his progress; the family was going to be late... could one be late to a *ton* affair?

Felicity couldn't stop herself from glancing up the stairs once again, but this time she was rewarded. The most handsome man she had ever seen was strolling down them, one hand on the banister, one in his pocket, and rakish scowl in place. She blinked, and for a moment she did not recognize him. And then she all but gasped as she realized it was the comte!

Tonight he looked every inch the aristocrat he was. He wore a dark blue coat of superfine, tailored

perfectly to show off his broad shoulders and wide
chest. It fit tightly, skimming down to slim hips that
were encased in dark breeches. The breeches were also
well-fitted, showing off muscled thighs. He wore the
requisite cravat, and it was starched to perfection, but
most surprising were the pumps. He wore the black
pumps every man wore with evening dress. Felicity
thought this must have been the first time she had seen
him with shoes on.

And actually, she preferred him without them. But
she could not fail to admire the spectacle descending
the stairs. He was the most beautiful man she had ever
seen. She wished she could loosen that cravat and free
his thick hair from its queue. She wished she had her
comte back, but this was the one who would go to the
musicale and who would woo all the ladies.

This was the comte who would find a woman of his
station to marry. If she had ever thought she deserved
or should aspire to that position before, looking at the
comte now relieved her of that flight of fancy. She
would never be anything more than a tutor, and he
would always be an aristocrat—whether his title was
revoked or not.

She realized quite suddenly she had been staring
and his eyes were on her. His scowl had grown
fiercer. Quickly, she stepped forward. "My lord, you
look perfect."

He faltered, glanced down at his attire. "I feel…"

She could see him grope for the word.

"Ridiculous."

"Oh, no!" His mother rushed past Felicity and
closed the distance between the family and where

he still hovered on the stairs. "Miss Bennett is quite correct. You look just as you should. Are you ready?"

His eyes cut to Felicity's, and she knew he was asking her the question. Was he ready? She took a deep breath. "Of course he's ready. My lord, have a wonderful evening."

He allowed his mother to take his arm, the tightening of his jaw the only sign of his discomfort at her touch, and descended the remaining stairs. Then he paused in front of her and offered his other arm. Felicity drew back. "My lord, we have been over this. I am not attending Lady Spencer's musicale. The invitation was for family only."

There was a long silence as the comte seemed to digest this information and find it distasteful.

"Armand," the duc said, his tone full of warning.

But the comte waved a hand at him. "I remember."

"Good. The carriage is waiting. Let's go."

The duc gave his wife his arm and led the four of them through the door opened seamlessly by the butler. Felicity stayed rooted in place, hands clasped, watching them go. This was her place, she told herself. This was her duty. She had tutored the comte in all he would need to know, and now she was to stand here while he went off and showed all he had learned. That was how things should be—and yet it hurt when he did not look back at her. It hurt when the door closed on his back and she was left standing alone in the vestibule.

She had a book in her room and had thought she would spend the evening reading or perhaps writing letters to her aunt or her friends in Selborne. But she did neither of those activities. Instead, she closed herself in her room, lay on her bed, and thought about the future. She didn't like to think about the future. There was nothing to be gained by traversing that path. Up until this point, she had focused on preserving her position as the comte's tutor. But now that he was progressing—speaking correctly, dressing correctly, hopefully addressing dukes' daughters correctly—how much longer could she expect this position to last? A month? Two?

At the most, three, and that was if the comte did not find a bride before then. And what would she do at the end of three months?

If the comte's appearance at the musicale tonight was successful, she might be justified in asking for an advance on her salary. Even ten pounds might be enough to hold off Charles a little longer. But if her position lasted only a few more months, would she receive her entire year's salary? What would she do if she could not pay Charles the twenty-five pounds in January?

He did not really want to marry her. Perhaps if she promised him more, he would give her a few more months. And perhaps the duchesse would help her find another position—one far away from London and the comte.

She might work for a wealthy family in the country, people who avoided Society and did not care about balls or musicales or gowns. She would be happy there, teaching cherub-faced children, and she would only occasionally think back on this position and the strange, handsome comte de Valère.

And that was the biggest lie she had ever told herself.

She knew that not a single day would go by that she would not think of the comte.

Armand.

She would think of him every hour, every minute. How could she ever forget him? Forget his eyes, his lilting speech, his mouth... oh, the things he could do with that mouth.

But, of course, by that point he would not be doing them to her. No, he would be married by then. He would be kissing another woman, the daughter of a duke, most likely. He would have children. Perhaps one day he would even engage a governess for those children, but it would not be she. She would be an old spinster by then. She would never have children. She would never...

Felicity closed her eyes. She did not want to think of the future any more. She would focus on the present. And at present, she was living in a duc's town house in Berkeley Square. She was tutoring a comte. She was in love with—

Felicity sucked in a breath of air and sprang to her knees. Where had that thought come from? That was a dangerous thought. She could not be in love with Armand—the comte. She would not be in love with him.

It was not love she felt. It was only lust. She wanted him to kiss her, touch her, and that was all there was.

And she would not allow any other thoughts—no matter how much they wanted to intrude—to enter her mind. She was not in love, and certainly not with an aristocrat! A man she could never hope to marry, even if Charles wasn't determined to ruin her.

There was a knock at the door, and Felicity quickly smoothed her skirts and grabbed her book, trying to look occupied. Trying not to look like a woman in love.

The door opened to reveal Gertrude, the maid who often helped her undress for bed. Felicity smiled at her, thinking an early night was probably just what she needed. After all, one could not think about—anything—when one was asleep.

"Gertrude, I'm glad you're here. If you could just unlace me, I can do the rest."

"But, Miss Bennett, I haven't come to help you undress. I've come..." She bit her lip and looked uncertain.

Gertrude was young, probably no more than seventeen, but she did not usually seem so unsure of herself. Felicity jumped off the bed. "Is something wrong? Did something happen?" Immediately the image of the shattered window and the brick on the floor of the dining room flashed in her mind.

"No, nothing bad has happened," Gertrude reassured her. "But I was told to come and help you dress. I was told to have you wear this." Now the door yawned open, and Felicity could see the dark blue gown that had been concealed behind it. Felicity frowned at it.

"What is that?"

Gertrude shook it out. It was silk and rippled like the waters of the ocean. "The dowager sent word you are to wear it. It was in her room."

Felicity laughed. "Why would I wear that? It's a formal gown, and I'm just going to bed."

Gertrude shook her head. "No, Miss Bennett. You see, the carriage has returned, and the footmen have a note from the dowager, requesting your presence at Lady Spencer's musicale."

"What?" Felicity groped for the bed behind her and sat heavily.

"I know! Isn't it exciting, Miss? They want you at the musicale?"

Felicity did not think it was exciting at all. Terrifying was probably the word she would have used. "The dowager sent word?"

"Yes, miss." Gertrude held out a slip of paper, and Felicity forced her wobbly legs to hold her long enough to stand and retrieve it. Now that she was closer to the gown, she felt her stomach clench. She remembered that watery blue material. The dowager had picked it out when they were shopping in Bond Street. Felicity had thought she was just being kind when she had mentioned a ball gown. Now, she could see the dowager had been more than serious.

Her hand shook a little as she flipped open the note. *We have need of Miss Bennett. Please dress her in the blue gown hanging in my room, and send her posthaste.*

It was signed with the dowager's initials, but they were unnecessary. The commanding tone was quite enough. Felicity looked up at Gertrude, and the maid held out the gown. "Are you ready, Miss Bennett?"

"No." Felicity shook her head. "No, I'm not."

"But, miss, the note said posthaste. The carriage is waiting."

"But my hair." Felicity chanced a glance in the mirror across the room. Her hair was a mass of untidy curls and rumpled coils. "And I don't have any suitable gloves."

Gertrude waved a hand, obviously unconcerned. "I can take care of your hair, and I'll ask one of the other maids if there are some spare gloves you might borrow."

"But..." Felicity tried desperately to think of another excuse, but none came to mind. Curses! She was actually going to have to attend Lady Spencer's musicale. As Gertrude helped her change into the gown, Felicity reflected it was not so much the idea of the musicale that alarmed her. She knew she would enjoy the entertainment. And it was not even the prospect of spending a whole evening among the cream of the *ton* that discomfited her, though she hardly relished the condescension she knew would be forthcoming.

What really bothered her was she would have to watch Armand—the comte—be introduced to other ladies. Would he flirt? Hold their hands and kiss their knuckles as he had hers in the garden? How could she stand seeing that?

"Miss Bennett, are you all right?"

Felicity blinked. "Pardon?"

"You're clenching your fists," Gertrude pointed out, fastening the last of the gown and bending down to straighten the skirt. Felicity carefully uncoiled her hands and peered in the glass across the room. Her hair was still rumpled, but the tutor in her serviceable beige gown was gone. Even without gloves, the blue gown made her look like a princess. Well, maybe not a princess but definitely a duke's daughter. She turned from side to side, admiring the way the gown shimmered and rippled. With its scooped neck, it showed off just enough shoulder and bosom to look interesting, but not enough to raise even the most conservative eyebrows.

Of course, the expanse of white flesh called out for adornment of some kind, but Felicity had no jewelry.

"You look perfect," Gertrude said, standing again. "Who would believe you were one of the staff?" Her eyes widened. "Oh, begging your pardon, miss."

Felicity laughed. "I *am* one of the staff, and I'd much rather stay here with you." But that wasn't quite true anymore. Now that she was in the gown, could feel its silky texture on her skin, she was eager to see and be seen.

And there was one man in particular she wanted to see her.

Gertrude guided her to the dressing table, and Felicity sat patiently as the maid pulled and combed and twisted her hair into some semblance of order. The style was simple, which Felicity preferred, and when the maid was done, they both studied her reflection in the mirror.

"It needs something around the neck," Gertrude remarked.

"I was thinking that myself, but I don't have any jewels."

"Me neither, though I do have something. Wait here!"

Before Felicity could ask what the maid meant, she was rushing from the room. A moment later, she returned with long gloves over her arms and a blue ribbon in her hand, almost the exact color of the dress. "Here, try this." She leaned over and fastened the ribbon about Felicity's neck, tying it with a small bow at the back. Then she held out the gloves and helped Felicity put them on.

Once again, Felicity was tugged in front of the full-length mirror, and she had to admit with the gloves, the ribbon, and the new coiffure, she looked entirely presentable. She smiled at Gertrude in the glass. "The ribbon is perfect, Gertrude. I think I shall actually blend in."

Gertrude snorted. "You'll do more than that, miss. You'll turn heads, I wager."

"Yes, well, let's not be that optimistic." But inside she was hoping there was at least one comte who would take notice.

"You'd better hurry, miss. The carriage is still waiting, and the dowager's note did say posthaste."

Felicity took a deep breath. "Thank you for your help, Gertrude."

The maid snorted again. "It was nothing. The next time I get summoned to a fancy party, you can help me."

Felicity grasped her hand. "Count on it."

She stepped out of her room and was surprised to see several servants, including Mrs. Eggers, the house-keeper, waiting on her. Within a matter of moments, she was pronounced acceptable and whisked down the stairs and into the carriage. As usual, the London streets were packed with conveyances. The carriage moved very slowly, and it was three-quarters of an hour before she finally climbed out of the carriage and stood before Lady Spencer's door. Lady Spencer was truly a neighbor of the Valères', and Felicity suspected that had she walked, she would have been at the door within five minutes. She smiled, thinking of the horrified reactions had she shown up on foot.

The door swung open, and a footman greeted her. "Welcome." He moved aside, and Felicity stepped inside. Lady Spencer's vestibule was not as grand as the Valères', but it was tasteful and well-appointed. She was goggling at the huge chandelier above her when she heard a man clear his throat.

She blinked and stared into the eyes of the butler. "Good evening," he said.

Felicity smiled. "Good evening." She peered past his shoulder, hoping she might catch a glimpse of the dowager or the duchesse. She was *not* looking for the comte.

"How might I assist you?" the butler asked, and Felicity brought her attention back to him. She could see the problem immediately. He did not recognize her, and he was being careful not to offend her by asking who she was and why she was there. It seemed butlers always knew who did not belong.

"The dowager duchesse of Valère asked me to join her party. If you could tell me where I might find them?"

His expression changed completely, his eyes lighting and the dour tightness of his mouth vanishing. "Ah, you must be Miss Bennett. Right this way."

Felicity had no time to ask how he knew her name or where they were going. She was led through a maze of rooms, all packed shoulder-to-shoulder with men and women dripping silk and diamonds. As she passed, their eyes touched on her, most showing little interest. After all, who was she?

The farther the butler led her, the more people

Felicity encountered. Who were all of these men and women? The duchesse had said they would attend intimate affairs. Such a crush of people would surely have alarmed the comte. Was that why she had been called? Had the comte been overwhelmed?

Finally they reached the music room, and Felicity saw a pianoforte was in the center, circled on all sides by chairs. A few of the seats were taken, but most were empty. Strange, she thought. Had she already missed the musical portion of the evening? She glanced at those seated in the chairs but did not see the dowager or any of the Valères. She was about to repeat her request to be taken to the dowager, when the butler bowed and said, "Lady Spencer, I present Miss Bennett."

The butler moved aside, and a woman of forty or so, dressed in a crimson gown with matching rubies, raised her eyebrows. She was a small woman and a handsome one, her dark hair showing only the faintest traces of gray. She notched her brow higher, and Felicity belatedly realized she should curtsey.

She did so, clumsily, and said, "A pleasure to meet you, my lady."

"Yes," she drawled. "I was told you can play and play well. Is that true, Miss Bennett?"

Play? For a moment, Felicity was confused, and then she saw the vacant pianoforte behind Lady Spencer. "Ah, if you mean play the pianoforte, yes, I do play. I cannot vouch for my skills, however."

"That has already been done. I'd like you to play a variety of pieces, something slow to start with, then more lively in the middle. Some Mozart might be nice."

Felicity stared for a moment. "You want me to play?"

Lady Spencer looked at her.

"You want me to play for your guests?"

The woman looked bored. "Yes, of course. Why do you think you were summoned?"

Yes, why had she thought she'd been summoned? Because the dowager hoped to introduce her to the *ton*? Because Armand—no, he was the comte, most definitely only the comte to her—had asked for her?

Ridiculous. She could see that now. She had been called to perform for the aristocrats. Nothing more, nothing less. To serve them was to be her lot at present, and if she was disappointed now, it was her own fault.

"Are you able to play, Miss Bennett? If not, then I fear I shall have to send everyone home. The maestro I had hired for the evening is in bed with a fever, and one cannot exactly host a musicale without any music."

"I see." And she did see now. She saw perfectly. "Of course, I shall play." She was already unbuttoning her gloves. "Would you like me to begin now?"

"Yes. I will gradually have everyone move into the music room. No point in making some grand announcement when the entertainment is one of the Valères' servants," she mumbled. "And Miss Bennett?"

Felicity stopped in her stiff-necked path to the pianoforte.

"If my opera singer deigns to make an appearance, I assume you can accompany her."

Felicity nodded, her neck cracking with the effort. "I shall do my best, your ladyship."

She sat at the pianoforte and tried to block out the noise, the tinkle of glasses, and the harsh sound of laughter. She was not nervous. She was too angry to be nervous. Why had the dowager not mentioned in her note that she would be playing? Then Felicity might have thought to take some of her sheet music along. Now she would have to play only pieces she knew by memory.

Across the room, Lady Spencer threw her an impatient scowl, and Felicity raised her hands. When she set them down on the keys, the sound was as angry as her emotions.

⁓

Armand could not breathe. He needed to find a way out of the masses of people before his hard-won control broke and he pushed them aside in an effort to escape. Beside him, Sarah talked away. She had introduced him to more women than he could count, and he had dutifully bowed and spoken of the weather to each. He did not have anything else to say to these women with their false smiles and their rouged skin.

He wanted to take off his shoes and rip the necktie from his throat. How could any man breathe in all of these clothes? And where the hell was the music? If the music started, then everyone might be distracted enough to allow him to escape. If he could only find a door...

"Lady Georgiana," Sarah was saying to another of the tight-lipped women, "might I present my brother-in-law, the comte de Valère."

The woman held out her hand, and Armand took it. He bowed, aware he was sweating now. He needed to escape. "A pleasure, Lady Georgiana," he said.

"Oh, but I adore your accent, my lord." The woman giggled, blinking at him six or seven times in rapid succession.

"Do you have something in your eye?" he asked.

"Armand," Sarah said, laying a hand lightly on the sleeve of his coat—a sign, he knew, he had said something inappropriate. "Lady Georgiana's country home is but a few miles from your brother's in Southampton. We are neighbors."

"Yes," the woman said, blinking again. "And now that we have been introduced, I shall have Mama invite you over for tea."

Armand did not particularly care to be invited for tea, so he said nothing. The silence dragged on a moment, and Sarah squeezed his sleeve again. Armand sighed. "Nice weather we are having," he said mechanically.

"Oh, but isn't it? Why just the other day I bought the most beautiful spencer, and now I wonder if I shall ever have the opportunity to wear—"

The first strains of a pianoforte sounded, mercifully interrupting the woman's babbling. Armand turned quickly to be certain the music was not his imagination. Others were craning their necks, as well, which meant they heard it, too. Now was his chance to escape. He needed to get out of this stifling room, but more than that, he wanted to go home, to make sure Miss Bennett was well. He had been away too long. What if she was hurt or in danger?

"Ah, it sounds as though the music has finally begun," Sarah said. "Armand, come and sit with me."

He whipped his head back to stare at her. Damned if he was going to be imprisoned inside this dungeon of people any longer. Even the music was not enough to calm him at this point.

"You go ahead," he ground out. "I will join you." He began to move away, but Sarah was in front of him.

"I think you will be interested to see the pianist tonight. Please, come and sit with me." She was hissing at him, so he hissed back.

"I don't care who is playing. Get Julien to sit with you." And he tried, once again, to step around her.

Once again, she danced in front of him. Her smile was huge and fake for the benefit of others who might be watching. "I insist you come and sit with me. Your mother will have saved us two seats."

She took his hand, and though the pain of her touch annoyed him, he allowed himself to be pulled along. Once they were seated, he could escape and be home, in his garden, in a matter of minutes. His mother was waiting for them just inside the music room, and she pointed to two empty seats beside her. Armand frowned when he saw they were right next to the pianoforte. He did not like to have so many people behind him. Sarah tried to pull him forward, but he resisted. If he had to sit here, he would sit in the rear, his back against the wall. That was the only way he would feel comfortable—if comfort was even an option in this small room crushed with people.

But as soon as he began to retreat, the music

changed. Something about it seemed familiar, and he glanced at the player.

His heart stopped for a full second when he saw her. She had that effect on him each time he came across her after any length of absence. And now, in a dress that was as blue as her eyes, she was even more beautiful than he remembered.

She was here, and she was safe. And he wanted her. The Rules be damned. He could not follow them any longer. Would not.

Tonight he would have her.

Fourteen

FELICITY SENSED A CHANGE IN THE AIR AS SOON AS THE comte entered the room. She didn't know how she knew he had come in, but somehow the temperature grew warmer, the colors more vivid, the sound of the keys more sonorous.

She looked up and met his eyes just as he saw her. He had been in the process of backing out of the room, but as soon as their gazes held, he paused. She could feel her cheeks heat at the look he gave her. No wonder the room was so warm. His eyes burned into her with a fierceness that made her blood race through her veins.

Did he look at every woman that way, or was it just her? For the moment, she wanted to believe that look of passion was for her alone.

Pulling her gaze away was one of the most difficult tasks she had ever faced, but she knew she must do so if she were to finish the piece without mistakes. She couldn't even remember what she played anymore, but she knew the next section was difficult, and she must concentrate.

That was easier said than done when, in her peripheral vision, she saw the comte take his place beside the dowager and the duchesse. With those eyes on her, burning into her, she could hardly breathe, much less concentrate on the music. Was he aware that he was sitting in the midst of so many people? She knew he hated to have anyone stand behind him, and he hated to be stuck indoors almost as much. Was he improving, or were these concessions to his comfort made for her?

She finished the piece to a smattering of applause and began the next. She chose only fast pieces now, to match the rhythm of her heart and because she wanted this performance to be over as quickly as possible. She wanted to speak with the comte, to be near to him.

The applause grew as she finished each piece, and she noticed gradually that the room was full. Several men, including the duc, lingered about the edges of the room, where there was now only space to stand. She thought playing for such a large, distinguished audience should make her nervous, but only the gaze of the comte could accomplish that tonight.

Finally, she played what she considered her final piece and rose to curtsey quickly, but Lady Spencer had other plans. She ushered in a lavishly dressed and coiffed woman of twenty-five or so, introducing her as the newest opera sensation.

"And I just know Miss Bennett will be thrilled to accompany such a virtuoso as this!"

Felicity sighed and sank back down on the bench. She was not at all thrilled to accompany an opera singer—virtuoso or not. She had not wanted to play in the first place, and now all she could think about was the comte.

But she dutifully conferred with the woman on the selections—mercifully, the singer had brought her own sheet music—and began the first piece. The opera singer was good, but Felicity heard little to nothing of her singing. She could not stop glancing at the comte, could not stop praying he would not leave yet. She knew the crowds were difficult for him. But if he could just hold out a little longer...

Then what? What exactly was she expecting to happen?

She knew what would most likely happen—she would be thanked for her services and sent back to the duc's town house while the comte stayed and flirted with more of the women deemed appropriate for him. Felicity could express her anger and outrage at having been used so, but would that accomplish anything more than making her feel better for a few hours?

She glanced at the comte again, felt the heat coil in her belly. Despite her best efforts, she was becoming more attracted to the comte each passing day. She would like nothing more than to kiss him, be held by him... go to bed with him?

Yes, if she was truly being honest, she wanted that, as well. And surely that would be the end of her position and, when she had to explain to Charles, the end of her betrothal. She did not think he would care—as long as she could pay him.

Finally, after what seemed an eternity, the opera singer began her last aria. Felicity played it diligently, but her heart was not in it, and she was relieved when the performance was finally over and the singer curt-seyed and blew kisses.

Felicity intended to escape while the crowds descended on the singer to congratulate her, but as soon as she rose and moved away from the bench, she found herself encircled by men and women eager to heap praises on her. With the pianoforte behind her, there was nowhere to escape. She was trapped with what now appeared to be an adoring public. Had she really played that well? She did not care. She craned her neck in an effort to spot the comte, but she could not see him.

Curses! He had probably fled, and now she would have no opportunity to see him tonight.

She tried to smile and look pleased at the congrat-ulations the crowd about her thrust upon her, but she could barely hear the accolades. She wanted to escape and had a moment of sympathy for what the comte must feel.

And then, at the back of the crowd around her, she noticed a commotion. Several people were being jostled, and someone was raising his voice.

Felicity's breath caught in her throat as she realized exactly whose voice that was—the comte. As she watched, he shouldered his way through the crowds, elbowing anyone who did not move aside quickly enough. The look on his face was almost feral when he finally caught a glimpse of her.

"No, my lord," she breathed, even though she knew he could not hear over the din of the crowd. "I am fine. I'm not hurt."

But he either could not see how she waved her

hands at him to stop, or he was too bent on rescuing her to care, because he continued forward, finally reaching her and grasping her hand.

"My lord, I'm fine. No one meant any harm. They were congratulating me."

"Come with me," he demanded, but Felicity dug in her feet.

"No, my lord. That would not be—"

"I don't care about your rules. I don't want another wife. I want you. Come with me now."

Felicity could only imagine the gossip that would already be circulating tonight. If she left with the comte, it would be ten times worse. She might not even keep her position through until the morning.

She looked him in the eye, prepared to resist, prepared to tell him in no uncertain terms that, under no circumstances, would she run away with him. But as soon as their eyes met, she knew she could not refuse him. She knew she loved him. All of her feeble protests were nothing more than lies to herself. She loved this man, and she knew she would do anything for him.

"I'll go with you." She put her hand in his, saw the way his eyes registered at first disbelief and then a male smugness that must be instinctual. He clasped her hand tightly in his and tried to pull her forward, but the crowds were interested in more than just the talented pianist now. They wanted to see what the comte de Valère was going to do with her.

The comte tried pushing them aside, and he made some progress that way, but he could not pull Felicity through with him. She was lost in the sea of bodies that closed in behind him, only their hands remaining locked against the wave of encroaching humanity.

Finally, he turned, parted the sea once again, and came to stand before her. Felicity was not certain what he was going to do, but the look in his eyes was enough to have her shaking her head. "No, my lord. No!" She barely eked out the last word before he swept her up into his arms and tossed her over his shoulder.

Felicity let out an undignified oomph and tried to catch her balance as her world spun upside down. She heard a gasp and a scream, and then she was bouncing through the crowds, which she noticed, parted quite easily at this point. She saw a swirl of faces, among then the dowager duchesse's. To her surprise, the woman did not look shocked. She looked almost pleased with what she saw. Felicity closed her eyes in understanding. The dowager had not arranged for her to be here because she cared whether Lady Spencer's musicale was a success. She had wanted Felicity and her son together. Perhaps she had even wanted this scene, the outcome of which would link Felicity and Armand together forever in the eyes of the *ton*.

The comte arrowed for the nearest exit and then through the French doors to the garden. Felicity blinked as the cool night air swirled around her. The lights from Lady Spencer's town house faded away, and she began to struggle.

"Let me down."

"Not yet. You're coming with me."

"Yes, well obviously you've given me little choice in that matter. You know you have broken the rules irreparably this time, don't you?"

"I don't care."

At the moment, Felicity did not care either. He swung her down, setting her on her feet but keeping hold of her arms. When her head stopped spinning, she looked about and noted they were standing at the back gate to the Valères' garden. The Spencer town house had been even closer than she had judged.

She looked up at the comte, saw his eyes glitter in the dark. "So beautiful," he said and reached out a hand to trace a lock of hair that had come loose from her coils. Actually, she could feel her hair tumbling down her back and curling in the breeze. It must all be loose.

"Your brother is going to be furious," she whispered as his hand slid down her neck. But she knew it would be some time before the duc and duchesse managed to escape Lady Spencer's. The gossip would have to be dealt with, the carriage called, and the return to the town house could take an hour in the crowded streets.

"So beautiful," the comte said again, and now he latched one finger under the satin material at her shoulder and pushed it down, revealing that shoulder and her upper arm.

"My lord," she breathed.

"Armand," he said, meeting her eyes. He caressed her shoulder, sending delicious shivers up her spine. "Felicity." Oh, how she loved the sound of her name on his tongue. He bent to kiss her, and she heard him whisper, "Mine."

As their lips met, she knew tonight she would be his.

This was what he had wanted. Armand knew the moment his mouth slanted over hers, that this was what he had wanted his whole life. He had thought he desired freedom, independence, land in the country. But now he knew none of that could compare to the feel of Felicity's mouth on his, her skin under his fingers, her soft moan when he pulled her close. She was not his wife, and this might be breaking The Rules, but he did not care. He had had enough of Rules forever. Enough of women who smiled at him with their lips but not with their eyes.

And he had had enough of crowded rooms and tight clothing and people at his back. He needed air and space—and he needed the woman in his arms. He was taking her.

He lifted a hand and ran it through her hair. He had wanted to touch that yellow hair for so long. It was far softer than he could have imagined—softer than his pet rat had ever been. And it was heavy. He fisted a hand in it, liking the feel of the softness against his skin. Touching Felicity never caused him pain, and he could not get enough of her.

Gently, he pulled her head back, giving himself better access to her mouth. He parted from her for a moment, pulled away just to look at her. With her head thrown back and her eyes closed, she looked more beautiful than he had ever imagined in his dreams. He wanted to kiss her mouth, her eyes, her face—every inch of her.

But not here. Not standing in the open garden. There were still men keeping watch on the house and the garden, and he wanted to be far away from their eyes. During the summer, he often preferred to sleep outside. In the back of the garden was a circular white structure. He had heard Sarah call it a gazebo. It was sheltered by trees and far enough away from the house that no one would see them. Putting his hand on her back, he led Felicity toward it.

"I was afraid you might leave before I finished playing," she said quietly as they moved toward the back of the garden. "I was afraid I wouldn't see you tonight."

"I couldn't leave without you," he answered simply. It was the truth. No matter how desperately he had wanted to escape that crowded house, he knew he must take her with him.

"Did you remember everything I taught you? I forgot to explain courtesy titles for the daughters of dukes."

He had no idea what she was speaking of, but he could see in her eyes she was concerned. "I did everything you said." They had reached the shadowy gazebo, and he pulled her close. "You ask Sarah."

"Somehow I doubt the duchesse will be too pleased with me after this." She moved into him, put her hands behind his neck, and stared into his eyes. Her face was a mixture of white flesh and shadows from trees. "But I don't care. All I want is to be with you. It's all I could think about tonight."

He leaned forward, kissed her lightly. His body was urging him to hurry, to move quickly to take what it needed, what it wanted, but he forced himself to move slowly. Everything about her seemed new and fascinating to him tonight.

"Did you kiss many women's hands tonight?" she asked, her lips whispering against his.

"Too many," he said honestly.

She pulled back, her eyes slanted in anger, and he knew that was the wrong response.

"I see. I'm sure it was a great hardship—all those rich, beautiful women vying to meet you."

He had definitely made her angry, though he did not know precisely what he had said or done. "You are beautiful," he said, coming back to the one word he knew very well.

She raised a brow. "Not more beautiful than those women."

He didn't understand exactly what she was saying, but he thought he knew her feeling. Jealousy? He almost laughed. "I do not want those women. Only you." And to prove it, he reached up and slid the material off her other shoulder so now both of them were bare and seemingly asking him to kiss them. He slid his hands up from her back until they touched the bare flesh of her shoulders. He knew they were white as snow, but tonight the shadows danced over them. Slowly, he pressed his mouth to one of the shoulders, let his lips explore the silky skin. He had never felt anything like Felicity's skin. Even in all of his time in prison, all the times he had dreamed of soft beds and soft clothing, he had never imagined a softness like this.

She moaned quietly and tilted her head away from him. That left her neck open, and he had the urge to kiss it, too. He could almost see where her blood beat beneath the white skin. There was so much he wanted to feel and to taste, and he hardly knew where to start.

Unable to resist, he touched his lips to her neck, letting his tongue trace her skin until he was right below her ear. She was trembling now and holding onto him, and he knew he was having as much an effect on her as she on him. And still he wanted more. What would her reaction be if he kissed her ear?

He did so, and she jolted then seemed to melt into him.

Now he slid a hand over her shoulder until it reached the smooth material of her dress. He wanted to touch what was beneath that—and he was not afraid to break The Rules this time.

"You never told me," he whispered in her ear, an action that had the effect of making her flesh rise like small pebbles. "What is this part called?"

His hand lowered and slid over the soft flesh of her chest. It was rounder and firmer than he had expected, and now he could hear her breath coming fast. And yet when he looked into her face, he saw she was red and obviously embarrassed. "Breast," she said, her voice choked.

"I like how they feel," he said, cupping both and testing the weight in his hands.

"Yes, well…" She tried to step away, but he pulled her close again.

"Do you want me to stop?" He did not know if he could stop, but he knew he must if that was what she wanted. He would never hurt another person or do something against their will. He had been the victim of the unwanted too many times.

"You should stop," she said in a tone he had heard many times before.

"The Rules," he said, knowing what she would say next.

"Yes, we are breaking them. Again." Then to his surprise, she stepped closer, put her hand on his chest. "But I don't care. I don't want you to stop."

She stood on tiptoe to kiss him, and while he enjoyed the feel of her lips on his, she must have loosened his neck cloth, because he could suddenly breathe again. He had forgotten how good it felt to be free, and immediately he pulled off the shoes, tossing them into the garden beyond. She laughed and he tried to strip off the coat. It took him a moment, because it was tightly fitted, but when she tugged with him, he removed it, as well.

Next were the upper buttons on his shirt, and then he decided he might as well do away with the shirt all together. He tore it over his head until he stood before her, in the cool night air, in only his breeches.

"Oh, my," she said, and her eyes were wide and round. "I don't think I've ever seen a man without his shirt before. It's…"

She didn't finish, and he did not care. She said too many words as it was. He preferred her actions, and now she reached out and traced a path from his throat to the center of his chest with one long white finger. His skin heated wherever she touched. He looked down, expecting to see she had burned the flesh, but it was unharmed. She moved closer, flattening her palms against him.

"You're so hard. Like steel," she murmured.

Now her hand cupped his upper arm. "And you're strong." Her touch tickled him, aroused him, made him want more.

Made him want to touch her in the same way. He opened his mouth to tell her what he wanted and then discarded the words. Words were his enemy with her. Words made her think too much about Rules. Actions were better.

He wanted the dress she wore off, so he could touch—what had she called them?—ah, yes, so he could touch her breasts, see them in the shadowed moonlight. He did not know how to remove the dress, so he tugged gently on it until the swell of the bare flesh he sought appeared.

The material was too tight to slide down any farther, so he touched that swell with his fingers then bent to touch it with his lips. "I want to kiss you." He touched the fullest part of her. "Here."

"Oh, I—"

He felt something hard in the midst of the softness, something small peak under his touch, and he rubbed it with two fingers. It was the right thing to do, because she moaned and pressed closer to him. Then she reached back, awkwardly, and a moment later, the material was loose enough to slide to her waist.

Armand reached out to touch her flesh and then frowned. She wore more clothing underneath the dress—and how he would ever remove it, he did not know. He glanced up into her face and saw she was smiling. "They are called stays." She turned her back to him, and glanced over her shoulder. "They lace in the back."

He could see now how the stays had been tied on. The laces were small and tight, and he would have preferred to rip them off, but he settled for fumbling to loosen them. To his surprise, they loosened easily and fell away.

She turned back to him, and there was still more clothing between him and those breasts. But it was less than before, and this layer was almost sheer. He could see the roundness of her breasts. They were as pale as her shoulders except for a dark circle in the middle.

"This is called a shift—chemise in French."

It was flimsy and loose, and he could see it would not be difficult to remove. He put one hand at the top and tugged it down, slowly. As he watched, the center of her breasts peaked and grew hard under the material. He reached out, touched that hard little pebble. "What is this?"

Even her neck was red now, but she answered him. "Nipple. I-I'm cold."

He looked up at her. "I will warm you." But not before he tore that material away. He needed to see her flesh, to see what he had been dreaming about. He gave the chemise a last tug, baring her to the waist.

She was more beautiful than he could have ever dreamed. Her waist was small and slim and her breasts round and heavy. He could not resist cupping them again, running his thumb over that hard pebble. The nipple. She moaned when he did so and arched her back slightly. That was something he had not expected, and it shot heat through him, making him even harder.

But as much as he wanted to do something with

that hardness, he was not through exploring. He wanted to taste her, and he leaned forward, putting his mouth at the swell of her breast. Her reaction was violent—her hands clutched at him, and she began to tremble. He darted a tongue out, tracing that cool flesh, noting how it seemed to warm as he touched it. Finally his tongue reached her nipple. He took it in his mouth, and she bucked against him as he teased it with his tongue. His hand rose up to touch the other, flicking it lightly with his fingers.

On a gasp, she said his name. Her fingers dug into the skin of his back, and though her nails raked into him, he liked the feeling. He liked that he was the one causing this reaction. Reluctantly, he lifted his mouth from her breast and moved below, to her stomach. The material was in the way again, but he tugged it to her hips, so he could explore further with his tongue.

Her skin tasted unlike anything he had ever known. It was sweet and slightly salty, and it tasted as he would have imagined she would taste—beautiful.

She was almost bare, and he needed to see all of her now. With one quick movement, he pushed the dress and chemise to the ground, revealing her body to him. Her hips were round and pale, and between her legs was a vee covered with the same yellow hair as that on her head. He wanted to explore that vee, but she was trembling, and he pulled her close to warm her.

He kissed her mouth again, feeling her bare flesh against his own. What would it be like to take off his breeches and stand naked beside her? But that would have to wait. She was still trembling, and he could see now it was not from cold. She was afraid.

"I'm not going to hurt you," he said, kissing her cheeks and her eyelids, allowing his hands to roam over those wonderful breasts and then down to her hips. How could she be so soft? So full? So warm?

"I know. It's only…" She swallowed. "I have never done this before. I've never been naked in front of a man before."

He had never considered that she had, but the idea of her sharing this with anyone else, revealing herself to anyone else, made him angry. He liked knowing he alone had seen her this way. That must be the marriage idea again.

"I have never done this before either," he said. "Would you be less scared if I was naked too?"

"No!" Her voice held a note of panic. "I mean, I understand the logic behind you saying that, but I think I feel more comfortable with you dressed—half-dressed—for the moment."

"Come here." He wanted her beneath him, and he led her to one of the benches around the edges of the gazebo. There were pillows scattered over them, making them soft and perfect for reclining. He had slept here often, enjoying the freedom of the open space and the open sky above him. He felt at ease here, comfortable. He wanted her to feel the same.

He eased her down onto the pillows on the bench and lowered himself over her. The skin on his chest brushed against her bare skin, causing a sensation he had never encountered before. It was not pain, but it was pleasure so acute that it was like pain.

He sank into her and the feel of her beneath him, her scent—the small noises she made when he began to kiss her and touch her—made the rest of the world, the rest of his life, fade away. When he was with her, his memories of prison faded away. The small man and his giant son retreated to the back of his mind. There was nothing before her. There was nothing but now, and he preferred it that way.

He kissed her lips, opening her so he could delve inside and taste her. She met him, her passion rising even as his did. Her hands slid along his back, pulling him closer, her nails urging him to kiss more deeply, press fully against her.

He moved to her neck, tasting it, tracing a path to her breasts, her belly, that vee he had been so interested in. As he drew close, she moaned, and when his hands brushed the yellow curls, she jumped and sat forward.

"What are you doing?" Her voice was raspy and breathless, almost as his had been when he had first begun to speak again.

"Exploring." He ran his fingers against her again, and she jumped even higher. "What is this part called?"

"My lord, I don't think we should…"

"Lie back down," he said, easing her back. Maybe this was one part he did not need named. "Let me touch you."

"My lord—"

"Armand." He rubbed his fingers over her again, and she jumped. But her reaction was less violent this time, and when he repeated the action, she rose to meet him slightly. "Am I breaking another Rule?"

"I—mmm—I don't know. I, oh dear."

He parted her legs, saw the flower between them.

"I don't know the rules for this," she whispered.

Armand smiled. No Rules. Perfect.

He ran his hands over her again, and this time she arched her back, her hips rising to meet his touch. His finger eased inside her, and he was astonished by how warm and wet she was. Yes, this was where he wanted to be. He could feel himself throbbing, needing to be inside that warm place.

His instinct was to strip off his breeches and plunge himself into her, but he knew that would scare her. Instead, he continued to rub her as he bent over her again and kissed her lips. He had no sense of time with her. Every moment ran together into what seemed an eternity, and then she was clutching at him, arching into him, and moaning his name.

He slid a hand down to unfasten his breeches, feeling relief when their tightness was gone. He stripped them off, aware she was watching, but her gaze was more curious than afraid now. And then before she could think too much, before she could begin to say more words, he was above her again, kissing her again, sliding his fingers into her.

And then he was inside her. He moved gently and slowly, but it was not easy. Every primitive need in him cried out for release. It would come, he knew, if he plunged into her. But he could feel how tight she was, how she stiffened when he moved too quickly. And so he moved slowly. It was painful how slowly he moved, but he was rewarded by her response. Gradually, she opened for him, her body taking his inside until he was fully encased.

The sensation was overwhelming. He had never felt

anything like it, and he knew this was only the beginning. Her hips were rising to meet his in a primitive dance both of their bodies knew, even if their minds did not. He moved with her, paying close attention to when her pleasure seemed the greatest. He wanted her to feel the pleasure he felt.

"Armand!" she cried out, and her hips seemed to race against his.

"Slow," he groaned. If she continued to move so quickly, he would not be able to hold himself back. But she ignored him, moving faster, her body bringing his to the edge of pleasure, the height of sensation.

And then she bit off a scream, and he felt her tighten around him. That was his undoing. He fell into her, fell into the sensations, allowed himself to tumble into that darkness.

For once, he did not care if he ever saw the light again.

Fifteen

FELICITY COULD NOT BELIEVE WHAT HAD JUST happened. She did not know her body could feel this way, that she could abandon all sense of propriety, all sense of herself, and give herself so freely. She did not know how else to describe what had happened. She had forgotten—perhaps discarded—all the rules of behavior and allowed herself just to act, to feel. The comte—Armand—had that effect on her.

And now he was lying on top of her, his weight heavy and satisfying, and she never wanted him to move away. She should have been worried. They were outside, naked, and the duc and duchesse were liable to be looking for them. How much time had passed? The Valères were going to be furious. If she looked as debauched as she felt, they would know exactly what had transpired out here tonight.

Armand nuzzled her neck, which sent tiny shivers through her. How could she still feel such pleasure? Surely he had drained every last ounce she had to give. Oh, she knew she should be worried about the Valères and about all the rules she had broken. About the consequences—and there could, would be, devastating consequences. But she could not worry about consequences. All she could do was arch her neck, giving Armand better access.

He rose up, hovered over her, his eyes searching hers. He spoke without words, letting her know the experience had been as profound for him as it had been for her.

Felicity smiled, ran her fingers over his cheek, touched his lips. He kissed her fingers, one by one, and then their mouths met again.

They could spend the entire night like this, she knew. And as much as she would have enjoyed that, she knew it was not possible. They would be discovered sooner or later if they lingered.

"Armand—"

He kissed her again, cutting her off.

"No words. Too many words."

Gently, she leaned back, broke the kiss. "I know, but words are necessary now. We can't stay like this."

"I like you better without words," he said, leaning forward to kiss her again.

"Yes, I like that, too, but your brother and the duchesse will have many words for us if they find us like this. We must get dressed and go inside."

He pushed back, ran a hand through his disordered hair. "Rules again."

Hoping he would not fight this next "rule," she sat and cleared her throat. "Perhaps it might be best if we did not mention what happened here tonight. We shouldn't tell anyone."

He frowned at her. "But we are married now."

Oh, dear. Was that what he thought? "Not exactly. There's actually a ceremony, a ritual, before marriage. We should be married before... doing what we just did, but without the ceremony, we're not."

"Then we will marry. Now." He leaned close, smiled mischievously. "I want to do this again."

She did, too, but she did not think it best to say so at the moment. Instead, she sifted through their discarded garments and began dressing. It was not an easy feat to accomplish on her own, and she asked Armand for help at several turns. When she was finally dressed again, she looked down and sighed. Her gown was wrinkled, her hair hung down about her shoulders, and she could not find one slipper. Armand had donned his breeches and shirt and that was all. He'd left the shoes, stockings, and tailcoat in a heap on the gazebo floor. She supposed that was about all he thought they were good for.

Now that she was dressed again, the hazy pleasure of the moment had worn off, and she had a flash of Charles's face in her mind. She knew now that no matter what the penalty, she could never go through with a marriage to him. She would find a way to get him the twenty-five pounds. But if she could not...

She did not like to think what that decision entailed for her future. If she were dismissed from this position, where would she go? If the duchesse blamed her for Armand's actions at the musicale, or if the family suspected what had occurred in the garden tonight, they would not give her a letter of recommendation. It was possible she would be dismissed from this position within the day. And then what? She could give

Charles her parting wages, but how would she live? Where would she go?

And if her parting wages were not enough, Charles could cause trouble. Some employers might overlook the gossip resulting from Armand carrying her off tonight. She knew there were many on the fringes of Society who might view the incident and her employment with the wealthy, powerful Valère family as giving her a certain level of cachet. But if Charles made their betrothal known, it would ruin even her chances with the fringes of Society. A governess swept off her feet by a comte was one thing. A woman betrothed to a military hero, which was how Charles would make himself appear, who betrayed the poor man with a comte, was something else entirely. She would be left without options, and how long would she survive on the streets before she was raped or murdered?

She did not like to think Armand would allow that, but what did he know of Society's rules and their consequences? And it was not as though he loved her. What if this passion for her was fleeting? She sighed. She supposed she would have to go back to her aunt's. There she would not only be a burden but a ruined woman, forever scorned by her upstanding neighbors. And what if Charles followed her there, demanded more money? Would her aunt demand she do her duty and marry him?

Armand put his hand on her shoulder, and she turned and smiled at him, not wanting him to see her worry. "I'm sure your brother and sister-in-law are searching for us. We should go in before they find us." She intended to hide for as long as possible.

He nodded, and she started back for the town house. He was right behind her. "I will tell Julien we marry tonight."

She sighed. "Armand, that's impossible. We need a license and a minister." And she would never consent. She was legally betrothed to another man. Would Armand want her when he realized she had kept that from him? If she tried to explain, would he even understand?

She felt heavy, thinking of the ramifications of what she had done tonight. Was the lovemaking they had shared worth the cost?

She glanced back at Armand, and he gave her a warm—a very warm—look. Yes, she decided, it was worth it. When they were close to the house, Armand took her arm. "We will marry as soon as possible."

She gave him a wan smile and wished that could be true.

"And then we will go to the country."

Now she frowned. "The country? Why?"

"There is a house there, in Southampton. That is where I want to live. I don't care for the city."

Felicity smiled. She could easily picture the comte living happily on an estate in Southampton. He would love the open space and the fresh air. And she knew he enjoyed working the soil, growing all sorts of flowers and plants. The country was the perfect place for him.

"We're in agreement on that point," she said. "I don't like the city either. But Armand, I can't—"

He put a finger over her lips. "We will have a dog or two or maybe more. And we can…" He gestured to the gazebo. "What is that called? What we did?"

She swallowed and felt her skin heat.

He put his hand on her cheek. "Why does your face turn red?"

"Because I'm embarrassed."

He frowned at her. "That is like shame?"

She nodded. "A little."

He stepped back, his eyes flashing. "I shame you?"

"No." She laid a hand on his arm. "No, but your question makes me uncomfortable. It's not something people discuss. The rules again."

He nodded, and she thought he must surely grow tired of all of her rules. "But to answer your question, it's called, well, I suppose we could call it making love."

"Love? That is what my mother says to me."

"Hmm. Well, that is a different sort of love. More physical."

"I see."

But Felicity wondered if he did see. Surely he had been loved and cherished as a child, but what did all of those years without love, without any human contact, do to one's capacity to receive and give love? Had she managed to fall in love with a man utterly incapable of loving her back? A man who did not even understand what the word meant? Perhaps all he knew was lust—primitive and instinctual. Was that all they had shared?

And then he leaned forward, cupped a hand to her cheek, and gave her such a look of tenderness she could not help but think he must have some understanding of love. He wasn't looking at her with lust now. There was a gentleness that made her heart clench, made her want to wrap her arms around him and kiss him until they were both breathless again.

He must have sensed her mood, because he ushered her toward the door to the town house—the same back door they had used the first night he had led her to the gardens. She could go to her room using this path without anyone seeing her. At least he had understood there was a need for discretion. She pulled open the door then noticed he did not follow.

"Aren't you coming inside?"

"Later," he said, his eyes tracking over the dark garden. Felicity followed his gaze.

"You think they're still out here somewhere? The two men who dug up the garden and threw the brick?"

He didn't answer, but she could see the way his shoulders tensed.

She laid a hand on his arm. "Your brother hired men to watch the house. You don't need to patrol all night."

"They will never give up. Never go away."

"Not until they have the Treasure of the Sixteen."

He gave her a sharp look and his lips thinned. His eyes grew haunted, and she could see her words had caused something to flicker in his mind. A memory? She should not push him, not after the magical time they had spent together tonight. She didn't want to ruin it.

And yet, would he ever be whole and complete if he did not face some of the demons that plagued him? Perhaps if they faced them together, it would be easier for him.

"What is the Treasure of the Sixteen, Armand?"

He began to turn away, and now she was the one who pulled him back.

"I know you don't like to think of it, of that time, but if you could tell us what this treasure is, then maybe we would know how to deal with those men."

"No." The word was harsh and simple and brooked no argument. He would not discuss the treasure. Felicity sighed. She had been foolish to think he would talk about it with her, foolish to think that together they could conquer his past. She would most likely be dismissed and out on the streets by tomorrow afternoon anyway. Perhaps it was better if they did not complicate the matter any further.

"Good night, Armand," she said.

He bowed. "Good night."

Felicity started up the steps, alone and shaking her head. His dismissal had been so formal, but then what had she expected? She had taught him well.

Her body still burned from his touch, and pleasure still thrummed through her, but had he been affected the same way? And what was she going to do tomorrow when the duchesse sent her away?

Curses but she was a fool! *You had to fall in love with him*, she scolded herself. *You couldn't just be his tutor.* Well, she was no stranger to the rules of Society and the consequences for breaking those rules. Now she would pay the price.

She slipped into her room and closed the door behind her, feeling lonely and lost—and more in love than she had ever thought possible.

❧

Armand walked every inch of the garden and the area around the town house until he was satisfied the small man and his son were not hiding on the property. Felicity had been right. They would not give up until they had the Treasure of the Sixteen. And was he so much the coward he could not allow himself to go back, to remember what the treasure was, why these men sought it?

But the snatches he did remember haunted him. He had no fear for himself—there was nothing they could do to him that hadn't already been done. He did not fear torture or death. But he feared for his family and for Felicity.

He wished he could have held her all night. Parting from her had been agony. He needed her skin against his, her lips against his. He needed to be inside her again, to feel her wrapped around him. He wanted her more than he could ever recall wanting anything— light, food, water, air, freedom...

He would do anything to protect her.

With that in mind, he marched up to the town house's front door, opened it, surprising the butler who had been standing in the vestibule, obviously attempting to overhear the discussion taking place in the dining room.

Armand paused, glanced at the closed dining-room doors. "My brother," he said.

The butler recovered quickly. "In the dining room, my lord."

With a nod, Armand walked past him, opened the doors, and stepped into the room. His brother, his mother, and his sister-in-law looked up at him. "What happened to you?" His mother was the first to speak. She rose. "Where is your coat, your shoes?"

Armand gestured toward the garden. "I took them off."

"Where the hell have you been?" Julien rose now, his scowl fierce. "And where is Miss Bennett? Do you know the problems you've caused?"

Armand shrugged, pulled out a chair, and sat. He was tired suddenly. "Rules again. I do not care about The Rules."

"Where is Miss Bennett?" Sarah asked, cutting Julien off before he could speak again. "Is she well?"

"She went to her room. She is fine."

"I'm going to go see her." Sarah rose, but his mother waved her back down.

"Let us first hear what Armand has to say. You know that you have caused quite a bit of trouble. You may not care about yourself, but now you have compromised Miss Bennett. This is serious." Her tone was stern, but it did not have the angry sound that Julien's did.

Armand nodded. "I want to marry Felicity."

Julien threw up his hands. "Oh, she's Felicity now, is she? Just what exactly happened after you left Lady Spencer's?"

He was tempted to tell them, but Felicity had seemed against it, and she knew The Rules better than he. "I want to marry her."

His mother actually looked pleased, but Sarah plopped down heavily in a chair and put her face in her hands. "Of course you'll marry her. What other choice is there?"

Armand ignored her. "But she says there is still a ceremony."

"There are many choices," Julien said. "Armand's

actions tarnish the girl, but he is not required to marry her."

Sarah wrinkled her nose at him, but he shrugged. "It's not my fault Society has a double standard. Besides, she's obviously looking for money or to advance her position." Julien folded his arms across his chest.

"Rubbish!" his mother said, "She was not the one who carried him off. Why should she pay? Besides, have you seen the two of them together? I think she is in love with Armand."

Julien scowled. "*Ma mére.*"

"Love." Armand nodded, recognizing the word. "Yes. I want to take her to the country after we marry."

"You're not marrying her! Haven't you heard a word I said?" Julien ran a hand through his hair. "And what exactly are you going to do in the country? Up until a few weeks ago, you couldn't even speak. And now tonight—well, how can I let you out of my sight?"

Armand stood slowly and advanced on his brother. "Just because I did not speak, does not mean I am an idiot. All of you treat me like I'm an idiot." He looked at each in turn, and Sarah lowered her gaze, but his mother nodded.

"I don't think you're an idiot, Armand," Julien said, "but I don't think you know anything about running a country estate."

"I can learn. I learn fast. I used to learn faster than you ever did."

He saw his mother purse her lips as though she wanted to say something, but she remained silent. No matter. He knew it was true. Julien may have been the eldest and Bastien the most adventurous, but he, Armand, was the smartest.

Julien sighed. "I don't know—"

"Did you take me from prison just to lock me in this house?" Armand turned to look at the dining room with its cushioned red chairs, its dark wood, and the sparkling light above the huge table. "This prison is beautiful, but if I can't leave, it's still a prison."

Color jumped into Julien's face, and he reached for Armand's shirt. A chair fell over as he lunged, but Armand did not flinch. "Who the hell do you think you are?" Julien roared, slamming Armand into the wall. The soft red curtains crashed down behind him. "Do you know what I sacrificed to get you out? Do you know how many years I searched for you? Do you know I am still searching for Bastien?"

Armand had not known, and it gave him a moment's pause. But he was still angry. "Do you want to lock him up, too?"

"You ungrateful—"

"Stop it!" His mother did not raise her voice, but the tone had them both backing down. "This fighting will not accomplish anything. Armand, you are not a prisoner here, and Julien, you are too overprotective. Your brother will do just fine at The Gardens. Give him a month, and he will probably run the place better than the steward you have there now—possibly better than you ever did."

Julien shook his head. "I'd like to see that."

"Give him the house. You do not care for it anyway. And that is not all." She raised a hand when

Julien would have turned away. "If he wants to marry Miss Bennett, I think we had all better give him our blessing. Armand was always a stubborn child and a decisive one. When he saw what he wanted, he usually got it. And he was usually right about it, too. He wants Miss Bennett. If she wants him, as well—and I think I have seen them together enough to know that she does—then why not condone the marriage? That will end the scandal broth tonight's incident caused."

Sarah raised her brows and glanced at Julien. "She has a point." But Julien still looked undecided. Armand shook his head. He was done with being treated as an idiot.

"You can't keep me here, and you can't keep me from marrying Felicity. You want to protect Sarah, Julien. I want to protect Felicity. There won't be any bricks through the window at The Gardens."

Julien raised a brow. "Really? You don't think the men who did that will follow you there? They found you here."

Armand clenched his fists because he knew Julien was right. It was his own weakness that he had not wanted to think of that possibility. He wanted to pretend he could escape from his problems. But there was no running. He looked at his mother and Sarah. Even if he and Felicity did manage to escape the father and son, that would still leave those here in danger. He could not allow them to pay for his sins.

Armand leaned down, righted the chair, and sat. He did not want to do this. He did not want to have to remember what he had seen, what he had done. The first few years in prison, he had driven himself mad going over and over everything in his mind. Finally, he had pushed everything down, everything away until his mind was all but a clean slate. It was the only way he had survived all those years of caged solitude. But now he would have to dredge all of it up again. There was no other choice. And hadn't he promised he would do anything to protect Felicity?

"I know something about the Treasure of the Sixteen," he said finally.

Everyone in the room grew still, and Armand could feel their eyes bore into him.

"I will tell you what I know. I will remember," he said, closing his eyes to keep the memories at bay for the moment. "Tomorrow." He was too tired, too drained to allow that blackness to seep in tonight. He needed to rest, to be sure this was the only way. He would need all his strength for what lay ahead.

"Tomorrow?" Sarah whispered. "You'll talk to us about—before?"

He nodded. His mother rose and put her hand on his shoulder. There was a stab of pain, but it was less than usual. He could almost ignore it. "Tomorrow will be soon enough. You need your rest. After all, we now have a wedding to plan."

He trudged to his room, feeling heavy and weary. He all but collapsed on the floor, forgoing even the luxury of a blanket tonight. The lights in the room burned bright. The window was open, but still the dreams started as soon as he closed his eyes.

Paris. He was a child again, and he was afraid for his father. There were more and more executions every day, and there seemed to be nothing anyone could do to save the doomed aristocrats—not that anyone wanted to do anything.

The peasants wanted blood, and there were days it ran in the streets like wine.

The first time he saw the small man and his large son, they had not appeared to notice him. Many men and women went in and out of the prison yard where his father was being held. Few paid any mind to a small, mute boy.

But he made the mistake of going there too often and at the same times, and soon, when Armand stood in the prison courtyard, he could feel the eyes of the small man on him. He was watched, assessed.

Armand knew he should stop coming to the prison, but how could he leave his father alone in there? He had never yet seen his father, but he had not been one of the haggard men and women loaded into the carts as fodder for Madame Guillotine. The duc must still be in the prison, and Armand hoped one day he would catch a glimpse of him.

He stood in the courtyard for an hour each day and stared at the windows, hoping to see his father's strong, dignified face. Instead, one day another man's face appeared before his. "You are beginning to attract attention, *mon ami*."

Armand blinked at him and then followed his gaze to the small man and his large son. The small man was staring at him, his gaze malevolent.

Armand glanced up at the new man. He was an

average-looking man, dressed in peasant clothing. He had a kind face but hard eyes that seemed to miss nothing. "I see you here every day, mon ami. Do you have a friend in the prison?"

Armand shook his head. To have a friend in the prison would mean he sympathized with the aristos.

"Then why do you come here, mon ami?"

Armand shrugged and looked down. He wanted to leave now, to go back to the tavern and busy himself until he was invisible again.

Now another man joined the first. They looked remarkably alike. "This is my brother, mon ami. His name is Jacques. My name is Jacques, as well. You can call me Jacques One and him Jacques Two." He laughed, showing a mouth full of uneven teeth.

Armand frowned. Both brothers named Jacques? But then he remembered many of the revolutionaries used this name in order to hide their true identities. Jacques Two leaned close to study Armand. "Do you have a name, mon ami?"

Armand stood silently, knowing any word would give him away as an aristocrat.

"Perhaps your name is Jacques," Jacques One said, laughing again. "You can be Jacques Three!"

Armand nodded then, smiling a little. He needed to get away now. The small man was still watching him, and the two Jacques made him nervous.

"Can't you speak, Jacques?" Jacques One asked.

Armand shook his head then put his hand to his throat. It was a gesture he made often to signal his voice would not work.

The Jacques nodded, exchanged a glance. Then

Jacques Two said, "Why don't you come with us, Jacques? We have work you can do. We could use a boy who works hard and won't be tempted to spread our secrets."

Armand took a step back, unsure if he really had any say in the matter. "I've seen you at that little tavern where so many of our fellow Jacques meet," Jacques One said. "You work hard. Why don't you work hard for us?"

The small man was coming toward him then, making his way across the prison courtyard. Armand watched him, praying he was not coming for him.

The Jacques turned, saw the small man coming. "And we can protect you from that one," Jacques Two said. "He won't touch you if you work for us. As it is now, he doesn't like you much, mon ami."

Armand swallowed. He could see the hatred in the small man's eyes, the suspicion. He looked at Jacques One and Jacques Two, nodded, and followed them out of the courtyard...

"Oh, Armand," Felicity said.

He looked up, surprised to see the whole family gathered around the dining-room table. The morning light streamed through the dining-room windows, and he squinted at it. He was not in Paris, and he was not dreaming. He had woken early this morning and been anxious to relay what he remembered to his family. Now they all sat around him, his mother dabbing at her eyes and Felicity's voice bringing him out of his reverie.

He glanced at her and, for a moment, he was caught by her beauty. The dirty streets of Paris, the Jacques, and the fears of a small boy were swept away. And then his brother spoke.

"And so these men took you in, took care of you, and protected you from the small man. What does any of this have to do with the Treasure of the Sixteen?"

Armand swallowed, not sure of the answer to that himself. It seemed information came to him slowly and in its own time. He could not force it, nor could he stop it.

"I don't know what it has to do with the treasure," Felicity said, giving him time to think. He gave her an appreciative look. "But the small man and his son. You said it was his son, my lord? Those are the men I saw in the garden. Those were the men digging the holes and who threw the brick at the window."

"But what are they doing here?" Sarah asked, sipping her tea. "Why have they appeared in London and after all of these years?"

"They want the treasure," Armand said simply.

"And they think you know where it is," Julien said. Armand nodded.

"Do you?"

Armand took a deep breath, and then the door opened. Grimsby gave a short, cursory bow.

"What is it, Grismby?" Julien's voice was sharp and impatient.

The butler cleared his throat. "I am sorry to interrupt, Your Grace, but there is a man here who wishes to see Miss Bennett."

Felicity's hand flew to her throat. "Me?"

"Yes, miss. He says his name is"—he held a card

by two fingers and glanced down at it—"Charles St. John. He claims to be your husband."

Sixteen

THE WORLD WENT BLACK. OUTSIDE, SHE COULD SEE the sun shining, the light streaming in through the drawn curtains in the cheery dining room. Carriages clopped past—horses' bells jangling jauntily and the coachmen calling out "hup." Men with their tall hats and women with their parasols lingered in the park at Berkeley Square, enjoying what might be the last mild day of the year. It was now December, but cold, dreary winter had held off a little longer.

Except that Felicity felt colder than she ever had before. She shivered, looked around, and saw all eyes were on her. The only gaze she could meet was Armand's. There was no condemnation there. Not yet. He probably did not understand all the implications of what the butler said.

"Shall I tell him to go on his way, Miss Bennett?" the butler asked. "We do not need rabble of that sort here."

Felicity swallowed. She would have liked to say yes and have Charles sent away, but she knew he would be back. She knew he would not be that easy to be rid of. "No, Grimsby," she said. "I had better see him."

The duchesse put a hand to her throat, and in her eyes Felicity could see all the censure the others must have felt. She did not know what Armand had told them last night, but she did know that this morning there had been a sense of acceptance about her. The duchesse and the dowager had welcomed her warmly, and even the duc had nodded at her. Perhaps they had not suspected. Perhaps she might have kept this position after all.

Now all of the family's earlier warmth was gone, replaced by suspicion and indignity.

"I…" She wanted to say something to reassure them, but what was there to say? Charles had not lied. He was, but for one small detail, her husband.

She rose on wobbly legs and made her way to the vestibule. The butler left the dining-room door open, and behind her, she imagined the Valères pouring more tea and going about their breakfast formally. Decorum demanded they give her privacy. But Armand had no such compunctions. He knew nothing of decorum and would not have cared if he had.

She could feel him at her side. He had risen with her, followed her into that cavernous entryway. She glanced at him, gave him a small smile. He did not smile back. Oh, how she wished she were still sitting beside him, listening as his rich voice—it grew deeper and richer with more use—painted a picture of revolutionary France. His slight accent drifted over her, until she could hear the voices and the sounds, feel his anguish at his father's imprisonment.

She wished she could turn to him now, throw herself in his arms, bury her head against his shoulder.

But when she looked ahead of her again, there stood Charles St. John.

"Felicity!" He stepped forward, holding out his hands. He would have taken her hands, perhaps taken her into his arms if Armand had not emitted a low warning sound beside her.

Charles jerked back, his eyes flitting to Armand and then back to her. Felicity knew what he must see—a man dressed in only a white shirt and trousers, his feet bare, his neck bare, and his long hair down about his shoulders.

Growing up, she had thought Charles St. John was the most handsome man of her acquaintance. But now that she had the two men practically side by side, Charles's looks paled in comparison to Armand's. Charles dressed in the height of fashion, but the starched cravat, embroidered waistcoat, and polished riding boots looked like an affectation beside Armand's careless style of dress. She had always loved Charles's blond hair, the way it curled over his forehead in a careful style, but now she could not imagine how she had found it appealing. Armand's wild locks were sensual and untamed. There was no affectation in the comte.

"Charles." Felicity tried not to allow her anger and annoyance to show. "I don't know what to say."

He laughed then, and she saw he was truly enjoying this. "You don't need to say anything. I can see it all in your face."

Felicity smiled tightly. She held her breath, waiting to see what he would do.

"You must be surprised to see me here."

She nodded. "Quite." She did not know what to say next, and she was saved from having to think of something when the comte stepped forward. Felicity watched him, unsure what he would do, and when he raised a brow at her, she quickly recovered her manners. "My lord, this is Charles St. John, an old friend of my family. Charles, this is the comte de Valère."

Charles bowed. "My lord."

"A friend of Miss Bennett's is a friend of ours," Armand said without any warmth. He moved to stand closer to Felicity, claiming his territory—or so it seemed to her. "I haven't seen you before, Mr. St. John."

Charles laughed again. "Well, it's the damndest thing. I've been in London for weeks and had no idea Felicity was here, as well." He winked at Felicity, and she guessed it was supposed to indicate they would keep their previous meetings here a secret. "Then this morning what do I see in the papers but a mention of a Miss Bennett playing exquisitely"—he glanced at Felicity—"that's the word the papers used, by the way. 'Exquisitely.' Anyway, I see that she had been playing for a Lady Spencer and that she was staying with the duc de Valère and family. Well, I knew right away that had to be my Felicity. No one can play like she does."

"I haven't seen the paper this morning," the comte said. Felicity raised a brow. She could not remember the comte ever reading the morning paper. But he was frowning, and Felicity knew he hated being caught off guard like this. She also had a feeling the papers had mentioned more than Charles was telling her. After all, she had run off—or been carried off—with the comte de Valère. Surely, no report would omit that detail.

Charles narrowed his eyes, and then Felicity was certain the papers had mentioned something about her dramatic exit. "I think you'll find it interesting reading, my lord." He focused his green eyes on her again. "How are you, my dear? You look quite well, considering you must still be in mourning." He seemed to take in her light blue gown with reproach in his eyes, though he knew as well as she there had been no money for any mourning clothes.

Felicity gave him a cold look back. "I am doing as well as can be expected." As always, the thought of her father brought her emotions to a head, and her words were tinged with pain, something she would have preferred Charles did not hear. Armand must have heard it, as well. He put his hand on her back, a gesture of comfort.

Charles saw it, too, and he frowned at the intimacy. "Again, imagine my surprise to learn you are here in London. I had to see you. I wanted to claim my bride."

She felt the comte's hand on her back tense, but he did not remove it. "Our butler said you were her husband," Armand said, his voice quiet—almost too quiet. "That means that you are married." He looked at Felicity for confirmation.

"No, but there was an—"

"Husband means married, correct?" he interrupted. She nodded, resigned. "Correct."

Armand's eyes met Charles's again. "Are you married to Miss Bennett?"

"The ceremony will be but a formality. Our marriage was her father's wish. I nursed the poor vicar during his last days. Before he passed away, the reverend signed an agreement betrothing me to his daughter. I have a copy of the agreement, if you'd like to see it." He glanced at Felicity, his arm hovering by the pocket of his tailcoat.

"No." She cleared her throat. "I've seen it."

"So you understand your father's wishes then." He glanced at Armand again. "The reverend promised his daughter to me."

Felicity did not want to look at Armand. She could not imagine what thoughts must be going through his mind, but she could not stop herself. She turned to him, just as he drew his hand away from her back. "I owe Mr. St. John a great debt." But there was no warmth in her words.

Charles waved a hand, dismissing her words. "You don't owe me anything, darling. I'm just so glad to see you, and I want to take you home."

His words were ridiculous. There was no home to take her to. He was trying to scare her, to let her know he wanted his money. "Now?" She floundered, unsure what to say or do. She did not have the money. "But... I..." She looked at Armand and then back at Charles. What would he say, what would he do, if she said she did not have his money?

"You can't take her now," Armand said. Felicity jumped in surprise, both relieved and apprehensive at his imperative.

Charles's eyes narrowed dangerously, and Felicity cleared her throat before he could speak. "What I think he means is I'm not ready to leave right this moment. Perhaps we should discuss this and make arrangements…"

"Of course." Charles waved that hand again. "I did not expect you to go with me immediately. We might go for a walk to reacquaint ourselves, as it were. We have much to discuss—in private." In other words, he wanted to get her alone to make his demands. And she was not the least comforted to speak to him in private. What was that but a veiled threat that he would go public with their betrothal, with any lie he chose, to get what he wanted?

Felicity looked at Armand, who looked right back at her. She knew he did not want her to go, but how could she refuse? She feared what Charles would do or say if she did refuse.

And she grew weary of being afraid! Perhaps she should allow him to do his worst, and then at least she might face the consequences instead of constantly fretting over them.

She thought about Armand and his family. Could she confide in them? Would they be angry she brought this horrible man and his blackmailing into their home? They were unsure of her now. The dowager and the duchesse seemed to like her well enough, but the duc didn't trust her. And all of them wanted, more than anything else, to protect Armand.

She wanted to protect him, too. What would the family think once they knew the truth of her situation? Would they suppose she had used Armand, played with his emotions when she was promised to another? Or would they believe her if she told them Charles had forced this engagement on her?

Would they help her? Could they help her?

She didn't know. But she still possessed some self-respect. Charles was her problem, and she must at least try once more to handle him and his humiliating demands on her own.

She blinked and looked down, unable to meet Armand's gaze. "I need to fetch my cloak. If you'll give me a moment, Mr. St. John."

"Of course."

With a bit of reluctance, she broke away from the two men and started up the stairs. A quick backward glance revealed they were standing face-to-face, not speaking. The dining-room doors were cracked, and she could see the rest of the family peering out. No doubt they had heard all.

She fetched her cloak and reticule quickly and then made her way back down the stairs. Charles was waiting at the door, and Armand stood at the foot of the stairs. She looked at both men. Why did she feel as though this walk with Charles symbolized something more to Armand? She wanted to tell Armand she was not choosing Charles over him. How could she, after all they had shared last night?

With a quick look at Armand, she walked to Charles. Grimsby opened the door, and Charles held out his arm. She turned back to Armand one last time, but he had turned away from her. He was making his way back into the dining room, where his family waited.

~✖~

"I don't understand why she never mentioned anything," Sarah was saying. Her voice was indignant,

Armand thought—not entirely certain that was the correct word, but reasonably sure. His vocabulary was slowly coming back to him. But her eyes did not match her voice. She was looking at him with pity in those brown eyes. He hated their pity more than anything else.

"Why would she say anything?" Armand asked, his voice harsher than he intended, but he had to wipe the pity off their faces. "They are not married yet. He said betrothed."

"That's a promise to marry. It's not taken lightly," Julien said, leaning back in his chair. He was the only one who did not look at Armand as though he felt sorry for him. "She didn't say anything because she wanted this position." He glanced at Sarah. "Would you have hired her had you known?"

Sarah shook her head.

Julien steepled his hands. "But why would he come here now? Expose her? I don't believe he just realized she was in Town."

"He wants something," Armand said. The man obviously wanted Felicity, but it was more than that.

"Money," his mother said on a sigh. "She might not have mentioned the betrothal because it was irrelevant and something neither party intended to honor. But he saw her name in the papers, associated her with us, and now he thinks he can get money."

Sarah shook her head. "But why would *we* give him money?"

"We won't," Julien said. "But she may have to if she does not want him to enforce the agreement."

"That's blackmail!" Sarah argued.

"Of course. He doesn't want to marry her. She pays him, or he makes it very difficult for her to find another position."

"She won't need another position." Armand stood. "I will marry her."

His mother shook her head. "It is not that simple. She is promised to another."

"She's mine."

"And if St. John discovers you feel that way, he'll want money from you, too," Julien said.

"Then we give him money." Armand turned, intent on going outside. The dining room—the house for that matter—was too confining. He needed air and sunlight so he could breathe and think.

And he wanted to make his rounds, to check the house was secure. If the small man and his son were in London, no one in this household was safe.

"We're not giving him money." Julien followed him out of the dining room. "I'm not going to be blackmailed. You think you'll pay once, but it never works that way. Better to let her go. I don't want this man raking the Valère name through the muck."

Armand stopped, turned to his brother. "I will not lose her." Even now it killed him that she was not with him, that he did not know where she was. Was St. John touching her? Holding her hand? No—she would never allow that.

But was she safe with that man? He should have followed them, been there to protect her.

But even a man such as he—a man who had suffered every sort of abuse and ignominy imaginable—still had some pride. He was no puppy to nip at her heels.

Julien ran a hand through his hair. "You may not have a choice, Brother. She's an independent woman. Perhaps she wants to marry this man."

"She wants me."

Julien laughed and shook his head. "You're far more confident than I ever was with Sarah." His eyes narrowed. "What exactly happened last night?"

Armand pushed through the French doors out into the cool sunshine of early December. He could smell colder air on its way. Perhaps snow in a few days. He scanned the garden and the walls. "We made love—at least that's what she called it."

There was a choking sound behind him, and he looked over his shoulder to see Julien stopped in midstride, his expression one of disbelief. Perhaps Felicity was right about not telling his family. Too late now.

"I hope to God that does not mean what I think it does."

Armand shrugged, and Julien pressed a hand against his eyes. "Damn it, Armand. I was afraid of this. I hoped it hadn't gone that far."

"It's against The Rules." He was scanning the perimeter again, looking for any changes since yesterday.

"Hell, yes, it's against the rules. A lot of rules—not just my rules. What if she's pregnant?"

Armand glanced at him. "Pregnant?" he struggled for a moment to place the word. "You mean like Sarah?"

"Yes. Like Sarah. How do you think she got that way?"

Armand had not really thought about that. Was Sarah with child because she and Julien had done what he and Felicity had last night?

"Hell, Armand, what kind of books did you read as a kid? You were always reading. Bastien and I thought you knew everything."

Armand thought a moment, but he couldn't remember reading any books about making love. He couldn't remember much at all about the books he had read, except there was one about wolves...

"It doesn't matter. It doesn't change anything. She can still marry St. John or—"

"She's mine." Armand gave him a hard look, stepped forward until he was nose to nose with his brother. "I will have her."

Julien threw out his hands. "Fine. Fine. How the devil did you become so bloody stubborn?"

"She's mine, and I will have her. We marry today."

Julien ran a hand through his hair. "She hasn't even agreed—"

"She will."

"Even if she does, a marriage today isn't possible."

Armand walked away, calling over his shoulder. "Make it possible." Then he grumbled to himself, "Rules."

❧

Felicity shivered. She wasn't certain if it was the cool morning air or the fact that she couldn't get the shocked look on Armand's face out of her mind. Why had Charles done this? Did he want the money now? Did he think, after what he read in the papers, he could get more?

"I know what you must be thinking," Charles said. Beside her he kept up a jaunty pace, his ebony walking stick striking the cobblestones with a measured thump, thump.

"Do you?" she said, her voice as measured as his pace.

"Of course. You're wondering why I came here this morning, what motive I could possibly have for revealing our betrothal."

"It did cross my mind. I was prepared to ask for an advance—"

Charles gave her an abrupt look. "You have been saying that for weeks, and yet I stand here, empty-handed."

"It's a delicate negotiation, and I have not been in the position for even a month. I needed the timing to be right."

He stopped, gave her a hard look. "Was it right last night? I read that the comte left Lady Spencer's with you slung over his shoulder. Perhaps when he was carrying you away, you might have begun those *delicate negotiations*."

"I can explain that," she began. But really, could she?

He waved a hand and began walking again. "I don't need your explanations. I saw it all quite clearly this morning. The comte thinks you're his. Well, you're not, Felicity. You're mine."

"No, I'm not."

He turned abruptly and grabbed her arm. "Oh, yes you are. Legally, you belong to me." There was no smell of alcohol on his breath, and his soberness worried her.

"No one would force me to honor that marriage contract," she hissed.

"Will they really need to force you? I can walk down to the *Times* right now and ruin you, stir up the scandal broth around the Valères even more. They'd have to turn you out. And then what other option, but marriage to me, will even be open to you?" The threat was clear. He would be certain she had no other options. "You don't think the comte would actually marry you, do you? You, a lowly vicar's daughter?"

She turned away, and he grabbed her arm. "I hope he does want to marry you. They'll pay through the nose to make this marriage contract go away."

She would die of shame before she allowed Armand to pay Charles for her. She didn't want Armand to know—anyone to know—that she had agreed to pay Charles to free her from the marriage agreement. That she had been forced to do so because her father had betrothed her to a drunk, a liar, a gambler. It was... humiliating. She wanted to leave her father—herself—some dignity. "I'm not going to marry the comte."

Charles sneered. "What you mean is he doesn't want you."

"Why are you doing this?" she asked abruptly. "I said I'd give you the money, and I know you don't want to marry me. You never even looked twice at me."

"But I'm looking now." He gave her a slow, steady perusal that made her skin crawl. "And I like what I see. I like the comte's whore, and I think I'd like a taste of what you're giving that idiot for free."

"He's not an idiot."

Charles laughed. "Did you hear him back there? He sounds like a five-year-old."

"You underestimate him."

"Yes, I am quaking in my boots." He released her

and made his way to a bench, propped one foot on it. She stood uncomfortably nearby, feeling the weight of the seconds tick by. With Armand, she was used to silence. Much of the time there was never a need for words between them, though it was her job to make him use them. But with Charles, the silence dragged on ominously.

"If, after last night, the Valères weren't already going to let you go, they will now."

"You made sure of that."

"I did, didn't I? But you won't go quietly. You'll demand a hundred pounds to keep your silence."

"Keep my silence? About what?"

He narrowed his eyes at her. "About what Society already suspects. The comte de Valère is a monster. He carried you off, raped you, beat you—"

"That's a lie!"

"Shut up! That's what you say, but Society will never believe it, especially not when the wounded fiancé makes a statement confirming you've been assaulted and ruined."

She shook her head. "No—"

"Yes. Demand the money and give it to me. Then we'll get you another position. Your connection with the Valères must be worth something."

Felicity gaped at him. "You're mad."

He leaned close to her so she could smell the perfume he wore. "I'm shrewd."

"This ends now, Charles. I won't be your pawn anymore."

He smiled as though this was what he expected. He looked at his fingernails. "I'm shrewd, and I'm ruthless, Felicity. Do you know what will happen if you don't do as I say?"

She opened her mouth to say she did not care and then closed it again, afraid when she saw the look in his eyes. There was something in them she hadn't seen before. Or maybe she had never been willing to look closely enough.

"Did you see the papers this morning?"

Confused, she shook her head. Bile was rising in her throat, and her heart was thumping wildly against her chest.

"Then you didn't see the notice about the woman they found dead. A friend of yours, believe it or not."

Felicity's head swam. What was he talking about? Charles truly was mad. "Friend of mine?" She had no friends in London. "You make no sense."

He grinned, stroked the handle of his walking stick. "Don't you remember Celeste?"

She shook her head. "No. I..." But she did remember. The demirep Charles had been with on Bond Street.

"Ah, I see you do remember." He smiled again. "She was found dead yesterday morning. Stabbed."

Felicity felt a chill crawl up her spine. She shivered and looked away. "That has nothing to do with me." Oh, God. She prayed it had nothing to do with Charles.

"Doesn't it? They're calling it a crime of passion. Jealousy is a form of passion."

Her head whipped around, and she stared at him open-mouthed. "Jealousy? I wasn't jealous of that-that woman, and I didn't kill her."

"Of course you didn't." He flicked the tip of his walking stick, and she saw the blade glint. "I did."

She was falling. The world was spinning. Desperate for purchase, she reached out and grasped the back of the bench to steady herself. Slowly, she lowered herself onto the seat. In the distance, somewhere far away, she heard Charles laughing.

"Shocked you, did I?" His face swam in front of her.

She could only stare at him, unable to speak.

"Would you believe it was an accident?" He chuckled, speaking almost to himself. "I didn't think so. I'm afraid I have a bit of a temper." Now his gaze lashed onto Felicity's. "You do not want to see my temper, Felicity, which is why you had better do as I say. If you don't, I'll have you charged for the murder of Celeste."

She almost laughed. Almost. "Me? Murder that woman? Don't be ridiculous!"

He didn't smile. "But you did murder her, Felicity. You were jealous because she stole your fiancé away. Dozens of people saw you confront the two of us on Bond Street. The night before last you decided to retaliate. You came to my flat, found her there, and murdered her. Then you got that idiot comte to help you dispose of the body. Only... the body has been found."

She couldn't breathe. A weight was pushing down on her lungs, and she couldn't move it. She whispered, "No one will believe that."

"Won't they? I think the public will gobble it up." He made slurping motions with his tongue. "A jealous fiancée, a mad comte, a dead whore. The press will adore you."

"But you can't prove it." Her voice rose, sounded a bit hysterical.

"Do I need to? You'll be stuck in Newgate, locked away. Perhaps you'll eventually be exonerated. Or perhaps the magistrate will find witnesses. They might find the bloody knife buried in the comte's garden."

"Charles—"

"You'll be hanged at Tyburn. What will you tell the crowd gathered there, Felicity?"

She glared at him, loathing welling inside her. "I hate you. I—"

"Oh, that won't garner you any sympathy." He smiled. "Now you know my terms. Do you accept?"

She swallowed. "Charles, I can't do this." She hated the pleading sound in her voice. "I can't threaten them. Give me time, and—"

"Time is up. I will be back tomorrow. You have a choice to make, *darling*." He stroked her cheek, and she shivered with revulsion. "Get that money from the Valères or spend the rest of your days in Newgate. Either way, the comte, your lover, is ruined."

With that, he turned and walked away from her, leaving her standing alone among the leafless tress and brown grass.

Seventeen

ARMAND SAT ON FELICITY'S BED, STUDYING THE FRILLY night clothing she had left on the coverlet. It was white and flimsy, with decorative patches that had holes. Armand thought the holes were intentional, because he had seen his mother with handkerchiefs that had this sort of small netted material along the edges. He held the night dress up, wondering what she would look like wearing the garment.

Just then the door opened, and he heard a gasp. "You're here."

He set the night dress down and studied Felicity. She was still wearing the blue outer garment, and underneath it was a lighter blue dress with a flimsy white ruffle covering her neck and throat. Her cheeks were red, probably from the cold outside, but her hair was still smooth and straight. It shone in the afternoon sunlight that filtered through the drapes he spread wide. He would have opened the windows, as well, but he was afraid she would be too cold.

She looked at the door, where her hand still rested on the knob, and then at him, and he could see the uncertainty in her face. Being here was breaking a Rule—he knew that.

He also didn't care.

"Close the door."

For once, she didn't argue. She closed the door. She stood looking at him for a long moment, and then she began to unfasten her outer garment, her fingers shaking slightly. "I hope you haven't been waiting long." She tugged the garment off her shoulders and shook it out before walking to the clothes press and opening it. "I didn't expect to be away for so long. We went for a walk." She folded the garment and placed it on a shelf. He could see from her slow, deliberate actions she was upset. St. John had upset her.

"You and your husband talked."

Slowly, she closed the door of the clothes press, her back to him. "He's not actually my husband. He and my father made an agreement."

Now he was off the bed. He snatched her arm and spun her to face him. She made a sound of protest, but he didn't give her a chance to speak. As far as he was concerned, she had spoken far too much already. "Why didn't you tell me? I want you to be my wife."

She closed her eyes.

"No." He shook her. "Do not treat me like a child. I know The Rules, but because I choose to ignore them does not make me a child. You will be my wife."

"I wish that were possible," she said quietly.

"It is possible. I told Julien, and he agreed to make the arrangements."

She blinked at him, obviously surprised.

"So you can forget that Rule."

"It's not that easy."

"No? Why not? Because St. John came here this morning? He has nothing to do with us."

"But he does, Armand." She shook off his arm, and though he did not want to let her go, he released her. "My father and he made an agreement. I want to make it go away, but… it's complicated."

"And so you will marry St. John."

She put her hands to her eyes, rubbed them. "No. No, I won't, but now that he knows you and I are… connected, he will make things difficult for me. For us. I think it's best if I leave. I don't want to cause your family any more scandal."

"The Rules?"

She nodded.

"You did not care about The Rules last night. None of them mattered when I had my mouth on your breasts and my hands on your hips. It didn't matter when you were laid bare beneath me."

Her cheeks had turned a dark shade of red at his words, and he knew he had hit a mark. "What is that called," he asked, "when your cheeks turn red?"

"Blushing," she said, lifting a hand to touch them.

"Why are you blushing, Felicity? Have you forgotten what happened between us? Have you forgotten that we made love?"

"No, I haven't forgotten, and you are right to be angry with me. I shouldn't have done that with you."

"I wanted you to. I want you again."

He saw her catch her breath, swallow, and then bite her lip. Interesting that words could have such an effect on her. He had always assumed touching alone could generate this reaction. Perhaps he had dismissed words too easily.

"I w-wanted you, too, but it was wrong, considering my betrothal to Charles. It was wrong because I should have known being seen with you might bring him here."

"But you still want me."

"Yes—no. I-I have to think what to do. I can't think…"

He was beside her again, his hand taking hers. "You think too much. The answer is easy. Do you choose me or him? That is the question I need you to answer."

She tried to pull her hand away, but this time he would not release her. "Perhaps I choose neither. Perhaps I don't want to marry. I love you, but that may not be enough."

"You love me?" Armand squeezed her hand. In his memory, he had heard these words only a few times, and those were from his mother. The only other time was once when Julien and Sarah did not know he was in the room with them. Julien had whispered to Sarah, "I love you," and then had kissed her. "Then we should be married," Armand said now.

"People don't marry for love alone, Armand. There's more than that. And it isn't enough this time."

"Why?"

She shook her head, looking suddenly so sad. He grasped her arm. He wanted to keep her close, make her happy. "Does your Charles love you?"

She laughed. "No."

"Does he care about you?" He tugged her hand,

drew her close so he could feel her press against him. "Does he make you feel the way that I do?"

"No." She sighed the word.

"Then give yourself to me." He bent, put a hand on the back of her neck, and kissed her. It was not a gentle kiss. He did not feel gentle today. He knew what he wanted, and he would have it. He would take it—whatever she would give.

His mouth slanted over hers, his tongue invading her until she moaned and wrapped her arms about his neck, pulling him closer. And then her tongue was imitating his, and he almost forgot about wanting to win and just allowed himself to feel the pleasure of having her body crushed against him, her mouth hot on his, and her scent in his nostrils. She ran a hand down his shoulders and put her palm on the bare skin at the base of his throat. Her other hand was under his untucked shirt, gliding over his chest, down to his belly. She brushed over the waistband of his trousers, and he jerked back.

"I want you," he said, ripping the little white ruffle away from her neck and chest. "Tell me you want me, too."

He bent to savage her neck, kissing it, finding the tender places that made her moan. She brushed her hand over the hand length of him, and he reared back again. "Tell me you want me."

"Armand, I don't think we should—"

"Lies. Your words are lies. Your body does not lie." He pulled at her sleeves, pushing them down until the roundness of her breasts was exposed. He lowered his mouth, ran his tongue over the swell, dipped into the valley.

"Tell me you want me." His hand was loosening the fastenings at the back of her gown, shoving it down so he could push her undergarments aside. There was the sound of material ripping, and then she was once again bare before him. In the light of day, he could see she was as pale as cream. Her nipples were dark and stood out like hard berries. He touched them, rubbing his thumbs over them, and her head fell back in pleasure.

He moved her backward, toward the bed, and eased her onto it. Pausing for only a second, he ripped his shirt over his head then freed his erection. She watched him through lidded eyes, her chest rising and falling, and he pressed bare skin to skin and put his mouth on hers again.

Her mouth was so sweet. He could not get enough of it, and she met his kisses with feverish ones of her own. His hand was under her skirts, trailing up her leg, past the knee, touching her thigh until he reached the vee he sought.

She was hot and wet, and his fingers slid easily inside her. "Tell me you want me." He looked down at her, her cheeks red, her eyes dark blue, her breasts rising and falling with her rapid breaths. He did now know if he felt this love she spoke of, but at this moment, it was the closest thing he could understand to it.

"I want you," she murmured. "I want you, Armand." He slid his finger in and out, and she bucked against him. "I need you. I love you. Oh, hurry!"

And then he was inside her, and he forgot all about winning, because she was his.

❧

Every part of her was on fire with need. She needed his mouth on her mouth. She needed his hands on her breasts—they ached for his touch—and she needed him inside her. Blissfully, he *was* inside her. She realized now she was still slightly sore from the night before, but her need was so great she could forget the slight discomfort. He was moving within her, his chest grazing hers, his mouth against her ear, and she wanted to scream *more*. She did not think she could ever get enough of this—of him.

"Felicity," he whispered, and she pulled him closer even as the pleasure began to crest. He moved again, sending her crashing over, and she called out and rose to meet him. She could feel his release, as well, feel him swell inside her, and then go still. She dug her fingers into his back and pulled him close.

"Armand."

There was nothing but the two of them in that moment. No Charles, no one hundred pounds, no looming scandal and prison. It was just the two of them, and she wished she could stop this moment, so it would always be this way. But gradually, the fog of pleasure subsided, and the world intruded once again.

Armand levered himself on his elbows and looked down at her, his cobalt eyes so impossibly dark she thought she could lose herself in them. And the look he gave her. No man had ever looked at her that way—probably no man would again. "You're mine," he said, his eyes boring into hers. "Mine."

She sighed and struggled to get out from under him. He rolled to one side, and she shoved her skirts down and tugged her bodice up. Outside the room, she heard the footsteps of a passing maid. Curses! She could only imagine her embarrassment if anyone should find them now. Had she even locked the door?

"Armand," she said, turning to him. She had to draw a breath quickly. He was so impossibly alluring. He sat naked and unashamed, his body surprisingly muscular for someone who had been imprisoned for so long. His hair was down about his shoulders. She longed to run a hand through the tangles and put them to rights. But that would ruin the dissipated look of him. And with his smoky eyes, his full lips, and the stubble on his jaw, he made quite the picture. Any woman would swoon.

She must be strong.

"Armand," she said more firmly this time. He looked at her and smiled lazily. It was the kind of smile that made her want to fly right back into his arms.

But she would not do that.

"I understand you want to marry me."

"Julien will arrange it. Then you'll go to Southampton. You will be safe there."

But she wouldn't be safe in Southampton. Charles could find her there. His accusations could find her there. She had never been a coward, but her every instinct told her to run from Charles, to hide somewhere he would never find her.

And that meant leaving Armand. "I can't think about marriage right now," she told Armand. But the more she looked at him, the more she wished it were possible. What would it be like to wake up every morning beside this man? To have those cobalt eyes look at her like that every night? To touch that body whenever she wanted...

Best not to think of that.

He was scowling at her. "Are you telling me no?"

"Yes."

He rose, put his hands on his hips.

"Really, you should put some clothes on," she said, turning away so she would not be distracted. "I'm not saying no, I'm saying I need time to think. So much has happened, and so soon. I need time to gather my thoughts and consider my options." She needed to think of a way to escape Charles, a way out of this mess. She would not allow him to hurt Armand. Charles could hurt her, but she would protect Armand.

Armand was behind her, his hands on her arms. Was he still naked? Of course he was! How was she supposed to have this conversation with him if he was naked? "You think too much, Felicity. You talk too much. You want me. Admit it, and we will be married."

"I do want you," she said because it was so obviously the truth. "But I must have time to deal with Charles and our betrothal."

He nodded stiffly, his jaw tight. "I'm not going to beg you."

"I would never ask you to. All I am asking is for time." Time to think of a plan, a way out.

"And what if we don't have time? Marius and his son will be back. They know I am the key to the treasure. They will not stop until they have it."

"Marius? Is that the small man's name?"

He looked momentarily surprised, as though the information was new to him. Perhaps it was. "Yes. I-I just remembered. The son... I cannot think—"

"That's all right. You'll remember, given time. And if you have their names, you can go to the magistrate. Those men can be locked away."

He shook his head, and the look on his face made her feel as though she were a child. "Do you think it's so easy?"

"I don't know, but I do know your brother is a powerful man. Perhaps there is something he can do."

"There is something *we* will do. We will face these men and kill them."

She blinked and took a step back. "I don't think—"

"It's the only way for me to be free. When they return, Julien and I will kill them. But I want you and ma mère and Sarah far away."

Felicity looked down and noted her hands were twisted together, and she was wringing them. "Have you told the dowager and the duchesse you want us to leave?"

"No. But I've made my decision."

Of course he had. Why worry about consulting others? That was just a social grace he had no use for. "Then I suppose I had better make up my mind soon, as well."

But her mind had been made up. She stayed in her room all night, grateful the family left her alone. She paced the floors until the wee hours, trying to think of a way out of her predicament. Neither of Charles's ultimatums was agreeable to her: accuse Armand of rape or face Newgate and a murder charge.

She might run, but would she have to hide forever?

What if she could acquire the one hundred pounds without accusing Armand? She could ask the duc. He would give her the money. But if she were able to acquire funds, wouldn't Charles simply want more? This nightmare would never be over unless...

Unless she were no longer available to blackmail. She did not want to face murder charges, but it was the only way. She would turn herself into the authorities and tell them the truth. She would tell them what Charles had said, his plan to trap her, and if she were not believed or if she were implicated, as well, then so be it. It would not leave Armand out of the scandal completely. After all, the two of them were linked, but it would keep him from being charged with murder. It might not save her.

The idea of prison scared her; the idea of hanging terrified her. But Armand had faced years of prison and survived. She might have to do the same.

What other choice did she have?

When morning came, she went over her plan once more then walked resolutely to the duc's study. She wanted to speak with him and Armand, tell them her plan, ask for their support. She wanted to explain all before Charles came for her.

But the butler informed her all but the duchesse were away from the house, and the duchesse was feeling ill this morning. Felicity cursed her indecision. Now she would have to wait until they returned to go to the magistrate. She hoped Charles did not come first. She gave the butler strict instructions not to admit Mr. St. John then went to the garden to wait for Armand. She knew he would go there immediately upon returning.

Outside the weather was cold and windy. The sky loomed gray and rain threatened. She pulled her cloak around her shoulders and paced. Finally, she made her way to the gazebo. The memories she shared with Armand there warmed her.

She heard steps and turned, expecting Armand. But her breath caught in her throat.

Charles smiled. "You thought you could avoid me."

"No. I—"

"You had the butler turn me away."

"I—" *Think, Felicity.* "I don't have the money yet. I was waiting for the duc to return with the funds."

He pointed his walking stick at her, and she couldn't help but think of the blade concealed beneath it. "Let's go for a walk."

"The weather is not conducive to walking." Indeed a cold drizzle had begun to fall. "Why don't we wait for the duc inside? You could have a cup of tea." She cursed herself for straying as far as the gazebo. She couldn't even see the house from here.

"I don't care about the weather." The wind whipped his greatcoat around his ankles. "You are coming with me."

She thought about screaming but feared he would hurt her before anyone could reach her. But once they were on the street, others would see her. She could run, beg for assistance.

She made her way out of the garden, Charles following. They took the side gate, but when they reached the street, Felicity did not see anyone about.

The rain had kept many inside today, but she knew someone would be along. She needed to distract Charles for only a few minutes.

Charles turned to face her. "Where is the money?"

Her heart pounded, and she tried to steady her voice and breathing. "I-I told you. The duc has it. If we could wait inside—"

"It's too late for that," he said, and she stiffened in alarm. She had her back to the street, and now she glanced from side to side, hoping to spot someone, anyone who might help.

"What do you mean?" she asked. Another moment or two. Surely a carriage would come along...

She waited for Charles to say something, anything, but he was silent. Eerily silent. He didn't look at her, seemed distracted by something.

"Charles?" she said when he still didn't speak.

He glanced at her briefly then away again. She didn't know what response she expected, but certainly not this one. Why did he not explode? Why did he not threaten her?

The sounds of the city filled the silence—a vendor calling out his wares on another street, church bells ringing, and the clop of horses' hooves as a carriage neared.

Thank God!

She turned to call out for assistance, but her cry died on her lips. The carriage had stopped and the small man—Armand's Marius—was coming toward her. She tried to scream, to run, but Charles grabbed her an instant before the holland cover was thrown over her head and her world went dark.

Eighteen

"WE THANK YOU FOR YOUR SERVICE, MONSIEUR. YOU are free to go now."

"Thank you, but I want to make sure she's unharmed."

Felicity blinked, still wrapped in darkness. She was lying on something hard and cold. Oh, how her head ached. The darkness spun, and she realized she must have hit her head in her fall. She tried to draw a deep breath and felt the stifling material suck in around her.

"You were not as concerned about that when we made our agreement. You have been paid. Your part, monsieur, is complete."

"What are you going to do with her?"

She recognized Charles's voice and knew he was talking about her. With some effort, she tried to sit, to scream, but the blackness just spun faster.

"That information was not part of our arrangement." That voice she did not recognize, but it was heavily tinged with French. "Now, say *au revoir*. You do not want me to get nasty."

Felicity shivered as the pieces began to come

together. The small man, Marius, and his son. Charles had given her to them, and now he was going to leave her, abandon her to whatever scheme they had concocted to get to Armand and the treasure. Perhaps they thought she knew something about the treasure.

Or perhaps they were just going to kill her. What had the brick said? *We will crush you?*

"You should have paid me, Felicity," she heard Charles say. His voice grew softer, and Felicity knew he was being led away. Led where? Where was she? She was no longer outside. They had taken her inside. She was lying on a floor of some sort.

"I didn't want it to come to this," Charles said.

She hated him, and at the same time she wanted to call out, to beg him not to leave her alone with these two men. How could he do this to her? This was far beyond asking for money. Had he sold her? Charles would not do that, would he?

"*Chérie...*" The voice was soft and close to her ear. Through the holland cover, she could feel the warm breath, smell its rankness.

She stilled completely, pretending to be unconscious. "I know you are awake, *chérie.* Your friend is gone."

Felicity squeezed her eyes shut. She had to think of a plan to escape. Charles was gone and would not have helped her if he'd been there. She had not seen this coming. But now that she was in this predicament, she had to find a way to return to Berkeley Square. She could tell Armand and his brother where Marius was hiding. Together they could go to the magistrate.

Suddenly, the holland cover was whipped away,

and she blinked as her eyes adjusted to the light. The world spun again, but gradually everything came into focus. Marius held a candle and squatted beside her, his son behind him, holding the holland cover.

"Ah, yes. You're a pretty one. I can see why he likes you. What is your name?"

She stared at him, keeping her mouth firmly closed. She was not going to speak to these criminals. She would not give them any information. She looked past the son, looked about her surroundings.

She was in a house, in a parlor of some sort. The place looked to be abandoned. What furnishings there were lay covered in white, and heavy drapes blocked out the windows. But she noted immediately the door to the parlor was open. If she could dash past her captors and reach the front door, she could make it on to the street. She didn't know her way back to the Valères' town house, but if she were away, she could hail a cab. She prayed she was still in London. She must be. She couldn't have been unconscious long...

"No answer?" Marius leaned closer, his fetid breath feathering over her cheek. "Ah, of course. How rude of me. I have not introduced myself." He gave her a short, mock bow. "I am Marius, and this is my son Claude. We are old friends of your lover, the comte de Valère. Perhaps he mentioned us to you?"

She stared past him at the door. Claude was so large that if she could move quickly enough, she might be able to evade him. Marius was small and possibly more agile, but he was not young.

"Are you thinking you can escape, *chérie?*"

She flicked her eyes to his and saw his knowing smile. His teeth were jagged, almost as though they had been filed to sharp points.

"You will not escape. We have plans for you." He signaled to Claude, who lumbered forward and, with no more strength than it would take her to lift a kitten, picked her up off the floor and set her on her feet. "Now, are you going to tell me your name, or does Claude need to ask you?"

She glanced at Claude, who clasped his hands and cracked his knuckles. She had the feeling she did not want Claude to ask her any questions.

"Felicity Bennett." Her voice was raspy and hoarse, but at least it did not tremble as her body insisted upon doing.

"*Merci*, Mademoiselle Bennett. And might I ask why you are living with the duc de Valère and his family?"

A dozen answers ran through her brain. Should she tell the truth? If she did, would that hurt Armand? But what if Marius knew she was lying? She looked at Claude again. He was studying his knuckles, which were the size of small plums. "I'm a servant. I was employed as the comte de Valère's tutor."

"Is that what they call it these days?" Marius smiled and glanced at his son. They seemed to share a private joke. "We saw you in the garden the other night. That was an interesting lesson."

Felicity shivered now in disgust. The idea that these two had witnessed something as private and intimate as her lovemaking with Armand made her ill.

"But I think you were hired to teach the comte to speak. We had heard he had made progress, and for that we thank you. We need him to speak to us, and you are going to help us with that."

Felicity swallowed. "How am I going to do that?"

"You are going to take a short voyage with us, mademoiselle. To France."

She was shaking her head, even as the words were out of his mouth. "England and France are at war. There's no travel between them."

Marius smiled at her as one might smile at a child. "I am not concerned with wars and politics. All that concerns me is the treasure. I think you can see nothing will stand in my way. I have waited years to have it, only to watch the comte slip through my fingers. For that the duc de Valère will pay."

Claude laughed and flexed his fingers. Marius turned to him. "But not yet. First we will have the treasure and the comte."

"The comte doesn't even know I'm gone. He was not home when I stepped out with Mr. St. John."

"Oh, have no fear, mademoiselle. He will find you, either on his own or with the help of his brother. The Valères can be quite resourceful. And once we have lured them to France, they will give us the treasure."

"They don't have the treasure."

"Then they will find it. And do you know why they will find it?" He leaned close, and she backed away. "Because if they do not, Claude will kill you."

Felicity drew in a sharp breath and felt an icy cold slash through her. She could see in Marius's eyes he meant what he said. They would kill her if Armand did not retrieve the treasure for them.

"Claude, gather our things. We will take Mademoiselle Bennett to the ship now."

"Wait." She grabbed Marius's sleeve, desperate now. She did not want to be on a ship with these men. Once she left English soil, she doubted she would ever return. Better to stay here as long as possible. She would have to think fast, think of a way to stall them. "I have spent weeks with Armand—the comte. He has little memory of what happened before. He's blocked it out. I don't think he knows where the treasure is. If he ever did, he cannot recall."

"Then we will jog his memory."

"But what if that knowledge was never in his memory?" She spoke rapidly now, her words almost slurred. "What if he does not know anything about this Treasure of the Sixteen?"

Marius paused and smiled at her, then pulled out a pocket watch. He nodded at what he saw. "Do you know why he was sent to prison, mademoiselle?"

"No. I don't think he recalls."

Marius shook his head. "The mind is a complicated thing, is it not, Claude?" Claude smiled and shrugged. Marius gestured to a couch, bare as the holland cover was on the floor at her feet. "Please, take a seat. We have a few moments before we need to be away."

Felicity did as she was told, not because she wanted to sit, but because it delayed their departure. Now she had to think. How could she escape? If escape was impossible, she must alert Armand. He would save her. Of that, she was certain.

"The first time I saw the comte, he was a dirty, skinny little street urchin," Marius said. "At least that was how he appeared. But I have a talent, mademoiselle. I can see deeper, and I knew he was no peasant boy. He came to the prison every day. I asked myself, why would that street urchin come here? The answer was simple. Someone he knew or loved was inside. No one but aristos were inside that prison, mademoiselle."

"And so you realized he was the son of a noble."

"Precisely. At that time, the nobility were hardly in favor. Times were hard. The price of a loaf of bread alone could bankrupt a man. But a little aristo boy, the price for turning him in could buy my son and myself both wine and bread."

She must have made a face of disgust, because he shook his head and laughed. "That was the time, mademoiselle. I do not expect you to understand. But just as I was getting close to the boy, my efforts to catch him were thwarted."

"The two Jacques," she murmured.

He nodded. "Yes. There, you see, the comte does remember. Yes, the two Jacques took him in, protected him, made him one of their own."

"Why?"

"I suppose they thought he might be useful. I am certain he was useful as an errand boy. He was an intelligent child. After all, he managed to evade me, and he convinced the two Jacques he was a mute. I suppose they thought their secrets were safe with him."

"What secrets?" She had to ask questions. She had to keep him talking.

He nodded to her in admiration. "Not bad, mademoiselle. You catch on quickly. The secret of the Treasure of the Sixteen. The Jacques wanted it. All of

Paris wanted it, but most thought it only a fable. It was too grand to be real."

"What was it?"

The answer did not come from Marius but from the figure leaning in the doorway beyond him. "The hidden royal treasure of Louis the Sixteenth."

"Armand!"

Marius was instantly on his feet, but Claude was already moving in. Armand, appearing unconcerned, held up a hand. "I'm alone and unarmed. But I still remember how to fight." He gave Claude a meaningful look, and the large man turned to his father for guidance.

"Leave him alone," Marius said. "For the moment." He sank back down, beside Felicity, who could not stop staring at Armand. It was as though he had appeared out of nothing. One moment he was not there, and then he was. How had he found her? Had Charles gone back and told him? She almost laughed at the absurdity of that notion. Charles had taken his payment for her and run straight to the gambling hell.

Armand must have seen her in the garden with Charles and followed the carriage here. Thank God.

Armand's eyes met hers and then flicked away. They were as hard as cobalt now, and she swallowed, feeling his displeasure. She knew he did not want to be here, did not want to speak of his past like this. But he would do it—for her.

A surge of love welled up inside her, but she did not want Marius and his son to see, and so she looked down. She did not want to give them anything else to use against Armand.

"It has been a long time since we have seen you, monsieur," Marius said. He spoke in French now, and Felicity, who had always daydreamed during French lessons, had to concentrate to understand every word.

"Not long enough." Armand leaned gingerly against the door jamb, and if Felicity had not seen him a few weeks ago, wild and unable to speak, she would not have believed he was the same man. He did not wear a cravat, and his hair fell loose and free about his shoulders, but he had donned a greatcoat and riding boots. His throat was bare, his shirt open at the collar, making him seem, for all intents and purposes, like a careless noble.

"I had hoped that your friend here"—Marius gestured to her—"would bring you to us. But I did not expect the pleasure so soon."

"You have me here now," Armand said, examining his nails as though all of this were tedious to him. "What is it you want to know?"

"You don't need me to answer that question, monsieur. I want what all of Paris wanted. The Treasure of the Sixteen."

"And what makes you think I know where it is? No one else has been able to find it. It's been over a dozen years."

"The Jacques knew where it was."

Armand shrugged. "They never found it."

Marius leapt to his feet, his small body quivering with excitement or anger. Felicity wasn't sure which. "They never had the chance—"

"That was your doing." He looked pointedly at Claude. "You had them killed. Pity you didn't realize they had imprisoned me for… safekeeping before you did so."

"I searched for you in every prison in the country. I bribed so many officials I spent a small treasure of my own. I know I searched for you in Le Grenier. I did not believe it when I heard the reports that your brother found you there."

"You must have bribed the wrong official. Either that or they had forgotten me by the time you searched."

"You can be assured, monsieur, that I never forgot you. And now we are going back to Le Grenier. I think there is something you left behind, yes?"

Armand's eyes darkened, but if the idea of returning to the prison troubled him, his face did not betray the emotion. "I will agree to return with you. But Miss Bennett stays behind."

"Oh, you think I am a fool, do you, monsieur? You think I would leave behind the only thing I have binding you to me? She comes, and if you do not give me what I want, she dies."

❧

Armand would have liked to put his hands around the little man's neck and squeeze until his eyes bulged and began to bleed. He would have liked to pull the sharp knife he had hidden in his boot and plunge it into Marius's belly. But he had to remind himself these two had not put him in prison. It was the Jacques. Marius wanted only what everyone else had wanted—the treasure.

Wealth, money, prestige. Men would kill for it. These two had.

Armand was not certain the treasure existed. What he did know was his life had been sacrificed to it, and that was enough. He would not allow Felicity's life to end on the altar of greed, as well.

But with Marius seated beside her, and his oaf of a son just a few feet away, ready to snap her neck at a moment's notice, Armand was left with little choice but to agree to the terms.

For the present. He would free her and then...

He did not know. Kill Marius and Claude? Return with them to Le Grenier? Seek out the treasure? He did not care for the money, but after all this time, he wondered if he had been imprisoned for nothing. He wondered if his suspicions would be confirmed.

"Very well." He spread his hands in a gesture he remembered seeing his brother make, a gesture common to his father. "I am at your service."

The words were barely spoken before he and Felicity were bundled into a carriage and driven across town. There was a ship waiting for them, a small, fast ship with a man at the helm who looked as though he had done his own share of throat-slitting.

A pirate, Armand thought. He had read about them in books. During a war, those pirates could call themselves privateers and make a fortune. He wondered how much Marius had paid the man to transport them across the Channel in the middle of the night. He wondered if the man could do it.

Not that he cared for himself. He didn't give a damn if he ended up on the bottom of the sea, but he would not lose Felicity. He walked closely behind her as they boarded the ship, trying to shield her from the eyes of the ship's crew. But strangely enough, not a one seemed to be looking at her.

All eyes were on him.

The captain, who was probably fifty but looked seventy, sauntered over. "Name's Wiggin—at least that's the name I'm using." He held out his hand, and Armand looked down at it. Was he supposed to kiss it?

After a moment, Wiggin pulled his hand back. "You look like someone I used to know. Someone I maybe still do know. What's yer name?"

"Armand Harcourt."

"French?" Wiggin's eyebrows went up. "He is, too. Or he was the last time I saw him. Probably dead now."

"This is all very interesting," Marius interrupted, "but we would like to go below—"

"What was his name?"

"He goes by Captain Cutlass. But I don't think that's his real name." He gave Armand a narrow look. "I once heard his quartermaster call him Bastien. Course could have called him Bastard for all I heard. I'd been in my cups."

Armand felt his throat clench, but he controlled the torrent of emotion that swept through him. "Sounds like a pirate. How would I know him?"

Wiggin shook his head. "Damnest thing. You look just like him."

"If you've had enough chitchat," Marius interrupted again.

Wiggin signaled to one of his men. "Take these four below. Get them settled. We leave with the tide."

Marius went above deck, leaving Claude to watch him and Felicity. The large man stood at the door to the captain's cabin, arms crossed, gaze never leaving them. Armand stood by the porthole, and Felicity sat on the berth, her hands in her lap.

Armand stared calmly out the porthole as the light faded to dusk. He kept his expression calm and composed, but inside, he wanted to scream. It was torture being locked in this tiny cabin. He could barely breathe, and it took every ounce of willpower he had not to plow through Claude, break down the door, and run for the deck.

He needed fresh air. He needed light. He needed freedom.

He looked at Felicity, at the unruffled way she sat, the way she looked at him every few moments, trust in her eyes. He could not leave her, as much as his instinct was to save himself. This cabin would not kill him, and he would rather be with her than anywhere else.

There was a knock on the door, and Claude opened it. His father gestured him outside, and the door closed behind the two men.

They were alone for the first time, and immediately Felicity jumped up. "I'm so sorry, Armand. I had no idea Charles would do something like this. He never mentioned Marius or the treasure, but I suppose if he made inquiries about you they might have sought him out." She reached out to him, and he took her hand, wishing she would be quiet for just a moment so he could think. "Can you ever forgive me? I know you don't want to return to Paris. I can't imagine anything worse. Perhaps we could plan an escape or—"

"Felicity."

She closed her mouth and glanced at him sharply.

"Stop talking."

"Very well. But what are we going to—"

He tugged her against him and silenced her in the best way he knew. He put his mouth over hers and kissed her long and hard. Not surprisingly, the kiss took his mind off the small cabin and the sense of being trapped. If he could kiss her all the way to France, he just might survive the voyage.

They parted, and when he looked down at her, her sky blue eyes were wide, and her cheeks were blushing. And she did not speak.

"We're going to sail soon."

She nodded, looking past him to the sinking sun.

"There is no way to get off this ship until we reach France. But I will protect you."

She nodded. "I know you will, but—"

He put a finger over her lips. "Once we reach Paris, you must do everything I say. No questions. No arguing. No talking."

She nodded, her eyes serious.

"I'm the tutor now." He bent and kissed her again, and the touch of her lips against his was like a drink of cool water. He wanted more than anything to wrap her in his arms and take her away from here, take her to Southampton, where she would be safe. But he would deal with Marius and Claude first, and then they would be safe wherever they ended.

She broke the kiss and brushed a hand over the hair falling on his forehead. "I just have one question before they return." She looked at the door as if making sure it was still closed and they were still alone.

He nodded. Had he really thought he would keep her from asking any questions? Words were like air to her, it seemed.

"Is there really a Treasure of the Sixteen?"

He understood the reason for the question. She wanted to know if he could give the men what they wanted or, if at the end of this, they would be forced to show their empty hands.

He was honest with her. "I don't know."

She let out a long breath. "I see. I'm sure we'll figure out something."

"But I have something I can give them. Something at Le Grenier."

She shook her head. "I don't want you to go back there."

"There seems no way to prevent it." And maybe he always knew he would have to go back. Even when Julien had walked into his cell and dug him out all those months ago, Armand had known that the dank little hole wasn't done with him. It had haunted him in nightmares, and now he was being driven inexorably back.

"I'm tired of fighting it," he told Felicity now. "I want to face it."

"Oh, Armand…"

He thought she would have kissed him again, but the door rattled, and Marius stepped inside. "Am I interrupting?" His face was a sneer. "Don't mind me, but I wanted to let you know we're about to depart. If the winds are favorable, we'll be in Paris in less than a day."

Nineteen

FELICITY HAD NEVER BEEN TO FRANCE BEFORE, SO she did not know what to expect. She had heard awful rumors of Bonaparte, but when she stepped off the ship two days later and gazed about Calais, the country seemed little different from England—with the exception that everyone around her spoke French. Considering that England and France were at war, she spoke as little as possible. Her rudimentary French and strong English accent would certainly give her away.

Armand was quiet, as well. They had little opportunity on the crossing to talk, but she knew from watching him, from meeting his eyes time and again, he was planning their escape. Relief swept through her every time she looked at him, brushed against him. He would save them. He would take care of her.

He would have to.

The more she observed Marius and his son, Claude, the more she realized that even if Armand were to lead them straight to the treasure, they would probably kill him anyway. They had even less incentive to leave her alive.

There had been a hundred times on the voyage she had wanted to touch Armand, just hold his hand, but they were kept on separate sides of the cabin. And he was as out of reach then as he was now, seated on the opposite side of a carriage on the road to Paris.

"It won't be long before we return to Le Grenier, monsieur," Marius said. He parted the carriage drapes, and she saw the sun was slowly rising. "I have connections there. We will stand in your old cell at nightfall." He smiled, showing a row of uneven teeth, and Felicity glanced at Armand.

He showed no reaction, seemed bored in fact. But she knew he must be struggling with the memories flooding him. They had arrived in France under cover of darkness, and now they would enter his prison in darkness. She shivered, thinking of the prison at night. Once they entered, would they leave again? Would this be their last sunrise?

Armand met her eyes, and she put away her fears. She had to be brave now. He would not allow anything to happen to her. Armand would protect them both.

Marius appeared to have all the papers and documents necessary to get them into Paris. They were waved through the city gates by soldiers who looked tired and hungry. The city looked tired and hungry, but all around hung limp French flags and banners proclaiming the French Republic. The city was bustling with people everywhere, buying and selling, living their lives. Felicity found it fascinating, but the men in the carriage did not even raise their eyes to peer outside.

It was only when they turned into a decrepit old street that she saw Armand stiffen. Beside her, Marius chuckled. "I see you recognize this place, monsieur. Yes, I thought you would."

The coachman stopped outside a dreary tavern, and Marius pushed opened the door and leaped outside. Claude pushed her to follow, and on wobbly legs, she climbed down. It was afternoon by now, and Felicity blinked at the bright sunlight.

"Inside, mademoiselle," Marius ordered. "I have rooms reserved."

The tavern was small and dark, populated by sour-faced men hunched over what appeared to be sour wine. They did not look up as the small group walked through. Marius seemed to know where he was going, and he herded them upstairs. Felicity followed dutifully, but she could smell fresh bread baking, and her stomach growled. They had little to eat on the ship. Once on the upper level, she and Armand were separated. She was pushed into a small room with a cot and a table, a ewer and basin. She did not see where Armand was taken, but she heard her door locked and secured. Footsteps trailed away, and she tried the door handle. It was indeed locked.

Sighing, she went to the table and lifted the ewer. It was empty—no water even to wash her face. And now she was alone in a room in an enemy country. She could not conceive how Armand would get them out of this. She could not conceive how she happened to be here. She, Felicity Bennett, was the daughter of a vicar. She had barely a shilling to her name. No connections, no position. And she had been abducted, taken to France, and was being held prisoner until the Treasure of the Sixteen was found.

If she hadn't sat on the ship crossing the Channel for two days and then a carriage traveling through the French countryside, she would have pinched herself to make sure this was real. It was just so unbelievable.

Her stomach growled again, and the last light of day began fading from the small window in the room. She looked outside and saw nothing but a long drop and a narrow alley. The grimy window was sealed shut, so she could not even call for help.

And if she were to call, what would she say? She was the enemy. Alerting people to her presence would only make things worse.

In the dim light, she heard a scurrying sound and turned to see a large rat dart under the bed. She closed her eyes and shuddered.

It was worse.

Somehow she had fallen asleep on the hard cot with the scratchy blanket under her. The rat had stopped moving long enough for her to cease imagining it jumping up and scampering over her face if she lay down. She had not intended to sleep, but her body was exhausted. Still as she lay there, hearing the sounds of the men and women below, part of her mind was listening.

When she heard the tapping, she turned over and tried to ease the ache in her back. But the tapping did not cease, and she finally opened her eyes. It was dark now, not full dark, but the darkness of evening, and she wondered if Marius and Claude had taken Armand to Le Grenier without her. The tapping grew louder, and she glanced at the window, almost screaming when she saw the face there.

But she clamped her mouth shut when she recognized Armand staring in at her. Good God! What was he doing outside her window?

She jumped up and ran to the window, stared out at him, trying not to think of the drop to the muddy alley below. "What are you—?"

He put a hand to his lips, silencing her. The action terrified her, as well, because it meant he was gripping the building with only one hand. He gestured to her to push the window open, and she gestured back that it was sealed. With a nod of understanding, he pointed to the blanket on the bed. Frowning, she brought it to the window. He made a punching sign, and she realized he wanted her to break the glass. Obviously, the blanket was intended to protect the skin of her hand.

Felicity glanced dubiously at the thin blanket, sighed, and wrapped it about her hand. If Armand could balance on a tiny ledge outside her window, she could break the glass. Only, she did not want to think what he would want her to do after the glass was broken.

She gestured for him to move out of the way, and then, taking a deep breath, she smashed the glass. Opening her eyes, she saw it had cracked but not broken. Her hand throbbed, but Armand indicated she should try again. Clenching her jaw, she did so, and this time she was rewarded as her hand punched through. Glass sprinkled over the alley below, and Armand reached through and grasped her tender hand.

"What are you doing?" she whispered.

"Escaping. Break the rest of the glass and climb out here."

She stared at him. His eyes were calm, his breathing calm, and though his hair was whipping wildly in the breeze, he looked mostly sane. "Are you daft?"

"I told you that when we reached France you would have to follow me."

"But I didn't think that meant plunging to my death!" She glanced down at the alley again. It was a daunting drop—probably not far enough to kill her, but she would be maimed quite thoroughly.

"We're not going down there, and I don't have time to talk." He said the word *talk* as though it were akin to horse manure. "Marius and Claude are going to find that I've escaped soon. Get out here."

She looked at him then looked back at the safe room. At least it appeared far safer than the tiny ledge where Armand stood. But if he could stand there, so could she.

Taking a deep breath, she punched out the rest of the glass and then dropped the blanket. Her knuckles were stinging now, but she ignored them and hoisted one leg out the window. Dizziness swept over her, and she refused to look down.

"Turn your back," Armand instructed. "Feel for the ledge with your foot." His voice was pedantic, and she decided she much preferred the role of tutor to that of student. She had an ominous feeling they had switched positions irrevocably.

Finally her foot grazed the ledge and, holding on with a white-knuckled grip, she eased her other leg outside. Her skirts whipped in the breeze, and she was painfully aware that if she made one wrong move, she would tumble to the hard ground below. But she was not going to think of that. She was going to hold on and close her eyes and concentrate on not falling.

"Climb," Armand ordered.

"What?"

He was looking up, and she followed his gaze to the roof. It was not as far as she would have thought. And still, she would not dare release the window pane.

"I worked here for months before I was imprisoned. Once we reach the street, we can easily get away."

"So you've done this before?"

He nodded and, using the natural ledges the misshapen bricks created, hoisted himself up a foot. "Come on."

Felicity looked up then back at the relative safety of the room inside the window. She had never even climbed a tree as a child, and now she was going to scale a building? In a skirt!

"Come on! We don't have time."

Armand was now several feet above her, hanging on to the side of the building like some kind of ape. But he was almost to the roof. It was not far…

"I cannot believe I am doing this," she muttered and reached for the first extended brick. She trembled violently as she released her grip on the window but tried to control her fear. She figured she could shake and cry from the roof—if she made it.

With agonizing slowness, she climbed higher, kicking at her skirts when they tangled her ankles. Armand was on the roof ahead of her, and he reached down when she was two feet from the top and pulled her the rest of the way.

She tumbled on top of him, and lay there clutching his arms. "I never want to do anything like that again. In fact, I think from now on I shall avoid anything above the ground floor." She looked up at him, and he raised a brow, looking pointedly around them. The rooftops of Paris glinted in the moonlight. "Oh, no." She shook her head. "You cannot possibly mean to travel—"

"It's the safest way to Le Grenier."

"Le Grenier!" She bolted upright. "Why are we going to Le Grenier? Let's go home to England."

"We will." He stood and pulled her to her feet. "After Le Grenier."

He began to walk across the roof, and she followed him, pausing at the far edge. "But why would you intentionally return to Le Grenier? This is our chance to escape!"

He looked back at her. "And have Marius come after us again? I want to be rid of him." He backed up a few feet, jogged forward, and leaped across the open space between the roofs, landing safely on the roof of the building beside them. "Come on!" He held out a hand. Felicity stared at him as though that hand were a venomous snake.

"I'm not jumping across."

"I'll catch you."

"I'm *not* jumping!" She backed up. "There must be another way." The man really was daft, either that or he was part feline. She was all human, and clumsy human at that.

"This is the way," he said, and she could hear the impatience in his voice. "Jump."

"No." She looked around her, searching for some other exit. And found none.

"Jump!"

"No!" But there was no other escape. And the worst part was after she made this jump, she would be forced to make another and another. She was sure of it.

"Jump, Felicity."

She threw her hands in the air. "Oh, all right!" She took two big steps back, lifted her skirts, and ran. For a moment, she felt the rush of nothingness beneath her—or at least imagined that she did—and then she was falling into Armand's arms. He was solid and strong, and she wanted to weep against his chest that she was safe.

But the feeling of safety was not to last long. He was already shepherding her toward the other end of the roof, and she just knew he was going to want her to jump again. The buildings here were close together, leaning into one another like old friends, but Felicity did not like heights, and she liked the idea of falling from them even less.

Armand did not give her much time to think. He dragged her to the edge of the roof, made a running leap, and then insisted she follow. They continued this way through half a dozen buildings. She made the mistake, only once, of looking down. Her world spun, her head seemed to detach from her body, and her legs wobbled. After that, she kept her eyes on Armand's.

The city was growing darker, and from their

vantage point on the roofs, she could see lights twinkling all over the city. It might have been pretty, if she were firmly planted. And if she were not headed for prison. She had no doubts now that they had escaped Marius and Claude, but she did wonder if they would escape Le Grenier. Surely Armand knew what he was doing.

Didn't he?

"Here." He gestured to a door on top of the roof where they had paused to catch their breath. "We go down here."

Felicity blinked. "We do?" That was welcome news. No more jumping off roofs. On the other hand, if they were going down to street level, they must be close to the prison.

"Are we close to Le Grenier?"

He nodded, taking her hand and leading her toward the door. It was old and rotted, hanging on one hinge. He propped it open so she could descend the steep, dark staircase first. Perhaps she had taught him some manners after all—if allowing her to be the first to fall and break her neck could be considered manners.

"We travel the rest of the way on foot," he said from behind her.

She was concentrating on finding her next foothold on the creaky steps, but she murmured, "Do you think we will reach Le Grenier before Marius?"

"If not, things will go badly."

Oh, good. Just what she wanted to hear. She paused, glanced back over her shoulder. "You could try a little optimism."

In the dim light, he furrowed his brow. "What is that?"

"Exactly."

They reached the ground floor and exited in a quiet residential area. Before she could even catch her bearings, Armand had her hand again and was pulling her past trees and houses and the last carts of tradesmen heading home.

They rounded a corner, and he stopped and stared. She followed his gaze but saw nothing of interest. "What is it?"

He nodded at an old stone building, yellow with age, before them. "That's Le Grenier."

She frowned, unimpressed. "That's it?"

He gave a short, humorless laugh. "It does not look like much from the outside."

She had to agree. It was wide and squat but formidable. Past the gate, where a lone soldier stood looking bored, towered a wide turret. It was probably three stories tall and ornamented with a heavy wooden door. Behind the turret was a rectangular building with few windows and no adornment. "Is that where the prisoners are?" she asked.

Armand only stared at the building. "Some of them."

She squeezed his hand, wished she could ease some of the anguish she saw on his face. Why had they come back here? She would rather run from Marius and Claude forever, jump every roof in the city, than see him so anguished. "Where were you?"

"In the garret. All but forgotten."

But that wasn't quite true, she realized. No one had forgotten him. They had not known where to find him. Perhaps in the end that had saved him. As a small boy, she did not see how he could have held on to the secret of the treasure's location and survived. "Are you sure you want to go in?"

"Yes. I will go back to my cell."

Wonderful. They would have to go all the way to the attic, deep within the prison. "And how will we get up there?"

Now he looked at her, his eyes confused. "You are not going. You will stay out here and hide until I return."

She gazed about the darkening street, eerily quiet except for the clank of prison doors and guards' keys across the street. "Oh, I don't think so. I'm not anxious to go inside a prison, but I'm not going to sit out here by myself, either. What if Marius and Claude come this way?"

"They will. You will hide."

She turned to face him. "I'll go with you."

"No—"

She put a finger over his lips. "We don't have time to argue. I go with you. Whatever happens to one of us happens to both. I'm lost without you in this city anyway."

She could see he didn't like the idea of her going inside with him, but she didn't like the idea of waiting outside—for hours, for days, forever?—for him to come back out. "Like it or not," she said firmly. "I'm going with you."

He scowled at her, but she stood her ground, and he turned back to the prison. "There is one entrance and one exit to the prison. You see it there." He pointed to the gate. "There is a second gate behind it."

Double gates. Her chest tightened. "How will we get inside?" she asked again.

"Leave that to me."

They crossed the street, angling away from the prison, so they would come upon it from the side. Once they were near the building, he gestured for her to stand back as he approached the gate with the sleepy guard. She tried to appear interested in the architecture as a cart passed. In the meantime, Armand paused before the guard and asked him a question. She could see him talking to pass the time until the cart was out of sight. And then, quick as lightning, he reached out, snatched the guard's bayonet, and smashed him over the head with it.

Felicity winced and felt her own head ache with sympathy pain. The guard stumbled, went down, and Armand reached into his boot, extracted a knife. Felicity rushed forward. "What are you doing?" The knife's blade glinted in the moonlight. "You're not going to kill him, are you?"

He looked up at her, his eyes laced with a savageness she had not seen before. "Why not? He did not care if I died in there. They brought me food once or twice a week, but you could see that they were waiting for me to die."

She looked down at the soldier, who was really just a boy, then reached out and touched Armand's arm. It was tense as a piano wire and hard as rock. "He's a boy, doing his job. Tie him up and drag him into those bushes. Hopefully, we'll be out before anyone notices he's not at his post."

She saw the hesitation as Armand flipped the knife

from one hand to another. And then he tucked it back into his boot, ripped material from the soldier's coat, and bound his hands. He dragged him out of sight and joined her at the prison gate. A set of keys dangled from his hands. "Let's go."

Everything in her wanted to back away, wanted to run somewhere—anywhere but this prison. After all, who in their right mind broke *into* a prison? But she could not turn back now. Armand needed her. And so instead of fleeing, she followed him into the mouth of the prison. There was a second gate beyond the first, and to her right was a door where she assumed the soldiers stood to admit visitors during the day. To her left was a wooden rack with bayonets and rifles lodged against it. The second gate was closed and locked securely.

Before her, Armand fingered the keys, and she heard the echo as they jangled. She tensed at the sound, certain it would send a whole pack of soldiers rushing to apprehend them. But nothing in the prison moved.

Armand selected a key, clanged it against the rusted, metal gate—a sound which made her close her eyes and pray fervently—then inserted it into the lock. *Please, please, please.*

But the key did not fit, and he had to reach for another. Time seemed to drag on forever, and she knew the longer they stood there in full view, the more risk they took. There were only five keys on the ring, but it seemed none of them opened the gate.

Finally, Armand lifted the last key. "Please," she whispered.

He glanced back at her, smiled. "This is it." And the
key slid home. He turned it, and she heard the loudest
screech she could possibly imagine, then the gate
creaked open, Armand pulled out the key, extracted
his knife from his boot, and they stepped inside.

Twenty

THE PRISON SMELLED THE SAME. ARMAND DID NOT know how it was possible. He recognized little else about the corridor they traversed, but he knew the smell of this place. He would never forget the smell.

It was the scent of death and despair.

If he had more time, if he had an army, he would have freed every man locked in here. He did not know if any really deserved to be imprisoned, and he did not care. He could not stand to think of anyone caged. Freedom was precious, and he had risked it all to return.

Felicity had risked hers, too. He hoped they had not made a mistake. He hoped they would get out alive and with their freedom intact, but he was not at all sure of that possibility.

Moving on instinct, he turned left and deeper into the prison. He was searching for a set of stairs that would lead him to the attic, to his former cell. He passed numerous cells, but none of the inhabitants even raised their eyes at him. They were bony heaps under their thin blankets, and the sound of snores, of coughing, and of weeping punctuated the steady drip of water coming from a leak somewhere within the darkness.

The stairs loomed ahead of him, rising like a dark cliff out of the hole of the prison. He paused, knowing where they would lead and trying to gather himself before he took that old path. He did not want to return to his cell.

Armand had no fear it would be occupied. Even the soldiers at Le Grenier were not so cruel as to throw another man in the grave at the top of the prison. They had left him there only out of fear of moving him, fear of violating a directive none of them probably even remembered being issued. Armand doubted his cell had been touched since his escape with Julien months before. What kinds of memories would seeing that cell again evoke? Could he stand, even for a few moments, to have his anguished past before him once again?

He looked back at Felicity. She had paused behind him and was nervously watching him, nervously looking about them. Fearful one of the soldiers would see them.

She should be afraid.

"Are you all right?" she whispered.

He shook his head. Even in the midst of this danger, she was thinking of him. He felt his heart tighten and constrict, wondered if that was what love felt like. "I'm fine. It's up those stairs."

She nodded, whispered as she followed him, "I don't see many soldiers."

"There was a garrison of about fifty here," he

whispered back. "But Bonaparte has probably called many to the front lines. The few still stationed here have done their duty for the day."

He grabbed a low-burning torch anchored in a wall sconce and used that to light their way. As they started up the steep stairs, she grasped his hand to keep from slipping.

"Be careful," he said, catching her arm and helping her to the landing. "And be watchful. The guards will make cursory rounds. Marius said he had a way in. Probably bribed one of the soldiers."

"They must have realized we escaped by now." Together they climbed higher, passing the floors of cells and traveling deeper into the maw of the prison itself.

"They will come here," he said as they reached the final landing. "They know we won't leave without coming here first. Coming for the secret in the attic."

"What secret?" she hissed. "What's hiding there?"

"I'll show you."

He stepped forward onto the gloomy top level of the prison. There was only one cell up here, the garret cell that had been his home for twelve long years. He could see the outside door ahead. It was closed. A single wooden door aged by time and neglect, but sturdy enough to withstand his beatings and pleas for release.

At least it had been when he had first been imprisoned. By the end, the prison was in his mind, and the door hardly mattered.

"Is that it?" Felicity whispered.

He stepped forward and put his hand out. It

trembled, and he clenched it in disgust. He would get through this. He would not break. Not now.

He pushed the door hard, and it creaked open.

The room was dark. At one time there had been a torch outside the cell. He turned back and saw its burnt husk in the wall sconce. He lifted it, waited until it lit, and handed it to Felicity. Still, the cell was dark, and he stood patiently, waiting for his eyes to adjust.

It did not take long, for he knew the cell and its contents well. The straw on the floor. The gray stone walls. The cold hearth.

The hearth. That was what he wanted.

He crossed to it quickly, bent, and felt inside. The chimney had long since been bricked in, so even if he had wanted to light a fire, there would have been nowhere for the smoke to travel. Was that just another way to keep him cold and miserable, or had the hearth been closed deliberately?

He felt the smooth brick at the top of the hearth and lay down on his back to peer up at it.

"What are you doing?" Felicity asked.

"I've explored every inch of this cell," he answered, scooting into the cold, dirty rectangular opening. "This chimney is bricked in."

"And?"

He reached up, felt the gray stone. It was newer than that on the wall. Or perhaps he had just not touched it enough to wear it down. "Give me some light," he instructed her, and she knelt, angling the torch so flickering light fell on his face. It did not illuminate the brick under the hearth much, but it was enough so his suspicions were confirmed. This brick was newer and of a different color than the rest of the cell.

He had never had enough light to see that before. He had explored this area of the chimney with his fingers and his mind. As a prisoner, he had never dared to do what he planned now. But he had done it in his dreams, both here and back in London.

After the brick with Marius's warning had come crashing through the town house window, he had dreamed about the hearth in his cell. He had felt that smooth brick with his fingers, thought again, after all those years, about the treasure.

"I never dared break through," he said, taking his knife and digging it into the stone. It was soft with age and dampness, and a shower of tiny stones fell on his head. "But one thing I always wondered about was the size of the garret. There's only one cell up here."

"And?" She was leaning over him, peering into the chimney at the stone he chiseled away.

"If you look at this section of the prison from the outside—something I didn't do very often, but they had to let even a dog like me into the exercise yard once a year or so—it's big enough to accommodate two cells."

The light faded, and he glanced up to see her peering out of the cell door. "This is the only door. There's just brick and stone at the end of the stairway."

"I know. That means this is the only entrance."

She knelt again, gave him more light. "The only entrance to the cell?"

"The only entrance to whatever is hidden up here.

The cell is just the beginning. I was in the cell. A watchdog, or maybe a—what is it called—false front?"

"Are you saying that the Treasure of the Sixteen is hidden up here?"

"Yes." His knife dug deeper, and he coughed as dust and stones fell on his face.

"Are you certain?"

"No. But I know this. After I heard the Jacques discussing the treasure, after they realized I was not the mute they assumed, I was imprisoned here. The last conversation I heard centered on where to hide the treasure. I always thought they were discussing where to hide it once they acquired it."

"But now you think they had already found it and were looking for a place to stash it." Her voice held a note of wonder. "The prison is brilliant. And with you in this cell, who would think a treasure was hidden here?"

"Exactly." The knife went deeper, and he almost had the large stone loose. He scooted back in case it gave way suddenly.

"The problem is that someone got to them first. Probably Marius. He killed them before they could reveal where the treasure was hidden. Either that or he killed them because they refused to say. And I was left here, forgotten."

"And if the Jacques had come for you?"

"I would be dead now. There!" The stone rumbled down with a thud, and he saw Felicity glance toward the door nervously.

"That was loud."

Armand pushed the stone out of the way and

wedged his large body into the hearth again. Looking up, he could see the long tunnel of the chimney. But he thought he saw something else, as well. "More light."

"Armand."

"I think I see something, but I need more light."

"Armand, I don't think…"

Impatient, he reached up and felt into the darkness. There! Something protruding out of the chimney. Something that definitely should not be there. A lever?

"I think the lady is trying to warn you of something, monsieur."

At the sound of Marius's voice, Armand jerked and hit his head on the low brick above him. He looked out to see Marius, Claude, and one angry soldier standing in the doorway of his cell.

His blood turned to ice, and he steeled himself for what was to come. "It didn't take you as long as I thought." He sat.

Marius nodded at the hearth. "So it is here. The key to the treasure."

He shrugged. "You tell me."

"I do not think so, monsieur. I think you will tell me. Claude." The big man reached out and grabbed Felicity by the arm. She looked surprised but unhurt as he wrapped one of his log-sized forearms about her neck. "Find us the key to the treasure, or we kill the girl."

Armand stared at them, feeling his blood boil. His grip tightened on the knife, but he knew he was at a disadvantage for the moment. "And when I give you the key to the treasure, you'll kill us both."

"No, monsieur. I give you my word."

Armand almost laughed. The word of a murdering criminal. "You don't think I know what you did," he said, his eyes never leaving Marius's. "You don't think I know it was you who sent my father to the guillotine."

"Your father would have gone to the guillotine with or without my help, comte." He sneered the title. "We had a mission—to exterminate the parasites, the aristos."

"My father was no parasite."

"Justice said otherwise."

"Justice? You had him sent to trial—if those ridiculous stage shows could be called a court—brought in peasants from our lands to testify against him. Paid them to lie."

"If the duc de Valère had treated his peasants well, they would not have said otherwise."

"They would have said anything for the price of a loaf of bread. They burned the château and then realized they were going to starve to death when winter came. It happened all over the countryside. The city was no better."

"Those were the times, monsieur."

"Yes, but not everyone was starving. You had money—and a taste for blood. I saw you at the executions, cheering with the rest of the mob. Blood ran in the streets, and the crowds all but bathed in it."

Marius gave a ghost of a smile. "Vengeance was sweet. But you, monsieur, had nothing to be ashamed of. Your father died well, as you know. You were in the crowd that day."

"I was, and tell me something, monsieur. Did it give you more pleasure to see an aristo have his head chopped off or to witness the tears of a little boy?"

"Oh, the tears, of course. You were such a pitiful sight. Poor little aristo boy. You should have been on the scaffold with him. I wonder"—he signaled to Claude, who tightened his grip on Felicity, making her gasp—"if you will cry again today."

"You want the treasure?" Armand climbed back into the hearth, grasped the lever. "It's all yours."

He yanked hard, and the wall behind him seemed to shake and tremble then split in two.

"Armand!" Felicity cried, but he was already moving away from the crumbling hearth. A shower of dust rained down and filled the room, obscuring Felicity from his view for a moment. There was a smattering of coughing, and then the soldier said, "I don't believe it!"

But Armand could believe it. The lever had destroyed the back wall of the hearth, and where the stone had been, there was a gaping hole, leading into another room. The hole was just large enough for a man to fit through on hands and knees. Marius pushed Armand out of the way and knelt before the entrance.

"It's in there!" he breathed, voice filled with awe. "I can see the glint of gold!"

"Let me see." The soldier shoved him aside, and soon both men were climbing into what had been the hidden room.

Claude, unsure what to do, stood holding Felicity captive. Armand's eyes met hers and saw only worry for him.

"Claude, come here!" Marius called. "We need you to help us carry this treasure."

Abruptly Felicity was released, and the big man squeezed into the hole in the hearth.

"What's in there?" Felicity asked. "Is it really the Treasure of the Sixteen?"

Armand nodded. "Gold, silver, diamonds. Do you want to look?"

"No. I want out of here. I want to go home."

"Then let's go."

"But…" She gestured to the hidden treasure chamber. "Will they let us leave? Will they come after us?"

Armand lay back on the dusty floor and wedged himself under the chimney once again. He reached up, felt the hidden lever, and shoved it back. Instantly, a stone door slammed closed over the opening to the treasure room. It cut off the light, and he could hear the surprised cries of the men inside. But the cries were muffled and difficult to hear.

Armand rose, dusted off his breeches and shirt, and took Felicity's hand. "I think we should leave them with the treasure. It's what they wanted."

Felicity stared at the sealed hearth. "Will they be found?"

Armand pulled her to the entrance to his cell, stood in the doorway, and looked back a last time. Then he pulled the door closed, flinching at the solid thud it made. He lifted the keys he had pilfered from the gate soldier and inserted one into the lock. The rusty tumblers closed into place, and he started down the dark stairway.

They made it to the first level before he turned a winding corner and came face-to-face with a surprised soldier. "What's this?" the man asked and drew his pistol.

Twenty-one

FELICITY JUMPED BACK, BUT ARMAND DID NOT HESITATE. She watched in horror as he brought his knife up and slashed at the man's face, slicing him across the cheek. At the same time, he pushed the man's weapon against the wall of the stairwell, effectively preventing the soldier from firing.

The two men grappled, and Felicity looked for some way she might aid Armand. The soldier regained some strength and, blood streaming from his face, pushed Armand back. Felicity heard the comte's head crack against the stone. But Armand looked unaffected. His foot reached out, catching the soldier under his ankle and bringing him down.

Unfortunately, the soldier took Armand with him. The two rolled down a half-dozen stone steps with Felicity chasing after them. Armand landed on top and, still struggling to keep the soldier's gun inactive, he glanced up at her. "Go! Get out of here!"

"I'm not going to leave you!" She watched as the soldier reared up and Armand fought to keep the man's arms pinned. Armand lost his knife, and Felicity heard it clank down several steps, into the darkness.

"I'll meet you at the tavern," Armand said through gritted teeth. "Go now!"

Felicity hesitated another heartbeat and then, knowing she could help most by freeing Armand to concentrate on escape, she danced around the two men's struggling bodies and stumbled down the stairs. She had dropped the torch at some point during Armand's struggle, and now the prison was dark and shadowed. Behind her, she could hear the men's grunts, but the stone was thick, and the sounds did not carry far.

As she continued down the stairwell, the sounds of struggle behind her faded. She said a quick prayer Armand would make it out alive. She never thought of her own safety until something underfoot clinked.

She paused and stood stone-still. And then she realized it must be Armand's knife. She bent, felt in the darkness until her hand closed on the sharp blade. She snatched her fingers back then felt more gingerly, until she had found the handle. She lifted the knife and crept down the stairwell. What if she encountered more soldiers? How would she explain her presence?

At the bottom of the stairwell, she paused and peeked around the corner. This section led into a long corridor flanked with cells. If she could make it down the corridor without being spotted, then she only had to get through the two gates. Unfortunately, Armand had the soldier's keys, but presumably the gates were still open and unlocked.

That was, if no one had discovered the missing entry guard.

The corridor was silent, and her shoes shushed along the worn stone. The only other sound was that of dripping water. An incessant drip that must have driven prisoners to madness after years. She avoided looking in the cells, but she felt eyes on her, knew she was watched. And yet, none of the prisoners called out or came to the bars to get a closer look. Perhaps they were too beaten down to care, or perhaps they did not believe what they saw.

At the end of the corridor shone a small beam of light, and she could hear the hum of voices. It had not been there earlier, but now she realized the door to the soldier's station was ajar. She crept closer, keeping the knife at the ready. At the edge of the corridor, she hid in the shadows and watched as five soldiers sat playing a card game. They were smoking and drinking and laughing, oblivious to her presence or to the fight taking place on the steps just a few yards away.

She could not get through the gates without passing in front of that open door. The soldiers were not looking at the door, but one could glance that way at any moment—especially if movement was detected.

She thought she was close enough that even if they saw her, she could run into the street and escape, but then the prison would be in an uproar. Armand would never make it out. She had to escape without alerting the soldiers to her presence.

She lurked across from the door for what seemed an eternity. The soldiers played hand after hand, and still

Armand did not join her. Had he lost the fight? Was there another exit? *Please God, save him.*

She could wait no longer. As the minutes ticked by, she could feel the danger of discovery grow. Sooner or later there would be a change of the guards, or one of them would leave to walk the grounds. She must go now.

Saying a quick prayer and taking a deep breath, she inched forward. One of the guards turned slightly, and she paused, held her breath.

But he turned back to the game, and she continued to creep forward. Another step and she would be visible to any soldier who looked. Should she go quickly and risk a blur of movement that might draw their attention? Or should she go slowly and risk one of them turning and seeing her accidentally?

Her heart was pounding, and her legs felt restless. She wanted to run, but she clenched her fists, her fingernails biting into the knife handle, and inched past the open door. She must go slowly for Armand's sake. Now that she was in full view of any soldier who looked her way, the lamplight felt as harsh and bold as a ray of sunlight. The doorway seemed to gape and go on for yards. Her muscles revolted, wanted to freeze. She wanted to fall to the floor and curl up in a ball, but she pushed herself farther. She pushed herself to the patch of shadow just ahead.

The room of soldiers erupted in a chorus of hoots and howls, and she bit her tongue to stop a scream. For one terrifying moment, her heart stopped, and she was certain she had been caught. But a quick glance at the small room showed her the soldiers were deep in their game, and she scooted the rest of the way without being noticed.

Once in that tiny patch of shadow, she raced for the first gate. It was still unlocked and slightly ajar, but she dreaded the squeak it would make as she wedged it open enough to allow her body through. Perhaps if she pulled it slowly...

She tucked the knife in her left hand and pulled the gate with her right. She inched it open, a fraction at a time, certain that at any second one of the soldiers would see her and call out a warning. In her mind, a fast sonata played. Her fingers raced over the keys of the pianoforte, even as she moved with tortuous slowness at the gate.

Finally, she had made enough progress to squeeze through. She did so, breathing in relief as she raced for the last gate to the beat of the sonata.

The Paris air had never smelled as sweet as when she cleared the last gate and stood outside the prison, free. She had been inside less than a half hour and felt immense relief. She could only imagine what Armand must have felt when he'd escaped.

Perhaps he was right behind her. Perhaps he would join her in a moment. She wanted nothing more than to hold him. She turned to look back, hopeful, and saw the blur of movement just in time to duck.

With a scream, she stumbled back. The guard they had left in the shadows by the gate lurched drunkenly toward her. "I knew you would be back," he said, moving forward.

The soldier beneath Armand was gaining strength. He was older, perhaps thirty, but in good physical condition. His cap fell off his head to reveal dark yellow hair, and his face was thrown into a patch of dim light. Armand sucked in a breath. He knew this man, remembered him. He had been one of those assigned to bring him food—if the paste he was given could be considered such. He had been one of the soldiers to beat Armand, trying to force information out of him, trying to discover why he was there.

"I know you," Armand spat. Straddling the soldier, Armand pushed his hands down, but he could feel his own muscles beginning to protest.

"And I know you. You escaped, caused us a lot of trouble. I should have killed you when I had the chance. Worthless scum."

Armand had lost his knife, but the soldier was deftly holding on to his pistol. Armand tried to shake it free from his grip, but if he concentrated on that arm, the other came up. And finally he was too tired to hold it down anymore, and the soldier's fist was free. Armand held the pistol down but took a glancing blow on the chin. For a moment, he saw white dots against blackness, and then he was flying through the air.

He hit his head on the stairwell behind him but managed to roll away before the soldier could jump on top of him. The only place to roll was down the steps, and the fall jolted his already bruised body. He landed on a wide step, looked up, and saw the soldier raise his pistol. "Now you die." The soldier smiled.

There was nowhere to hide, and Armand closed his eyes, waiting for the hot sting of the bullet.

But all he heard was the click of the hammer.

Armand opened his eyes, smiled, and said in French, "Misfire."

The soldier roared, tossed the gun aside, and leapt for him. Armand met him halfway, and the clash of bodies sent them both tumbling down the steep stairs. Armand, conscious that they were nearing the bottom of the flight, doubled his efforts. He would be doomed if the soldier was able to alert the others to his predicament. Felicity would be doomed. He was not a praying man, but he prayed now. Prayed hard that she was safe and far away. He could not go on if anything happened to her. He could never forgive himself.

He saw the fist coming, but his reflexes were slower now, and he ducked too late, taking a blow to the eye. His world spun for a moment, and then fury swept through him. With renewed vigor, he slammed the soldier back against the stone wall. He heard the man's head crack against the hard surface. "Now you see what it's like," he rasped out. "Now you see how it feels." The soldier looked momentarily stunned then charged again. This time, Armand deftly sidestepped, and the man's unchecked momentum sent him tumbling down several more steps.

Before he could rise, Armand was on his back, arm wrapped around the soldier's throat. The soldier struggled, beat his feet on the floor, and then ceased the fight.

He wasn't dead. Armand knew he was only unconscious. Something in him wanted to keep squeezing until the man was dead. He could make this man pay for all he had suffered. It was time someone paid.

But Felicity's face swam before his eyes. Could he face her? Could he ever look in her eyes again if he became the monster he had always feared lurked inside him?

Slowly, he released the soldier, allowed the body to slump on the steps. He rose unsteadily to his feet, his breath coming in quick gasps. He had only a few minutes until someone came this way and discovered the soldier. Then the alarm would sound, and it would be too late for both Felicity and himself.

If it wasn't too late already.

He stumbled down the steps before him, praying Felicity had made it out of Le Grenier.

❦

Felicity's hand felt heavy and clumsy, and she fumbled with the knife. The guard stumbled toward her, and still she could not seem to find her grip. She backed away, trying to raise the knife in self-defense, but it almost slipped from her fingers. Finally, as the guard was all but on top of her, she managed to hold it, blade out, before her.

"Stop. I don't want to hurt you."

He cocked his head at her, and she could see his brown eyes were bloodshot and there was a trickle of blood running down his temple where the wound that had incapacitated him earlier must have bled. His uniform was ripped, and the tattered material that had bound his hands dangled from one wrist. "You're English," he said in French. "On top of all this, you're English!"

Felicity winced. She should not have spoken. Her French was adequate, but her accent very poor.

"Come here, little English girl." He reached for her, and she squealed, ducked, and skittered out of his grasp. He lurched forward then swung around again. "I'm going to catch you."

"Not if I can help it," she muttered in English and brandished the knife again. Brandishing was about all she was capable of. She had never used a knife against another person before. She could not even conceive of hurting a rabid dog, much less a person. She looked behind her. The street was clear. She could run, and even if the guard alerted his cohorts, she would probably be away before they could catch her. The guard was in no shape to chase after her.

But she had to think of Armand. He was still inside. If she alerted the soldiers that the prison had suffered a break-in, he would never escape. She could not be the one responsible for his imprisonment. It would be better that she were caught, that she were killed by this guard than to have to think of Armand locked in the garret cell again. If she could just distract the guard, keep him busy a few more minutes, perhaps Armand would have enough time to join her.

The guard was coming for her, and though she was backing up, he was closing in. His head wound must have opened up again, because fresh blood flowed down his cheek and into his eye. He swiped it away, creating a macabre crimson smear along one side of his face.

Her back rammed into the outer prison gate, and she felt the sharp metal dig through the thin material of her gown, scratching her skin. As she watched the guard advance, she knew she could still evade him. She could still escape.

But she stood still; she stood patiently. She waited. It struck her that this was love. That right now she would fight to the death for Armand. She was prepared to go to prison in his place. Yes, if she were caught, she could distract the soldiers long enough to give Armand the opportunity to escape. She did not delude herself about the consequences of being caught breaking into a prison. She was a woman who would be remanded into the hands of half a dozen angry soldiers. She was a foreigner and an enemy of France. She would be imprisoned for a very long time—and that would not be the worst of what she suffered.

And still she stood and waited. The guard was on top of her now. He was leering, the blood trickling down his cheek a thick red river. She held up the knife, and he sneered. "Try it."

He stepped closer, and she swiped at him. He jumped back, but his reflexes were too slow. The knife grazed the material of his coat. Unfortunately, it was a glancing blow and did no harm.

Except now the guard was angry. "Little bitch!" He leapt for her, and she stuck out the knife. But he was ready for her, and he evaded the blade. His hand came down, striking her arm, and she buckled in pain. Her reflex was to release the knife, but instead she bit down hard and held on. She ducked under his arm, but he was right on top of her. He grabbed her arm and twisted it back, holding her far enough away that she could not strike with the knife. He yanked her arm up hard, behind her back, and she stifled a scream of pain. Screaming would only bring the soldiers sooner.

"Drop the knife," he breathed, yanking her arm

up until the pain was almost all she could think of. It burned through her, made her vision flicker, caused her knees to buckle. But through the haze of pain she saw Armand. She had to be strong for him.

She held out the knife. "I'll drop it."

"Do it!" the guard hissed.

"You're hurting me," she cried, trying to make her voice sound as plaintive as possible. It was not difficult, because tears had sprung to her eyes from the pulsing ache in her arm. Any minute now he would break it. She could feel the muscles screaming, feel the bone dangerously close to giving way.

But her cry must have worked, because he eased his grip just enough that she could see clearly again, and then, turning into the pain, she swung the knife at him. It was a wild swing, but she was lucky. She caught him, felt the resistance as the blade swiped and saw the blood as her hand came around again.

He cried out, but to her dismay, he did not release her. Instead, he yanked up her arm, and she swore she heard something pop.

This time she could not stop the scream of anguish from bursting forth. Her knees gave out, and she sank to the ground. Immediately, he was over her, reaching for the knife in her free arm. She would have given it to him. She would have done anything at that moment to make the pain stop.

But then she saw Armand. Not the image of him. Not this time. It was he in the flesh. She blinked, not trusting her eyes, but he was running through the gates, coming for her. His eyes were wild, savage, intense. Oh, how she loved his eyes, loved that they were fixed on her. The guard reached for the knife, and in one last moment of resistance, she brought it up—and felt it ram into something soft.

He screamed, and she fell forward as he released her. She hit her forehead on the cobblestones, but the pain of that was nothing compared to the scream in her arm.

And then Armand was beside her. She heard the guard's screaming, and Armand had her in his arms, had her on her feet, and was pushing her to stand, to move. "Run, *chérie*. Run!"

She wanted to tell him she couldn't run. She didn't have any strength left, but she had never been able to tell him no. And so she ran as the guard's screams echoed behind her, and the sound of booted feet grew louder.

They ran for what seemed like hours. Her lungs were on fire, her arm was on fire, her legs were on fire. At one point, she stumbled and almost fell, but Armand caught her, carried her for a moment until she regained her footing. The night was dark now, but Paris did not sleep. It was not long before they were in a busy quarter, surrounded by lean, hungry people who had more to worry about than a woman with blood on her dress and the savage-looking man running beside her.

"Please," she wheezed. "I can't go any farther."

"We can't stop yet." He pulled her along, and she plodded after him. But her legs felt encased in lead. She could barely lift them.

"I can't. Armand." She grabbed his shoulder, turned him to face her. "I can't."

330330330330330330330330330330330330330330330330330330330330330330330330330330330330330330330330330330330330330330330330330330330330330330330330330330330330330 SHANA GALEN

He looked ready to argue, but then his face softened. He pushed her into the doorway of a shop that was closed for the night and pulled her into his arms. She sank into him as soon as he touched her. Even after days of travel and with the grime from the prison on him, he still smelled good to her. He still felt good to her. His arms were solid around her, and she closed her eyes and laid her head on his shoulder. She wanted to stay like this forever.

"How is your arm?" he murmured.

She rotated it gingerly. "Sore but not broken."

"Good. We need to get out of here." His voice was a rumble through her bones. "Once the soldiers at Le Grenier sound the alarm, the city will be closed off. We'll be locked in." She could hear the undertone of worry in his voice at the thought, and she pulled away, cupped his face.

"We'll hide. They'll never find us."

"We need to go to Calais. If we can find the captain Marius hired, convince him to take us back to England, then we'll be safe. That's the only way."

She nodded. He was right, of course. They had to get out while they had the chance. "What do you propose? I'm too tired to walk all the way to Calais."

He nodded. "I'll get us a horse and cart."

"You have money?" she asked.

He shook his head. "A few pounds, which won't do me any good here. I'll have to steal him."

Oh, Lord. It seemed her sins continued to add up. Soon the tally board would be lopsided. "What if you're caught?"

He raised a brow at her. "I won't be. Stay here."

She grabbed his sleeve as he moved away. "But what if we can't find that captain once we get to Calais?"

He shrugged. "Marius paid him to wait. He'll still be there."

"But you're not Marius."

"No. I'm something better." There was an uncharacteristic ghost of a smile on his face. "I'm the brother of Captain Cutlass."

❧

Stealing the horse and cart was almost too easy. His brief life of crime in the streets of Paris had taught him skills he was unlikely ever to forget. And Armand was surprised at how quickly those criminal skills came back to him. While he was feeling adept, he stole a loaf of bread, several apples, and a cloak. Paris was cold, and Felicity had been shivering when he'd left her.

He'd hated to leave her, but bringing her along on his mission would only have drawn more attention. Now, he hoped she'd stayed put and would use the knife he'd pulled from the guard and given her on anyone who had tried to get too friendly.

He directed the horse through the crowded quarter until he reached the dress shop where he'd left her. He jumped down as soon as he saw the flash of her yellow hair. "I can't believe you actually did it," she said, admiration and something like censure vying for dominance on her face.

"This is only the beginning." He hoisted her into the seat beside him and started for Calais.

As he'd expected, Marius's captain was still waiting.

The captain didn't ask many questions after ascertaining that Marius would not be returning. His fee was a concern, but Armand used the Valère name, promising payment when they returned.

The trip back was not as uneventful as that to Paris. A winter storm made the Channel rough and caused several days' delay. Armand used part of that time to speak with the captain. He hoped the man could answer some of his many questions.

Later, he joined Felicity in the captain's cabin, where they had been given quarters. She wore only her chemise. She had taught him both the English and French names for that garment, but he preferred the French term. He could see the outline of her body in the candlelight. He realized, as he came through the cabin door and the sight of her fired his blood, that he had not touched her since the last time they had been together in London. It wasn't that he hadn't thought of it. But she had been tired, and when he'd seen the bruises the guard had given her on her arm, he had been too enraged to do anything but prowl the ship's deck, even if the swells threatened to pitch him into the icy waters.

But now the color had returned to her cheeks, and the bruises were fading. He felt his hands go slightly damp at the sight of her yellow hair—she had told him the term was blonde—falling over her shoulders and down her back.

As he closed the door, she turned to look at him. "I thought you'd never be back. Were you with the captain this entire time?"

"Yes."

She raised her brows. "For someone who doesn't like to speak, that's a great deal of talking."

"I let him talk."

She smiled. "Of course. What were you talking of?"

He wasn't prepared to discuss it with her. He wanted to speak with Julien first, and so he shrugged and crossed to her, putting his hands on her almost-bare shoulders. "You look cold."

She raised her brows. "That wasn't what you were discussing, and I am a little cold."

"I'll warm you."

He pulled her to him, wrapped his arms around her waist, and lowered his mouth to hers. She was eager to kiss him back. He had not expected that. He had grown used to her initial reluctance, to having to persuade her, but now her fingers were in his hair, and she was urging him to deepen the kiss. "I need you, Armand," she whispered against his mouth.

The words puzzled him. She had never seemed to need anyone, most especially not him. Even when he had emerged from Le Grenier to find her on her knees with the guard towering over her, she had looked a moment away from turning the whole situation to her advantage. And it had been she who had dispatched the guard, not he. She had not asked, and he would never tell her where her knife had landed. But when he'd extracted it, he'd known the guard would never see again.

He kissed her more deeply, wondering if this satisfied the need in her.

"Do you need me?" she asked, pulling away.

It was a strange question, but perhaps it was

something typical of lovers that he was unaware of.
"Of course," he said, bending to kiss her neck. "I
needed you from the first moment I saw you."

She stepped back, away. "That's not what I mean.
I don't mean do you want me. I mean, do you need
me? Do you love me?"

Armand frowned. Those seemed to be two different
things to him. He understood need. He needed food
and water. He needed to hold her, to feel her touch.
But he did not understand love. What was that? He
took her face in his hands, marveling once again at how
soft her skin was. "I need you. You are the only one
who can touch me."

She blinked, and he saw the question in her eyes.
"Armand, *why* can I touch you? I've watched you. I've
seen how you react when others touch you. It looks
like you're in pain."

He nodded then shrugged. "Too many years
without touch. Like too many years without talking.
You lose the taste for it."

"But I can touch you." As if to illustrate, she ran her
hands down his arms then up again, and over his chest.

His skin grew warm where her fingers trailed, and
he had the urge to kiss her and end the discussion right
there. Why did she have to talk so much? "You're
different." He bent, but she put a hand between them.

"Why? Why me?"

"I don't know." And that was true. He didn't know
why her touch was like a drug to him, whereas others'
were painful, though truth be told, he was beginning
to get used to touch. It was no longer excruciating.

"Do you think it's destiny? We're destiny?"

He knew the word, had read it as a child, but he didn't know anything practical about it. "I don't know. I don't care. *I* need *you*." He bent to kiss her, and this time when she tried to ask him something about fate, he brushed a hand over her breast, felt her nipple pebble, and made sure she forgot all about words.

He eased her back on the berth, careful of her arm as he undressed her. But he wasn't looking at her body, as much as it fascinated him. He was looking in her eyes, because there was something new there, something he didn't remember seeing there before.

And he had a feeling that he finally understood what it was.

Twenty-two

ARMAND PULLED DOWN THE STRAPS OF HER SHIFT, kissing her shoulders as he did so. It amazed her how at times he could be so gentle and other times he could be so fierce. He was gentle now, kissing the skin at the base of her neck, teasing the hollow of her throat with his tongue, tracing a fiery path from her throat to the swells of her breasts. And then his mouth was there, as well. She could feel the material of the shift bunched at her hips, feel his hands on her, his mouth on her, exploring, teasing, tantalizing.

She opened her eyes and looked down at his soft, dark hair. She wanted to cradle him to her, to hold him, but then he took a nipple in his mouth, and she felt passion stirring. Tenderness was pushed aside for the moment as she arched up to meet his eager hands and lips.

"You're wearing too many clothes," she murmured. She didn't expect a vocal response, but he obediently stood and began to pull off his tattered shirt. She knelt on the berth and grasped his roughened hands. "Let me do it."

He raised a brow but lowered his hands compliantly. She liked this side of him, this obedient, compliant side. She knew it would not last, but she liked that, for the moment, she had control.

Slowly, she drew his shirt up, allowing her fingers to trail over the smooth, bronzed skin underneath. She wondered how his skin had become so bronzed. Was he outside without his shirt? She could imagine that scenario quite easily. Armand would never be a man who cared about fashion or its rules. She tugged the shirt over his head and allowed it to fall in a snowy heap on the cabin floor. Now, in the dim candlelight, she saw the ravages the night in the prison had cost him. She traced the outline of dark bruises on his ribs and chest.

"You're hurt," she whispered, looking into his cobalt eyes.

He shook his head as though to say it was nothing, then captured her hands and kissed her knuckles. He began to draw her into another kiss, but she resisted. *She* was supposed to be the one in charge. "You're still wearing too many clothes," she chided.

"And you are talking too much."

She gave him a sly grin as she slid her hands out of his grasp and down his chest. She could feel the skin pebble under her fingertips. "In a hurry, are you?"

She did not think he would answer, and she knew he would not once she dipped a finger into the waistband of his breeches. She could feel the tip of him, just an inch below that waistband, knew he was hard and ready. And still she took her time. She extracted her hand and ran her palm over his hard length. He groaned with pleasure, something she could not remember him doing before, and she worked her way around to caress his behind.

Now she could see the impatience in his eyes, his face. He reached down and began to flick the trousers open. "No, no," she chastised. "Allow me."

He gave her a look that said his passion would override his patience any moment, and so she went to work on the fastenings to his trousers. They fell open, and she eased them down his legs. Hastily, he kicked out of them and reached for her, but she moved more quickly, wrapping her hand around his hard length.

Armand went utterly still at her touch, and she was so surprised by his shock that she wanted to see how else he might react. Her hand slid down that hard, velvet length and then back up again. When she met his gaze, his eyes were fastened on hers, so dark and so intense. "Again," he rasped.

She smiled. "Now who's talking?" But she complied, rewarding him and herself with his reaction. He reached for her, but she shook her head. "Felicity." His voice was husky and sent shivers up her spine.

"Wait." She ran a hand down the length of him, felt him jump in her hand. She was learning so very much! And she wondered...

She met his dark gaze, leaned forward, and touched her tongue to the tip of him. His hands were instantly on her shoulders, his body rigid with shock and... yes, that was pleasure in his eyes. "Again?" she teased.

He didn't answer, but the look in his eyes was enough. She repeated the action, this time closing her mouth on him. He groaned, loudly, and she hoped there were no sailors passing by the cabin. The groan was unmistakably one of pleasure.

She liked that she could give him that pleasure. That she could cause this reaction. She bent again, laved him with her tongue, learning the taste of him and the feel of him. He was smooth and hard and seemed to grow more so the more of him that she took inside.

Finally, his hands gripped her shoulders tightly, and he pushed her gently back. "My turn."

"But—"

But his compliance was at an end. She could see in his face that he was taking over. She had a moment's disappointment, and then he was pulling her shift over her head and his hands were on her. They were rough hands, not the pampered hands of an aristocrat, and their roughness excited her. She liked the way his calluses felt on her skin, tripping over her nipples, running along her belly, skirting up her thighs, and... oh—

He eased her back on the berth—or perhaps she fell back, and his finger teased that nub at her center. She was alternately hot and cold, impatient and then unwilling for the sensation to ever come to an end. He spread her legs and knelt between them. She wondered if she should feel self-conscious before him this way, but she did not. She knew he was the only one for her, as she was for him. She saw admiration in his eyes and wonder, and it made her want to open for him, want to take him in.

She could see his erection between them and

knew he was ready, but he did not move over her. Instead, he smiled.

Felicity frowned. That was not like him. "What are you thinking?"

He bent and put his mouth to her belly. His breath was warm and ticklish, and she squirmed from pleasure and excitement. She wanted him inside her, wanted his heat and his hardness.

Instead, he licked a warm trail from her belly button to her center. She knew what he was doing now. He was showing her what she had done to him. As much as she wanted him inside her, she wondered how his mouth would feel.

And then he touched his tongue to her, and she all but convulsed. Instead of withdrawing, his hands grasped her thighs, held her steady, parted her for him. He licked her again, and she arched against his mouth, fisting her hands in the bedclothes and crying out with the intense pleasure of the sensation. He never spoke, but she could feel his pleasure at her reaction, could feel his eagerness to see how she would react when he touched her this way or that. And she could not help but indulge him. She was panting, almost screaming when release finally came. She could feel his eyes on her, see she pleased him, feel his eagerness as he entered her and brought her pleasure to greater heights.

She bucked hard, wanting him deeper, wanting him to fill her, and he obliged. He was rough and fast, and when he exploded inside her, he called her name.

No word had ever been sweeter to her, and she caught him as he collapsed against her, his hair falling on her pillow, his chest crushing her breasts with a pleasant, sated heaviness.

"I love you, Armand," she whispered, and he nuzzled her neck tenderly.

She thought they slept for a time, entangled and in one another's arms. When she woke, the sky through the porthole was hazy and gray. It might have been dusk or dawn, but she could feel the ship's gentle rocking and knew the storm from the last few days had passed.

Armand's eyes were closed, and he looked so peaceful in sleep. She could feel her heart constrict with love. He opened his eyes then, and though they were tender and filled with what she thought might be love, she was not certain. She wanted the words. She wanted to know he felt what she felt. That there was more to this than just attraction and pleasure. She wanted his heart, not just his body. And, as always, she wanted his words.

She smiled, "How long have you been awake?"

In answer, he kissed her, and they made love slowly, leisurely once again. It was not everything she wanted, but for the moment, it was enough. A few hours later, after washing and eating a very satisfying meal of bread and cheese, they lay on the berth together and dozed. She could not ever remember having been so lazy, but she was tired, and she did not know what awaited them in London.

The Valère family would be there, probably frantic with worry and demanding explanations for their sudden, unexplained disappearance. And what could she tell them? She had been betrayed by Charles. And if he was still in London, the danger he posed was very real. He could still accuse her of murder. She could, in turn, accuse him of kidnapping. Either way, the Valère family and Armand would be exposed to scandal.

"What's wrong?" Armand breathed into her hair. She turned her head and met his gaze. "You're stiff."

"I'm thinking about when we get back. Your family will be upset."

"But we're alive."

She had to agree with that logic. "Of course they will be happy we're well, but they will still want to know where we've been, what has happened. They must be worried sick with no word from us."

"A lot of words."

She nodded. "They deserve an explanation."

"We'll give them the words, and then I will take you away."

She rose on one elbow to face him. "What do you mean?"

"I want out of London. We'll go to The Gardens."

"Your home in the country?"

He nodded. "There is a pianoforte there. You can play any time you wish."

She laughed. "I'm sure you'd enjoy that, but we can't exactly run off to the country together. We're not even married."

He shrugged. "So we marry."

"It's not quite that easy." And for so many more reasons than she wanted to explain.

Now he rose on an elbow, a look of annoyance in his features. "Why not?"

She could have told him a dozen reasons—from

objections his family might have to the logistics of the special license. Instead, she blurted out, "I'm not good for you."

He frowned at her, uncomprehending. "You are very good for me." He traced her breast with a long, aristocratic finger. "You are mine."

Not yet, she wasn't. She wanted to be his, she truly did, but how could she marry him knowing she would expose him to charges of murder. Knowing if she accused Charles of kidnapping, it would bring to light Armand's past—a past she knew he wanted kept very private. It was better for him and for his family if she disappeared. Perhaps they could give her some money, help her find somewhere to hide. Maybe one day she would return…

He must have seen something of her dilemma on her face, because he sat and scowled at her. "So you will not marry me?"

She sat as well. "I don't know. There are other problems, other reasons."

He spread his hands. "Such as?"

"I'm already betrothed."

"St. John."

She nodded. "After what he's done, no one could expect me to honor that agreement, but he can make things difficult for us. He can cause a scandal."

Armand waved a dismissive hand. "I don't care about scandal."

"But your family will. They'll be humiliated to be at the center of such scandal. And Charles—"

"Is dead. I'll kill him for what he did."

She sat, grasped his elbow. "Armand, you can't.

You'll go to prison." His back was to her, but she felt him tense.

Slowly, he turned to look at her. "Only if they catch me."

Oh, dear. She stood hastily before him, putting a hand on his chest. "I don't want you to kill him." His eyes flashed a warning at her, but she continued. "It's not because I have any feelings for him. I love you, only you, but he has power over me, Armand. Do you know what that means?"

"He sold you to Marius. I got you back. He'll never get close to you again."

"He doesn't need to. He can hurt me without ever coming near me."

"Tell me."

She hesitated only a moment before the words and the story seemed to pour out of her. "My father was ill, very ill. I didn't realize how ill he was, and he sent me to stay with my aunt for a fortnight. At least it was supposed to be only a fortnight, but my aunt needed so much help—she has six children—and she asked me to stay longer, and I agreed. I didn't know that my father…" She broke off, her chest hitching as she tried to hold back the sobs.

"He died?" Armand's voice was matter-of-fact and yet full of compassion. He knew what it was to lose a parent. To be unable to offer comfort at the end.

She nodded. "While I was away. I might not even have known if Charles hadn't sent a letter. He lied and told everyone in Selborne he had gone off to fight in the wars, joined the military, but while I was away, he came back. He nursed my sick father and was with him at the end. He wrote me of his death, asked me to come home. And when I did, he showed me the betrothal contract. My father had agreed I should marry Charles. He wrote he wanted me to be taken care of."

Armand's hands had fisted when she spoke of marriage, and now he stood and paced away from her. "You will not marry him. You're mine." She could feel the anger and heat radiate off him, and she went to him, laid her head on his broad back.

"I am yours. I never wanted to marry Charles. When I returned, I saw what he was. A drunk and a gambler. He must have thought he could make some profit by nursing my father, but we had nothing. I told him I would never marry him, and he threatened to reveal the contract to everyone and to tell them that I would not honor it. First I had to promise him twenty-five pounds. Then it was a hundred."

"You will pay him nothing."

"You don't understand. H-he's killed a woman. A prostitute. I saw them together when I was out shopping with your mother. People saw us speaking. Now Charles says if I don't give him one hundred pounds, he'll accuse me of the murder. He'll say I was jealous of her and you were an accomplice. We could both go to prison, Armand. And even if we don't, the scandal—"

"I will take care of him."

"Armand, I told you, I don't want you to kill him. I don't want you to go to prison. He's not worth that. At first I thought I might go to the magistrate and tell him what happened, but now I think it's best if I go away. Perhaps if he cannot find me, you and I will both be safe."

"But not together,"

She looked down. "No…"

He notched her chin up. "We will be together. Leave St. John to me. I won't have to kill him."

She wanted to ask him what he meant, but a knock sounded on the door, and the captain announced the cliffs of Dover were visible on the horizon.

After that, the time seemed to rush by, and she didn't have another minute to discuss Charles with Armand. It wasn't until they were in a hired hackney, on the way to Berkeley Square, that she had the chance to ask him about Charles.

Not surprisingly, he didn't answer her, and she was forced to throw him evil looks and entertain herself with looking out the window as the landscape changed from dingy, noisy poverty to the tree-lined, quiet streets of Mayfair. The jarvey called out when they stopped in front of the Valère town house, and Armand was out of the vehicle a moment later. He grabbed her about the waist and swung her down, then gave her a stern look. "Let me talk."

Both her brows shot up. She couldn't help it. It was the last thing she expected him to say. He marched up the steps, and she stood on the curb, watching in mute disbelief. The jarvey called after him about the price of the fare, and Felicity assured him he would be paid in a moment.

Indeed, the butler was out of the house in second, hastening down the steps to pay the jarvey. A moment later, the duchesse was at the door, rushing to bundle

Felicity inside and chattering nonstop about how frantic with worry everyone had been. Her greeting was warm, almost sisterly, and Felicity was shocked by it, shocked at how she felt as though she were coming home.

But as she stepped into the vestibule, she was greeted by the duc, and he did not appear brotherly at all. She could see he wanted an immediate explanation, but Armand was ready.

"Can we speak in your library?" he said.

If the duc was surprised by the polite request, he didn't show it, merely nodded his head and followed Armand into the room.

Felicity watched as the door closed behind them.

Armand began his explanation before Julien was even seated. He kept it short and to the point. When he had to describe going back into Le Grenier, Julien rose and poured him a small glass of the amber liquid his brother was so fond of. Armand had never cared for it, but he took it now and drank it without hesitation. He needed something to keep the recent images of prison at bay.

When he finished his explanation, Julien leaned back in his chair and cursed softly under his breath. "So the treasure was there all the time."

Armand nodded. "I was the watchdog, but Marius killed my keepers—the Jacques."

"Do you think Marius will be found?"

Armand shrugged. "Either way, he won't be back here."

"And you're not back for long." His gaze shifted

to peer through the French doors into the barren December garden beyond. "You want to go to Southampton and take Miss Bennett with you, as well, I suppose."

Armand's silence was his assent.

"I don't suppose I can talk you into staying. Ma mère will miss you."

"She can visit. You can visit."

"You can't take Miss Bennett with you until you marry her. That will take a few days to arrange."

Armand stood, went to the window, and gazed out.

"You *do* still want to marry Miss Bennett?"

"She's mine," Armand said quietly. "But…"

He could see Julien's reflection in the window, and his brother sat forward. "But?"

"But there are complications. We will deal with St. John."

Julien nodded. "Of course. I have some information on St. John—"

Armand waved his hand in dismissal. "We will deal with St. John in a moment."

Julien raised a brow. "Is there something else you'd like to discuss?"

Armand clenched his hands in frustration. Finally, he rounded on Julien. "She keeps talking about love! She seems to need this love to be happy."

"*Do* you love her?"

Armand threw his hands out. "How the hell do I know? What's love?"

"That's a good question."

Armand walked away from the window and leaned his hands on Julien's desk. Julien looked decidedly uncomfortable now. He reached up and loosened his neck cloth. Armand wondered why he wore one when it was obviously so uncomfortable. Maybe The Rules said he had to wear it when he went out, but he was home. "The answer?" Armand demanded.

Julien ran a hand through his hair. "I don't know. This is the sort of thing women talk about. I guess... love is a feeling."

"I have feelings for Miss Bennett."

Julien raised a brow. "More than just wanting to see her naked?"

"Of course. She..." He hesitated. How could he explain how it was when he'd first seen her, first touched her, realized she could touch him without causing him pain? How could he explain how she had made him want to live again, to crawl out of his safe hole and risk all for her? And how could he put into words the fear and desperation he'd felt when he thought he might have lost her at Le Grenier? Nothing had ever terrified him so much. Nothing ever would.

Julien was smirking at him, at his lack of words. "That's the problem. And, by the way, your solution."

Armand frowned at him now, watched as Julien rose and poured another glass of the amber liquid. "You don't make sense."

"Love doesn't make sense." He swallowed half of the liquid, and Armand clenched his fists again. He felt like throttling his brother.

"It can't be this complicated. I want Felicity to be happy."

"Tell her you love her."

"How?"

"You have to go into detail. You have to say when you realized you loved her, and how, and why, and how you'll always love her."

Armand felt his stomach sink. "A lot of words."

"And she'll want to hear them over and over again. Even Sarah still asks if I love her. I must have told her a thousand times."

Armand sank into a chair. "I can't just show her?"

"Haven't you tried that?"

His brother had a point. He swallowed. Somehow he would have to find the words. "Will you take care of The Rules for the wedding?" he asked.

Julien raised a brow. "Certainly. I'll get you a special license. When will you be leaving for Southampton?"

"Not right away. I have something else to do first."

"Are you ready to talk about St. John?"

Armand nodded. "He pays for what he did."

Julien leaned back against the wall and crossed his arms. "When you disappeared, I did a bit of investigating into the life of our friend Charles St. John. I think I have the perfect solution."

Twenty-three

CHARLES DID NOT WAIT LONG TO FIND HER. THE MORNING after they returned, Felicity was in her room when she heard a commotion downstairs and the sound of a man's raised voice. She rushed to the marble stairs overlooking the vestibule and felt her heart clench when she saw Charles standing there, arguing with the butler, Grimsby.

"Sir, you shall have to leave now. The family is not at home."

"I know Felicity is here, and I'm going to stand here and wait until you fetch her."

"Sir, I will have these footmen"—he gestured to two burly footmen who had emerged from one of the doors off the vestibule—"escort you out."

"Then I'll stand outside and make a scene. You won't get rid of me until I—" He broke off and smiled as Felicity descended the stairs. "There, you see. That wasn't so difficult."

Grimsby turned and scowled at her. Felicity rather had the idea that he would have preferred tossing Charles out on the curb. "I will take care of this now, Grimsby," she said. "Thank you."

Grimsby gave a stiff bow and hurried toward the duc's library as though he had an important errand. Even with the footmen still standing guard, she felt quite alone at the moment. She wanted Armand but was glad he was away. She worried what he would do if he and Charles met face-to-face.

"What are you doing here?" she said stiffly.

But Charles either did not hear her tone or ignored it. He rushed toward her, and when she put up her hands, he grasped them warmly in his. "Darling! I was so worried. Are you well? Are you hurt in any way? I came as soon as I heard you were back in Town."

Felicity shook her hands free of his grip. "Do not touch me. Get out of here."

He stepped back and smiled. "Not quite yet," he murmured, low and menacing. "Did you forget our little discussion? I'm sure the magistrate would be interested in any information I can give him about the murder of poor Celeste."

She almost laughed. "After what you did, do you still think you can scare me with threats?"

"And what have I done?" He gave her a blank look. "It's your word against mine. I've been worried sick about my fiancée. And while I fretted here in London, you and the mad comte de Valère cavorted in a secret hideaway."

"That's not true."

"Who cares? The magistrate might think you ran away to avoid suspicion. No matter. *The Times* will sell thousands of papers once I tell them my story of the mad comte and the jealous fiancée."

She wanted to protest, to cry out, to beg and

beseech him, but she knew those methods would fail. She was ashamed she had ever tried them in the past. No, she would not beg or plead. And she would not allow Armand or his family to be dragged through the muck. It was too late to run away. She had to stand and face her fate. She had to protect Armand.

"Fine," she said, smoothing her gown. "When the comte returns, I'll have him escort me to the *Times*. We can speak to the reporters together. After that, we'll see the magistrate. We'll see whom he believes."

Charles raised a brow. "I know a bluff when I see it."

She shook her head. "I'm not bluffing. I'll tell my side of the story, and you tell yours. We shall see in whose favor his opinion turns." Her side of the story would leave out everything about her relationship with Armand. She would paint him and the Valère family as generous benefactors.

And if she were not imprisoned, she would leave on the first coach.

"You won't do it." Charles sneered. "Not when you can give me five hundred pounds, and this all goes away."

"Five hundred pounds now?" She smiled. "That's impossible. I'd rather go to Newgate."

"But what about Valère?"

She could see Charles was worried now.

"I heard he wants to marry you."

"I've refused him. I won't bring any more scandal on the family." She meant it and let Charles see her intent in her face.

"He won't let you go," Charles stammered. "Valère went after you in France. He rescued you. You'll end up marrying him, and if you think I'm going to let you get away with that for free, then you've forgotten what I have." He pulled out the familiar paper with the agreement between her father and himself. Her betrothal.

Oh, Father. If only you'd seen what I see now.

"I haven't forgotten, and I don't care. We'll go to the *Times* today. I don't want to waste any more time with you."

"But—" And then the surprised expression on his face turned to anger. "Why, you little slut!" He grabbed her arm in a punishing grip, all but lifting her off the floor. The footmen called out, but Charles didn't release her. "You are mine, and if you think I'm going to let you go that easily, think again."

"Get your hands off her."

Felicity whipped her head to the side and saw Armand standing in the vestibule. She had not heard him come in, did not know how long he had stood there. Charles was surprised, too. She felt him jump, but still he did not release her.

"This is my fiancée. I have the papers from her father to prove it. If you want her, you're going to have to pay."

Felicity saw the look that crossed Armand's face and closed her eyes. It was nothing short of pure rage—caged rage she had no doubt he could use to destroy Charles, as he had promised to do. "Armand, don't," she warned.

Charles laughed. "No, Armand, do. There's more than one way for me to get payment for my betrothed."

Armand stepped forward. "Get your hands off her before I remove them myself."

"You want her?" Charles said, shaking her. "You can have her, but if you want this agreement to go away, then you're going to have to pay for it."

Armand stepped forward, and Felicity hissed, "Let go of me or you will regret it."

"One thousand pounds," Charles said triumphantly. "For that, I'll disappear, and you'll never see me again. I'll even give you the marriage contract. We can pretend it never happened."

But Armand was no longer listening. His eyes were cold and flat as he drew back his fist and slammed it into Charles's face. Shocked, Charles released her and reeled backward. He lost his balance and tumbled to the floor. But he was up again in a moment. "You'll pay for that!" He leapt at Armand, and Felicity jumped back as Armand easily sidestepped, drew his arm back and hit Charles again. This time blood splattered in an arc over the pristine black-and-white marble floor.

"Armand," she cried. "Stop!"

For a moment, it did not appear he heard her. He reached down and took Charles by the collar, hauled him up, and hit him hard enough that she heard something crack. Charles made a rattling, wheezing sound and dropped to the floor when Armand released him.

"Open the door," Armand said, looking over his shoulder at Felicity.

"What?" She blinked in confusion.

"Open the door." Armand gestured to the door, and she finally managed to force her legs to move. She grasped the cold door handle and pulled it open. Outside stood two hefty men dressed in coats and breeches but with the look of thugs. A third man was smaller and more effete. He tipped his hat at her. "Madam. Your butler sent for us. I believe a friend of ours is here."

"Pardon?"

The man smiled and gestured behind her. Armand was standing over Charles, looking disgusted.

"May we?"

Understanding filtered in. These men were Charles's creditors. Armand must have contacted them, and Grimsby sent for them. She tried to feel sorry for Charles, for what would happen to him, but hadn't he brought this on himself with his gambling debts?

"Yes, I think you may," she said. Felicity moved aside so the two henchmen could enter. Armand moved away, nodding his approval. In a moment, the men had bundled Charles into a black, nondescript carriage. The remaining man tipped his hat politely. "He won't be bothering you again. He owes us quite a deal of money. We shall be certain he repays it. Thank you, my lord." He nodded to Armand. "Good day."

And he retreated down the steps, stepped gracefully into the carriage, and was gone. Felicity stood in the doorway for a long minute and stared at the street. Charles was gone. He was really gone. She felt as though a brick had been removed from her shoulders.

Slowly, she closed the door and turned back to Armand, who was studying his bruised knuckles. "Was that—were those—?"

"Acquaintances of St. John's. They had been looking for him for some time."

"What's going to happen to Charles?"

Armand shrugged. "Debtor's prison? Nothing he doesn't deserve."

It was true, and still she had a headache forming between her eyes. She reached up to massage it away. Things were happening so quickly. She needed a moment to think.

"Felicity, you're going to marry me."

She opened her eyes and saw he was standing before her, holding out a piece of parchment. At first she thought it was Charles's copy of the marriage contract, but it was crisp and new. She took it from him, unrolled it, and gasped. She looked up. "It's a special license. I–I've heard of them, but I've never seen one before." She knew they were expensive and difficult to acquire.

He stepped closer, and she could see he intended to kiss her. She skittered back, needing a moment to think. Was Charles really gone? Was she really free?

"St. John is gone," he said matter-of-factly. "My brother helped me acquire the license. Julien and Sarah want us to marry. You have no reason to say no."

He was right. After hearing of their ordeal in France, the Valères had made her feel welcome, like one of them. The dowager had treated her almost like a daughter, and the duchesse had been warm and friendly. Even the duc had softened toward her—as much as she imagined a man like that could. She desperately wanted a family again, and it was beginning to dawn on her she would have one. "Armand, I—"

Armand held up an imperious hand. "There is something else I must say."

She furrowed her brow. "I was going to assent."

"Not until I tell you."

She raised a brow, waiting.

He swallowed, opened his mouth, closed it again. Felicity couldn't imagine what he wanted to tell her. Had he changed his mind? Did he not want to marry her?

"I love you," he said.

Her heart stuttered. She actually felt it stop and then start again. It was painful and caused her blood to rush through her veins until it was pumping so loudly in her ears she could not hear anything else. "Wh-what?" Her voice sounded far away and shaky, not like her own voice at all.

He shook his head, reached out and took her cold hand in his large, warm one. "Julien said you would want the words. I'm not good with words."

"Try," she whispered, because she did want the words. Could he love her? She had loved him for so long. Her heart clenched, and she felt she had to force it to keep beating.

"I loved you the first moment I saw you." He gestured to the stairs. "You sat at the pianoforte, and I had never seen anything as beautiful as you. I wanted to be near you, and I had not wanted to be near another human for so many years. But I wanted you."

"I felt it for you, too."

He grinned then looked serious again. "And then you touched me. No one could touch me. I had been beaten for so many of those early years in prison, touch meant pain to me. And then there were years with no touch, no contact. I almost would have welcomed a beating if it meant some sort of contact. When Julien rescued me, I found any touch was pain. It still is pain. My mother can't touch me, my brother can't. But you can. Only you." He lifted her hand, put it to his heart. Because he wore only a thin linen shirt, she could feel the warmth of his skin through it, imagined she could feel his heart beating.

"Love is wanting to be with you when I wake up, yes? Love is doing anything for your smile. Love is dying for you. I would, if it came to that."

She felt tears well up in her eyes. Her heart felt too full, felt as though it would burst. "That's how I feel about you. That's exactly how I feel."

"Love is wanting you to be mine. Always." He gestured to the special license she held in her trembling hands. "Marry me."

"Oh, Armand—"

"Wait. Julien said there is a rule." He knelt before her on one knee, put her hand to his mouth, kissed it. "Will you marry me, Felicity?"

She couldn't say what seeing this wild, untamed man kneeling before her did to her heart. She did not want to tame him, but having him love her was more than she could have ever dreamed. She knelt before him, took his hands. "Yes, I'll marry you. And I love you, too."

He was up and pulling her into his arms before she could finish the words. "Good. Let's go marry now."

"Armand!" She laughed, and he wrapped her in his arms. "I don't think we should marry this instant. I'll need a dress, and I want my aunt to come. And

I'm sure your mother has some people she would like to invite."

Armand gave her a look that said his patience was all but exhausted, and she took his face in her hands. "Soon. As soon as we can." She kissed him, and when he kissed her back, she could feel his love infusing her with warmth and joy.

∾

He finally had her. It had taken a week to make all of the arrangements. Armand didn't understand why they were all necessary, but Felicity seemed to think them important. And it made his mother happy. And Sarah. He thought Julien would have rather they married right away, but men didn't make The Rules.

And now that he was at home at The Gardens, he really didn't care about The Rules anymore. It was snowing outside, which wouldn't normally deter him from his daily walk, but Felicity had cajoled him into sitting in the drawing room. She had a fire blazing in the hearth and his Christmas present—a black mongrel puppy—was dozing on the floor at his feet. She was at the pianoforte, playing a slow, dreamy song. He loved listening to her play. And now she could play for him anytime. All the time.

The clock chimed three times, and her hands stilled. He frowned. "It's already three?" she said. "They'll be here any moment, and I'm not finished with the wrapping."

No one would care. He had told her this before, but it hadn't seemed to make any difference. She wanted Christmas to be perfect.

"Do you hear that?" Now she was up and racing to one of the windows. "Those are the horses' bells. Yes! They're here! Come on."

He would have preferred to sit where he was, but she grabbed his hand and pulled him to the door. Before their butler could do his duty, she had it open and was out in the snow, welcoming Julien, Sarah, and his mother. There were words and hugs and kisses, which Armand tolerated because he could see how happy it made Felicity to have family around her. She told him she wanted a large family, and when he realized what that entailed, he was happy to oblige her.

Sarah was noticeably with child now, and he wondered how Felicity would look, her belly round with his son or daughter.

A few moments later, they were all inside, and Felicity had the housekeeper pass out warm cider and chocolate. Julien insisted Sarah lie down in her room, and his mother went to settle her in. When it was just the three of them and the dog, Felicity sat at the pianoforte again, playing quietly, and Julien stood at the large hearth.

"I looked into the information you gave me about Captain Cutlass."

"Who's Captain Cutlass?" Felicity asked, her hands never pausing.

"A pirate who's been harassing the English Navy for the past several years. He attacks foreign ships in and around the English coast, steals their cargo, and probably makes a tidy profit selling the luxury items. The Navy has been trying to capture him for some time, but they haven't been successful. My information is that he actually enjoys engaging them, thinks of it as a game."

Armand nodded. "That sounds like Bastien."

Now her hands stilled. "Bastien? Your brother? I thought you were talking about a pirate."

Armand looked at Julien, and his brother nodded. "I think they might be one and the same."

"But how is that possible?"

"We'll have to ask him," Julien said. "I've been making inquiries, trying to find the best way to contact him. If we're successful, we can reunite the whole family."

Armand went to Felicity, put his hand on her shoulder.

Felicity covered it with her own. "I hope you find him—even if he is a pirate. I can't think of anything better than having your whole family together again."

"Neither can I—"

"Julien, I am not going to lie down all afternoon. I'm not tired." Sarah's voice floated in the hallway, and Julien scowled.

"That woman refuses to rest. I didn't even want her coming all this way in the carriage. It jostles her. I'll be right back." A moment later, Armand could hear the couple arguing, Julien firm and Sarah just as stubborn.

Felicity stood. "Perhaps next Christmas your brother Bastien will be here, as well."

He put his arm around her, drew her close. She sighed contentedly, and together they stared into the crackling fire in the hearth. At one time fire had represented destruction, his life in ashes. Now, with Felicity beside him, he welcomed the warmth. He looked at his wife bathed in the soft glow of the firelight. With a smile, she kissed him. "I love you," she whispered.

"I love you." And he finally knew all that the word meant.

Acknowledgments

As always, thank you to my husband Mathew for all of your support and patience as I struggled through this novel. Thank you to Christina Hergenrader and Linda Andrus for reading this book over and over *and over* and always offering a fresh take and new suggestions. Thank you to Deb Werksman for your suggestions and encouragement. To my agents Joanna MacKenzie and Danielle Egan-Miller—thank you for believing in me and all your hard work on my behalf.

About the Author

Shana Galen is the author of six Regency historicals, including the Rita-nominated *Blackthorne's Bride*. Her books have been sold in Brazil, Russia, Turkey, Spain, and the Netherlands and featured in the Rhapsody and Doubleday Book Clubs. A former English teacher in Houston's inner city, Shana now writes full time. She is a happily married wife and mother with one daughter and one spoiled cat. She loves to hear from readers: visit her website at www.shanagalen.com.

FROM

The Making of a Rogue

COMING IN APRIL 2011
FROM SOURCEBOOKS CASABLANCA

France 1802

"That's him," Percy whispered. "I'm almost certain of it."

Raeven Russell glanced at Percy. He looked nervous. There was a fine sheen of perspiration on his pale, freckled skin and his white-blond hair stood up in all directions as though he'd run a hand through it half a dozen times. Which he probably had. Percy Williams was purser for the *HMS Regal*, and while Raeven knew Percy adored her, she also knew he abhorred any action that violated her father's rules.

She reached over and slung an arm around him in the jaunty way she had seen men do time and time again. "You look nervous," she said under her breath. "People will wonder why."

"I *am* nervous," he hissed. "You're going to get yourself killed."

"That's my problem." She shifted away from him and scanned the men around her. Which one was Cutlass? There were several likely candidates.

Raeven stood like a man—legs braced apart and hands on hips—to survey the seedy Brest tavern. Dockside taverns the world over were the same, she mused as she studied the crowd. They were filled with sailors looking for wine and women, ship's captains hiring additions to their crews, beleaguered serving girls skirting men's too-free hands, and whores working to entice any man with the coin to pay.

She didn't know why she should feel so at home. She certainly didn't belong here and had gone to considerable trouble to disguise herself as a young man before sneaking off her father's ship and onto a cutter with the crew members going ashore legitimately.

If her father knew she was here… She shook her head. She could hear his booming voice in her head. *The daughter of a British admiral should behave with more decorum, in a manner befitting her station in life.*

But what was her station in life? Her mother had died days after her birth, and she'd been sailing with her father from the age of four—when the last of her relatives had given her up as incorrigible. This certainly wasn't the first tavern she'd visited. It wasn't even the first time she'd sneaked off the *HMS Regal*.

It *was* the first time she'd found Captain Cutlass. After six months of searching for the murdering bastard, she was about to meet him, face to face.

"It'll be my neck when your father finds out." Percy swallowed audibly, and she suppressed a smile.

"Then you won't be long in following me to meet our maker. I'll put in a good word for you."

He gave her a horrified look, which she supposed indicated he didn't think she'd be a very good envoy.

He cleared his throat. "I prefer a little more time on this earthly world."

"I'm in complete agreement. Now, tell me which one he is again, but don't look at him or gesture toward him."

"Let's go sit at the bar," Percy said. "You can see him better from there, and we'll be less conspicuous."

"Fine." Remembering to play her role, she swaggered to the bar and leaned belligerently against it. Percy ordered ale and she did as well, though she had no intention of drinking it. She needed all her wits about her.

When the barkeep moved away, Percy studied his mug and murmured, "See the man in the far corner?"

Raeven allowed her eyes to roam lazily over the tavern until she focused on the corner he meant.

"He's dressed as a gentleman—navy coat, white cravat, buff breeches."

She saw him now and nodded. "A gentleman pirate." She shook her head. "Contradiction in terms."

"The rumor is he's a deposed marquis whose family fled France during the revolution."

She scowled at him. "Don't tell me you believe that rubbish. All the pirates concoct romantic stories. Just because one claims he's a duke, doesn't make him any less of a thief and murderer."

"Of course I don't believe it. I'm telling you the rumor."

But she could hear in his voice he had believed the story, and now that she'd set her eyes on Cutlass, she could see why. The man did have the air of the aristocrat about him. It wasn't simply his clothes—any man could dress up as one of the quality—but there was something in Cutlass's bearing. He was sitting at a table, his back to the wall, facing the door to the tavern. That much told her he was no fool. There was a man seated across from him, and Cutlass was listening in a leisurely fashion to whatever the man was saying. Cutlass's arms were crossed over his chest, and his expression was one of mild interest. He had a glass of something on the table before him, but she hadn't seen him drink from it. Nor had she seen any whores approach him.

He was doing business then. It would have better served her purposes if he'd been drunk and whoring, but she didn't have the luxury of choosing when to strike.

Her gaze slid back to Percy. "He's handsome," she remarked and watched the purser's eyebrows wing upward. "I hadn't expected that."

The reports she'd had of him rarely mentioned his appearance. Captain Cutlass was known for his stealth, his agility, and his slippery escapes. It was rumored he'd boarded over a hundred vessels. That was obviously exaggeration, but even if his record was a quarter of that, it was an impressive feat. Of course, he claimed he was a privateer, and she knew he sailed under the Spanish flag and with that country's letters of marque. She didn't care for privateers any more than she cared for pirates and made little distinction between them. Neither pirates nor privateers should dare attack ships of the British Navy. Neither should dare to kill a British naval officer.

She felt the anger and the blood pump through her and took a deep, calming breath. She couldn't afford to be emotional right now. She had to put emotion away. And she couldn't afford a schoolgirl crush on the man either. Yes, he was handsome. His dark brown hair was brushed back from his forehead and would have grazed his shoulder if not neatly secured in a queue. His face was strong with a square jaw, plenty of angles and planes, and a full mouth that destroyed the hard effect and hinted at softness. But the eyes—the eyes did not lie. There was no softness in the man. She couldn't quite see the eye color from this far away—it was something light—but under the sardonic arch of his brow his eyes were sharp, cold, and calculating.

A worthy adversary, and she'd spill his blood tonight.

A *Duke* TO *Die For*

BY AMELIA GREY

THE RAKISH FIFTH DUKE OF BLAKEWELL'S UNEXPECTED AND shockingly lovely new ward has just arrived, claiming to carry a curse that has brought each of her previous guardians to an untimely end...

Praise for Amelia Grey's Regency romances:

"This beguiling romance steals your heart, lifts your spirits and lights up the pages with humor and passion." —Romantic Times

"Each new Amelia Grey tale is a diamond. Ms. Grey...is a master storyteller." —Affaire de Coeur

"Readers will be quickly drawn in by the lively pace, the appealing protagonists, and the sexual chemistry that almost visibly shimmers between." —Library Journal

978-1-4022-1767-8 • $6.99 U.S./$7.99 CAN

A *Marquis* to *Marry*

by Amelia Grey

"A captivating mix of discreet intrigue and potent passion." —*Booklist*

"A gripping plot, great love scenes, and well-drawn characters make this book impossible to put down." —*The Romance Studio*

The Marquis of Raceworth is shocked to find a young and beautiful Duchess on his doorstep—especially when she accuses him of stealing her family's priceless pearls! Susannah, Duchess of Brookfield, refuses to be intimidated by the Marquis's commanding presence and chiseled good looks. And when the pearls disappear, Race and Susannah will have to work together—and discover they can't live apart...

Praise for *A Duke to Die For:*

"A lusciously spicy romp." —*Library Journal*

"Deliciously sensual... storyteller extraordinaire Amelia Grey grabs you by the heart, draws you in, and does not let go." —*Romance Junkies*

"Intriguing danger, sharp humor, and plenty of simmering sexual chemistry." —*Booklist*

978-1-4022-1760-9 • $6.99 U.S./$8.99 CAN

Lessons in French

BY LAURA KINSALE
New York Times bestselling author

"An exquisite romance and an instant classic." —
Elizabeth Hoyt

HE'S EXACTLY THE KIND OF TROUBLE SHE CAN'T RESIST…

Trevelyan and Callie were childhood sweethearts with a taste for adventure. Until the fateful day her father drove Trevelyan away in disgrace. Nine long, lonely years later, Trevelyan returns, determined to sweep Callie into one last, fateful adventure, just for the two of them…

"Kinsale's delightful characters and delicious wit enliven this poignant tale…It will charm your heart!" —*Sabrina Jeffries*

"Laura Kinsale creates magic. Her characters live, breathe, charm, and seduce, and her writing is as delicious and perfectly served as wine in a crystal glass. When you're reading Kinsale, as with all great indulgences, it feels too good to stop." —*Lisa Kleypas*

978-1-4022-3701-0 • $7.99 U.S./$8.99 CAN

SEIZE THE FIRE

BY LAURA KINSALE

New York Times bestselling author

"Magic and beauty flow from
Laura Kinsale's pen." —*Romantic Times*

AN UNLIKELY PRINCESS SHIPWRECKED
WITH A WAR HERO WHO'S GOT HELL TO PAY

Her Serene Highness Olympia of Oriens—plump, demure,
and idealistic—longs to return to her tiny, embattled land
and lead her people to justice and freedom. Famous hero
Captain Sheridan Drake, destitute and tormented by nightmares of the carnage he's seen, means only to rob and abandon her. What is Olympia to do with the tortured man
behind the hero's façade? And how will they cope when
their very survival depends on each other?

"One of the best writers in the history of the
romance genre." —*All About Romance*

978-1-4022-4683-8 • $9.99 U.S./$11.99 CAN